The OVERLAY for the UNDERPLAY

by DaNeana Ulmer

Nelymesha Publishing • Minneapolis, MN

Copyright ©2009 DaNeana Ulmer
First Printing 2009

All rights reserved. No part of this book may be reproduced or transmitted in any form or by any means, electronic or mechanical, including photocopy, recording, or any informaton storage retrieval, without permission in writing from the publisher.

This book is a work of fiction. Any references to historical events, real people, or real locales are used fictitiously. Other names, characters, places, and incidents are the product of the author's imagination, and any resemblance to actual events or locales or persons, living or dead, is entirely coincindental.

ISBN: 978-0-9820870-7-7

Library of Congress Control Number: 2009932452

Published by
NELYMESHA Corp.
P.O. Box 65804
St. Paul, MN 55165

Acknowledgements

First and foremost, I would like to Thank Jesus Christ, my Lord and Savior.

I want to say a big Thank You to my daughter Meisha for helping me get this book out and Roshae for all your hard work and support no matter what!!!

Special thanks to my editors B. Givens, Jacquelyn Smith and Rachelle K. White and to Jernell McLane at Black Phyr Productions for doing my cover designs.

Thanks to all my supporters that believe in my work and want to see me do well. Thanks to Duane Martin for being a grandfather to my daughter Meisha and to Aasim S. and you all for lighting fire under my butt to get the next novel out. Luv ya!

Thanks to Chell at Starr Hair Design for keeping my hair and attitude in order when it needs to be corrected.

Thanks to Digital City and Mike Spicer, Boise Jones and F.G.Entertainment for showing me love when I first came home- your support was greatly appreciated!!!

Thanks to Angie and The Favors Café for giving me my first book signing with class and style.

Uncle Howard and Auntie Helen- I truly miss you.

Sam, thank you for your kindness and coolness whenever we hit your town.

Thank you Ms. Naomi "Buh" Glass for showing me love anytime I entered your home- you are missed.

Thanks to Al Flowers from Twin Cities Public Television for my first live interview and Al McFarland from Insight News for my first radio interview.

To all the cliques and posses that made Minnesota what it was and still is in our hood:

Perfection, Cutie Pie Posse, Get Fresh Crew, Iowa Posse, Short Mac Clique, T.K.O., Nike Mobb, Whopp Security, UMOJA, Hill Top Hustlers, Dozen

Cuzin, TC Squad, Capital City, Champagne Queens, Gucci Girls, Jelly Bean Crew, Minneapolis Body Breakers, Dropp Topp Productions, International Breakers, World Class Lovers, Raiders, C.A.N., R.A.N. and Dark Side Posse.

Thanks to all the places that kept us entertained at all cost:

L.B's., Oxford, King Center, Inner City, Bernadette's, Library, Industry, Roller Gardens, The Dust Bowl, Star Dust, Gatsby's, River View, Glam Slam, People's Choice, Hip Hop Shop, D-Boys After Hour on Broadway, Valley Fair, Arnellia's, The Metro, First Avenue, South Beach, Cristal, Twisters, Willard's, Johnny Baby's, The Legion, VFW, Eddie Webster's, Boys & Girls Club, Top Fun Center, Pop Shop, Mom's Sweat Shop, Varsity, The Hub, Oak Park, June Teenth, Rondo Days, Plymouth Days, T.C.'s, Elks, and the Warehouse.

Anybody that was somebody took you to grub at:

Ms. Ann's, Amos & Amos, Fish House, Lucille's Kitchen, Art Song Wings, Milda's Café, Nankins, Slice of New York, Jim Bo's, Golden Chicken, Rocky Rococo, Rudolph's Bar-B-Que, Jakeeno's, Wing Joint, King of Wings, Runyon's and Zantigo's.

R.I.P. to all my people that meant so much while they were riding through the hood:

Robin J., Big Coke, Jason "411" B., James "JJ" W., Larry "Buck" W., Ronald "Hud" N., Binky, James J., Clarence J., Charles J., Robin J., Anna G., Cousin Boobie, Javis, Ronnie S., Jeff, Brice, Bruce, Dirty Dre', Do Dirty, Lil Rick, Kenyatta, Clarence STP, Big Roy, Jamar, N. Sleep W., Raymond, Lon B., Sinbad, Cousin Ricky, Duck, Tycel N., Romain, Silas, T-Money, Tiny, Big Jerry, Rome P, Bucket, Shawn "Dirty Loc" E, Pianche, Big June, Ricky C, C "Yellow Boy" B., Shonda and Lisa Ware, and Sharise D.

To know me is to love me. Don't hate on me, get like me...you'll feel better Suckas!!! Hating is yo fault, so just kill yo self cause I ain't going no where... Ha-ha

Last but Least...Big Ups...to all my Haters!!!

Chapter 1

"Kick Back Baby Girl"

"Mommy Mommy" I screamed as I heard the front door of my grandma's house getting kicked in.

"Shine, Shine are you ok?" my mom yelled.

"Yes Mom, I'm ok."

All the loud strange voices and heavy footsteps were coming up the stairs at me. I pulled my old Winnie the Pooh blanket to me and covered my head. Suddenly my door swung open with a loud BAAAAAAAAAMMMMMM.

"It's the St. Paul police, is anybody in here?"

I was terrified and all I could think of at eight years old was them taking my Mommy (grandma) away from me.

"Don't shoot in there please, my grandbaby is in there" my Mommy screamed at the police. I lifted my head from beneath my blanket. As I looked around the room, it seemed like the whole police department had guns pointed at my head.

"It's ok Shine, come out my sunshine, nobody's going to hurt you, it's ok." I sat shaking and trembling with fear, as the salty tears came streaming down my cheeks.

"Mommy, why are all these police here?"

The big cop next to my bed spoke with a gruff voice. "Honey, we'll put the guns down when you show us your hands." I sat there quietly looking at the cops, and then at Mommy who was still yelling. Suddenly, I started peeing all over myself.

"She is just a baby, she don't have no weapons or nothing" my Mommy yelled as the cops lowered their guns.

"See I'm clean," I said and stood in my bed with my hands raised up.

The cops put their guns down and at the same time hot piss was running out of me like rain forest.

"Ok honey, I'm about to pick you up and bring you out there with your mom and grandma."

Mommy broke in "you better not hurt her motherfucker."

"Honey, we're not going to hurt you, but we have to search the room for narcotics and weapons" the cop said.

At that age, I didn't know what narcotics, weed, cocaine or heroin was, but I did know that Mommy had a lot of company. When this old tall skinny black man, who wore the big belt that went around his waist twice, would come over and sit, he would leave laughing every time.

"Why would you tell an eight year old some shit like that, you dumb dick donut eating motherfucker." Mommy was going off on the police like it was the law. She started pushing and pulling to get in the room with me and I realized what I had hidden in the basement in Chico's, our black Chihuahua, dog kennel. He's probably what they were looking for.

"Stop Mommy please, I don't want them to kill you, please stop." My Mommy looked on with tears rolling down her face. "Mommy, Mommy calm down, they're not going to find nothing, because it ain't nothing." That set the tone right there once Mommy looked at my mom as the cops arrested her. See in her eyes, seeing that the house wasn't dirty, she was straight.

"Ok honey, put your hands down and grab your pooh blanket so you'll feel better." It was so embarrassing; I just stood there soaking wet.

"Come on now kid, I was nice, now I'm about to grab your little nappy headed ass and throw you across this damn room cause I know there's some dope up in here" the cop said.

"Don't call my kid nappy headed you son of a bitch" my Mom yelled. She tried releasing her hands from the cuffs so she could get to the cop for calling me names.

My grandma yelled "You white powder head undercover buying pussy at the Belmont for $100 dollars ass pig, you better watch what the hell you say to my grandbaby."

"What did you say to me?" The cop looked at my grandma and his face turned as red as a ripe tomato. He was so mad he looked just like a tomato with horns coming out of it.

"Ha ha ha", I laughed and pointed. "You look like a pink, purple and red tomato, you pig." I tried to copy my grandma by being disrespectful.

"Ok, I'll show you how to talk to your elders" he yelled and picked my little butt up by the back of my onesy. He grabbed my butt so hard and all I could feel was my little panties and a part of my jump suit all up in the crack of my butt. It was going to take a saw to cut this pissy ass suit off me.

"Oh shit, this little black bitch pissed all over me" he screamed as he held me in the air.

"Let me down sir please, I'm sorry" I cried. No one could understand my pain right now. Everybody looked at me and started laughing. "I'm sorry, I told you I didn't want you to pick me up, you scared me and made me pee-pee all over myself."

 As the cop put me down, he must have felt bad as he looked himself up and down. "I guess I won't take you to foster care but you better tell somebody the next time you have to use the bathroom." I put my head down in shame.

"You fucking racist asshole, my baby don't have to bow down to no donut eating ass pig like you" Mommy screamed. I just sat there with my pooh blanket filled with pee and watched the cops raid my grandma's house. That was the start of it all. Mommy introduced me to hustling. The police never found nothing because I hid my grandma's Crown Royal purple and gold bag with the weed in it in Chico's kennel. Thank God Chico didn't poop all over it because he was known for having accidents.

"Shine, get up baby, are you ok?" my mom asked. My mom got up for work every morning and couldn't understand why Mommy never did. I guess that just wasn't her thing and my mom hated it. After I got up and pulled all those stinky clothes off me, my mom ran my bath water and made sure I got in the tub.

"You wash up real good and don't half ass do it either" she said. I'm going to get us our own place so we don't have to go through this anymore."

"What mom, I like being here with Mommy" I said with tears in my eyes.

"You'll understand in time" my mom said.

"Shine" my grandma yelled from the basement.

"Don't you say a word about what I said to you, do you hear me?" my mom said with that evil look. When she gave me that look, she meant business.

"I know mom, I won't ok." I was going to tell my Mommy as soon as I got a chance. I put my Punky Brewster pajamas on and ran downstairs with my favorite fuzzy pink slippers. When I made it to the bottom of my grandma's big brown wooden steps, I looked up to see the old man, Mr. Z, that lived down the street.

"Hey Sunshine, give Z a high five" he said. As I jumped up, he lifted his hand up higher so I couldn't reach it.

"Aw Mr. Z, that ain't fair, you moved" I said while laughing. I kept jumping to reach his hand.

"Yeah, I'm moving cause that's how the world is and if you don't reach for success by any means, you'll stay down with the failures" he said.

"I ain't no failure" I said jumping and yelling. I was so out of breath, so I snatched his arm down, stepped on his feet and slapped his hand.

"Whoo lil Shine, you got one on me" he laughed.

"I told you I never fail" I said out of breath with my hands on my hips.

"That's the lil girl I know, lil Miss Sunshine, always reach like your grandma, run with the best and you will be the best" he sang.

All that stuff Mr. Z talked, I never paid any attention to until I got older. He was so funny and I enjoyed the funny noises he made while smoking his joints in Mommy's chair on the front porch.

"Ok Mr. Z" I said as I walked past him and all the clothes, food and plants in Mommy's living room. I had to talk to Mommy before my mom made it downstairs. I could hear Mr. Z asking my auntie did the police find anything.

I made it. "Mommy" I said, while trying to catch my breath.

"What, didn't you hear me calling you girl?" Mommy asked while looking around for her stuff.

"Yeah Mommy" I said out of breath.

"Catch your breath girl, you don't want to have a heart attack at your age" she said with a chuckle. "Shine where… where is my purple bag? I saw you playing with it" Mommy asked.

I went right to Chico's kennel. "It's right here Mommy" I said while pulling it from behind the dog food. My grandma's basement had three hidden rooms and an old fashioned toilet, making it look like a real bathroom. It was made real hood style. I guess Mommy had to have somewhere for all her alcoholic, joint smoking partners to use the bathroom.

When I got to school the next day, some people from Child Protection Services were waiting for me in my class. My teacher said, "Veronica, please go with these people in the hallway honey." As I walked, I could see that the man had a badge on his waist, and his chubby partner looked like the old lady with the raspy voice from "Throw Mama From The Train." I knew something was up.

"What?"

We need to ask you some questions about your grandma."

I was trained by the best to never talk to the law about my Mommy's business.

"I need my Mommy here first" I said with an attitude.

They both looked at each other and shrugged. His partner, the chubby one, kept staring, as if she wanted to hurt me.

"I'm going back to class now" I shouted and tried to turn the knob to my classroom door.

I went to Webster Magnet Elementary. I loved my school. It was the coolest at the time because of all the programs they offered.

"No Veronica," the ugly white women yelled. "We need to ask you some questions about your mom and grandma."

Sweat was pouring down my face and my little hands started shaking as I cried. My teacher opened the door so I made a quick dash in the room and hid behind all the coats hanging up. I hid my face in both hands and cried. "Please God, don't take me away from Mommy, I won't tell where the weed is, please" I begged.

"Veronica, come out of there right now" my teacher yelled.

Then I heard my mom's voice "Roni, Roni come on baby."

My mom snatched me from behind all the coats as all my friends looked on. One boy, who taught me how to play dodge ball yelled "Veronica, where you going, you still owe me a kiss." I smiled.

"Maybe when she's eighteen" my mom said as we walked out the classroom.

The whole class laughed. I was glad all the attention was on me and my mom. St. Paul was so small, that whenever anything exciting happened, folks were all in your business before God got the news. True to her word, six months later, my mom moved us to Minneapolis.

— Six Months Later —

We moved to South Minneapolis across the street from Powderhorn Park. I hated it. I was only eight years old and trying to find my own identity. My dad Percy, at least the only dad I knew, was working on my Mom. They had been seeing each other for sometime, but I didn't think they were on the verge of marriage. I was really irritated with my mom because I couldn't understand why she never explained to me what happened to my real father. Every time I asked, I was told that he was killed by his friend over a girl his friend had a son with.

"You know tomorrow you're going to have to catch the bus on your own" my mom informed me.

"Why mom, Francis doesn't have to" I complained.

Francis was my step-dad's daughter, four years younger than me. She was cute and quiet until she got to know you, then she was all over you.

"I'm too young to walk that way by myself" Francis said. Fox was her nickname.

"Who asked you Fox" I yelled and rolled my eyes.

"Nobody, I was just talking to you" she said as she put her head down.

"Roni, you're not going to keep making her feel out of place. She has a place here just like you do" my mom yelled. "You two are equals, so don't forget it."

Ooh, I hated it here already. I wanted to go back to Mommy's house, but I knew I couldn't because there was too much going on at my grandma's from the raids to the dope dealing and weed smoking. My mom wasn't letting me pee no more.

"I hate her, she always gets her way, ohh you make me so..."

I was stopped mid sentence by a slap in my mouth. "Ouch" I cried. "What you hit me for mom?"

"You are so evil girl and you talk to much to be so young. I know it's from being at Mommy's house and that's why you ain't going back!"

Those words made me hate it here even more. At that point, I was determined to wreak havoc in my life. If I didn't like it, I was taking control. When I walked past Fox, I got my lick back and slapped her in the head.

"Ouch... ouch, Ginger" she yelled as I stomped to my room.

"It's ok Fox, don't worry about her because she's on punishment for two weeks" my mom yelled out. I could hear my mom talking about me to Percy and Fox. I was glad that Fox had her own bed so she couldn't pee on me anymore I thought as I fell asleep.

Chapter 2

"New School, New Rules"

"Hey girl, who are you?" asked a light skin, medium height girl with short hair and a fresh Nike sweat suit on.

"Who are you?" I asked as I rolled my eyes.

"I'm Taylor Hardaway, the girl that has a locker next to you and you are always gone when I get there."

"What you waiting on me for" I said looking her straight in her eyes.

"Well I won't no more!" "Your stuff is going to get stolen if you don't get no lock on your locker dummy."

My eyes got big as I stood back and pointed my finger in her face. "Who you calling dumb... you high yellow heifer."

Taylor stood there with her arms crossed. "You...I was just trying to be cool because you're new here, but I won't no more" she said while walking off to class.

Dang, every time somebody likes me, I mess it up. The next few days were cool. I started making my own friends and from what I heard Taylor a.k.a Ty, was the most popular girl at Wilder Elementary School. She was trying to recruit me to be in her clique of 6th and 7th graders that she hung with. What she didn't know, but later found out, was that I was my own leader.

Chapter 3

"Summertime"

I met this girl named Wonnie on my last day of school. She had a lot of family members and they told me about the Boys and Girls Club on 37th and Chicago Avenue. The club was kind of far from my house, but I had another friend that Wonnie knew really good named Fay that lived right by me on the other side of Powderhorn Park. I would cut through the park and meet Fay on 35th and Elliot. At the club, we would shoot pool, play basketball and sell pancake breakfast tickets. By the time we made it home, we were beat.

"Roni, the phone's ringing" Fox yelled from outside on the steps.

Since I was so mean to her by not taking her with me, I decided that today I would let her hang out. I went downstairs to answer the phone and knew that it was Wonnie or Fox.

"Hello."

"Hey girl, this Fay and Wonnie, we got you on three way."

"Hey y'all." Minneapolis wasn't as bad as I thought it would be...

"We wanted to know if you wanted to go hang out at the City Center." Fay said as Wonnie listened."

"Umm... I'm only 10 years old and I don't think my Mom will let me."

Wonnie broke in "I'm 12 and Fay is 11, so it's ok and we'll catch the number 5 bus over on Chicago Avenue."

"Where's that Fay... is that by your house?" It was real confusing trying to figure out how I was going to get it together with old Ginger.

Wonnie said "No Roni, I live on 34th and 5th and Fay lives on 35th and 10th. We meet on 35th and Chicago and get on the number 5 bus that takes us to Lake and Chicago."

"Then what do I do Wonnie, I mean, I'll be by myself you know?" I wasn't really trying to hang downtown Minneapolis, shit, that's where Prince made Purple Rain. My grandma used to be Prince's manager so I got to meet him and hang backstage at First Avenue.

"Girl listen, with your scary self... walk down 14th and go to Lake Street. Catch the 21 bus to Chicago Avenue and get off right in front of Roberts Shoe Store where they sell all the tennis shoes with the fat laces... do you remember now"?

"Yeah, yeah, now I remember."

"Ok, and remember that dope boy that called you a high yellow heifer because you wouldn't talk to him"?

"Yeah Fay... ha ha, I remember."

"Well ya dummy, the bus stop is kitty-corner from that bar where they sell drugs at... its called Sunny's."

"Ok y'all, I'm not dumb, I do remember that bar."

"Well let me know that then" Wonnie yelled.

"Ok, I'm on my way" I said hanging up.

By the time I hung up with Fox and Wonnie, I was already putting my long ponytail to the side. Huh, most girls only had a pigtail calling it a ponytail, but not me- I had buttas. To top it off, I put my blow pop sucker on top of my ponytail with two red and white ribbons.

"Roni, who are you talking to?" Fox asked walking in my room.

"I don't have time right now Fox, leave me alone." Damn, she was always in my business.

"Hum, since you getting smart, I'm telling Ginger you going with your friends to be fast with boys."

I gave her the most evilest look and started to slap the piss out of her golden shower giving ass, but then I thought about it. If I let Fox go with me, my mom and Mr. Percy won't be tripping and I could get some extra money from Mr. Percy.

"Give me my doll Roni and stop being so mean to me... big head."

"Spell it" I yelled as I laughed and lifted her cabbage patch kid up higher than she could reach.

"No... punk."

I really hurt Fox's feelings, so I knew I had to make it right.

"Shut up before my mom comes up here. I'll take you with"...

"Shut up Roni...what are you doing to Fox? I know you up here bullying her."

"No mom, I'm not." I nudged Fox to say something.

"Nothings wrong Ginger, I'm just mad because I can't find my doll" Fox said throwing my mom off.

"Ok, calm that noise down. "Roni"?

"Huh mom?"

"Your Granny E is on the phone and she wants you to come over this weekend so you need to get your stuff together."

Damn, what am I going to do? I hated going over there because my uncle was always feeling on me. At ten years old I wear an A cup, my hips are a 32 and my butt is bigger than most older women. But, that's still no reason for a grown ass man to tell you he'll pay you $20 dollars to let him rub his penis up and down your ass. If Ginger knew she would kill him and so would

Grandma E. One day she caught my nasty uncle trying to make me change in front of him after getting out of the pool and she whooped his ass with the telephone cord. I knew he was wrong for what he was doing and I didn't like how he made me feel, but I could use the $20 dollars.

"Nah... I'm cool; I don't want to go because I'm taking Fox downtown to the Skyway Theatre on 7th and Hennepin to see Willy Wonka and the Chocolate Factory" I yelled as I took my tooth brush and laid my baby hair down.

"Fox, hurry up and get dressed. We got five minutes and we have to walk all the way to Lake Street."

"I'm ready."

Poor thing was so worried about me leaving her that she put on anything.

"You up girl... you're not going to have me looking good and you looking busted... what you thought."

I took my time ironing a crease in Fox's pants; we had a pair of "white girl" tennis shoes in every color. I put on white and she put on black.

"Thanks Roni."

"Yeah yeah whatever... don't make it a habit."

As we walked down the narrow porch steps, I could hear Mr. Percy talking to the old Professor that worked at Sanford Jr. High School; the school I would be attending in the fall. The Professor had that scary laugh like the ones you heard on TV. The men were sitting on Mr. Percy's old leather couch that smelled and had rips all in it. I hated that couch and insisted he throw it out, but he said he's had it since his college days and wasn't going to get rid of it. Since this was his house, those were his rules. Any chance I got I spilled kool-aid, milk or whatever I was drinking and made the rips bigger. I always did this on the sneak and nobody noticed.

"Roni, what time are you and Fox going to be back, and why don't you want to go to your Granny E's house"?

"I don't want to talk about it right now mom... it's hot and we're going to be late for the show."

"Humph... that's weird, I thought you loved being around Prince and Time. I mean, you said you met Vanity from the group called Nasty Girls."

Shit, why is she sweating me... can't she see I'm not trying to go over there. I crossed my arms and rolled my eyes. "Mom... if I said I don't want to go, why are you trying to make me... I don't like my dad's brother."

"Your uncle... why Roni?"

Oh, I wasn't about to tell her. A friend from school told her mom that her brother and her Mom's boyfriend had grinded on her and the crazy woman sent her to St. Joseph's- a group home. So no, I wasn't having that. My life wasn't that bad...

"If my dad was here today and knew what his brother was doing to me..."

"Roni, is he messing with you?" Fox whispered.

"Come on Fox, we're going to miss the bus." Mom, we'll call when the movie's over so you can pick us up, ok."

I grabbed Fox's hand and made a dash for it. She saved me. I didn't feel like going through the whole reason of why when I came from my Grandma's house I sometimes had $20 or $40 dollars. The stories they told me about how ruthless my dad was.... man, he's probably turning over in his grave right now.

Wonnie and Fay had an attitude when we finally met up with them. "Damn Roni, what took y'all so long?" Wonnie asked while rolling her eyes and crossing her arms.

The bus was approaching as I was ready to respond. I didn't like Wonnie talking crazy, but she was my friend and I wanted to fit in. I didn't have any friends in Minneapolis, so I'd have to bite my tongue and go with the flow. When we all got on the bus and sat down, I peeped a bunch of dudes sitting in the back of the bus. This made me smile and I forgot all about Wonnie and her attitude.

"Roni, sit back here and let Fox stay up front with the bus driver" Fay yelled.

"Fox are you ok... sit right here so you can see all the people that get on."

"But I don't want too" she whined.

Oh goodness, would she just do what I said. I gave her the look. "Fox, I'm trying to... oooh you make me..."

"Be quiet, I know you want to sit back there with those boys."

"Shut up!" Two older people busted up laughing as I slapped her upside the head.

"Ouch... ok I'm sorry, please just tell me when we're going to stop so I don't fall."

My eyes lit up. "I will and you better not tell on me ok."

I didn't even hear Fox respond. I ran straight to Wonnie and Fay. I sat down next to this medium built ball headed dude who was looking at me like I was crazy as I swung around the pole and jumped right next to Wonnie.

"I'm so excited, are we going to see any more fine soup"?

She gave me a half look because she was in a deep conversation with some older dude on the other side of her.

"Yes, will see way more now."

As she turned around, I stuck my tongue out. I didn't appreciate nobody trying to treat me like big me, little you, just because she was older than me. We finally made it downtown to the City Center, and I loved how everything was all lit up. 7th and Hennepin was where all the pimps, prostitutes and dope boys hung when the police weren't around. We went in this music store called "Northern Lights." They had everything from Salt-n-Pepper to Prince. As I stood in the window and waited for Wonnie and Fox to buy a t-shirt, Fay pointed across the street to where Prince drove his motor cycle out of the alley in *Purple Rain*. We went in this big department store called Dayton's and I saw all the clothes that rich people wore like Gloria Vanderbilt, Cross Colours, Tommy Hilfiger and Girbaud. We walked around looking at boys and sampling every piece of candy and popcorn in this store called Candyland. I called my Mom to pick us up because Fox was getting tired, whiny and getting on my nerves. Fay and Wonnie got on the number 5 bus with the 'Guardian Angles'- a crime fighting street team who walked the streets in high crime areas to make the streets feel safe.

Chapter 4

"New School, New Rules"

"Hey…hey… excuse me" I heard this boy yelling at me two lockers down.

"Huh", I said while grabbing my paper to find my next class. It was my first day at Sanford and I was starting to get used to the changes that my mother was putting me through. I've been to five different schools and I'm only 10 yrs. Old. I didn't like all this moving around, but I've learned to adjust to any environment.

"Do you know a boy named Bobbi"?

 I thought about it for a minute before I said "yeah", with excitement. "That's my homie from the Peter."

"Yeah, he told me that you and your friend Bird snuck in his dad's house one night after a library party downtown St. Paul, and 'yall were with Bird's big brother."

"Yep, we sure did… what's your name?" I wanted to keep it moving because I didn't even know dude.

"Oh, my name Zimbie…I'm on the basketball team with Rabi."

"Oh you are, how can I get on the cheerleading team?" We stood there talking and he seemed real cool- already like a brother. I hoped he could show me around and I could keep meeting more of his friends. I was getting tired of going to the Boys & Girls Club with Fay and Wonnie all the time.

"Yeah I can keep you and you can meet my best homeboy named white boy." "Ha ha dang why would y'all name him that." "Because he has real curly hair and very red skin and looks like a white person... ha ha he doesn't care." "Um ok I'm going to have to get to class." "Oh yeah... let me show you how to get there."

Chapter 5

"End of the School Year"

I enjoyed Sanford my Mom and Percy were having grown up problems that were starting to wear on my schooling once again. My Mom informed me today that after 5 years were going to move right back to St. Paul with Mommy my grandma again. Man I was tired of this. I couldn't get stable with no relationship at all. "What's wrong Roni." White boy said while putting his arm around me. The tears started to roll so hard that he pulled out his team shirt to cover my face, "Here wipe your eyes with this so nobody would see you and be all in your business." Man he was on point. I didn't want anybody all in it because I only had a few friends and most of them were dudes. Zimbie had become so cool like a brother. I just didn't want to put all of my stuff on him today. "Thank you white boy... I got much love for you." I said as I hugged him back. I seen in his eyes that he wanted me. I thought he was cute but I really wasn't attracted. I liked much darker dudes and I wasn't ready for my cherry to get popped yet. I'm only 12 and boys weren't supposed to be on my mind. "I have cheerleading practice white boy can you walk me home?." "Yeah." He said smiling. "Ok I'll meet you in front after 6th hour. I was so stressed and didn't know how to cope with nothing. I was in between wanting to have sex, a period that ran out of me like a blood bath 3 days a month, and pimples that took away my true beauty. Even though all the boys loved my size 6 jeans and D cup breasts at 12, I still didn't get the attention I wanted. "Hey... Roni you better get your umbrella cause it might rain."

White boy told me as I put my uniform in my locker. We walked a long way. It was at least 2 ½ miles from my school to my house. White boy didn't complain at all. I poured all my feeling out and felt good doing it he explained to me that he always talked for therapy because his Mom was dead and his grandma took care of him. His closeness came from grandma just like mine did and whenever she told him it was going to be alright it was. As he spoke highly of his grandma I remembered that I was about to move right back to Mommy's house with all that chaos that went on in her house. I cried "Roni what's wrong? …I thought you were having fun walking in the rain." "I'm ok…I just don't want to move back to St. Paul… White boy it's so boring and slow." He looked confused with nothing to say. "Um… you can run away and I can hide you in my room… my granny never comes in there." I laughed a little. "No boy my Mom and Grandma would be worried your grandma would go to jail." That was sweet… even though I enjoyed the walk , I was soaked and ready to get home. "Ok… stop right here white boy…. I have to give you a hug here." "Why…you live a block in a half down." He just didn't get what I meant about my Mom. She didn't play when she no boys. That meant no boys. "I know I do boy dang just stop"… I hug you here." He thought about it for a minute. "Ok I no….um well since you got to go I'll…." "wait no." He just kissed me real fast and that felt a little weird. "I'll see you tomorrow White Boy ok." I said while getting away from him. "Ok….I'll watch you until I see you go in ok." He said yelling down the street. "White boy …don't call my house make your little cousin call so my Mom won't get mad ok." I hope he heard me. "I will Roni…..I like you a lot baby." I hurried in and slammed the door. As I stood on the porch and took my wet clothes off, I could hear my Mom yelling at Percy telling him that it was over. A prostitute called our house and told my Mom the whole story about him tricking and treating. Percy looked real scared because he knew by being a big computer analyst He was going to be paying some big bucks for adultery when that divorce went through. Thank God for him that I wasn't his biological daughter because he would be paying $2,000 instead of the $1,000 that he pays to Fox's mother.

Chapter 6
"Ramsey"

"What's up Southsider." I could hear Rabi yelling through the hall. I was so happy to see some people I knew. "Hey boy I thought your butt was still whining from when your pops whooped it in front of me and Bird." I could see that Rabi was tired of me bringing it up, so I switched the subject and gave him a big hug. "I missed you homeboy …I thought you was moving over to Minneapolis." "I know! I missed your butt too." He said while hugging me back. Rabi let me know my home girl YoYo and Sana was in the lunch room and that Nella didn't hang with Sana anymore, because she moved down to Texas with her dad. I let him know that I had my eye on all the dudes at Central High because boys my age were too immature. "Ha you're crazy Roni girl one of them nigga's is going to bust that cherry open…." "Nah I can hang Rabi." "You act like you already had some….you're only 13 Roni…..what you gave up that nappy dug out already?." I wasn't a hoe…Huh not yet anyways. "Nah Rabi…I would of stood on the IDS building and told the whole Minnesota fool." I said while pushing him. We stood there and kick the willybowbow (talked)so long when we looked around and seen nobody in the halfway we walked to the gym and sat down like we were apart of their class. Rabi informed me that he wasn't a virgin and that he still had hopes and dreams of being the paper in between bird scissors. I busted up laughing so hard, that was my boy Rabi and Zimbie had mad love for me. "So when are you moving over North?" "I don't know my dad be tripping still and my Mom got a big enough house for me to come back now….remember she just had my one brother and me and my middle brother stayed with my dad. "Oh….nah I forgot….but um Rabi tell me how it feels to not be a virgin…I got to know playa because they about to send my ass to St. Agnes man." Rabi stood back laughed, pointed at me with one hand over his mouth and said "girl you better wait ! or wait until you get with somebody older so they can teach you and have more patience." I thought about it for a minute. "I got you homie but when I do I'll let you know."

Chapter 7

"St. Agnes"

"Wait….please…..Wait." I yelled as I tried to catch the school bus on the corner of Grotto and Aurora Avenue. Man I hated being in St. Paul again. I'm a Southsider and the people over here seem so slow to me now. Something's always happening at my Mommy's house and I can never do anything without somebody catching me. When I made it to the bus everybody on there looked identical. I wore a navy blue sweater, light blue button up shirt a plaid skirt with white tights and blue with a white and red stripe Fila's. I sat down next to an older dude that looked like he sold weed. Since nigga's wasn't into the heavy shit at the time that would be about the only thing he could be selling or his people's had some paper. "What's up?" I turned to size him up. "What's up." As I turned to look straight ahead. My leg got to shaken and a tingling sensation went from my left butt cheek to my clique as I sat there hornier then Luke from the 2 Live Crew. I tried to make myself not look anymore but I couldn't help it. "what's wrong…you nervous on your first day. I'll take you around." Oh just what I needed- an older dude to pop my cherry …yes. "Ok that would be nice." I said with a smile I knew my ponytail and bangs were in place because my Mom had just helped me put a dark and lovely in my hair the night before. Why would she pick a catholic school I don't know but I'm so mad. I think she was so mad at Percy for cheating and lying to her that she just spent all that divorce money on everything that would make lives better. As my new boyfriend escorted me off the bus somebody tapped me on the shoulder. "You can let go of his hand now….this brother belongs to me baby girl." The tall slender light skinned chick with long hair pushed me real hard to the side. "Wait bitch you don't know who you are fucking with." I said while thinking that this older girl is going to beat my ass but she wasn't bout to see no punk in me. Better to tell it first then you have time to know it later with all your might, I put my dukes up. She grabbed me so hard by my ponytail that I screamed and all the attention went on us. The dude turned around in shock so this was my chance to show out. A upper cut right in her stomach she went over and hit her self. So I went to town on her head and face. The dude and the bus driver broke us up and walked me only to the office. "Hey let me go....she hit me I didn't do nothing." I knew playing the victim wasn't going to get me far but I'm going to try like I always do. "Yes you did....duh you just fought the principle's daughter." The dude said while the bus driver watched him take me to the office. "So what she hit me because of your ass." I snatched my arm from him and sat down. When I looked up I seen her high yellow ass looking at me with blood in her eyes and hair all over her head. "What bitch? what?" I said and jumped at her. I lost it for real, not realizing and totally disrespecting god. Even though it wasn't a catholic and I was a member of M.T Oliver church. I knew I was way out of pocket. All the Nuns and students in the other class rooms came out. It was so quiet you could hear a mouse pissing on cotton. I put my head down in shame. Oh I just want to disappear instantly. Her dad came out in a nice gray suit and asked me to step into his office. After putting me on release suspension and no basketball tryouts for three months. He topped it off with staying after school with all the thirds graders and cleaning out the boy's bathroom. I just took the punishment and didn't have to tell my Mom thank God. So much for the lusting after that older nigga. No plan to get my cherry busted now. Man I guess that was my punishment for disrespecting the Lords house. I never did get the dudes name because he was in high school and we barely seen the bigger kids. They moved me to another bus and as it got hot outside I started walking to and from school.

Chapter 8

"Cherry Poppin"

Oh it is too hot out here, I said to myself after thinking of how many days left of school. My Mom moved on with our new apartment on Fairview and Ashland Avenue and her new boyfriend I didn't know which one I was more happier about. "Roni....Bird is down here asking do you need a ride to work." My grandma yelled as I ripped that hot ass uniform off. "Tell her to wait Mommy I'm coming." Thank goodness that honey had to work for his. My Mom thought I had to work until 10:30 PM so I had until 12:00AM to make it to her house. It was Friday night I was feeling good. "What took you so long girl?." Bird asked with a lot of attitude. Her brother was looking at me through the rear view mirror like I was a piece of meat. "What's up slurp?" I said too Bird's brother as he drove us to Oxford recreation center. That's where everybody hung out at until 10:00 PM then they would take to the block on Selby Avenue. Every dope boy, prostitute or wannabe was there. If anything was to kick off I knew hanging out on Friday night was going to allow me to see it all. "What's up? Roni how you doing with your sexy thick ass?" Oh I just got a tingle in my butt and it shot straight to my clique. I've dreamed of him busting my cherry every since I first laid eyes on him. He's 16 and I'm only 13 wow what would the grown folks that hang at Mommy's house think of me right now. "I'm doing fine Slurp what you going to get into?" I saw Bird huffing and puffing. "He ain't doing shit that got to do with us girl! We got thangs to do." She always got mad that her brother wanted me. Bird never wanted nobody messing with her brother because she always felt that would ruin her friendship amongst people. "Shut up girl… She got her own mind…I ain't going to hurt her at all." Slurp said to Bird while pushing her head. "Stop boy I'm going to tell her you trying to get in Roni's panties and you going to get it cause she's too young." Wow, Bird knew just what time it was, Damn I wish she shut up cause I'm ready. When we made it to Oxford, Bird jumped right out the car and ran into her boyfriend. She totally forgot about me so I just sat in the back seat. "See your girl just left you with her hot tail ….she talking about me! I'm going to tell Mom she messing with that grown man, huh nigga is 19 yrs old what is he doing with a 14 yrs old." "He doesn't know that Slurp…he thinks she's 17." "Oh so you think he don't? Shit, she ain't that grown acting." I jumped in the front while Slurp went on and on about his little sis messing with older boys. He got so tired of whooping on dudes so he just let her do what she wanted as long as they didn't hurt her. It started getting dark outside and I was a little nervous. When we pulled up to the house Slurp kissed me and stuck his tongue in down my throat. He sucked my bottom lip then I followed and twirled my tongue around his. I instantly got horny as he felt my breast with one hand and pulled me close by my hips with the other hand. "Come on....you're not going to let me get it in the car are you?." He asked as I scooted away and wiped my mouth. "Nah boy....you will never get nothing from me in a car but a kiss." I rolled my eyes and closed the door. "Do you have a rubber?" I know he was shocked that I would even know such a thing. Yep Mrs. Vick never played that. Since my sister died at five months and I came right after her death. My Mom always vowed to keep me upon every move any man could make. She taught me the birds and bees in baby steps all I've seen at this point in life hell, it was past all that anyways. "Ha ha....yep I got a rubber from the health department." "Huh you must have been burning if you got them from downtown." I said with my nose turned up. Dudes don't usually tell things like this. "You be tripping Roni....you think you are the bomb girl....watch your mouth when talking you somebody like me for real." Slurp had a attitude and I was glad because now that it's time I was ready to chicken out. He walked past me real fast and opened the screen door to the porch. When I seen him open the house door and stand in the doorway, I just stood there with my hands in my mini skirt pockets. Why would I have on a skirt it definitely wasn't supposed to happen like this. "I ain't got to watch my mouth huh you want me I don't want you." I said with my hands on my hips and standing in the fenced in yard. He looked at me with shock and then smiled. I didn't realize he was waiting to tear my little ass up. He started walking towards me and I got nervous. "Come on girl we don't have much time before Bird notices that we're gone." He said while grabbing me by the arm. When we made it up to his bedroom I sat down on the edge of the bed. I didn't realize my legs were shaken. As I turned to look around he was naked from the waist down and his THING was at full attention I swallowed and sweat started pouring down my head. "Come here Roni I ain't going to hurt you I'll be gentle." I started to walk very slow to him and decided to act like the girls I seen in movies Risky Business. Even though I wasn't going to be sucking on him. I had to at least act sexy. "Where's the rubber at." I asked and pulled my panties off. "Right here." He showed me the ones that they give out in sex education. He laid me down on the bed and caressed my double D's. When he started sucking them sensation went through my soul. He rubbed me up and down, kissed me all over my neck and face. He was a pro because he used his right hand to put a rubber on and his left to play with my clique. I felt some kind of liquid running out of me and I watched him get more excited. "You ok baby." "Yes…go ahead do it Slurp." I was a loose cannon. He opened my legs wide as they could go and pushed. "Ouch…oh….wait wait Slurp." "You have to relax Roni or it's going to hurt worse." He started kissing me and fingering me. That felt good and I thought that since his finger felt good, his thing would too. He went down and kissed all around my stomach and between my legs as he came up he tried again. "Oh…cum no." "Just relax shit." He said with frustration and glory in his eyes. Beads of sweat was pouring off the both of us. I didn't move at first then when I did it was the wrong way. "Nah…baby move like a hula hoop." Dang I'm so embarrassed. "Ok….you act like I've done this before." He told me to get on top, when I did I sat down on him with force. "Oh…my God…no." Pain shot right to the top of me and I felt a burning sensation. "Take it out girl." I took it out. "Now take it and rub it on your pussy so I can watch." I did as he said and the pain went away a little. He leaned up and cupped my tittles and started sucking them. "Now put it in slow and act like your hula hooping." I went down slow and moved around like he said. "Yeah baby….that's good right there." He yelled out and grabbed my hips. We were moving on the same accord. As he got ready to release he was speeding up. "Come on girl go faster." "I can't I'm not a pro boy." He took it out and made me lay on my back once again he opened me real wide. "No…Slurp." He ignored me lifted my butt up and went in deep. "You like that huh?...yeah its mine huh?" He kept yelling I felt like the ceiling had a hole in it and a rain storm came threw. He was sweating like a pig. "Oh..oooh…I'm cummin girl….you got….good." "Oh ohh." He really didn't finish any of his sentences so I guess that meant I did a good job. He laid on top of me for about two minutes. "Get up boy…Bird is going to find out we were here." He jumped up and so did I. We went to the bathroom together and both washed up. I had blood all between my legs and was so embarrassed he was such a gentlemen. "Here…I see my Mom use these…she said it make her feel clean." He handed me a pad. After that I wasn't so embarrassed because he was three years older and had more experience with girls then I did with boys. We jumped right back in the car and off to Oxford we went. An hour in a half had passed and everybody was on their way to walk up to Selby and kick it. "Where you been….I been looking for your ass girl." Bird yelled from across the street and scared the shit out of me. "Tell her you had an accident and had to go get some pads." Slurp whispered and kissed me before walking off. Bird made it over to me. "Girl Mommy needed me to do something for her…plus I started." "Oh…you did finally girl all the boys going to want you now…that means you're a women just like me." "Um huh." I felt so good not having to tell Bird what happened right then. Dang I'm a women now wow. Yep now I can get all the dope boys with the money and nice cars.

Chapter 9

"Riding- N- Flowing"

"Run, Run, Run Annie." I said as I pulled out my mace. I'm trying but the bitch is too far away. "Huh wait girl I'm out of breath." Annie and Veronica was chasing a dope fiend that ran off with their dope. As hard as school was these days their single parents wasn't given up no extra doe. Getting paper the best way they knew was all that was on their mind. Hardaway a.k.a. Annie and Veronica Gittens a.k.a. Shine were the infamous "Cutie Pie Posse." Yeah! That would be me the leader of the click at least in my mind, Moca Anderson O.k. Hell Girl, Barbie Langford O.k.. B.B Olivia Goodman O.k.. Ola, Heather Jones O.k.. Sip, and Taylor Hardaway O.k.. Ty, we had the hood on lock. Not just the North side but the Southside of MPLS, MN as well. "Damn Annie, that was all our shit that Strawberry (crack hoe) took from our ass, we only got re-up money left" Shine said. Annie was all out of breath from running and didn't feel like hearing my mouth, but so what. Ignoring me, she said "Shine where in the fuck are we walking to now?" I mean the bitch got away." Annie threw her hands in the air and continued to walk towards McDonald's on Plymouth and Penn Ave. I knew the bitch was peed off, but so what, that was my new Dooney & Burke, and my money to get my buttas whipped. I would beat the brakes off that bitch if I would have caught her ass. "Slow down hoe, damn... I know you ain't in that much of a hurry and you let that crack head take our shit." Annie rolled her eyes and ignored me again. We made it to McDonald's and she ran right in to make an order. As I made it in, I sat to warm up. Shit, I'm too cute to be in below zero weather trying to get some paper. For real all I got to do is fuck one of these dumb ass D boys to get what I need. These old niggas out here be sweatin a bitch. I ain't tripping though, because I like to get and have my own. Niggas be trying to take that shit back if you don't act right. I guess I could do what my Momma taught me, use what you got to get what you want and never let no nigga know what you really need cause when he knows you need him he'll be on to the next chick. "Shine.... Shine what yo ass want to eat?" I'm over here checking this nigga out and she's all in my mother fucking grill. "Get me what you get, damn. "Damn nigga." Andre Franklin O.k.. Bull, was looking me right in the face. I turned around sucking my teeth. It's not to be like that, baby, damn!... you was eyeing a nigga down and now you acting brand new. I know this tall, skinny, bean head looking nigga ain't trying to check me. I thought Rolling my eyes and crossing my arms. "Whatever, your ass was looking me in the grill... Um please.... Hurry up, Annie." I look good and I know my beautiful red skin with my chinky eyes and shoulder length hair was irresistible as shit. I'm the flyest bitch at North High School and I knew his ass heard about me. "So now you going to act all hard and shit ..... like you wasn't just eyeing a nigga or something, huh." "Yeah I saw you... but you saw me too. Damn this bitch better be well worth it. I ain't going to keep playing with her fine ass. She know she heard about me and the "Shorty Mack Posse." Shit I'm the most caked nigga out here and I got to have her fine ass. Her damn mouth is going to get her ass kicked in if she don't shut the fuck up. "Yo, why ain't you eating... you cold or something?.... I see you your feet and shit." Well if yo ass is wondering if I'm cold and hungry.... Yo ass sho ain't doing shit to change it, damn." "Yo baby, Shine, What up beautiful." "What's up sexy." Some dude was trying to holler and fucked Bull's game all the way up. Let me see how he handles this. "Yo chill playboy, I got this." Bull said while sliding in the booth and putting his arm around me. "Oh that's your nigga, Veronica?" "No he... " "Yo I'm bout to be so move around playa." Bull said while standing up and putting his mad dog on the handsome, chocolate, 6 football playa. "Alright then homeboy, my bad... but hey don't slip cause I might just be there to catch her fine ass. He walked off and winked at me. "Damn niggas be at yo ass, don't they." This turned my ass on, yeah. I knew my profession was to fuck these niggas for dough until I made Hollywood but hell I guess I'm getting an early start. "You act like you don't see why they wouldn't be." "Shut up, with yo stuck up ass." Pushing her in the head as he said it and went to pay Annie for her food. It was packed in here tonight because everybody was trying ' to warm up before the bus came. It was Friday night, skate night at the Roller Garthens in St. Louis Park. It was right outside of the hood. So you knew if niggas called themselves tripping' , it was guaranteed that they were going to jail. The most could happen was your nigga was going to be pushing up on the next bitch from St. Paul or the Southside. Them blood hoes always got into it with the girls. Shit them hoes rolled deep but wasn't nobody scared cause if the shit got to popping off, me and my posse rolled deep as hell. They just felt safer at the garthens because they were closer to their territory. I had my bitch beater, box cutter and mace as always to handle me hoes. Shit nobody was getting past hell girl and B.B. Them was my big manly built home girls that didn't take no shit. "Here goes food, Shine." He handed me my food while Annie looked confused and happy at the same time. We all sat and ate while watching drug transaction go down. "Um I'm full as at... could you go get me a shake... Bull." I threw that charm on his ass cause he acted like a bitch had two heads or something. He wiped his mouth and looked around to see if anybody was listening or looking. "Yeah bay, I'll go get you a shake." I watched his ass walk off as I got my plan together. Shaking the shit out of me, Annie was amped up. "Girl shine do your ass know who the fuck that nigga hoe is?... he's paid the fuck up girl." Placing a piece of gum in my mouth after checking my teeth IN THE NAPKIN HOLDER. "Yeah... and ... So... So... So... Annie put her hand on my forehead to make sure yo ass is all good cause you slippin 'on yo pimpin'. "No... hoe I ain't." I got this... I told your ass I ain't no joke when it comes to playing a nigga." "Yeah right he going to have yo ass selling his shit and stashing his shit in yo Momma's crib before you know it." "Um! I'm glad you think so... watch this over lay for the under play B-I-T-C-H." Bull l made it back to the table and caught the end of the conversation." Ya'll call each other out your name like that." He frowned up at the both of us. Annie looked and said "It's a girl thing, you wouldn't understand" and slapped my hand. I smiled at her and winked my eye. What's up ya'll need a ride somewhere?" "yeah we got to pick up my girls and we bout to go skating." "Oh yeah... Um ya'll wild like that huh." "What you mean wild?" Shine stood up to fix her clothes and put her coat on. "Yo I'll take ya'll... but if you going to be my girl all that shit going to stop." Damn this nigga ain't even got no pussy yet and his ass already trying to lock the shit down. "What ever nigga, just take us to my home girls crib and shut up." Annie got her coat on quick, She couldn't believe her ears. Veronica was talking way too slick to Bull. His ass was known for whopping on niggas and smoking whoever got in his way. He had two sisters and an uncle that ran the whole Southside and Northside of Minneapolis. He had every drug trade sold up. But If were some outsider trying to get paper in his hood, he was sending somebody after your ass. The whole state was scared of his uncle because of how large his organization was. The thing about it was no one knew who belonged to his gang. So your best bet was to just follow the rules at hand. They got in his black Chevy two door Yukon. I felt like a dip (pretty girl) because all the hoes waiting to get on the bus for skating rolled their eyes and pointed. This pumped my head even more. I knew Bull had a girl somewhere! I didn't care but the nigga ain't got started yet, he only bought some funky ass Mickey D's. We made it over to Ty's house. B.B., Hell girl and Cocoa, were waiting on us. Annie and I ran in the crib to check them out while ignorant ass Bull stayed in the truck. Annie flew in the crib before me, so she could run her damn mouth. "Yo... ya'll guess who Shine just snatched up?" She announced Everybody continued to put their clothes on but looked at her like she was crazy for busting up in the crib. On one accord everybody said "who." That nigga Bull... Girl his ass bought us something to... "what... huh who bought ya'll what?... with your big ass mouth! Cocoa came her hating ass from out the bathroom. She made me sick because she was Hell Girl's older sister and always had to make herself known for something. They always telling peoples business. Hell Girl always lied and says she don't tell her sister shit about us but when our shit gets out its always said that Cocoa said it. I threw my hand in her face. "Shut yo old ass up Cocoa ain't nobody talking to ass." Cocoa got quiet so she could hear more details. "Hey ya'll... hurry up, I got us a ride to skating. "When was you going to call us?" Hell Girl said while combing Ty's hair. "Yeah when... and yo big mouth friend told us. "watch yo self Cocoa shit!" Annie was getting pissed off by the thought of Cocoa trying to hate on her. "Damn Annie let me tell my own business shit." I was pissed. Annie was more amped about the nigga then I was. "I was just happy for you that's all." "So who is this nigga?" B.B. said while pulling her Gucci sweatshirt over her head." "That nigga Bull, girl!... Nigga ain't impressed me yet, shit a burger, shake and fries, shit. I can buy myself that and more! I told him, yo ass better be trying' to lick that nigga for that doe... you know his whole family got the shit on lock." "I know... I know Annie told me everybody in the city buys their dope, blow and weed from them." "Ya'll finish so I can go back to work on this nigga" I told them. Everybody finished getting ready as I made my way back to the car. I wasn't really feeling it but me and my girls had to meet up with the rest of the click. The blood girls known as the "Champagne Queens" would have thought we were scared if we didn't make our appearance. So you know I had to make myself known. Nobody punking me and my clique. Skating was the shit, as usual, the Champagne Queens were there. At first the nigga Bull tried to act like he wasn't coming in. Then when he saw how thick it was he fell off in there. Most people that came skating were older kids around Cocoa's hating ass age. I guess they were rejected by their crowd or was just a little too young to make it to the bar. Shit I know when I got 18 I would make my way to Cali anyway I know how. Whether it's Hollywood or Holly hood, I'm doing it. I'm going to dress the stars no matter what the fuck I got to do , shit. For real. I dressed better than all of them. Mary J, Sharon Stone or lil Kim couldn't rock shit like I can. "Yo B.B. that 's our shit girl." Big Pimpin by Jay-z was blaring through the speakers. "Yeah girl lets kill the dance floor." I ran right past Bull to let his ass know I see him. By the time he turned around to see me he winked and waved at me. Annie, Ty and Hell Girl were already skating around the rink. That's one thing all three of them could do. Shit I could skate only you know regular. They all were skating like they were winning some grand prize or some shit. "Hold on Hell Girl wait for me." I was really trying to catch up. I couldn't so I just did my own thing so I wouldn't fall. You know a dip like me couldn't fall and mess up my outfit I had my tight stretch DKNY and matching shit on. My personal booster Tuesday got it for me. Annie and I broke her off a little somethin' somethin' to get us all the shit other hoes won't have. Nobody else in the clique hustle like me and Annie. I guess they don't have the guts. They would rather flat back (have sex). Boost, write checks or wait on their Momma to do some shit. Oh no not me never, shit my Mom works her little 9 to 5 and that shit barely gets us by. Skating was just about over and hoes had already started tripping'. While everybody was in line waiting to get their shoes, a fight broke out. The Queens were standing against the wall acting like they didn't have shit to do with it. If the owner caught yo ass scrappin' he would bar your ass for a year. Since this was the hottest shit poppin' on Friday nights, hoes had enough sense to not be in the line of fire. Some Bitch named Princess stole off on Cocoa. Cocoa's ass ain't no fighter in no kind of a way, so Hell Girl jumped in. The bouncers broke it up and pushed them outside. I had my own skates, so I had to wait for Ty and B.B. to trade their skates in so they could get their shoes. "Let's go… what the fuck you standing 'around for and yo girl don't yell at me shit. I'm waiting on Ty and B.B. Bull walked off threw his hands in the air. His boys all looked at me like I was crazy and I flipped them off. "Hurry up y'all shit… this nigga is tripping like I would leave my people's to get whooped on or something." B.B. made it to the front of the line and got her shoes, Ty had to d-bow her way threw and caused a whole stir. Everybody started pushing and shoving and screaming at the white people about their shit. After Ty grabbed her shit, we ran outside and it was on. Some bitch name Pearl tried to sneak me and it was on. "Come… co… come on bitch you tryna fight bitch?." "blow, slap bam." I stole that hoe and slapped that bitch three times before she even got a lick. "This is Champagne bitch y'all hoes better recognize me." All of them yelled and just charged our ass. The police took damn long to get there. Bull jumped in to help me and a gang of Blood niggas rolled his ass. His boy tried to help but they got putting rolled up too. After it was over and the po po started grabbing people and putting them in the patty wagon, we all started running to Bull's truck. Hell Girl, Cocoa, Annie and Ty made it there first. "Yo B.B. are you ok?" I helped her off the ground, her and Fay were still rolling' around on the ground fighting. "No… I'm going to kill this bitch." B.B. was landing hay make's and stomping the shit out a that hoe. I backed the fuck up. Shit her big ass wasn't going to get out of here… girl the police is going to take us to jail." Po po being mentioned made her jump straight up. "Um stomp ' bink bink ' hawk spit… Now bitch take that shit back to them damn Champagne bitches." Me and B.B. ran and made our way to the truck. Cocoa got started. "Where the fuck was y'all at when shit went down?." B.B. didn't even give her a chance. "Shut the fuck up! Cocoa, Shine and me was fighting Jay and Pearl… shit where the fuck was yo scary ass? Shit… Hell Girl had to handle yo damn business." Hell Girl felt embarrassed because her older sister had no guts just all mouth. Everybody in the truck snapped on Cocoa's ass for starting the shit. Bull's boys pulled up and told everybody to shut the fuck up before we all go to jail. "Yo chill before I start stealing on y'all ass." Bull was trying to pull off and everybody kept yelling. "Click clack… Did y'all here me… shut the fuck up." Bull pulled his heater(gun) out on our ass and everybody shut up. "Now since we're all quiet, stay cool and we can get the fuck away from the po po." Everybody was looking me upside my head. Hell Girl started whispering to me." "Yo dude is wild as hell… you better watch his ass." I rolled my eyes and turned around. As I looked at everybody through the rear view mirror, I saw everybody nervous, so I busted out laughing." What's so funny , Veronica?" Annie asked as she smirked. "Y'all… hahahah… y'all ass is scared ass hell" I said. Everybody else laughed but didn't want to start off to much because they didn't want Bull to start again. They was unsure if his ass would shoot them. Bull had his mad dog on. He was pissed that he got rolled up. I didn't even have to ask him what was wrong because the look in his eyes said bloody murder. "Bull when we get over North lets get something to eat… then me and you can go sit down, eat and talk." I told him he looked at me and didn't say a word, he just nodded his head "yes." By the time we pulled up on

Broadway everybody was still out. We were bout to pull in the gas station but the po po had it surrounded. Bull pulled over to find out what happened. As soon as he jumped out everybody got started. "So Shine are you going to fuck the nigga tonight or what?" I busted out laughing cause my girls had me fucked up. Number one rule, never give up your drawers too soon because the nigga will sho nuff act as if he don't know you the next day. "Now y'all know damn well I ain't fucking that body." I said "Yeah right... and don't tell yo Momma you stayed at our house neither. That shit had me pissed off. "Cocoa what da fuck? You think that I got to say I'm staying at yo crib?." I told her Ty was irritated by the jealousy so she spoke up. "Yo Veronica, you can say you was with me and Annie, shit. You know my auntie is out of town, so she'd never be able to tell if you was lying or not." "Thank you homie. You make sure you use a rubber girl... I heard that nigga be hitting a gang of hoes." "h-uu-l- I'm not going to F-U-C-K him damn, y'all." I yelled B.B. just handed me a rubber anyways. Bull made his way back to the car and was a little happy. "Yo what the fuck y'all want to eat and who am I dropping off first?." He asked everybody got to looking at each other and arguing about how much money they did or didn't have. "Yo shut up... damn, I got it... shit. I just want y'all ass out my truck shit." We pulled up to Taco Bell and my girls tried to break Bull ass by ordering everything on the menu. He knew them, and told them about themselves. Everybody but me and Bull ate their food. "Shine why ain't you eating?... I know Burrito Supreme's are your favorite." He told me Hell Girls was shoving the damn Burrito down my damn throat. "Na girl... I'm cool." Bull started rubbing my leg. Y'all don't worry about her, I got this alright." Everybody sniggled and looked at each other. We rolled back past the gas station on our way to Cocoa and Hell Girl's house. The po po had people stretched out on the ground because a shoot out had broke out. We dropped off Cocoa and Hell Girl. To my surprise Cocoa said thank you, and sorry for being a bitch. Bull was shocked, but knew that shit wouldn't last so long. Cocoa always apologized but never meant it. We made it to Ty's house and Annie and B.B. jumped out. I had to run in and get some under clothes. "Yo baby girl, I thought you was Rollin with me." Bull said I was going to play his ass. "Um, I have a bigger plan. "Quit tripping... I got to get me some fresh gear." I told him he grabbed my arm and shook his head. "Na... I got you covered, I told you." I gave everybody a hug and told them what to say if my Mom called. I told them I'll page them when I'm on my way tomorrow. "Don't worry about Sunday." Bull said while pulling off. I didn't say a word the whole ride. I went with the flow. I started looking through his music selection and popped in an old Mary J. Blidge CD. We rode around and talked. He told me all about his crew and how his uncle basically had an iron fist over his head and him and his boys was tired of his ass. People from Chi-Town, Cali and New York were moving in on the territory and it was getting harder to sale dope anywhere in the city. He didn't trust me enough to go to his Moms crib so we went to his sister's instead. "Hi, what's your name?" His sister said while laying across the couch with her boyfriend, I guess!" My name is Veronica." I told her, Her man was looking me down my damn throat. He was fine as hell. He stood about 6'3, had gold teeth and was bow legged. I didn't want to make myself look obvious so I turned my head. "Yo Cat we going to crash in the baby's room, ok." Bull said and grabbed my hand and walked me to the room. After Bull put covers on the bed and went and got me and him something to slip on I felt relaxed. He was a gentleman. He never tried to touch me. He did the regular thing everybody does. Took his body and held it against my booty. He rubbed my tittles and kissed me softly as we laid there and kissed until we fell asleep.

Chapter 10

"Bait"

"Roll Call... and if your friend next to you is not here don't try to make excuses for them." "Na na na... oh shit, na na na... I can't miss this class or be late damn!" I was running up the stairs to make it to zero hi, when you fuck up in school and you don't want your hard working Momma to know shit, you can make it up in the "fuck up" class. I'm here... a a... MO. I'm here." "Young lady I'll talk to you after class." "Ok" "Fuck her shit! She's getting paid either way it goes why would or should she give a fuck. Its just math something I hate but love to count. It's hard enough trying to make it to school, have a tender boyfriend, and beat my feet (sale dope). I'm going to make it through, the lord knows, I am. My Mom ain't having no more D's. Shit I thought it was cool that I didn't get any F's. I know I constantly here it. "No man wants a woman without a brain, Veronica or a pretty face always gets old, or beauty with no brains is useless even to a rich man." I get so tired of hearing about that, I had a bad ass headache from the weekend with Bull. He never tried to get pussy but he let me know he couldn't wait to get it. In my own way I let his ass know he won't be getting shit until he drops some paper. It was easier than I thought. Saturday started out with a good breakfast at Milda's on Morgan and Glenwood. It was a cool little white folk's restaurant that everybody goes to. After seeing a couple of haters, we made our way to downtown. I got 4 pair of Nike Airmax in different colors, three pairs of k-Swiss, 3 pairs of red cream and black boots. And a gang of panties and breeziers, he wanted to see me in. Then he bought Seven pairs of jeans with matching shirts and three coach bags with three dresses to match. Oh, I was impressed, I must say. Shit, after I dropped all that shit off at Annie's, I wanted to drop my draws then. Nah, I just chilled. My fine ass was going to get more before it was all over. Sunday we ate good. We went to some place called Red Lobster that shit was fire. I will be making his ass take me more often. Since I had a headache the whole weekend. That was enough reason to not fuck, huh, that will be my excuse to always make it to Red Lobster. I made it through class. I had to listen to MO, lecture my ass about school, and how intelligent I was if I would just try harder. She didn't tell me shit I didn't already know. "Yo what's up, beautiful?" Oh shit here comes this fine nigga trying' to holla. I wouldn't want Bull poppin' up no where. "What's up." I said while walking away. "Hold up… damn the nigga got you like that already." I ignored his ass and kept walking. "You ain't paying' me to talk… shit! I got to get to class." "Paying' yo ass… P-L-E-A-S-E hoe… yo pie ass ain't got it like that." He yelled loudly Oh no his ass didn't call me pie. "What you mean pie." I grilled his ass with my hand on my hip. "Yeah like I said Pie… you fine as hell, but you look funny than a motha-fucka with yo big head." He said "Big head… Big head shut yo haten ass up… shit you just mad cause Bull got on it before yo ass could!." "Yo home girl, who's that you wild'n out on?" Annie said and she rolled up and she heard my big mouth going off!" Girl nobody but that haten ass Gov… his ass mad cause Bull…." "I ain't mad at the shit, girl… a …you better shut up before I have somebody… " I started "Somebody what?"… nigga please ain't no hoes running up on the Cutie Pie Posse." "Yeah nigga our clique rolls deep" added Annie. I let his ass know while Annie checking on his ass. "Alright I'll see." He said as he walked his punk ass on. Annie and I contemplated on skippin 5th and 6th hour to go to the block. Shit we had missed the whole weekend because I was chilling with Bull. "Shine… I got an idea!"Annie blurted out Oh goodness… you and yo bright Ideas… What now you already let that hoe take our shit, left… "Shut up… already damn… yo ass just don't let shit go." "So… so what, hoe… that was two quarter ounces, bitch… you should of… " "Ok… we ain't going to keep arguing about week old shit, alright… now that nigga Gov's boy, shortcut said I could come over his spot and make some paper." "What… Nah girl that nigga, Gov." "No… it ain't what you think… just cause they hang, don't mean they always do bidness together." Annie ass scared me. I thought about it for a minute and shit. What the hell. I could work on that nigga Gov, if his ass do come through. "Alright, but let me see if Ty and them got something planned." "Damn we can get this paper… shit you know them hoes ain't on the curb game like we are." I thought about it for a minute. Shit if the jump out boys come then that's less we have to worry about. Everybody has to play there position in life. Moca, Barbie or Tylor ain't fit for the game so taken them would make us worry about them snitchen! "You right… if we hit a good lick tonight… we just treat them to something '… alright." Annie wasn't feeling that shit. Even though Ty was her cousin. She didn't always feel up to sharing. "Whatever girl… let me page that nigga so we can head over there." We walked past the block. To my surprise they were runnin' right up to me and Annie. I had to go get the rest of my boulders(50 pieces) from my tennis ball in the bushes. Even though I told Annie I'll let that loss ride. Um, I wasn't taken no more loses. "A Shine lets go… I seen an undercover… and he keeps eyeing my ass." That's all, I needed to hear shit! There was no need to stick around. When you hear shit like that, yo ass best be out. On our way to shortcut's spot, we saw Bull. I told his ass I'll get up with him later. He didn't really question me because he had his home boys and two bitches in the car. Nobody was in there for him doe cause he let that be known when he got out to give me a kiss. I was glad I saw him in that bucket ass Malibu. That was his DC(DoLow) car that he used while doing business. I never let him know my next move cause I got to get my own paper. We made our way to shortcut's spot. It was a 4-plex on 6th and Morgan. I was a little leery because there was no emergency exit in case of a raid. To my surprise I was impressed when we made it in. "What's up Pie Pie." Shortcut's ass haha jokes and I wasn't in the mood. I had money on my mind and that it. "Don't start shortcut she ain't tryin' to hear that shit." "Don't tell him shit Annie I'm going to give his ass a punk in head in a minute." After gropping Branda's and slappin her ass. "I'm just playin' girl… I heard about what happen in school today." "Um you did huh… I hope his punk ass ain't comin' through." "Na he's chillin' he ain't sweatin' that shit." I walked through the house to check it out. He had PO PO scanners, walky talkie's and iron bars across the doors and windows. There wasn't any traffic at the time so I just chilled. After about two hours the shit got to pumpin." "Yo I got 3 for $45 or 2 for $40." "Na na Shine we ain't going to do that like that right now." The dope fiend stood, looking confused but he knew not to question shortcut about his dope, "A…A…A…let baby girl handle her own… " M-o-th-a-f-u-ck-a don't tell me how to run my shit nigga." Shortcut slapped, kicked and punched the clucker (dopefiend) all in his head. He started out the door. "Wait…a… hold up… I got you dog." I grabbed him by da arm and walked him to the hallway so Shortcut couldn't hear me. "Yo next time just ask for me alright." The clucker was scared as hell, but at the same time he was glad to be getting a deal. "What's yo name?...a… what do I tell all my people?... a… you know who I ask for… cause I don't wanna fuck over Shortcut, him and his boys are crazy." I knew right then I was coming into big doe. Yeah my pager was bout to be jumping'. "Yo just tell everybody to look for baby girl… either on da block or up in dis spot." I got my loot and pusher his ass out da door. "Cause traffic was thick. For some reason I knew Dirty Red was going to be bringing my love. His appearance on the outside was dusty but I seen in his eyes he had heart and wanted a little more in life. I made it back in the apt. "Yo don't never leave out dis spot without me or Branda'e." "What...nigga you said I could get doe so I'm a get mines... damn." I went and sat on the couch while him and Annie stood and counted money. "Chill Shine... he just looking out for you." "I know but da nigga can check you not me." He stuck his hand down Annie's pants and smelled his finger then sucked it. I turned my nose up. "Yeah see if yo had a nigga like my boy Gov to do to you what I do to Branda 'e then yo ass wouldn't be so uptight." Annie just stood there smiling from ear to ear." "Um cool... I'll get what ever I want... when I want." "Yeah baby... she ain't hurtin ' for dick." "Let that nigga know Annie." He showed me how to get my doe through the window. I opened the window just enough for them to slide the paper (money) through and gave them their dope. I didn't let Shortcut or his boys see me give them extra. I just said "baby girl let da hood know." They caught on real quick. "Branda's take the cutty and go get us something to eat." Alright baby!!... and call me Annie so these cluckers don't know my government." "I'm going with you." I stood up to grab my coat. "Na stay... so you won't miss no doe." Ah man this damn Annie done set my ass up. You know when yo girl leaves yo alone with her dude. Um in Annie case her tender cause shortcut is just her fuck buddie. I didn't like how this looked. I didn't want to be left in da crib with my home girl's peoples. That shit just ain't straight. "You like that doe you getting huh? Shortcut said while ploppin ' his dick next to me. I rose up off the couch and walked to da window. "Yeah I appreciate that homeboy." I said as I made my way over to the window to finish seven them fiends. His ass got the point because he instantly started stressing me about Gov. He was tryin to convince me that his homeboy was better than Bull. He started hatin like most niggas do. I'm glad I was talking to his ass cause I found out a gang of shit about Bull and his peoples. He had two sisters named Cat the one I met and Trina. His sister Cat had a boyfriend named Rock and they also called him Zero because his ass was black as hell. I know that was that nigga eyeing' me that night at his sister's crib. That nigga zero is the man. Shit Shortcut say that nigga is hooked up wit some Cali nigga's and they bout to take the Sota over. Right when Shortcut was about to tell me some more juice here come Annie and that nigga Gov. My heart started pumpin ' cause I saw two ugly hoes standing ' right behind his ass. "What's up… Pie pie." I was unsure about my response so I better watch his actions…"What's up big head?" Everybody in the spot was laughing ' their ass off. "Oh so you got jokes huh." "Nah… yo do… Annie gemmed at food." She thought that shit was so cute. I didn't. that's why I pinched her ass. "ouch… girl… stop." "You play too much." "Nah… when I was coming in the door him and them two cluckers ran up behind me!." "Um so they ain't his goon squad?." "Nah… I think they buy work (drugs)from him." "Oh… ok." The rest of the night went cool. The damn door and window was jumping all night. I was hearing "Baby girl, Baby girl" all damn night. When we ran out of dope, Annie had to recop (buy more) from that nigga Gov. It was about 4 o'clock in da damn morning and dis nigga was feeling on my ass. "Nigga don't touch me." I said and slapped his ass in the head and tried to get up. "Yo just chill… you said you needed some work don't you." My mind started racing. His ass was a baller and I could come up off his ass. Shit but if I fuck his ass right now he'll throw that shit all up in Bull's face. I tried to move him off me but he wasn't havin ' it. "Stop Gov… quit… damn move your damn hand." I told him "I could feel his dick all on my ass. Damn his shit was big as hell. He started blowin ' and lickin' in my ear. I was getting weak as hell but I wasn't letting ' that nigga get shit. "You know you want dis dick… Uh huh, yeah let daddy do what that nigga ain't doing baby." He said and pulled my pants halfway down. "Gov… stop nigga damn." I started screamin ' on his ass cause my pussy was wet ass hell. "Sh!… sh!. Sh!. Girl… damn I ain't going to rape you shit." "I know you ain't cause you ain't… getting shit… he covered my mouth with his hand I felt even weaker. The nigga smelled so good and his lips were soft ass hell. Between breathes I said "Gov…chill please… I got somebody." He wasn't listening at first and started sucken and lickin all the way down to my hair line. He came back up as we played tug a war with my jeans." Huh… let…let me eat it. "Nah… not up in here he looked me dead in my eyes all sweaty and shit." Nah… I think you a raw bitch… I'll pay you!… just to let me taste you." I was getting weaker when shortcut came knockin ' on the door. "Yo…what y'all doin ' up in there?" He laid his ass on me harder."

We straight dog." "Why Shine yellin and shit?" "Oh she's cool..." "Yo Shine." "I'm straight, shortcut... thank you." He walked away from the door. I could hear him and Annie snickering. I know they thought I was given up my pussy but I wasn't. "How much... you got." He pulled the know out. Damn, the shit looked like at least 3 or 4 g's. "You impressed?" He asked "Na...but if you got that just to taste it...shit I'll let you...... but you ain't fucking and you know Bull... is my tender." He pulled my pants down to my ankles. He pulled his shirt off, pulled his pants off and got butt ass naked. Damn my pussy was jumpin like a rabbit. He started stretching ' so I could see every curve of his tightly toned body. His dick was big like a fucking horse. Long and thick with a slight curve to it. I was leaking all over the couch and my nipples was at attention. "You sure you ain't going to let me hit it... Nobody will ever know... shit, I got hella rubbers!" He was smiling 'and rubbin 'his dick. I'm strong though. "Na... you said eat the pearl tongue and that's it." I answered He laid on top of me and put his money in my coat pocket. He started rubbin my tittles, kissing me and lickin in my ear. "Um, yes baby... oh... shit Gov... you said you was going to suck it. "His dick was right between my legs and touching my click. "Yeah... you feel that don't you...Uh huh... he kissed me softly down to my click and sucked it while havin his finger in me. I was going crazy. I didn't make much noise because it started getting light outside and I knew Annie would be knockin ' for us to go to school soon. He turned me over and licked my pussy from the back. "Gov... Gov... stop... baby." He didn't listen, he was fingering me and blowin and lickin my ass. I still wasn't going to fuck him. He blowed and licked while watching me grind his finger. "Yeah... I like how it looks... baby just let me feel you." He said and grabbed my waste from behind. Kissed me up my back and rubbed his dick up and down my ass hole. He was lickin ' on my ear and neck." Is that enough for you... you feel... good don't you...see I can make you feel better." He said and turned me around and made me sit on his lap with my jean around my ankles still, so my legs was over his head. "You already sitting right here on it you still ain't going to let me get it." He said while kissing me. "um... no... I can't... not in dis spot... and not dis soon." I told him he held me tight and kissed me for what seemed like an eternity." "I respect that... baby... dis between me and you... don't go round telling yo girls I broke you off." I was tripping. Not dis nigga Gov. Got it going on, ballin, hoes tripping, off him and he wants me, paid to eat and didn't even fuck. Yeah and they say I ain't da flyest bitch at North High. "Nah...I won't even tell Annie or your girl." I said kissed him one more time because I knew it would be a minute before I was around his ass alone again. We dozed off for about two hours in each other's arms. We were woken up by Shortcut blasting Jay-Z's, "can't knock the hustle." Gov's crazy ass jumped right up and put his clothes on. He gave me a peck on da lips and offered me to wear one of his jogging suits to wear to school. I took the suit and one of his Gucci sweats that some clucker brought through the night. "Y'all looking all happy dis morning, Um...what did y'all do when we was sleep." Annie and Shortcut had jokes and I wasn't letting up on shit. I didn't have to." "Yo Cut tell yo girl to mind her bidness man." Gov was a little irritated by them being noisy. "Yo Annie she will tell yo ass when y'all get to school!" Annie just looked at cut and laughed. "She sure is baby." Me and Annie washed up. We didn't have any toothbrushes with us but we had some at school in the locker. You know a girl is always prepared for a booty call. Shit that booty call paid off for me, Um, I didn't know about Annie but I was leaving' school early to go shopping'. I know my Mom had been looking for me so I was going to pick her up a little something. "Yo... I got some mouth wash if you want some... or you can use my toothbrush." Gov stood in the doorway saying as he watched me butt ass naked at the sink taken a hoe bath. "Thank you... I'll take the mouthwash." He stood there being entertained with soap dripping 'off me. He stuck his head in and sucked my nipple. And said "Damn you still fine ass hell in da morning." I smiled and shut the door so I could finish. Gov dropped us off at school. For some reason he wouldn't take us right in front of the school. I didn't trip cause when I was in the bathroom, I counted the loot. It was $4,500 plus six hundred in food stamps. Shit me and my Mom was going to be eaten for a grip(longtime). He kissed me and told me "Yo... between me and you... you owe me next time... and da loot will be bigger depending on what you do." I looked at him and turned up the Biggies ""wanting" and said "as long as that paper is correct then its whatever." Annie was looking me all upside my head. We made it into school and the first person I saw standing by English class. "Where... have yo hot ass been?" Bull asked I got to get to class... I'll see you at lunch." Annie hurried up and ran off before he got to questioning her. I could barely look him in the face. "What" "you heard me... I kept calling Ty's house and I went over Hell Girls and she said she paged y'all all night and you never hit them back." I rolled my eyes and sucked my teeth. Damn I'm barely his girl and his ass is questioning a queen. "Me and Annie was getting doe... you know that... don't act like I don't make my own money nigga." I told him in my class cause the bell rung. "Hold up." He said and grabbed my arm. "I'm going to let you get your school on... but don't disrespect me after I spent all that lost on yo ass." His grip was kinda tight and I knew right then he was going to fight me if I got out of line. I'll page you when I get out ok... ." I kissed him before he could start questioning me about this over sized Nike suit I had on with DKNY gym shoes on. "Alright I made it through school like a champ. I couldn't get that nigga Gov's scent off my hands. I know he wore that Calvin Kline well. Annie and I caught a cab out to Ridge dale shopping mall. That nigga Shortcut broke her ass off with a G(thousand dollars). Plus she had 3G's from what we made in the spot. Half was mines as I told her to use my half for recop. She let me know Shortcut gave us a quarter key (9 ounces of coke). I was cool cuz, I thought Annie was slippin on her pimpin. Shit she came up a little better than I did. I guess that was the price of the hot girl's pussy nowadays. "I wanna go in Banana Republic first." "Alright... but we ain't buying all that shit today cause I wanna buy my Mom's coach bag." We walked all over that damn mall, ate everything in sight and bought everybody a little something. Annie didn't question me about Gov. She just assumed that we fucked. I was going to let her know but I decided not to. Shit, it was my business. On our way home I thought about buying a car. I was only fifteen and in the 10th grade. My Mom was disappointed in me but not much because I hadn't had any babies. She had me at sixteen and had already been through a bad marriage. I had a cute little step sister and step dad that cared a lot about me. Me and my step sister were close even though my Mom got a divorce and moved on to a new boyfriend. We were raised together from childhood. My step dad loved me like his own and helped me get over my depression. When I was younger I was introduced to sex by an old friend of the family and by the time I told my Mom it was too late. She cried and apologized to me. It wasn't her fault and I let her know that. Any sick motha-fucker that messes with kids will pay in life and the after life. God knows that and he's watching them. She also feels that the reason why I was sexually active s because of it, and that maybe at least I'd get paid for it. My dad made me pray it off my mind as a kid and it works. So before I lay my ass down to sleep. I thank god for my blessing and for delivering me from evil. "Annie you wanna stay at my house for the rest of the week?." I asked Annie was tryin to get back to Shortcut and I knew it." "What about that dope Shortcut got?" Just like knew it she couldn't even let the nigga miss da pussy. "If he gave it to us... damn... Annie you weak for da nigga already." I asked her "Weak... girl please I just don't want the nigga to change his mind you know." "nah... he ain't going to change shit that Gov gave us." I assured her "Oh yeah... you right...alright I'll chill all week plus I got to study." "Cool ok... and my Mom asks where we got dis hoe, tell her ass we been working for the telemarketing place and they pay us everyday,ok." "ooh...cool girl you know yo ass be comin with them stories." Annie commented "I got to stay on my toes." "We made it to my house. My Mom and her boyfriend left a note saying that they were going to the show and if I left to let her know before I disappear again. I was glad she wasn't right there shit. I looked like Santa Claus and X-mas was months away. I made a promise to put my school work first and I did. Me and Annie studied until my Mom got home. I put her two coach bags and three pants suits on her bed. Her boyfriend knew I sold dope but would never disrespect his house by havin dope in it and I didn't. The number one rule you learn from the streets. Never ever have shit where you sleep, trust no one and slow money is foe sho money. When you rush the block or never leave it and give it a rest. You will get fucked. "Oh so I see y'all studying tonight." My Mom said"Yeah Mom we need to" "good! Branda 'e does your Mom know you are over?" "I left a message with my cousin Ty cause she's out of town." "ok as long as she knows... you guys make sure you secure the door when you leave in the morning." Mom must have been in a good mood cause she didn't question me. Before I went to bed I called Gov and Bull. Gov never called back, so I kept paging Bull. He was given ' my ass the silent treatment and I was pissed off.

Chapter 11
"All About Bull"

Over the next 6 months things got a little fucked up. The nigga was beaten my ass every chance he got. Everybody said it was my fault because I wouldn't keep my mouth shut. Bullshit I wasn't letting no mother fucker talk to me any kind of way. That shit use to cost me though, I was in love. To make it bad the dick wasn't even all that. He wasn't eating pussy so it couldn't of been that. Annie and I wasn't getting no money. She was, it was I had my head stuck up Bull's ass. When ever he paged me, I better call him back or that was a black eye. It was his regular thing to embarrass me in front of his friends. His ass was so damn slow he didn't know that the Shorty Macs was waiting for da opportunity to fuck. Especially little Butchie. His ass always smiled at me. Told me if I ever needed help slangin my dope or if shit kicked off on the black with other hoes and my clique, the little nigga was ready to scrap with us. The nigga Pig Pen use to run around the hood and snatch all the cluckers dope, slap or punch them, then sell the shit right back to them. His big brother Jack was a fucking jokester. One time he invited me and the clique to spend the night in the projects with him and the Shorty Macs. He was gone off that beer, Cisco. That shit was liquid cocaine he was putting beer on people's feet and butt, then putting a match to them. They woke up screamin and not knowing what the fuck was going on. By the time morning came, we was wet with a pile of roaches crawling around our ass. Boo, Gotti and Spanky held that nigga down and let us whoop his ass. It was fun then. Their Mom was cool as hell. She let us smoke weed in da crib and drink but don't get caught fucking! Nah she wasn't having that at all. Spanky's crazy ass was the only one that would bust a hammer (gun). One time some nigga from the Gangsta Souls came through set trippin'. He had two of his peoples with him and a dog. All the Shorty Macs rolled them nigga's up and they started making the dog. All the girls was running and screaming Spanky came from out the bushes and got to bustin that hammer. The dog got hit and died instantly. Word around the hood was to not fuck with the Shorty Mac's, especially that nigga Spanky. He loved that shit. Asking did we want him to kill anybody for us. All them niggas were under 16. Shit we all were young. It was about to be the eleventh grade and summer was breakin '. When it gets hot, niggas don't know how to act. "Yo shine... Shine... you hear me girl... go wit B.B. and Hell girl." Bull told me I was getting some paper and that nigga Bull was haten on me. He was mad cause that nigga Gov came through and gave me, Annie and Ty a sweet deal he couldn't pin point where it came from so he wanted me to leave... "Nah... I got to get this off before I leave... my Mom needs groceries." I told him "Shit you been havin ' all them food stamps for the past 6 months...what happen?" he was talking about that old shit from Gov. He thought he was slick enough to find out where it came from but nope. "That shit been gone." Slap... slap... Bang. Bull slapped the shit out of me, then punched me in the top of my head. "Come on Bull, damn... not today boy... if you going to hit her then why you with her?" said Olivia was da home girl. She was down with the Cutie Pies but she was about her paper so we only kicked it once in a while. "You shut the fuck up and stay out my business!." He said and charged at her to hit her. B.B., hell girl and I rushed his ass. "Leave her the fuck alone!" I said while picking up a stick. His boy Doo Rod tried to grab B.B. from behind. I walled his ass across the head. "Ouch... bitch I'm a ...beat yo ass." He yelled I took off running and he couldn't catch me. I ran and B.B. was behind me. Olivia was still standing there arguing with Bull. B.B. was glad I hit his ass and got away with it because he use to whoop her ass. Him and Bull thought they was running shit. Bull's cousin Tomp was fucking ' Hell Girl on and off. She wasn't having him beaten ' on her, that's why she never helped too much when it came to getting in the middle of me and Bull's shit. She was a hater sometimes, always tryin to encourage me to cheat on Bull and talked shit when I wouldn't. Then dry snitch and tell him shit if I didn't. I was pissed because Hell Girl thought the shit was funny. What if that nigga Doo Rod would of hit me. She was acting like she didn't have my back. "Yo... come here Shine." Bull started coming close to me. I knew he was going to hit me so I stood on the other side of the car. "What" Hell Girl was laughing ' her ass off. "Ain't shit funny girl "I yelled. She thought it was cute cause Tomp wasn't whopping on her ass. "Yeah it is… I told you he ain't going to hit you no more she was confident that nigga wouldn't hit me. Doo Rod came from one way and Bull came from the other. "Hah…help B.B.…help Olivia." I was running and screaming my ass off. "stop… stop Bull." Olivia was tryin to stop Bull but he pushed her back. She started crying, after getting up off the ground. He grabbed me after Doo Rod pushed him off me. "See what you made me do to your little friend… now say sorry to my boy." He said as he had a tight grip on the back of my neck and arm. "No fuck him… and fuck you." I said and I tried breaking loose. He continued to fight me and I was fighting his ass back hard ass hell. "See I can't take this shit… just leave his ass alone." Olivia threw her hands in the air and started walking away. B.B. and Annie started walking with her. After Bull quit his shit and Doo Rod stopped chanting him on, I ran and caught up to Olivia. She was still crying so I gave her a hug. "I'm going to leave him, Olivia… I am… I promised." She just hugged me back. "I'm not going to be around you if he keep fucking with him… I can't do it…. I mean his ass is going to kill you." I couldn't blame her. I didn't really care about my appearance anymore, I constantly made sure I smelled good and kept my hair in a ponytail. The booster, Tuesday, came through the back and showed us love with all the gear but I only could wear it if I went somewhere with Bull. This relationship shit was getting on my damn nerves. Every time I got out of school his ass was right out front, waiting on me. I never understood, me hanging ' with him and his boys. Later on that shit will catch up to him. "You don't need to go to school tomorrow!" I hate his ass. How in the fuck is you going to tell me, I don't need to go to school. "What… hello… what." "You heard me girl don't go to school tomorrow." What signal was he tryin ' to give me. "Bull cut the shit… what's up." "I ain't about to be explaining shit in the phone…come meet me on the corner of yo Momma's." I put my clothes on. I felt cute today with my guess daisy dukes with matching ' shirt and gym shoes. I had to cover my black eye with foundation and put brown lip stick on so you couldn't tell my lip was busted. I made it to the gas station on Penn and 26th . I seen Bull sitting in the car with a girl. Not this shit, this nigga got a bitch in the car? To my surprise it was his sister Trina. Me and her were cool but I could tell she was a little jealous of me. "Come here." Bull grabbed me by my ponytail. "OOOuch... stop...you already fucked me up." I said as his stupid ass sister just sat there with a smirk on her face. "Quit Bull before somebody calls the police out here." She said after getting out the car to make him stop. "Get in the car?" he told me. "No." I tried to run in the store but the people in there wasn't having it. They locked the door on me and the women shook her head, no. I guess in my neighborhood people knew not to get in other peoples business. I walked with him to the car and sat down. We was Rollin through the hood with the window down bump in '. His sister turned the music down. "Veronica remember when we was drunk at my house?." I already knew what she was about to say. She thought her fake ass was slick. Yeah she was known for putting a whopping ' on a bitch but I wasn't no punk. "No... uh... when?" "When you and yo home girls was talking about getting doe on the block." This bitch is about to bring that nigga Gov up. All this time, damn near a year and nobody ever brought that nigga up. "Yeah... Trina... what the fuck you getting at." "Slap...a ...don't curse at my sister." Quit Bull. "She faked like I was grabbing his hand back. "I ain't getting at shit... with yo smart ass...now I wasn't going to tell Bull but I am now." She knew damn well she was going to tell his ass cause she was mad Gov didn't want to fuck her ass. "Now didn't you say Gov be breakin you and Annie off." "No." "Yeah ...you did girl...and you said the nigga broke you off to fuck him." Before I could answer, Bull's fist was all upside my head. I was crying ' hysterically and just covered my face. "I... I... I... I never fucked him." "I didn't say you did... I said he paid you to!" Bull stopped , and him and his sister got to arguing. "Yo dumb ass told me that she fucked him recently girl." "No...I said she gets dope from him and Shortcut and she was going to fuck ..." "No you didn't bitch." They went back and forth about who said what and how his sister was lying. I tried getting out the care but neither one would let me. "Don't touch me bitch." I tried hitting Trina Bull stopped me. "Alright... I'm going to let her whoop yo ass." She tried swingin ' on me.

"Nah... don't tell her shit...I'm going to get her." Bull never said sorry but tried being nice and taken me to get my hair done. The bitch Trina got dropped off at Cat's house. Bull ran in while I sat in the car. Cat yelled hi out the window and I ignored her ass. Her man Rockma' came outside acting like he was going in the trunk of his car. He winked his eye at me. I just smiled at his fine ass. This made his ass come over and speak. I really didn't want him seeing me with a black eye but it wasn't shit I could do about it. "Hi...how you doing?" He slid halfway in the driver's seat with his feet hanging out the door... "I'm cool ...I guess." I slid over closer to my passenger door in case Bull or Cat came out tripping '. "You don't have to be scared...ain't nobody going to hit you with me right here." I felt a little more at ease. He musta heard about Bull beating on me I'm sure. He seen my face all fucked up. We talked for a minute about me hitting the block and how or who I could get deals from without Bull knowing. He let me know that he was about to get the fuck away from cat and her family. He was tired of Cat's uncle running shit because he was his own man. He told me all about him and his boy T.T.M (Talk To Much) who gets the hook up from his peoples, Nathan and Derrick as he was about to finish Bull came running out the house. Rockma told me, "Keep that on the low... if I see you know how to be quiet I'll hook you up." He blew a kiss at me and headed back in the house. He slapped Bull's hand and told him to chill with whopping ' on me. "Yo... what you tell that nigga." He was talking as he backed up out the drive way. I was still pissed off at Trina doing that shit. So I wouldn't talk, I just cried for him to take me home and leave me alone. "I'm sorry ...I won't... "Yes the fuck you will...you bitch." I was shaking and crying ' with snot and buggers comin ' out my nose. His bitch ass started laughing and tried to cover my nose. We made it back over north. It seemed like forever getting to the beauty shop from Hopkins. Yeah da nigga Rockma ' had him and Cat a cool spot way out there so niggas couldn't run up in their crib. When we pulled in front of 'head hut' right off on Broadway and Penn I just jumped out and grabbed my purse. While I was crying ' I saw his dumb ass look through my purse and put a couple of hundreds in there. "Oh...you ain't going to say thank you." On my way in I saw Bull's homeboy Tweedy. His ass was so light skinned that the hood gave him that name. "You alright Shine?" It wasn't his fault his boy beat my ass. So I just ignored him cause I wanted to go off on somebody but it wasn't nobody's fault except Bull. He gave me a hug before walking out the door. "It's yo own fault …just leave the nigga." He was right! It wasn't his fault and I shouldn't of treated him like that. Everybody in the shop watched me like a fucking piece of meat. I forgot I was in the hood with a big shining black eye. As light as my ass was you could see any flaw I fucking had. I got a roll n' set and tipped the woman $20. She was grateful because people stopped going to her after finding out she was a crack head. Even though she left me about three times to get high, shit I didn't care. The job was well done, so I mind my own business. I called B.B. up there to get me. She pulled up with Hell Girl and Ty. "Damn how… that nigga still whopping ' on yo ass." Here goes Hell Girl and her shit. "Shut up hoe… you just worry about Tomp's ass not fucking up your ass." Ty and B.B. busted out laughing. "I ain't got to worry , that nigga know what not to do." "Yeah right." We rode on after I told them about Trina and that snake shit she pulled. They was tripping ' because she was much older and knew she shouldn't get into her brother's business. Shit she knew his punk ass was fucking a gang of hoes. I heard she be letting the nigga fuck her friends and fuck at her crib. Shiesty bitch um I got her though. "I told yo ass to stop fucking with that nigga's family…you be hangin ' with that hoe Dana and that other cousin of his… shit them hoes probably be telling him shit too …and to make it so bad you won't even cheat on the nigga." "I know Ty… but I love him …I …I just don't want to cheat on… I mean a year ago it was cool to fuck for doe… but shit I'm bout to be 16 and that ain't cute you know." "Shit… please that nigga DooRod don't know but I gets my fuck on… especially for some money please." "all y'all hear about how them niggas be fucking, y'all be snappin '", "shit I don't." "Hell Girl, Hell girl… please y'all remember that hoe Shawn that fucked Tomp and his brother and was smiling in Hell Girl's face?" Everybody looked at each other Hell Girl held her head down. "Yeah Hell Girl beat the shit out of her in front of the Marriott Hotel." Everybody started laughing. "Yeah we remember ." "Um hum…Hell Girl what's wrong? Cat got your tongue baby?" I shoved her on her shoulder and pushed her head. "Quit before I slap you." She bucked at me because everybody was laughing at her. "Don't play hoe." You know I fight wild as hell." I made her smile, she was pissed but had to suck that shit up. "That was different anyways... shit that hoe was skimming ' and grinning in my grill and tryin to be my friend... then called herself fucking Tomp after fucking his big brother." I let Hell Girl have that shit. She knows damn well she was fighting over Tomp and her hard ass wouldn't admit it. We rode back over to my house and I told everybody bye. It had been a couple of days and I hadn't seen Bull. I was tryin to wing my ass away from him. Annie was still hitting the block everyday but I wasn't feeling it. For two weeks Bull was pagan ' me and I wouldn't answer his ass back. Every time his ass came up to my school my teacher would tell him I couldn't take a break to talk to his ass. My Mom finally seen my black eye. She told his ass if he ever out his hands on me again then he's going to jail and she didn't give a care who his family was. Damn my Mom had more guts than me. I was going to have to stand up to this nigga. Money was getting low so instead of going in my stash I asked my Mom for some money. "What? I can't believe you came down from that attic." She was looking me up and down for any signs of injury. "I know Mom... I've been given da streets a break." Her boyfriend smiled at me and said "good... cause they will wear you out before your time." "Yeah Veronica... don't rush to get older... take your time...here goes a hundred dollars stay away from that women beater." "I will Mom... I will." I know me getting beat made her very uncomfortable. It showed in her beautiful eyes. No matter what I was going to get the fuck away from his ass if it's the last thing I did. I walked over to Olivia's crib. I'm so glad she was there so I could explain to her how much she meant to me. I sat and talked with her for about two hours. Annie started paging me 911. So I had to hit her back. "Ring, ring" "Yo Annie what's up?." She started telling me and Olivia over the phone that it had been a big shootout. So Chris's niggas came on the block talkin about how their little nigga's better get their shit off and ain't nobody going to stop them. She said that Rock's boy Iowa Posse and the Shorty Macs came through, they couldn't match it. She said basically T.T.M told the Shorty Macs that they had a choice to be with the Iowa Posse or them. The Iowa

Posse just knew that the Shorty Macs were down but they weren't. They acted real fucked up and told T.T.M to put them on. Rockma was sick about it. He caught the Shorty Macs one by one and gave them a choice. He told them flat out. "either you with me or against me, so don't get caught slippin." "So who had the shoot out." "All I seen was that nigga Tomp and his brother go up to T.T.M and two dudes that was with him." "was Bull there?" "No he came after it was over." "Um hum just like a punk… yeah his bitch ass will fight me but won't fight no nigga huh." "I… know… hoe let me finish… niggas came from Logan and Knox and lit the whole block towards Logan, so that let me know they set that shit up." "Where in the fuck was yo ass? Seeing all this shit?." "I was shocked Annie had all this damn info shit! Fucking CNN could of hired her ass. "I was in shortcut's cutty with my head halfway up." Girl you lucky you didn't get killed." "I know Olivia girl I was scared… I'm bout to come through alright!" "Who's with you… oh I got the Shorty's Mya and Myrecal with me." "Oh let me tell Shine." She took the phone away from her ear. "Yo Shine do you want Annie to come through with Mya and Myrecal?" "Um I don't know about those girls. Shit their only a year and years under me but we got enough hoes in the clique. "it's yo crib Olivia… shit if you was tryin to hang because of our status. The hoes all around wanted to be down ' I wasn't that find of them because their Auntie was hangin ' with them sometimes and the girl use to talk about Bull. She said he got a big dick but couldn't fuck, I was Rollin ' cause it was the truth. I always wondered why their name was Mya Myrecal but they wasn't twins. They was like a year apart. When they pulled up they just honked the horn. "Come on y'all the block is still hot." "Yeah it's money out there! Come on! Mya and Annie was yelling from the window. Me and Olivia jumped up and ran to the car. "What's up y'all." "Hi!"… where we going?" On Morgan to get the work (drugs) and then we going to walk (drugs) and then we going to walk to the block from there. We made it to the block and it was on like popcorn. Shit as soon as we hit the set, all I heard was "baby girl"… where you been… niggas is spooked and it's money to be made! The clucker Dirty Red rushed me as soon as he seen me. "I been chillin '… just bring um to me and I got you." Olivia went up on Penn by McDonald's. She had to get her doe on her own. I respected her for that but to me that's how you get robbed. If your friends, police or enemies see yo ass up here by yourself that gives them a reason to fuck with you. When we finished our shit Annie wanted these two leeches to hang with us. I was ok with Mya. She seemed cool but Myrecal was sneaky. "Why do they call y'all Mya and Myrecal and y'all ain't twins." "Yeah we are only... 14 months apart." "Oh...that makes sense I guess." Myrecal ass was going to be a hater. I could already see it. I'm bout to let Annie know they are her friends and not mine. "Yo...yo Bull come here." See what I mean now this bitch Myrecal knows I fuck with Bull and she calling his ass over here. "A... don't do that, I don't want to be bothered." "So ...that's my homie." See I knew my instinct never served me wrong. "No... Myrecal." She said she don't want him coming over here trippin ' Mya spoke up to her sister cause she knew I was pissed and she didn't want no problems. "Yeah... you wrong mycreal." Annie wasn't feeling her ass on that one. I started walking back towards the car. I seen Tuesday with a big ass bag. Annie Olivia and Mya was right behind me. "Yo Tuesday what you got?" We all looked in the bag it was hella shit in there. She had shit in all our sizes, even my Mom and sisters "I don't know... you tell me!" I knew what she meant. See Tuesday was one of those smokers that only smoked primo's (weed and crack). She kept herself up and always wanted money and dope together. "I got you... meet me at the car... and put the bag in the back seat until we come." We stood on the corner kickin ' the shit and served a little more people in front of Tomp's spot. Shit them crip nigga's had shit shook up and niggas wasn't around. We waited for that slick bitch Myrecal to come and she finally made it. "What took you so long." Mya was looking ' her sister up and down. "Nothing, I was hollering at Tomp's little brother... I got his number too...Bull is suppose to hook me up with the nigga." I felt a little at ease but I still felt like the bitch was lying '." Did that nigga Bull is suppose to hook me up with the nigga." I felt a little at ease but I still felt like the bitch was lying '." Did that nigga Bull ask about Shine?" I walked towards the car so Tuesday ass wouldn't leave. Just because she's cool don't mean she won't give nobody else my shit. "yeah... nosy Annie she did." "What did he say?" I could hear Mya and Annie questioning her ass as we walked to the car. Olivia was already there looking over the shit with Tuesday. Olivia was a booster herself so she wasn't letting Tuesday get over on us, because if she wanted it she could get it herself. "Yo don't be taken all the good shit." They looked at each other. "Didn't I tell you she was going to trip." "Yeah you sure did… hah hah Olivia said she was waiting till you came before she picked shit out." "Ooh I like that… man I want it. "Oh my god that's bomb." Myrecal and Mya was admiring the gear Tuesday had. I gave her a quarter ounces and 4 hundred dollars and she rushed off. "Damn bitch you came up…that's enough shit for everybody." "I know that's why I wouldn't let it get by." We split the shit up. I let Mya and her sister get them a couple of things after Olivia and Annie got what they wanted "thank you Shine… and I wouldn't sleep or creep with my home girl's man." Myrecal tried to say in a convincing voice but I wasn't moved. "Yeah, thanks Veronica…hum sometimes too nice." "I know girl but it's just in my nature." That night ended up hurting me in the long run.

Chapter 12

"Bad Luck"

Summer done kicked in the door. Damn, Bull done let up off of me a little. He's too busy goggling women. In the past couple of months I caught him with three bitches. Yeah I said I was going to leave him but of course I'm still here. I'll give him the silent treatment for a week and then he'll come to me with a couple hundred, Red Lobster and some make up dick! After two days or a week, it's back to the black eye or busted lip. My whole clique talks about me like a dog behind my back. Shit all they got to do is step to me about the shit and I got them. Every bitch I run with is weak for a nigga but I don't check them about shit unless they get in mine. That's where shit gets fucked up everybody judging me but ain't looked in their own shit. Only God can judge me, so when hoes realize that, they be alright. "what's up Veronica?" Tweedy was the first person I seen on the block at 5 in the morning. He was a true believer in the early birds gets the worms." "Hay…Tweedy is there any paper out here?" "yeah a little… hay why you out here by yo self?...where's all the home girls at." Bless his heart he was always concerned about me in a brotherly way. I guess that comes from his parent's passing away at a young age. He was left to live with his older sister and she's done a great job at raising him. "They ain't like me Tweed... I'm tryin ' to quit this shit and move out to Hollywood... I want to be in movies, make movies or dress the stars." He busted out laughing. "Girl you're funny as hell!... but I guess that's what our brain is for you know... it's for us to use and take advantage of any situation." I was moved by his positivity. If I would of shared my thoughts with anyone else they would of shut my ass down and laughed in my face. "I guess we're taking advantage of this situation now." I took off running over to dirty red before Tweed paid any attention. "All now... you got me ha." He was killing himself laughing. "That's alright I'm bout to go in dis spot right here!" He walked over to a duplex across form where I was standing by the townhouses. "Hold up... let me holler at him." "alright I got you." I had to talk to Dirty Red cause I hadn't seen him in a while. "Baby girl... you ain't never stable baby...how you going to reach yo quota if you ain't never around." "Damn... I know Dirty but ...a...I've been doing other thangs." "Yeah... I know like getting yo pretty face kicked in...you know a lot of people care about you and you let snakes run all around you and fuck up yo shit." "I know Dirty Red... I know ...it's almost over though... I turn 16 in August so I am going to pursue my dreams." "Ok but quit letting that nigga whoop on you... shit it ain't like he don't got other bitches." Damn here he goes. Everybody knows this nigga don't appreciate me. I'm going to get this doe this summer and move out to St.Paul so the nigga can't track my ass down. I made my way into the upper duplex where Tuesday was standing on the balcony. There were two people sitting on the front steps before I came in. The girl looked like a dope fiend and the dude looked like he was something. " What's up...y'all live here?" "yeah... we just moved here from out of town... " "Oh ...alright. I started to walk up the stairs. "excuse me... hey." I turned around. "what's up?" "do you got something?" I don't know dis blood like that for her to be asking me shit. "Nah." I ran up the steps and locked the security gate. Yeah Tuesday spot was like shortcuts. Her ass had a big ass gate with a dead bolt lock on it. "What that clucker ask you?" "if I had something?" "Oh... shit she owes me a c-note (hundred)... I don't know why she asked you like you wasn't going to tell me." "I know... you want me to whoop her ass?." "ha... quit trippin girl... that ain't how you do bidness." His ass was too damn nice. I would of beat her ass if it was my dope. "That's how I do bidness... ha." "Yeah and yo ass will have the police on you a lot more." I took in all the little game Tuesday was tryin' to run by me. Even though I'm a good person, I know the game can get ugly. If you're not hard or don't have any guts then you will lose. Bull lectured me about having an attitude at him that time I seen him in the shop. I let him know it's all love and I know he got my back. We kicked it for a couple of hours and made plenty of money. A couple of the Iowa Posse came through talking about Bull's uncle and his iron fist. The old man was back in prison for tryin to take somebody's shit that wasn't having it apparently. Even though the Crips have the best deals in town there was still money to be made. Tuesday and I talked about Bull having a big head because the big homie Chico put him on to getting some real 20money. His uncle didn't know about that though. Um hum his ass even wanted to be a Crip with T.T.M. Chico let his ass know he ain't got to flip because he ain't no Crip. Chico had done time for smokin' a nigga 5 years ago. Bull knew not to ever cross his ass because he heard about him handling his business. Bull was bringing Chico at least a 50 g's a week. So for every Kilo Bull bought Chico fronted him two. The best thing for Bull to do was to stay on Rockma's good side. Yeah that was the only reason Bull's ass was on. He was just about to fuck himself. Bull was bangin' that Iowa Posse shit and Chico heard about it. He told him a real man tryin' to get paper in da streets don't gang bang... fuck a gang. In between Bull's lies and the dice game, he couldn't keep up with the flow. "Yo Tuesday I'm bout to call over the crew... alright." She was serving' somebody through the gate. The home boys Mistro and Doo Rod was smokin a blunt and drinking some yak. "That's cool... but if they don't come before 9:00pm they wont get in alright." "alright." I called everybody and asked them did they wanna come through and smoke. Of course everybody was game. Annie brought Mya And Myrecal. B.B. and Ty weren't there but Annie told me, Olivia was chillin with us until Tomp, his brother and Bull came through. "Oh dis where yo ass been all day huh?." Bull said and pushed me in my head. "Quit trippin...and tryin' to front me in front of niggas." "Alright but we going to talk later." Tuesday pulled him over to the window and let him know not to start. I was relieved that he was cool. The clique and I was discussing the next party at the Varsity on the U of M campus. E.P.M.D., second to none and D.J. quick was going to be there. I didn't want Bull to hear because he would be out of town that weekend and I was going no matter what. "Bang Bang Bang." I ran to the window to see who it was. "Yo Tuesday I'm bout to let Ty and Hell Girl up." Niggas started slappin' hands and toasting drinks. I guess cause Ty was a freak and they was going to see who could take her to the telly (hotel) that night." I told y'all niggas once they came... nobody ain't leaving '." "Shut yo drunk ass up Tuesday." I ran down the stairs to let them in. On our way up the steps, I let them know who was in the crib. "That nigga Tomp better not be trippin '." "Nah... he's been cool." "Yeah till his ass see me and gets drunk." "What they say bout me?" "Ty's ass was stressin about that because she was the freak (slut) out the clique. "There in here bidding on who's going to hit." Me and Hell Girl busted out laughing '." All I know if yo trifling ass does fuck a hoe you better get paid!." "Hold up... Hell Girl... don't tell me what to do with my fucking pussy... alright... and when have you known me not to get paid bitch. Ty was pissed at hell girl. See I told you. She flip flops one minute, she loves you and you're her friend the next minute, she's siding the next bitch against you." Oh shut up...shit just get the paper like I said." "A y'all get in here... shit 5—0 can come through here and snatch y'alls dumb ass up." Tomp said while snatching the open door. "Alright boy...quit trippin '." That put a smile on Hell Girl's face. We kicked it all night. Myrecal's ass didn't know if she was going to fuck Mistro or Tomp's little brother spade. Yeah Ty let me know she fucked Mistro and Bull was tryin' to hook her up with spade. I use to fuck with Mistro when I was younger and running with his cousin Spade . I use to fuck with Mistro when I was younger and running with his cousin Wonnie. She lived on the other side of town but I still consider her my best friend even after she fucked the dude that broke my virginity. Yeah fucked up I know. I was taught not to cross that line. I never slept with any of my girl's man or none of their fuck buddy's. That's kind of the reason I quit fucking with her but I still love her. The night was bought to turn into morning and everybody was laid out anywhere that was comfortable. Bull's auntie ran the apt because it was in her name. She smoked so much she never came out the room. Ty was laying across Doo Rod's lap, I was combing Bull's hair, Annie was kicking the Bow Bow with Tweedy and watching the windows at least that's what they was supposed to be doing. Mya was checking the back door, Myrecal was jumping from Spade to Mistro. Everybody was so into the mood that nobody but me, Hell Girl and Tomp paid attention to Ty's trifling ass laying across Doo Rod. If B.B. was to see her ass, boy it would be on. "Y'all peep that." I... but I ain't got shit to say." "Yeah mind your B-I-D-ness... baby." "I am boo I am." Hell girl is lying. As soon as her ass sees B.B. was going to tell her or hint around to it. "Boom... Boom... MPLS police Department... oh shit...where's yo shit at ...girl." Bull said, while pulling me against the wall. "What the fuck is going on." Bull's aunt finally came out the room behind her. "Mother-fucker don't say my damn name." The police weren't prepared for that gate, so they kicked the door to the house open. Everybody ran to the back of the house. "Bull and Tuesday... I know y'alls punk ass is in there with some good ole dope... I'm here to get y'all." Everybody got to finding a spot on the wall so they couldn't see our face. "Auntie come here." "I can't." "crawl your ass over here." Everybody was whispering "Oh my god... my man Is going to kill me if I go to jail." "What are we going to do?" "Bull... Tuesday...y'alls ass ain't going to juvenile Hall...y'alls going to jail with the big boys. Where they take your manhood." "Oh shit Tuesday that's that pussy dick...damn he been trying to catch our ass." "We're scared Bull... what they going to do to us." He ignored us as we sat on the floor against the wall. The backdoor had a gate on it with a dead bolt on the second door so it was harder to kick that door open. "Bull please we scared." Mya and Myrecal eyes were about to pop out they head. Hell girl, Ty and Annie and I were shook up but ready to ride with whatever. "Bull give me the shit puma stuff it." I seen his auntie take everybody's dope and put as much as she could up her pussy." I see a girl in there with y'all... you let her ass know once we get in there and y'all got some dope she's going too." The punk ass dick saw Myrecal sitting by the window. "It's police around the house." "Sh...sh...." Bull I can hear them on the walkie talkie." We sat and listened to them in the stairway as they tried to get a warrant and pry the door open. "Yo dog... they ain't got no warrant." "I know Mistro that's why they don't got the hammer to knock that gate off the hinges." They continued to yell out all the Shorty Macs and Iowa posse one by one. They let it be known how they had been watching the block, the high rise and this duplex. Nobody said a word. "Give me some of that dope." I told Bull's auntie. I knew she was tryin to get as much up there she could so she could keep some. I don't know what made me take his shit when I had my own. The hammers were put up in the ceiling by Hell Girl. They had a secret compartment up there in one of the rooms in the closet so we didn't have to worry about that. Y'all they leaving... they leaving." "yeah we leaving for now cause you got this gate on this door I guess New Jack City taught your ass something you little fucks...but when you slip I will be there to catch all of you... even your little girlfriends." I was sweating my ass off. I didn't want a no felony on my record. Everybody stayed in place and chilled for about ten minutes. "Yo... yo... y'all can come out." "We heard a voice say from downstairs. "Who in the fuck is that Tuesday?." Tomp ass high was gone. He was nervous as hell. He had just got out for dope. He didn't want to go back for dope again by the same cop. Everybody jumped up and ran to the front of the house. "Y'all come here." "Mistro seen the dicks in the alley. We all looked out the window as he pointed to every spot the dicks and the undercover were. "Man...I'm bout to go." Hell girl reached for the door. "Chill girl... yo dumb ass will go to jail if you seen from leaving from here." "A y'all wait about 20 minutes and I'll circle the block." "That was the clucker that lived downstairs. The dude that didn't say much when I first walked in . Yeah they wanna work off that debt they owe Tuesday. "Well since we waiting...nigga's wanna shoot dice." Spade was a gambler at all cost. "Man we bout to go to jail and yo ass wants to shoot dice...stupid." Bull said while shaken his head and watching the window. We all got to talking and everybody acted like they forgot what was going on except me. "Yo... y'all can come out but... I seen one of the under covers with a camera and binoculars… they look like they got it positioned at the door." The man was yelling from downstairs. "Alright… playboy… I got you …and forget what you owe alright." The clucker was cool, Tweedy chalked his debt up. "Hey I got some people for you that want something down here alright." "alright." Tweedy shut the door and everybody got to plotting about how they was getting out that house and never coming back to that hot spot. I'm jumping off the balcony in the back.." I headed towards the back and everybody followed. Mistro grabbed me as Bull watched. "A… be careful… let me help y'all." Bull turned his face up. He knew Mistro was sweet on me but he didn't wanna make it look like he was jealous. Tweedy busted up laughing and was pointing at Bull. "Shut up nigga." Mistro helped us jump off the balcony one by one. When I seen all my girls get down, I broke out. "huh… huh." I huffed and puffed all the way to the bus stop. "Wait for us Shine damn." I heard the whole clique yelling at me but wouldn't stop. Fuck that, I wasn't going to jail and I knew the popo was somewhere around. "I ain't stopping until I see a cab or a bus." I ran all the way up Emerson Ave. I wasn't stopping. I could hear everybody laughing at me. As I heard their voices in a distance the next thing I knew the hoes pulling up on the side of me." "ha ." They was laughing and pointing while I'm all out of breath. "huh… who o y'all got jokes so early in the morning." I wiped the sweat off my head. "Come on stupid get in." I had them drop me off at my house first. Everybody else went out to Ty and Annie's. After that bullshit I needed a break from all that shit. It was summer and I wasn't bout to spend none of it in jail. My Mom was gone to work. The house was a mess and her boyfriend was on his way to work. I knew his ass was about to be questioning me. "What you doing coming in here this time of a morning?." "A… I was over my friends and… "look your Mom hasn't tripped because it's summer and I've been keeping her off your back… don't take advantage of that alright… and don't be lying about shit." Damn I can't get shit pass his ass. I didn't lie , I was at my friend's house. "I won't… it won't happen again… a… I appreciate that." "Yeah… and yo mother left something for you to do around here since you don't have a job." I looked him up and down cause I was tired as hell. "alright." He slammed the door. It was time for a calgon Moment. I took a long hot shower, because I was about to clean the house from top to bottom. My Mom told me to cut the grass, clean the basement and my room. By the time I was done my phone was ringing off the hook. I never answered it. I took a long bath after washing the grass and bugs out my hair. My Mom felt that chores were a way to make a person have responsibility. Yeah I guess so. I never minded cleaning but this was too much shit for one person. I laid in my bed eating pizza and watching MTV raps. Doc One and Ed Lover was silly as hell. I forgot that shit I had my pussy in the raid was on the counter and I heard my Mom calling my name. "Oh shit... a huh." "Get down here... now!" Damn she's bout to beat my ass. "Oh" I slipped on my pajamas bottoms and ran down the stairs. I seen my tennis ball laying on the floor. "What's this!" She was standing there with a fat bank roll. "A... I got it from..."I know that damn boy...that you let beat you." I seen the dope on the floor next to the flower pot. I got to keep my eyes on her so she won't look down. "He don't beat on me no more Mom... look I cleaned the house and cut the grass like you said. I had to stroke her ego so she would go to her room. "Yeah... don't try changing the subject... I'm about to change my work clothes and me and you is going to talk. She headed towards her room and I got out her way. "ok Mom." When I heard her bathroom door shut I raced over to the ounce the it was broken down in little pieces. "Damn I got to hide this shit outside." I put it all in the tennis ball and threw it between the neighbor's house they didn't have a dog so I didn't have shit to worry about. "Veronica Renea Gittens... what are you doing." I made it back up the steps . "hah... Mom." "Get in here" she said while grabbing my arm. "Now tell me why you have all this money... I mean what are you doing to get it?." "Nothing Mom... my boyfriend gave it to me." "Oh yeah... and what does he do to get it?" "a... I never asked." "he sales drugs... and you know it." "Oh man somebody done told her some shit. She never tripped this hard. "Mom you're trippin." I tried to walk away but she grabbed me. "You don't tell me I'm trippin little girl... if you know what's good for you...you would leave that no good boy alone." "I am Mom... I hardly ever see him." I was lying and she knew it. "I tell you what if I see you on Plymouth Ave, as you kids call it... the block or hood... whatever I'm going to embarrass your butt... you hear me!" "Oh snap she talking about coming on the set and putting me on front street." "Mom... come on don't do that." "That... what kind of English is that... I can't wait for school to start back... so you can use correct English girl." "Uuh...she always talking shit about the way I mean... don't come in the hood looking for me....that... I mean that ain't cool." She raised her finger and put it right in my face." I'm the adult you're the child...you don't tell me what to do." I was hot and knew that I better not raise my hand to my Mom. She was asking for it. "Whatever... you won't find me out there." I walked off while she was nagging. I ran up in the attic and slammed the door, She continued to yell and threaten me at the bottom of the steps. I let her run her mouth and vowed to never let her catch me out there. Shit if she would have caught that shit in her house she would have flipped the fuck out. I called up everybody and told them to be on the look out for my Mom. I checked my messages and Gov, Mistro and Bull called. Gov was just checking to see if I was ok. He heard about me being in the middle of that raid that was about to go down. He hadn't seen me in a while and was concerned about how Bull was treating me. After hearing him tell me about his girl suspecting me and him fucking. I told him that she was picking him because I never even told Annie and plus we never fucked. It's been a whole year and I still didn't cheat on Bull. Mistro thought he could convince me to leave Bull but I wouldn't. I don't know but I was use to him. Getting beat was normal I was use to it. I told Mistro, Myrecal wanted to slide him some pussy so holler at her. He laughed and told me take care and he was always there if I needed him. Now Bull. Oh shit he always brings the drama. "What's up Bull." "What's up ...it took your ass long enough to call back." Here goes the argument and I ain't giving it to his ass. "I had to stay in the house today cause my Mom was trippin." "O... yeah what for?." "Cause she's tired of hearing about your ass whoopin on me and she questioned me about you selling dope." His ass got quiet because he knew how my Mom was. "O...um...and what did you tell her." "I didn't have to tell her shit ...I'm just going to give you a break for a couple of days." He got quiet again." "Damn its like that...I was hoping you would come over... so we could talk." "about what." "Us ...um ...I'm not going to hit you no more...my Mom and sister Cat been snapping on me about it." "I wasn't convinced. Shit to me Cat was shady just like Trina. "Nah... I'm cool... I'm chillin from you like I said..." "Ok...well I just wanted to make sure you was ok form the police earlier...I know y'all was shook huh." I was getting bored off this conversation and he was reaching because he felt guilty. "Yeah... we alright." "Well...would you call me tomorrow." "Maybe." "Maybe... all your trippin...click." He called my phone and paged me all night. My Mom yelled upstairs for me to answer my phone because he was calling her line but I wouldn't . "Ok Mom... I will." He started circling the block calling my phone while sitting in front of my house. "Look motherfucker... I'm done with yo ass... call some other bitch alright." I cut my ringer off and after 20 minutes his ass left from in front of my house. I never realized I missed my period that month until I used the bathroom before going to bed. That's why I had a bad attitude. So I just cried myself to sleep.

Chapter 13

"Zero Made His Move"

Damn I done fucked around and got pregnant. Yeah I'm five months into it now. I just told my Mom a month ago and she's pissed off. She cried because Bull's Mom still knew before she did. Man, I wasn't trying to hurt her but I just didn't want to disappoint her. "Veronica... get up." I heard her but it was Friday, this damn baby was kicking and I didn't really feel it today. "Veronica Renea..." "Ok... ok Mommy I hear you." "Well get up then. Just cause you're pregnant don't mean I won't stay on you, you have to get an education for that baby." "I know but I'm tired." "So what!... what you going to tell that baby when it starts crying...wait...no you can't do that." "I'll have you help me." "Um huh... is that right after you told me "women beaters" mother you were pregnant first... like she can help you... please." I knew she was still pissed off. "If you don't get up now!... you can pack stuff and go live with them people." That was it I lost it. I jumped up and ran downstairs to face her once and for all. I didn't even have a meeting with the sink first. SO you know that little them on in my mouth was kicking. "Mom I'm tired of your threats... every time I turn around you bring that shit up." She slapped the piss out of me. As I grabbed my face she thought I was raising my hand up to her so she grabbed my hand. I started crying hysterically. "who you think you are…raising your voice like you pay bills… huh…you don't run nothing around here." "Mom I said… screaming… I'm sick of you …you ain't making my life any easier since I fucked it up." "What do you mean easier…and stop cursing in my face." I stormed off to pack my stuff up. "Where you going… huh?...Nobody's going to make their house your home… you'll see…you'll be back." She was being so nasty to me. Emotions was flying and I could see tears in her eyes. I guess she was making me lay in the bad I made. After getting everything together, I finally made it to the sink. I took care of my face, hair and breath. "Where are you going… huh?." I ignored her as I walked down my block at 6:30 in the morning. "Leave me the fuck alone." I put a pep in my step in case she decided to come slap me again for cursing. "You better be glad your butt is damn near down the street… don't come running back here when you have that baby… you hear me!." I waved her crazy butt off and kept walking. Where was I going I don't know. I had two g's on me and I thought about catching a cab to the hotel and staying for a couple of days. That idea went away real quick, shit this was all I had so I had to stretch it. As I walked towards school I seen Bull's cousin Dana. "Hay…Veronica where you going this early with all that shit in your hand?." I knew her ass was being nosey so I played on her sympathy. "My Mom put me out!." She looked real sad. "Damn for real… you wanna put your stuff in my house until you find somewhere to go." "Just like I knew. Yep her nosey ass wanted to be down so bad, she had no choice but to help a pregnant girl. "What's your Mom going to say?." "She won't know… she's at work." Her Mom was crazy as hell. She was known for snapping out on people for nothing. One time Bull left some work in her yard and she seen him put it there. She took it, sold I, and then talked big shit after she did it, and lied and said she didn't do it. Damn most of the people in Bull's family was shady except Dana and his Momma Steen. "Ok girl…but I don't want her taking my stuff… and I need to jump in the shower." "Cool…I'll put your stuff up and you keep all your money on you." We went to her house and I cleaned myself up. We walked to school and had a long talk. She told me that we could stay Cat's house tonight because she was out of town. She ran her mouth o and on about how Cat ran off with Zero's boy. "Who is Zero?" "You know... Cat's boyfriend... oh you know him as Rockma or rock?." "Yeah ...that's what she told me his name was." "Yeah... well he changed his name to Zero because he ain't down with the family no more." "Straight up." "Um huh... he still be hanging cause he loves Cat... but he hangs with them crips now... he ain't down with Bull at all." "Oh yeah... how does Bull feel about that?" What can he feel shit... that's a grown ass man... plus he can't whoop Zero." I busted up laughing. Damn his cousin was way more real than the rest of his family. Her school was two blocks away from mine. She went to Franklin Jr High and I was with the big girls at North High. My counselor informed me today that I would be going to City Inc. It was an alternative school that Bull went to. I was pissed off because I had to go. Not realizing how many days I missed. Then I had to deal with his Mom Steen. Shit she was cool but I didn't want her being my teacher. What's wrong with you Veronica? You don't look like yourself today." Some nosey bitch in the hall questioning me. She just wants to see if I'm really pregnant. "What am I suppose to look like?... mind your bidness and worry about you hoe", I rolled my eyes and walked off. "I was very concerned that's all. "She was still looking me up and down. So I flashed her ass." "Damn you see... I'm pregnant hoe." She ran off laughing and covering her mouth. I was real emotional today so I went in the bathroom and just cried. I don't know why but two blows was enough shit, I just knew something had to get better. After gathering myself, I went looking for Annie, Ty and B.B. They all went to school. I hadn't seen them much while I was in my beginning stage of pregnancy. This is the time I needed them the most. Olivia paged me everyday to check on me. I never wanted to impose on her because she lived with her boyfriend now. Hell Girl was two years older and almost out of school. She went to PYC. She had credits to make up because she went to school less than I did. A week went by and I found out I was having a little boy. I decided to name him Victor Depaul Franklin. I know it sounds funny but I named him Victor because of Young and Restless. I loved that soap. I only got to see it every now and then. I was spending the night from house to house and it was beginning to wear on me. I felt the most comfortable at Hell Girl's house. Even though Cocoa was fake, she wasn't that bad to me while I was pregnant. Their Mom and dad always welcomed me with open arms and I appreciated that. When they would ask me if my Mom knew where I was, I would just ignore them or say "She doesn't mind." I didn't lie but I wasn't totally honest either, so I tried to stay out their way. I always cleaned up behind myself and others. When I felt like my welcome was being worn out, I went to my next house. My Mom was blowing my pager up. It had been three weeks since we argued and the school had called her to inform her that I was transferred to the City Inc. I never called her back. I decided to spend the weekend with Dana and Peaches, Bull's other cousin. Since Cat and Bull was in Chicago on business, Cat left the house to Rockma. He said we could come over and kick it so we did. "Girl… Cat and Rockma be having all kinds of food… you are going to get full." That was music to my ears. Peaches just didn't know. "Would he mind if I come with y'all?" I knew he wouldn't but I just wanted to see where their heads were at. Looking at each other and laughing. "Girl no… he don't care about that… shit… I told you call him Zero ok…he been trippin about that." Peaches looked a little confused. "What he still mad at Cat from running off and fucking his Homeboy?" "Hell yeah… shit you would be too… but he been chillin at their crib cause he went all the way to chi, knocked on homeboy's door and asked him where Cat was. "Oh my God… and what happened girl?" "Shit his boy looked at him a little crazy…went in to get Cat and her dumb ass stood in front of the house and talked to him." I was shocked as hell. This hoe was bold as hell. "So what did Rick, I mean Zero say to her." "I guess nothing… but I know his sneaky ass got a plan… I hope he kill her or do nothing stupid… he's crazy." "Oh so that's why his ass was winking at me. I see now, he's not using me to pay her back. Plus I'm bought to be family so I ain't crossing no lines. "He won't do that… I'm sure he went down to the Chi to see if she really was going to leave him… Um he loves her." We continued to talk until we made it to Hopkins, I found out that Peaches goes to the City so I'd have somebody to run with. When we got out there Spade, Tomp, Tweedy and two other dudes that I didn't know were there.

"What's up y'all." Tomp opened the door and felt on my belly." "What's my little cousin in there?" That felt good to be welcomed like that. I'm fine... I'm having a boy." Tomp started clapping and acting crazy. He was high and I was getting a contact. "Hey y'all she's having a boy." Tweedy and Spade got up to give me a hug. "How you doing in there." They was talking to my stomach. "Y'all ass is crazy." They were into the Nintendo game so they really didn't pay me, Dana and Peaches any attention after that. Dana went looking around, "Yo where that nigga Zero at." None of them said a word, they kept playing the game and smoking their weed. So I asked "where's the men of the house at":. Tweedy looked up and pointed to the back. Spade looked at me, "he don't want to be bothered... he knew y'all was coming... he said we're welcome to whatever we want." "Ok... y'all wanna help." "We will but we can't cook. "They both said while laughing. We or should I say I started cook that shit up. Dana and Peaches talked and smoked weed while I did all the work. I looked through the cabinets. They had every kind of seasoning and food you could think of. Cat didn't have any kids that I saw so I never understood the reason for all that food. I guess they have a lot of company. "A Dana... I don't see the salt... Do you know where it's at?" She was so into the game talking to the dude on the floor that she just waved me off. Peaches was on the phone. "Go ask Zero..." I looked at her crazy." "Quit trippin girl...hah... he don't bite ...he's in the room... I just left out of there... he ain't sleep or nothing." I walked to the room and opened the door. It was dark as hell. "Zero... a do you have any salt?" I was yelling over the music and fan. "What... what you say." He looked up as he laid on his stomach across the bed. I walked a little closer so he could hear me. As I bent down to get closer to his ear. He jumped up real quick. "Smooch." He kissed me dead in my mouth. I jumped back and held my mouth as I looked around to see if anybody saw that. He watched me with a smirk on his face. "Ah...ah... do you know where the salt is." I said while walking backwards. "You don't have to be scared... it's in the cabinet... eat what you want... don't make the baby starve." "Ok... ah... thank you." I walked back to the kitchen really quick. I had to regroup myself. "Hay... hurry up with that food." "Yeah... girl that shit smelling good as hell... I'm starving like Marvin." The munchies was getting to Spade and Tweedy. "Ok...I'm on it." I didn't want them to detect anything so I tried my best to act normal. We ate like pigs and I was sleepy as hell. The whole house was laid out after eating. Me, Dana and Zero were the only ones awake. "Where we going to sleep." Zero came from out the back room. "Y'all can sleep in the room... I'm bout to go." He looked dead at me and whispered "Between me and you remember." I was spooked as hell. Dana could detect something but she didn't hear what he said. She really didn't care what he said. She really didn't care from what it seemed like. "Dana" "huh" "Here goes the keys... tell Cat I'm done with her... here get you and the pregnant girl something to eat." She looked at the wad of money and her eyes bucked. "Thank you... thanks Zero." "Yeah... and just give her that message." Me and Dana split the thirteen hundred. We both took five hundred and gave Peaches three hundred. I knew right then me and her would always click. Shit it was new to Peaches, she didn't care as long as she got something. We crashed in Cat's room. We looked through the drawers to see if we could find something to slip on and seen that Zero snapped out. He cut up all he shit and poured bleach all over everything. We could smell it coming out of the closet. He bent and broke up all of her jewelry. When he left we seen him with a small safe but his jacket was covering it up. We left everything the way it was and went to sleep. The next day was hell. Cat came through at about 6 in the morning. "Who the fuck is in my bed." She yelled snatching covers off me and Dana. "Damn... what's going on." I was in a daze and could barely see with the light gleaming in my eye. "What's going on... what's going on is y'alls in my bed... where's Zero's ass at... did y'all fuck him or something." Dana woke all the way up. "What...are you fucking crazy...! We don't want him... and one's pregnant." I didn't say a word. I got up and went to the bathroom and locked the door. While I was in the tub, I could hear Bull's voice out there questioning Tomp, Spade and Tweedy. Cat came bangin on the door. "I'm sorry Shine... girl you hear me... take your time in there with my little nephew in there ok." I could hear her whole attitude change. They must of told her I was having a boy. I could hear everybody snapping about Zero fucking up all Cat's shit. She was ranting and raven about how she didn't give a fuck and how she was going to fix his ass. Man I wanted to be around for this shit. My baby was kicking I guess from all the stress so I got my ass from out of the tub. I heard you could have a miscarriage that way if you're not to far along. "Where you been." Bull done started questioning me. So I played the over lay for the Under play. "Where has your ass been." I was lotioning my body up. I guess I was looking good cause his attitude changed. "I told you I went out of town on bidness." "Nah… you never told me that." He did but I was just making him spill his guts. "Well I'm sorry… but Zero been trippin so Chico don't really wanna fuck with me no more… so I had to go see if my uncle's friend would hook me up… you know." Now he has never spilled his guts like this. I always have to find out from the streets. "Um… so what happened." "Oh… oh… I got on… and you and the baby will be straight." He started pulling his clothes off. "What you doing?" I said while trying to put my panties on. "Come on now… you about to give me some pussy… shit I ain't seen you in a month. "Well his dick was hard as hell. This is my baby's dad… I guess I could get a quickie." I never realized that Spade and his friend were in the closet listening to us. Bulls bitch ass let them motherfuckers hear us. As I was ridding him, Spade and his friend ran out laughing as I had my back turned. "huh… oh my god… what… who was that. "He smirked and ignored me. I tried lifting up but he wouldn't let me." "Wait… oh… yeah… dis pussy …is –good-wait baby." "No… No… crying… No… let me go." "I jumped up off of him and cried my heart out. You bitch…you let them mother fuckers watch us fuck… how could you… how could you do that… I got your fucking son in me nigga." Cat came rushing to the room. "Bang bang… Bull what are you doing in there." "Nothing she… just trippin." The bathroom was connected to her room so I just took another shower. I cried. He let his friend and cousin watch me and him fuck. I was going to pay his ass back. It was bad enough that I heard he fuck Ty over Cocoa's house. Yeah you know Hell Girl can't hold water. Cocoa's fake ass even told me. I guess Bull's money he paid wasn't enough to keep her big mouth shut. "Knock… knock… Veronica… are you ok… it's Dana and Peaches." I turned the water off and started drying off. "I'm cool… I'll be out in a minute." I could hear Cat out there going off and putting Bull out. He was trippin because she wouldn't let him take a shower in the other shower. After getting dressed and walking to the living room, Tweedy , Peaches, Dana and Cat were all talking. "I'm sorry baby girl… I'm sorry that my boy heated you like that. Tweedy was always taking up for Bull. He had his back no matter what. I just hope whenever Tweedy needs him that he's there for him. "It ain't your fault Tweedy… what the hell you apologizing for my brother for." Cat was just as confused as I was but I understood that's all." Dana and Peaches just looked at me and I shrugged my shoulders. Cat cleaned her house and we all helped. She let me know that any time I wanted to stay I could. I really didn't take her serious but she was. Trina called and told me hi and congratulations. I hadn't forgot about what she did to me, so I was real shitty towards her. We all took a cab over North and I thought about going home. I would love that but to be hard I changed my mind. "Yo… Dana and Peaches…y'all wanna go on the block with me?" They looked all excited. "Yeah." They said together. "You bout to cause a problems. "You sure are." Tweedy and Cat didn't agree with me on that. "What y'all me?… cause a problem?… Shit they wanna be paid too." Cat didn't say shit but Tweedy said, "You going to turn them out and they might not know when to stop." "Shit… y'all act like we are kids." Everybody laughed as soon as we got out the cab. People were running up to us. "Baby girl… yo… your Mom's been out here looking for you." I felt an instant pain in my stomach. I knew it. After ignoring her she couldn't take it. She was coming to embarrass me. I walked around and made a little money. Not too many people would by from me because Bull told them not to. His haten punk ass. I kept feeling this fucked up pain in my side and felt some kind of liquor come down. "Dana… hold this… I'm bout to go over here and pee." I started walking towards Tweedy's spot. I seen my Mom's car hit the corner so I ducked behind a car. As I ran in the duplex I seen somebody pointing at me. "Bang bang… yo Tweedy open please… Boy my Mom is looking for me." He was on the balcony making noise because he wanted me at home too. "ha ha… Mom…she's over here." He was waving off the balcony but my Mom couldn't hear or see him. "Stop… Tweedy she put me out boy." "So… you're pregnant you need to be with your Moms." He was right but he needed to understand my point. After 10 minutes he let me in and my

Mom finally pulled off. Thank goodness. When I used the bathroom it burned and I had a bad smell. I knew that I had took a good two showers today so something was wrong. I made it out the bathroom and I was heated. "What's wrong." Tweedy seen my face red. "Nothing…I'm going to kill Bull." I ran down the stairs and walked up and down the set screaming. "Anybody seen Bull." Everybody knew I was pissed about something. No one knew where his bitch ass was. "What's wrong Shine… are you ok… slow down." Peaches couldn't keep up with me. "I'm straight… I need to find Bull." Cat and Dana came running to catch up to us. "Slow down girl, What's wrong." I was going to tell them but fuck that. I started screaming "that nigga burned me, he fucking burned me." They all looked at each other. "How do you know… I mean are you sure he was the only one you been fucking." "fuck you… Cat fuck you…. who would I fuck at six months, huh." I was screaming and Dana or Peaches wouldn't touch me. "Well I didn't know… shit I thought y'all cheat on each other." "No… that's your problem you don't know me… I never cheated on your brother… never… but I will soon as this baby is out I sure am." I stormed off up Plymouth Ave away from her ass. With Dana and Peaches on my trail. "Wait up Veronica…we got love for you don't be like that with us." I know it wasn't their fault. I was mad though and I felt like fuck everybody. From out of nowhere here comes my Mom making a U-turn. "Oh shit… run y'all run." We were running through the liquor store parking lot. We weren't fast enough because she made it through the other side and caught me. She jumped out and chases me. "Leave me alone Mom." I tried to fight her off. "Didn't I tell you I was going to catch you here huh." She was beating me in the head. "Stop… stop Mom… I'm not coming home." Dana and Peaches and a whole crowd of people just watched. "Whoop her butt… she don't talk to you like that." Some old lady yelled to my Mom with a bottle in her hand "Yeah… show her ass who's the parent… I'm tired of young kids hanging out here every night." The owner of the liquor store said. That started a whole back and forth conversation. My Mom boy friend open the car door and my Mom pushed me softly in the back seat. As we pulled out the parking lot I saw Zero standing next to Dana and Peaches shaken his head. I was crying and he mouthed "it's going to be alright." Dana put her pinky to her mouth and her thumb to her ear for me to call her. "Oh and I'll wash your clothes." I nodded my head ok. Back to the old drawing board, home sweet home. But my Mom sure wasn't making it sweet.

Chapter 14

"Baby having a Baby"

For the past two months I've been taking medicine thanks to that damn Bull. I'm in my eighth month and this little boy is really stressing me. "Mom... ouch... ah...Mom." It was nothing but the baby kicking me in my rib. "What girl... wait I'm on the phone with the doctor." I had to get up and put a hot towel over my belly. My Mom was trying to see if anything was going to be wrong with the baby, "Ok... what... what's wrong." "My stomach hurts... please rub it." "You big ole baby... girl... see that's why you should of waited to be married. .. then your husband could have been doing this." I put big smile on my mother's face this morning. I was glad of that because I need her. "I know Mom... maybe next time... oh what did the doctor say about the medication... I'm not going to be sterile or anything." "No... thank god... clymidia will only make you do that if you don't catch it in time ok baby... see that's why you need to protect yourself... you know HIV doesn't have a name... and anybody can get it... you can stop taking the medication now." I was happier than a sissy with two dicks. Today was the E.P.M.D, DJ quick and 2nd to none concert, I had to call up Olivia to see what was poppin. "Ring, ring, ring... H-e-l-l-o." Damn she was in a damn good mood." "Hay Olivia ...O ski... what's up." "Nothing girl." "You sure sound jolly this damn morning." "I know... I'm ready for the concert tonight." "Yeah that's what I'm calling you about." "What... shit as big as you are... you can't go... you could get hurt." That's always O ski... she has to look out for me. "I won't be getting hurt so shut up... plus I know y'all got my back... shit I've been I this house for two months and ain't been no where but school." "Ok... hah... you bought me." "Good what time y'all coming to get me... oh who's driving with Mya and Myrecal and Ty's shady ass thinks I believe she didn't fuck Bull. "You know I'm not riding with Annie if she got Myrecal or Ty with her." "Oh… I know girl… I don't blame you… B.B's driven or my cousin Wonnie got a car… she been asking me about you." That was cool. I remember when me and Wonnie were like sister. She's still my ace I guess. "What… has she been doing ?… how's that nigga Lumpy been treating her?… I know she ain't still playin seconds… hah. "She busted up laughing." "Well… oh… yeah she's still his other women, , , she's happy with that… that's her so you got to be happy if she likes it." "Oh… no trip I just thought she would get tired of that shit." "Well… lets talk about that later." "Aight… when you coming." "It starts at 8… so I'll be over around 6 or 7." "Ok… ye." I let my Mom know what I was doing. Of course I had to hear her mouth. Damn she needs to understand I'll be a mother in a month and I won't be able to kick it. I'm going and that's it. I wrapped my own hair and sat under the dryer. Annie called to see if I wanted to go with her, Ty Mya and Myrecal. I told her "Hell no! ' She never questioned me about why because she already knew. She was disappointed because we had plans to all kick it. I let her know that I see her there. My hair was dry so I got into the shower so I could paint my nails. I wore a polo over all jumpsuit and the matching polo boots with a polo tee shirt under it. I looked pretty with a chunky face and feet. My damn feet looked like I was walking around with balloons in them. My hair had grown down my back so I was excited to get my floss on. "How do I look Mom?" I made sure I asked her while she was on the phone. "You look beautiful baby…" she took the phone away from her ear. "Hay… don't you be out all night… you know I'll come looking for you." I started laughing. "Ha ha… you are funny Mom." "I'm not playin as in your language… if you ain't here by a reasonable hour imma give you a pumpkin head." "She's bugging now. "ha… ah… what you know – bout that?" Um… more than you think." She kept into her conversation. "Honk… come on Shine." I grabbed my tickets and purse. "Smooch… bye Mom… love you." Pulling her ear from the phone. "Don't forget what I said… be careful… stay away from that…" "Mom… dang… I know Bull. Bull with his disease infected… ass… oh…oh I'm sorry… I mean boy." "All right… I love you." I felt good and was looking fly even being fat. I saw Wonnie. She was still very pretty and I still couldn't understand why she let nigga's play her. Then she's the first to talk about you or somebody else like a dog. "Give me a hug... with your cute chunky butt." I gave Wonnie, Olivia and Mistro a hug. This is about to be like old times if only we don't see Bull. "Bitch betta have my money... Bitch betta have my money." I could hear DJ quick rappin through the speakers as we were standing in line. "Hay... bitch betta have my money. I was doing a little step and shaken my ass. "Girl you better save all that energy for later." "Why...what's up?" "We going to the after party." "Yeah... well it's right here in this building... Wonnie." She looks as if she didn't know. "Oh... do your thang. "She joined me with the dancing." We made it in and everybody was waiting for E.P.M.D. to go on stage. "Come on Veronica I see Annie and them." I looked around and saw them over by the picture stand. I'm not about to take a picture with Mistro. Bull is jealous of him for nothing. He's scared I might mess back with Mistro because we're still good friends. "Come on... why you staggering girl." I ain't mistro... I just don't want you and Bull to get into it... you... you think da nigga will run up on me... please... and ain't going to fight you." I know Veronica... you're my best friend and we haven't been able to kick it don't worry about him." "Ok Wonnie...just watch my back ok." Reaching out to hug me and tell me it's ok. Olivia seen Tomp. She didn't want me to get scared so she just pointed him out to Mistro. "You ready to take some pictures." Annie and her crew said while greeting me. "Put big Momma in the front..." "Yeah... and we all put our hand on her belly." Mya had Myrecal was tryin hard to make them. "Are you ok with that." "I'm cool." Annie knew I still wasn't feeling them but I wasn't going to ruin the fun. I stood in the front with Wonnie on one side and Mistro on the other, Olivia bent down by my feet, Mya laid on the floor and Annie and Myrecal were on each side. "Ready... 1... 2..." "hold up... how y'all going to forget us." Here comes Hell Girl, B.B and Ty. Yeah wait." The picture man was getting real impatient. "Ok... is everybody ready." All together everybody cheesed. "Go head." "Ok... 1...2 ...3... snap. ' We picked up the pictures. We had copies made they wanted to have their own. You know you can never depend on a nigga to get copies of shit, you'll be waiting forever. As we watched E.P.M.D. rock the stage I seen Tomp, Tweedy, Bull and the whole Iowa Posse. It looked like some shit was about to go down. The Shorty Macs were taken pictures with everybody. They was ball in hard and had on the same outfits. Mya and Myrecal were jumping in everybody's picture. "Come on Shine...it's over." I had nodded off in my seat I guess. "Yeah we bout to take you home." I woke up instantly "What...hell nah...I'm kicking it Olivia." "I heard that Bull was looking for you ...he said he's whopping your ass and he's drunk." I felt an instant pain in my stomach. I haven't seen this fool in two months. "I'm not letting him take my fun away." "ok well... we all going to fight his ass." B.B. was ready for him. After everybody went outside to see what was up. Shorty Macs was arguing with the Iowa Posse. "Y'all crab ass nigga's flipped." Bull was yelling at Butch, Pig Pen, Spanky and Gotti. "Fuck y'all niggas...y'all mad cause we getting dis paper." Spanky yelled as the rest of them through up gang signs. Mistro was just watching like the rest of us because he was still a part of the Iowa Posse but he was cool with the Shorty Macs. Annie and Hell Girl was all in the middle of it. From out of no where the Cali boys came through and started spraying. "Oh... oh my goodness." Everybody was screaming and running . "Wait... get up please shine." Olivia and Hell Girl helped me up. We ran as gun fire flew past us. I started crying. "Come on ...don't cry just keep up." All out of breath we made it to the car and waited for everybody to get there, Wonnie, Mistro, Ty and Annie came running. "Ha ...ha... woo... open the door." "Hold up... everybody can't fit in here and Shine is pregnant." "We just wanna tell y'all what happen...we got our own car." Annie and Olivia was bout to go at it and started mugging each other. "Yo...yo... shut the fuck up...shit...we ain't about to have this shit tonight." Everybody stopped, looked at me and busted up laughing. "Ok um...sorry...T.T.M. and Tomp got to fighting... then Bulls punk ass was running from that nigga Zero" "oh...my goodness...did he whoop his ass." "Yeah... Wonnie girl... Bull was running so fast he slipped and fell then them Cali niggas rolled his bitch ass up." I was glad to hear that, I was hoping more would happen to his ass. "Good... I wish I could of watched... I can't wait for this baby to come out." "I know cause we going to kick It." "Yeah and I can't wait for you to be with somebody else." B.B never really spoke on that until now. Annie never really cared for Bull cause she felt I should of gave a chance.

"I'm hungry…lets ride around and go get something to eat." I was starving and nobody was going to make me wait." "Ok… we can roll through the block so I could stop by my house… then… we can roll through the block so I could stop by my house… then we can get some McDonald's." "We going to follow you Olivia." B.B and Annie got in their and followed us. We made it back to the hood and it was packed out. Everybody was in crowds laughing and talking about who got shot, or taken to jail. Everybody just knew Bull was going to hide out but they were wrong. After everybody was walking up to McDonald's from the side of the police station here came Bull and his crew. I tried to duck but who could I get behind with a big ass belly. "Oh shit… just keep walking." "Hell Girl you talk to him and I'll go get the car." Annie walked back to get her car. Olivia go this way." I grabbed Olivia and B.B put her arm around me, I was shook the fuck up. I know he was mad and embarrassed about getting his ass whopped. We started walking faster and so did he. "Don't run bitch… cause I will catch yo ass." That did it, I wasn't no punk bitch, and I just lost it. "Come on… mother fucker… I'm so tired of your bitch ass." I was screaming and a crowd of people formed. "What… you wanna jump bad huh." "Yeah… hit me bitch… hit me." I put my fist up." Slap…" He hit me so hard and fast. "Oh no… She's pregnant." Olivia came to my rescue and Annie pulled up in car. "What happen" she said while jumping out the car with an even more crowd. "I'm going to get the police." B.B ran in the precinct to get an officer and Bulls bitch ass took off running. "Look at that bitch run …you bitch." Wonnie was screaming as I cried and held my face. "Girl… your eye is black as hell." I never said a word. I just cried as we walked back to the car. B.B was tryin to get me to talk to the officer and I wouldn't. I just wanted my Mom. "Come on… the police wants you Veronica… put that nigga in jail… please." Olivia was saying and crying at the same time. "No… Just take me home." Everybody talked shit to me about not pressing charges on his ass. I don't know but I just didn't have it in me to tell on nobody. Even though he deserved every damn thang but I didn't want to be the one to do it. I made it home and my Mom waited up for me. I tried to cover up my face but messed up hair, a black eye and dirty clothes wasn't easy to cover up. "Come here… don't walk past me… let me see your face ." The whole crew was at the door explaining to my Mom what happened as they all cried. "Mom stop crying... I'll be ok." "No... damn it... you won't... you are going to go back to him... do you know that the hospital will take that baby if they think you're in an abusive home." I didn't realize I'm due any day now and what if I jeopardize me and my baby's life. "Ain't nobody going to take me baby... you watch Mom." She was really mad and just looking at me... "Ok everybody... Thank you for your concern... Veronica will call y'all when the baby comes." Everybody left and my Mom laid into my ass. She talked about how beautiful I was and how I've really let my self esteem down. Being pregnant is a gift and I should appreciate god's blessing and not take advantage of him. I listened to her for an hour and it all sunk in. "Oh...and I'm calling that school to get your homework because you're not going back to school until that baby is born," "ok" "And I might change your school I don't know." I started walking up the stairs. "I don't like it here anymore... so we might be moving back to St.Paul... I already bought house for me, you and the baby." "Ok... that's fine Mom... whatever." I never realized my Mom's relationship was going sour. She was strong women. When her husband cheated and she had proof she left. When her boyfriend cheated or tried abusing her she dumped him. I admire her for not giving no man a second chance. She showed me that at a young age and that I value. HE obviously was cheating so it was no use in me asking. Whatever it was,, it wasn't my place to ask if she didn't work . Her boyfriend tried explaining to me that he didn't do nothing to her. I told him don't try to convince me cause I can't change her mind. We moved in our new house my grandma lived over here in the hood but I wasn't sure if I wanted t live back over here. Oh what the hell, it should be good to get the hell away from Bulls ass. My due date was in three days and my black eye was still shining like it just happened. "Mom... you want me to call my friends over to help us unpack?" I was tired of watching her do all the work. Her ex-husband offered to come help but she turned him down. He was still tryin but she shut his ass down every time but she still remained his friend because of me and my step sister Fox. "I don't care... but that don't have to." I called up Hell Girl, Annie and B.B The only one that felt like spending the weekend was B.B "You wanna catch a cab over... my Mom will drop you off to school Monday." "Ok... I'll bring enough clothes." "Ok... bye... click." I helped as much as I could. My Mom ordered pizza for me and B.B. "I hate your face being messed up Veronica... I really hope you done with that boy." The door bell rang and I let B.B in. "I know Mom... y'all will see... I am watch." I paid for the cab and took B.B's stuff upstairs." "Here... let me take it you don't need to be going up and down stairs." I felt helpless and couldn't really do much. So I just watched my Mom and B.B bust a sweat while moving furniture, hanging pictures and cleaning all at once. We ate all the pizza up and talked while my Mom went to sleep. The next day we watched movies all day. The phone started ringing and so did my pager. It was an unknown number on my pager so I wouldn't call back. "You want me to call?" "No B.B I know its bull or somebody in his family... I'm done... I'm not fucking with none of them people and they ain't seeing this damn baby." She just listened to me as I vented. "Veronica get the phone." "Who is it Mom?..." I knew it was somebody in his family. "Some girl... named Trina... don't start with given this number to everybody." "B.B how in the hell did they get this number?" She looked at me confused. "I don't know." "Veronica... get the phone." "Huh... ok Mom." "Hello... look don't call my Momma's house no more..." "Wait... now we didn't do shit to you and my Mom was worried about you and my nephew." "What... w-h-a-t... the fuck y'all worried about me for?" I was going off on her so bad that B.B hung up the phone and my Mom made me sit down to calm down. "Oh... Mom... I'm having pains shoot in up my back... ouch... please help." "Lay on the floor... so if your water brakes you won't have to pee all over my couch. "Me and B.B was cracking up. "You just worried about this pink couch ain't you hah." I sure am... I worked hard to get this plush set... and it's mine." "I won't mess your couch up... lady '. She propped my feet up and me and B.B kept watching movies until we fell asleep. I turned my pager off because Trina dumb ass kept paging me at 5 in the morning , my water broke. "Ooh... shit B.B. get up." She was snoring and didn't hear me at first. "B.B. girl... I peed on myself." My Mom jumped up out the bed and ran in the living room. "Get up, Get up off my couch girl... your water broke?." Ha... ouch... I'll clean it up." B.B. rolled over out of her coma.

"Girl I thought I was dreaming." "No... hell no these pains are real." My Mom called the doctor and informed them we were on the way. We were there for six hours and his little ass only contracted 5. "Oh Mom... it hurts." The nurse and doctor kept coming in to see how far apart I was contracting. My Mom wanted the epidural to be the last result because I was only 16 and she didn't really want me taken more medication. B.B. called everybody and the only people that made it in time was Bull and his sister Trina. My Mom flew out the chair. "Get out... No... right now." She chased Bulls ass to the elevators. His sister was looking stupid. "How you doing Shine?." She made me sick but I was in too much pain to complain. I'm cool... my Mom wants you to leave." "Well... Bull's gone... why I have to go... I wanna see my little nephew." My Mom came back in with my Auntie. "You can stay... but you tell that low life brother of yours he's not welcome here." She didn't say a word because she knew my Mom was upset. I'm going to call my Mom and Cat and tell them not to come. "My Mom's auntie and friend looked at her crazy. "Nah, don't tell them that, yeah tell them to come so they can see my baby's face... while she's having a baby." "I understand you being mad... but that's still my brother." My Mom got mad and started roasting her ass. She called Bull every name but the child of god. "Mom... Mom my contractions are getting closer." Everybody stopped arguing. "I'll go get the nurse." My aunt went to get the doctor. "You should leave ok...no hard feeling but I don't want to see anybody in your family." Trina left and told B.B. to tell me congratulations. "How far apart are your pains now" "Ouch... I don't know Doc... Um about two minutes." He whispered something to my Mom. "What happen to your eye... Veronica." I was a little scared now because my Mom warned me about this. "Ah.... Me and my boyfriend got into a..." "You know you shouldn't be going ..." "Oh Doc she won't... not in my house see she wasn't at my house when it happened. The Doctor got the point because he shut up about my eye. "Well... Ms.Veronica... we are going to have to get your mother's permission to give you an epidural. "I really didn't want that because it's a shot in my back and even though I won't feel no pain during labor, it could paralyze me. "Go ahead... but be careful with my baby..." "I will... we need to take him now because she's only at seven but she's been in labor for twelve hours already." "Dang Doc it's been that long." "Yeah… you won't feel a thing." My Mom made everybody leave the room. B.B. called everyone under the sun. Annie and Hell Girl was going to come later so they could name him. During labor the Doctor said that they would have to use little dent on the side of his cheek. "Ouch… oh what was that." "That was the after birth honey." "Damn that hurt… I didn't feel my baby but I sure felt that." Everybody laughed. I took a three hour rest and woke up to my baby crying and a room full of people and gifts. "Hay you finally woke up." Bull's Momma Steen was standing there holding the baby. "How long have y'all been here." It was Dana and Trina with her. "Ever since you had him." My Mom had an attitude every time they asked her a question. Dana and Trina gave me a hug and was tryin to ignore my eye. "Y'all going to stay…" "No… Um we just came to show your mother that we care as well." My Mom kept her conversation going with everybody else and ignored them. "Ok… well thank you, Steen. …I'll call you when we get home." "Oh… what are you going to name him… you know this is his first and he should be a Jr." My Mom almost broke her neck "No. ….no way… he will be cursed… No." Steen didn't want to make a scene so she ignored my Mom. "Look I don't like that you are sitting here with a black eye… I understand how your Mom feels and if you were mines I would feel the same… but at the same time Andre is my son and I won't listen to her disrespecting me talking about him, so I'll just leave… call me baby… whenever you need me." I was so weak and stressed I just reached up to give them all a hug. Annie and Hell Girl made it up there and had jokes for everybody. "I know you didn't name my little god son." "No, Hell girl. She was dancing around with little Victor in her arms. "What's his name." "Annie you know I love young and restless. "ok his name will be Victor Depaul Franklin." "No his name will be Gittens like me and my daughter." "All… come on Mom… he has to have his daddy last name at least." Hell Girl was right as she convinced my Mom. "Yeah Mom she's right don't you think." The doctor came in with the woman to make me sign the birth certificate. "Are you sure that baby will be in a non abusive home." My Mom was looking at the child protective services right in the eye, that's who the woman was. "This baby is going home with me and he will be fine... I live in my own house... come check it out." "My Mom snatched the baby away from Hell Girl. The Doctor never said a word but my Mom mean mugged him hard. The woman with the certificate asked my Mom a few more questions and she left. Boy was I glad to see her leave. It could only get better.

Chapter 15

"It on an Poppin!"

Drama, Drama and more Drama. Bull can't take it. My son is ten months and I've been through hell with his ass. It's over, why can't he just get over it. "Ring, ring... Hello" "Hi Shine." What the fuck does she want this early in the morning. "What Cat... for you to be calling this early , you must be on some bull shit." "Damn you talking to me like I've done something to you." "Nah... you haven't... but... ok what is it." Now while I'm talking my son is tossing and turning. "Um... I... I heard you was waiting on your section 8 to come "ok ...and." "Well I got a way you can make some money...you know so you can get some furniture and maybe a car." "What did I have to do." "Pause" "She's on some bullshit, she wants me to do something that no one else should know about. "Hello . ....Cat you still there." "Ah... Um I need you to fly out to Cali to get something for me..." "What...for what." She wants me to do some illegal shit." You know to get something.... Bull or nobody don't have to know... please I know you're down and I could trust you." "You know what... Cat... me and you ain't even like that... you got me fucked up... click." Who does this old bitch think I am tryin to set me up. I ain't taking shit on no damn plane unless it's for me. Ring Ring Ring... Hello." "Shine... please don't hang up on me... I'm tryin to get you on your feet." "It don't sound like it to me." "A I'll tell you what, meet me on the block so we can talk aight." I thought about it for a minute. Maybe I should go see what she's talking about. "What time." "About six... meet me in front of Tweedy's" damn I don't feel like being bothered with Bull today. "Ok... I'm going to be out there for no longer than an hour and I'm up... a... don't let Bull know I'm coming." "Aight... Bye." I got my son dressed and took him to my auntie's for the weekend.

She let me know that if she doesn't work Monday she'll keep him. "Ok auntie…thank you." "You're welcome baby…. don't hang out to much." I caught a cab over North to Hell Girl's house. She wasn't talking about much. Tryin to get me and Bull back together because he and Tomp was on good terms. I let her know I was hanging out with Wonnie a little more now that it was summer. She turned her nose up because her and Wonnie didn't too much care for each other. "Aight girl I'm bout to go and see what's on the block." "Ok I'll be down there later." When I was leaving Hell Girl's house for some strange reason I felt that she was on something sneaky. As soon as I made it down there I seen everybody. "Yo… yo cutie what's up." Dudes were yelling at me out their cars. "You baby" that felt good since I haven't been out. The baby had kept me up all night or school was taking over my life. I had missed so much school that it was guaranteed I was graduating late. I didn't care as long as I graduate. Better late than never. "Tuesday Tweedy hay… boy I missed you." I gave him a big hug. "Hi girl… you came to make some… ?" you got something for me?." "Yeah but…it's hot out here so we got to go to this spot around the corner… I don't want you getting caught up… that little God baby of mines needs his Mom." He gave me another hug. "Thank you… you care more about me than Bull… I'm glad I haven't seen his ass in months." "Oh shit… I don't wanna be in the middle of the shit… I hope we don't see his ass neither… shit I get tired of y'all always arguing." "I don't argue… if he just would understand I don't want his ass." "Yeah… that's your fault… you must got some gold between your legs or something." "ha ha…shut up boy." We kicked the shit for a while. Dirty Red was working the block for Tweedy and me for now. Cat came Rollin through in Zero's black and gold 5.0. It was tight as hell. The music was beaten up the block and the gold D's was sparkling. "What's up Shine… get in." I wondered how she knew I was down here so early. Tweedy got in with me "Where we going Cat?" Tweedy really didn't want to leave this money out here." "Oh um… bought to give y'all an offer." "Girl this car is bangin ass shit." I was trippin off of the peanut butter and black seat with custom made mats on the floor. Nobody wasn't eating in this ride no time soon. "Oh girl… Zero just let me use this for a minute…He really don't fuck with me no more… but I guess since I'm pregnant then he was being nice." "How far along are you... are y'all going to move back in together ?." "I don't know... hay... he wants to know will y'all go pick up some work for us..." Tweedy looked at me like he was game. "Nah...I ain't wit that... shit if y'all won't go get your own shit then something must be up with that." She got an attitude. "Well fuck you... get out of my car." Tweedy started laughing. "I will...shit I ain't no fucking flunky... I work for my shit." I slammed the door and started walking up the block. I could see her given Tweedy something out the corner of my eye. "Yo... Shine... wait... girl huh... damn you mad cause she tryin to help us get some paper... girl you crazy." As we were talking Bull rolled up, jumped out the car and ran over to us. "I ain't letting nobody use me... you can but I ain't. "Bull looked back from me to Tweedy. "What... y'all fucking or something?" Tweedy laughed and I threw my hands up in the air because I can't explain myself. "Nah... I don't fuck my ex mans friends... but we know you do." He tried grabbing me and Tweedy grabbed him. "A... man chill... how in the fuck are you going to say some shit like that... she's my sister... I don't want her." Bull checked himself after Tweedy went off on his ass. "Don't keep explaining yourself... you know you ain't never tried to holler at me... he's the one guilty for fucking hoes that smile in my face." "A... let me talk to you." He tried walking along side of me but I started walking faster with him and Tweedy behind me. "Veronica stop... please quit going off do you see how many people are watching this... this is what they wanna see y'all fighting... y'all got a baby to look after." Me and Bull continued to argue and fight while the whole hood instigated. "If y'all don't stop... I'm through fucking with y'all...stop arguing... Damn." Tweedy said while walking in between us. "I'm done... I said all I have to say... he's just a snake ass nigga." "Nah... you are ..." "See I'm bout to go." Tweedy walked away because he refused to watch or listen to me and Bull argue. I'm mad because that's the last I seen of my homeboy.

— Two Weeks later! —

"Ring Hello." "Veronica... you heard from Tweedy?" Bull sounded like he was nervous wreck. I haven't seen or talked to his ass since we pissed

Tweedy off. "Nah… Why?" "cause… um he's missing." My stomach dropped to my feet. I felt something was wrong and I couldn't detect it. "What do you mean missing." "Missing nobody hasn't seen his ass in two weeks… he owes some people and their looking for him… thinking he ran off." "He… he would never run off… he's good peoples… Nah not my brother." "I know… I know Shine… I'm nervous as hell… I hope he's

ok." I got on the next bus and caught it over North. Bull ran right up to me. "They said the last person who walked him to that house… I mean that duplex was dirty red…yeah and if I find that… that dope fiend mother… ' "Yo… chill let's not jump to conclusions." We walked around the hood as the word spread around. Spade, DooRod,Tomp and a gang of new friends that their clique accumulated gathered around. Everyone exchanged stories of who saw Tweedy last and who he was with. Spade said that he was getting his dick sucked by a strawberry and Tweedy said he didn't want none. At about 2 I'clock in the morning Doo Rod walked him down to the duplex we use to sell dope at. The people that moved up here from out of town had still lived in the downstairs house. So then Doo Rod said that Tweedy road the bike and he walked along side him. When they made it in front of the door Doo Rod was asking him where he was going to sleep that night. Then Tweedy turned up his nose and said he didn't wanna stay at Bull's anymore because he was tired of him arguing wit me and he didn't want to hear it. Bull looked at Doo Rod with an attitude and Cat jumped in. "Don't look at him like that… he did say that because me and Zero was laughing when we caught Spade getting his dick sucked by that clucker." Some people laughed and some just looked at Bull. He tried changing the subject. "Yo ain't that Dirty Red over there." Everybody looked and headed for him. "Let's get him…" "Yeah let's kill that nigga." Bull was the leader of the pack and all of his flunky's followed. Me and Cat stopped everything so we could hear his story. "Wait… wait y'all… stop… no… don't hit him." "Bull… I'm telling Mom… quit." We were getting pushed back and forth while blows were being thrown our way. "I didn't do it… no… please… come on y'all…why would I come right back out here." They stopped dusting Dirty Red off and made him start talking. Like Doo Rod said, he explained that Tweedy had nowhere to sleep and he was going to crash at the spot. He saw him last at the duplex. The dude and the girl wanted to spend two hundred dollars and he went to serve them. Nobody had seen him ever since. Everybody got to scratching their heads and comparing stories. We walked right back in front of that duplex. "Damn Bull it stinks out here like a mother fucker." Everybody started smelling the foul odor. When Cat started questioning the girl downstairs she looked a little nervous but nobody really paid attention. The bike that the dude had pulled up on looked like the bike Tweedy had bought from a smoker. "Hay... Bull that's the bike Tweedy was riding." "Where... where at Dirty Red." He was wiping his tears away. "Right there." He was pointing and moving around. "Right there... the dude that lives in this downstairs house... ol man... this shit don't feel right... I don't feel right." Bull went over and checked the dude about the bike and how he got it. "ah... um... I bought dis from him... the other day." Bull, Doo Rod and Spade knew the dude was a little shaky but they had no proof of anything. Cat started grilling the girl about her suggesting that Dirty Red killed Tweedy. She continued to stand by her story that her and her man gave. Tweedy's brothers and sisters came to the duplex to check out everyone's story they were hurt and very concerned of their brother's whereabouts. Their sister didn't like the drug infested environment and she informed everybody that she would be contacting the police. I was very sad, angry and confused. I don't know any one who would want to hurt Tweedy. He was a good friend and from the looks of it a great brother. "Man it stank so bad out here... that might be Tweedy's body out here stinking." "You're stupid... why in the fuck would you play like that." I ran away from Bulls ass. At a time like this you never say hurtful shit. "Wait...come here Shine... I was just playing... he ain't dead... don't think like that... I'm sorry." I walked so fast up Plymouth avenue. I didn't know where I was going. I made my way up Penn Ave and then down Broadway and got on the bus. I was so hurt and cried while people watched and asked me if I was ok. I never talked to anyone on the bus. I was ducking down when we made it downtown. I saw Bull's truck ride past with the whole Iowa Posse hanging out the window and looking up in the bus to see if they see me. I'm so glad I got the hell away from his ass so he couldn't try nothing. I really had to brace myself from not stealing on his bitch ass after that comment he made about Tweedy. I don't play like that. If Tweedy comes up dead then his ass is going to feel real fucked up. I had to transfer buses to the 16, that would take me right around the corner from my house. "Ring Mom... I'm waiting on the bus... what are you and the baby doing?" "Nothing... little Victor is sleep... when are you coming home? I heard that one of your friends are missing... everybody has been calling all day for you. "I know Mom... his name is Michael Broadway... so if you hear anything before I get there let me know." "Ok... you just get out them streets... your son is waiting for you." My mother was so much of a blessing. All she wanted me to do was graduate and become something if I don't do anything, I'm going to get her a diploma. I enjoyed the rest of my ride home. I cried, laughed and talked to myself thing about Tweedy. I know everybody thought I was crazy. When they stared at me I just stuck my middle finger up at them.

— One Week Later —

"Veronica... Veronica get up." I just went to sleep about an hour ago. Victor had my ass up all night. "What... what's wrong... Mom I'm..." "Girl get up and look at the new." My stomach fell to my feet. I knew it was devastating news. I took time to get downstairs so I would have to hear it. "Veronica... I said get down here... you need to see this." I heard the phone and my pager going off as I walked down the steps washing my face. "Who keeps calling here... dang my pager keeps going off." My Mom never said a word she just looked at me with a sad face. I turned the T.V. up. This is CBS reporting live... we are in front of 1105 James avenue north where a maintence worker for Hennepin county, went into the downstairs apartment here and found a gruesome discovery. A male who looked to be hog tied with his hands and feet bound together and looked to have been dead for a week or two. Medical Examiners have not been able to say a name or age to this victim because maggots and rats have eaten his face off. Family and friends reported a Michael Broadway missing two weeks ago. This is all that I have at this hour... I'm Shelia Lang reporting live from CBS." My legs buckled and fell to the ground. "Get up... get up Veronica...

you need to be strong... it's going to be ok." Mom you just don't understand... he was a good man... he helped me always... he never hurt anyone." The phone wouldn't stop ringing "What" I screamed in the phone. "Dang girl...that ain't how you answer the phone." "Who is this?... I'm pissed off right now... I don't have time for games." It was Ty, Annie and Hell Girl. "We just called to tell you what happened to Tweedy." I calmed down a little. "I just seen it on T.V... what was a main'tence worker doing the basement?" "He went to check the meter... whoever was at that house at that time didn't know that the body was down there and let the man go in the basement. He smelled a foul odor and seen maggots coming from under a closed door, opened it up and ran up out of there and called the police." I just cried and so did they. Look how he suffered. None of us thought that hustling could lead to death like that. "Who... w-h-o-... who would do this." Annie and Ty couldn't talk they were crying so hard. "That girl and dude that lived downstairs from that spot, the girl asked him to come serve them something. He road his bike down there and knocked on the door. As soon as they opened the door the dude hit him in the head with a board that had nails on the end of it which knocked him unconscious. Then the girl used her purse strap to tie around his neck to keep choking him. Then another girl we never saw before used her purse strap to tie his hands and feet together. Then they threw him in the basement in one of those rooms and he died from dehydration and starvation. He lived for about 12 to 16 days. Then the rats started eating at him. I cried uncontrollably. "What... what Hell Girl... what in the fuck did they want... I mean they couldn't just take the money or dope and let him live. ' He had hope for his life girl." "I know... I know Shine... I've been crying every since Bull made that comment that day about... we might be smelling Tweedy's body." Look were his sense of humor got him. I bet his ass will remember that shit he said for the rest of his life. "Yeah... and we was standing right in front of that building looking for him that day... man that odor we smelled was his body." I never answered the phone for Bull. I needed a day or two to get my self together and re- think my life. Tweedy was a good example of why I needed to stop selling dope. He always said to not go up in nobody's spot alone. He made that grave mistake of not following his own orders.

— Two Days Later —

I went to take the baby to see Hell Girl and her Mom. We found out that the man and two women wanted in connection with a murder in Dallas, Texas too. The man had murdered somebody in cold blood. The two women witnessed it and brought him on the run to Minneapolis. They are set to go to trial and testify against each other blaming each other of the murder. "Let me see my little baby." I gave Hell Girl Victor as I stepped out the cab. "Where is your Mom… is she going to watch him… tomorrow while we go to the funeral?" "Um hum… you know she loves him… of course she is." I laughed and kicked it with Hell Girl, Cocoa and their Mom. It was early so I decided to go to the block to just see what it looked like since Tweedy was gone. I had Victor with me since it was only 2 o'clock, I didn't think too much drama would be around. As I pushed little Victor towards Logan Ave, where the murder happened from out of nowhere. "Slap" I turned around with my fist drawn. "Who the… fuck." I looked right into the eyes of the devil. "Why… in the fuck you got my baby out here… bitch… and why you ain't answer my page back?" I tried swingin on him and he laughed. Cat pulled up and headed towards us as we tussled. "Fuck you… what part don't you understand… I don't fuck wit you… go fuck Myrecal and Ty… I shouldn't of brought them up because that makes his ass think I still want him. "stop y'all… th e baby is crying." I ran over to get my baby out of the stroller. Cat kept reaching for him but I let her touch him. "No… leave us alone." I snatched away from them with Victor in my arms and trying to walk away with the stroller. "Give me the baby bitch… he's mine to bitch… you got me spending money on shit and he can't wear it cause you won't let me see him." He started walking back and forth with me as me and my son cried. "So…so what… shit you more worried about who I'm fucking instead of him." He started walking back and forth with me as me and my son cried. Cat just walked and watched. She tried telling everybody it was ok and we ain't fighting. "I ain't worried about you bitch… I got hoes now n-o-w b-I-t-c-h." He screamed as loud as he could. "Good… you see I've moved on. My baby had snot coming out of his nose he was crying so hard. "Yeah… um huh… Myrecal told me you stole that 1000 dollars from me that I was looking for. "Oh …shit that fake bitch snitched me out. I knew they was fucking. That's why her ass wouldn't let me buy her ass shit. "Whatever boy… as many people that beat your Moms… shit anybody could of took…" "Pow… pow" "Screaming." My baby let out a horrifying scream. "Oh god you… you hit my baby" Blood was squirted everywhere. I could taste it in my mouth as the baby screamed and cried. "Give me the baby… Shine… let him go girl." Cat yelled and snatched Victor out of my hands. I fought Bull so hard all my breath was out of me. "I'm sorry ha ha… quit girl…I wasn't tryin to hurt my son." He said while running from me. Cat started walking with him towards the car. "Wait …oh um… where you going with my son?." "His head is bleeding bad… I'm taking him to the hospital." After examining him I hugged and kissed him and sat on the curb and cried. I watched her leave with him and got angry again. "You bitch… I hate you." I screamed and charged at Bull. His friends held me back. "You punched me so hard in my head… you bitch… you made my front two teeth go down in the top of his head." He felt so stupid as the whole block watched the incident go down. I promised on my boy Tweedy if not for life in my body I'm done with his ass. I waited on Cat to come back. He had four stitches in the top of his head but he was smiling and happy. Bull tried kissing on him but he was scared of him and started to cry every time he tried picking him up. "You see… you made my baby hate me." "I didn't do shit… he see your fake ass tryin to hurt his Mom… he knows you hurt him… bitch." I got in the car with Cat and Bull stood outside the car tryin to apologize.

Chapter 16

"Funeral Day"

Everybody from the block came clean as a whistle. Rockma and his crew came in a black and grey Cherokee jeep that said RIP to the homeboy Tweedy. "That was very nice of him. Even though he's not on good terms with Bull, Cat and their crew. He took the time out to represent for a good dude. Tweedy's face was eaten off by maggots and rats so he had a closed casket. The whole Cutie Pie Clique, Shorty Macs and Iowa Posse listened to the preacher as he talked about the drug and crime infested neighborhood that we called home. There wasn't a dry eye in sight. After going to the funeral, we rode around and got drunk. Hell Girl was driving a trap car that some dude gave her. Shortcut and Gov didn't come but they showed their love and gave me and Annie some money. Nobody wanted to see us on the block anymore. Everyone thought that all the smoker would think that they could do this. "Let's roll to that house where Tweedy died at." "Nah... it's soon... I ain't that." Hell Girl always wanted to do something stupid. She make me sick with that. "Yeah... Shine we just wanna pay our respects to the homeboy." "We just did... damn... y'all listen to anything that man just preached about." That bumpy face (gin) was taking over me, I think I drank to much. "Yeah... I heard him that's why I wanna go." I was out numbered everybody in the car wanted to go. "Fuck it... go ahead... I ain't tryin to ruin nothing for y'all." We made our way to Logan Ave. Once we hit the block it was packed. Everybody from the funeral was there. Pouring out liquor, dropping flowers and reminiscing of good times. "See I told you... listen to me from now on... it might get you somewhere in life." "Yeah... my ass to Hell." Everybody busted up laughing. "Look Shine... ain't that Myrecal all up on Bull." Everybody looked at Ty when she said that. The only reason she saying that was cause she think I forgot about her ass fucking Bull. "So... I don't fuck with him no more... good she can have my left over's... shit just like the rest of these hoes out here... she fucked Mistro too... that let's me know the bitch wants her pussy to be like mines... That hoe will never be me. ....y'all better tell your little friend. Everybody laughed and we got out the car. As soon as Bull seen us he ran away from Myrecal. She stood there looking stupid as we both locked eyes. I knew right then me and this bitch was going to scrap. Not over Bull but over respect.

Chapter 17
"Pimp, Tip And Low"

"What you running for bitch... don't back up hoe." I struck Myrecal right in her mouth. The young bitch gave me some go. "I ain't running bitch... I just ain't fighting over no nigga." We kept scrapping. "Stop... please y'all stop... you're suppose to be my friend Shine... you're wrong..." Mya was crying as she watched me and Myrecal go toe to toe. Nobody won that fight. I felt a little bad by what Mya said. Even though her sister was a nasty ass hatin bitch, that didn't mean I had to get her while she was with Annie and Mya. Well I didn't feel like waiting. "Shut up... before I whoop you too." Mya just cried as everybody broke us up. "You wrong Veronica... you are wrong." "Shut up Annie... you picking sides now." "Nah... you don't even fuck with Bull... you got a new man... and you fighting over his ass." "Nah... correction I'm fighting cause the bitch keep fucking behind me. She smiled in my face and fucked behind me. That's just respect... you don't do that. Or don't try being my friend shit. "Whatever." Annie walked off with her friends. I was done with that hoe from that day on. Shady bitch. I guess when you go M.I.A. (missing in action) for a while people's real actions come out. I hate fake ass hoes.

— 3 Months Later —

"Ring... hello." "Hay... dis is Tip what's up." I didn't feel like being bothered with his ass. Little did he know I just wanted his paper so I could get my furniture. "I'm chilling... you got that doe so I can buy some thangs I need." The number one rule in pimpin any man: Let his ass think you are buying something that he can't take back like a trust fund or always make him think you're paying a bill. He can't take shit back that he don't see when he gets mad at you. "Yeah... you going to give me some pussy?" "Um hum... but I need you to bring that doe so I can pay my deposit." "Bet... I'll be through in a minute." His ass think he's slick. He's going to use a rubber for sure. He fucks everybody in town and I know his ass got a woman. On time he brought me a thousand dollars. That was chump change compared to the doe that Pimp was tryin to spend. He was a big time nigga that ran an enterprise with his boys and his Mom's long time boyfriend from Memphis. I just met him so I'm going to take it slow with him. Me, B.B and Tip's cousin Bird, sat downtown St.Paul in front of the section 8 office. We were #'s 81, 82 and 83. I was first of course because I'm the one who heard about them accepting applications. We didn't have to wait over night because one of the case workers sat out there the night before to pass out numbers. The next day we all went to our meeting and was informed that by four months we should have our section 8. I informed my Mom that I could move out of my roach infested little two bedroom apt. that had nothing but a small TV on a TV cart that was falling apart, a nice eating table, a small amount of food for me and my son had a bedroom set that I got from my Mom's house. His dad finally bought him something to sleep on. I had to go through great lengths to get a order of protection against Bull, after he tricked me over to a hotel he was on his way to. He told me he needed me to ride with him to pay Rockma his money and that he might get me a good deal on some work. My dumb, money hungry ass believed him. Knowing damn well Rockma don't fool with him. He got me way out in Brooklyn Park and raped me. I cried and he punched me in my mouth continuously. After he finished he taunted me and stated nobody would believe me because I got a baby by him he poured more salt in my wound as he laughed and talked about how I was just a whore for letting our family friend molest me as a child. I told him that as a confession when we were on better terms. This made me hate him for real. Why on earth would you believe that you could crush somebody's heart by making fun of something they had no control of, like child molestation. He never understood from that day on I hated him, I wanted something bad to happen to him, I waited on something bad to happen to him. So when he called about his son I would refer to him as "What bitch, no hoe, or punk ass nigga." I was over the wounds of child molestation I thought. I guess me fucking at an early age, getting pregnant and disrespecting myself was so easily to come by. I summed it up by using the excuse of making a nigga pay me for pussy or conversation. Open the door... Bang... Bang... Veronica open the door".. That was Tip at my window and I had company over. "Who the fuck is that..." "Oh... this dude that thinks cause he helps me out he can drop by when he want to." Damn I was just about to get this Cali nigga for his paper. "You want me to handle him or something ..." He showed me and Bird his strap. "I'm bout to go... Shine don't put my cousin in the middle of no shit girl." "I ain't." I frowned at her and his boy walked up to her apartment. "Nah... wolf... don't do that... just leave aight." He was just about to break me off so I just decided to let him stay. "Veronica... you going to play a nigga like that... huh after I just ..." Be quiet before you make the neighbors call the police... damn." Bird and her friend was being nosey so she went and let him in. "What the fuck was you doing... huh?" He looked around and saw my company laying on the floor watching TV. "Yeah... I was going to let you in... damn quit tripping." I rolled my eyes and tried to move past him. "hold up... who is that nigga." He grabbed me by my arm, slapped me then pointed at homeboy on the floor. "Stop... nigga... I ain't your girl." The dude watched Tip but he didn't say a word. "Oh I ain't your man... huh... stop... slap." "Click... click... a... nigga you ain't about to be hitting on no women in front of me." Tip's punk ass stopped hitting me. I started crying because I didn't want no incidents behind me. "Yo... chill... he's my cousin... Shine... you shouldn't of had company... knowing Tip was going to trip." Bird was mad at me, like it was my fault that her cousin was jealous. This nigga couldn't handle being my booty call and wanted to get serious. I told his ass I wasn't looking for nothing serious. "Tip... should of called me first... what the fuck you mad at me for... this nigga is the one who's fighting me." "Yo... so you don't fuck with me and I just gave you a G a week ago... I break your ass off everytime we fuck and now you going to trip." He just knew that this was making me look bad but really he stepped my game up. "You knew that we wasn't no couple from jump... don't trip now nigga... everybody pays like they weigh around here." "Fuck you... bitch..." He left and slapped all my pictures off the wall. "Chill... baby... let his ass go." Homeboy was about to follow him out to the car. "That's how people get killed baby... you going to have niggas getting smoked around here...in L.A. that nigga would have been done... slapping on you and shit... you must have some good pussy." Everybody busted up laughing. "I'm just glad my cousin didn't get killed over no pussy." "Wasn't nobody going to die Bird... quit trippin." Bird didn't like the situation because her brother got killed over a girl when we were younger. "You know how I am ...you know I don't like that shit." I understood her pain and I also understood that I couldn't run her while fucking her cousin. O knew for some reason Tip wouldn't take this lightly but I also knew his ass was all bluff. If he wasn't put in a corner or his ass didn't have his whole family with him then he was all mouth. I wasn't really feeling this Cali nigga. His ass had a long ponytail and looked black and Puerto Rican. I mean I don't give a fuck who they are if I've been put on by then, three days with the fools and the paper is right I'll break them off. Oh and he has to be magnum strapped. Ain't nobody running up in me without a rubber. Bull fucked that shit up for everybody. The next nigga hitting me raw will have to prove them self's. "A... so... since you ain't give homeboy his money's worth tonight... ah...why don't you take this and let me take you to the Marriott or something." See now his ass came off too damn easily. He think because he gave me 2000 dollars that it's that cool. Nah, I see now he's just trying to give me more than Tip did. "I ain't like that baby...I've been messing with Tip for a couple of..." "Oh that's...that buster ass nigga's name." Bird looked up while she was entertaining his boy. She kept her mouth shut. "Yeah and... I can't be having nobody hitting on me... I've been through that shit and I'm done with that." "So you just out here being a hood rat since one little nigga broke your heart huh?... that's stupid." "who the fuck you calling stupid." "Yes the fuck you did nigga... and I ain't no hood rat... correction... I'm a hustling ass hoochie if anything." "What's the difference... shit why would you refer to yourself as a hoochie." "Nigga... please... like I said I'm Hood then a mother fucker and I'm a chic to the fullest nigga." "Damn I never understood the shit... women... women... women they make up the dumb...I mean craziest names for themselves... I guess that's the same as you calling your home girls bitches... but as soon as a nigga says you're a bitch you try and fight them." Bird jumped in with me. "Damn right..., it ain't the same." Me and Bird snapped on them nigga's until they shut up. She felt me. Right on time I didn't even have to tell her the game, she already knew to play. I'm getting tired and I know you ain't comfortable here... plus I got to get my son from my Moms in the morning. I knew that would work every time. "Ok... for real... I understand you tryin to tell me to leave huh." Not like that... but you know it's 3 in the morning and I got to pick him up at 8." He stood up and yelled for his friend to come on. "Well you got cool conversation... maybe you'll let me take you up on the offer." Before I could respond, he pulled me close and gave me a long deep kiss. "Think about that ok." That shit made me wet as hell I had to keep up the game. "I sure will baby." I winked at him and wrote my house number down. I never do that but I couldn't forget about that 2 G's he just broke me off. Bird just swore I gave him some pussy before. I never had, the conversation it just that good. Since it was that easy I won't be dropping my draws no time soon neither.

— 3 Months Later —

"Ring... Hello." The person didn't say anything at first. "H-e-l-l-o...dumb bitch." I got up and fixed Victor Something to eat. "Mommy...was that my daddy." His ass still thought we should be together. "I don't know baby... probably not." I try my hardest not to say anything bad about the asshole in front of him I don't want him blaming me for that when he get older. "Mommy... da phone going again." "Get it for Mommy." At almost two years old his but can do a lot for himself. He was potty trained before he could walk. That damn heart murmur may have slowed him down from walking but not for nothing else. My baby is going to be a pro at something. "Mommy... somebody said tell you they sorry." I was tryin to get them damn eggs off the stove. "Who is it Victor." "It's Annie... remember Annie... hi Annie." I snatched the phone from him. "What... what the fuck you want hoe." I scared Victor when I talked like that and he started crying. "What's wrong baby... Moms ok... don't cry." "I... don't... want you to fight Mommy "I had to calm down. He still has flashbacks of Bull hitting on me. "Mommy not going to fight ok baby." I gave him a kiss and sat him in front of his TV so I could finish fixing his food. "Hello... yeah... like I said what you want?" "Um I just wanna let you know I was wrong." "Oh... hum you, Mya and Myrecal must of fell out huh." She sat quiet for a minute. "Yes ...but I've been wanting to call cause I missed little Victor and I missed your crazy ass." I missed her too but I wasn't letting her off that easy. "How do I know you won't pick another mother fucker over me… huh…I mean what the fuck you think I am." "Quit trippin Shine… you know you my home girl… that Pimp been asking about you too." That was music to my ears. Money… money" Good… I needed some doe too. "He got plenty of it. My Mom helped me get a car… it's cool enough to get around in… I'll come get you." "Ok bye." Damn see how god works. When one nigga is gone he blesses you with another. This nigga is paid the fuck up. I know he can put me on my feet! I made my way over t pick up Annie. She had a gang of clothes with her. I knew that either Ty or her Mom was getting on her nerves and she didn't want to be bothered. "Let's roll by Sunny's to see if Pimp is out there hustling." Damn she was right on it. "On Chicago and Lake?" "Yeah… we can get something to eat… plus… we can make some paper out there." We made It up on the set. It was all new to me because I was use to hustling over North. The Southside had new faces and new rules. "If he don't come through while we working up here then we can go on Park and Franklin… he might be hanging in the park." It's cool… I mean you been getting paper out here… you know who the police is and shit?" She looked at me and laughed and started walking up the block. "Wait Annie…I ain't bugging… I'm just concerned from Tweedy… you know." "I understand.… but this is a new girl.… quit trippin." We sat up in KFC until Annie sold all of her shit. "You out yet." I was a little nervous around these parts. I didn't fit in at all but I was going to have to learn how to adjust because I couldn't get paper in Bull's domains anymore. "Almost… a let's walk so you can get some clientele." "Cool." We walked up and down Lake street. I seen Tuesday and let her know that I was going to have something in a few days. She ran that shit about how she don't be doing too much but boosting. Yeah right I let her know we been in the game to long. She can run that on somebody else. "A Tuesday… that's Dirty Red ain't it." I grabbed Annie by the arm and ran towards the laundry mat. "yeah that's him… wait up… Shine you running your ass off." I was so happy to see him. It's been almost a year since I seen him. "Dirty Red… Dirty Red… don't act like your ass don't hear me nigga." He turned around from the dude he was buying dope from. His eyes light up like X-mas. "Hey… baby girl… man I ain't seen you in so long."

He gave me a hug and let me know he'll do whatever for me. I told him that I've been clean of Bull and that I'm sorry he had to go through that bullshit about Tweedy. "I knew I didn't kill Tweedy... I don't even roll like that baby girl... but I still wanna get them nigga's one by one." "Shine enough with all dis... let's go see if pimp is down on Franklin." I was mad at her rushing me but this was her new stomping grounds. "A... y'all need a spot...Pimp ain't the only one holding." "Here ...take my pager number, Dirty Red and I'll hit you back...I don't even know dis nigga pimp... you know I got to feel him out. Annie was looking at me like I didn't trust her but I still had to see the nigga myself. We made it to the car when a brand new grey and white Suburban truck whipped on the side of us. "Who is that Annie." Tuesday ran off thinking it was under covers. "I don't know but I wish they would get that damn light out our face so we could see. "Yo Annie ...come here girl." We could see it was two people but we was still unsure. "A... Annie I ain't getting in my car... that might be a set up." She felt me so we started walking up away from the car. "Wait...they know my name so it must be a homeboy or something." "Girl come here... it's Pimp." I felt at ease. Who I thought we was getting robbed or going to jail. "Turn that light off nigga... you got us spooked out here." I started walking towards my car door cause it was a little chilly. He turned the light down. "Yo... to fine ass can come too." "Come on Shine... we get in the truck and listen to her mumble about some rawchy (heroin). I knew nothing about it so I thought they was talking about dro(weed). "How you doing." I sat in the back before answering. "I'm fine." I didn't want to be to eager to meet him but it was cool. "Yo get in the front." Annie started laughing cause his boy wasn't feeling that. "Why you want me up here." He was looking me up and down. "So I can get to know you." He said while passing Annie something in a little aluminum foil package. "What's that?" She hit his seat and shook her head no. "What Annie... y'all got secrets now." I got real agitated. I don't know what the fuck she was on. "Nah... baby don't trip... here... let's smoke." He passed me a big ass zip lock bag of hydro and the shit smelled good. "You got some blunts." He turned the music up and I started Rollin. We pulled up into the gas station. He passed me a hundred dollar bill. "Go get a couple of swisher sweets." "Damn... so go get... you can ask better than that." He looked at me and smiled. I can tell he wasn't use to girls talking to him like that and I knew his ass was high off something other than dro. "What you want me to say damn girl... ok... can you please go get some blunts... I gave you a whole c-note shit." I got out and went in. I seen Annie and Pimp talking about something heavy while I was in the check out line. When I jumped in the truck they both were wiping there nose. "Y'all up to something Annie... take me back to my car." They thought the shit was funny and ignored me. I just watched them both as Annie talked to the dude in the back and Pimp tried spitting game. "Sniff... sniff so... um what's your real name." "Veronica... what's yours?." He pulled up to a park that looked like New Jack City. "Pimp...you get to know me a little better... I'll tell you my name." I didn't say shit cause that was weak as hell. Nigga didn't want me to know for some reason. He got the truck and all the smokers surrounded him. I watched him walk to the corner and his boy stood there and collected his money from all his workers. "You see how much paper he making... see this is the spot out here... Shine... I'm telling you get in good with him so we can get paid." "It seems like you are already." "Nah stupid... why would I try and hook you up with him." She was right but I just didn't like that sneaky shit they was doing. "You right... he better try and holler at me shit." "Girl... he just gave you a c-not for some damn blunts girl... he didn't ask you for the change did he." "No... but girl... that's chump." "Slow down miss queen B." "Shut up ha." We laughed until he came back. His boy walked off somewhere else." Did you roll that up? "Yeah... two of them." "Cool give me them... roll one for us to smoke now...and keep the rest for y'all to smoke later aight." He came back with a better attitude. I came up with 95 dollars and about four hundred dollars worth of dro. "Did you think about what I said." He started driven back towards my car. "Yeah I did." "And" "And what?" "You... look at your fine ass... um... got to be hard huh... miss hustler." I'm glad his ass knows it. "I ain't hard... I'm just me." I put my charm on his ass as he kept staring at me. We pulled in front of my car. "Here ...take this and get y'all something to eat... and write my number down." After he passed me two hundred Annie jumped out the car to give us a little privacy. I gave him my pager and wrote his down. "Thank you" he got out and came to my side as I was about to walk to my car. "Hold up... I can't get no kiss or nothing damn..." "What you think I am... I don't know." I kept walking and cheesing from ear to ear. He undressed me with his eyes. "That's cool... I like what I see... you got a fat ass... good boy and you might get to taste this fat ass. We laughed at his ass and pulled off. Again I was being way blessed without Bull's ass.

— One Month Later—

We going out tonight. "Annie had been acting strange over my house lately." I don't have no money or shit to wear Annie. I just wasn't feeling it. "Watch! Let's just go... you can wear what you got on... your hair is done." I just went to get a weave ponytail from this girl from Cali. She whipped up Annie's hair she did hair in her house. "You right let's go." We rolled up to Gatsby's since it was the new shit poppin at the time. When we got there we seen Mya and Myrecal and hoes were in our ass. "Hi y'all... what's up?" Mya came over to us talking as we stood in front of the club waiting for everybody to come out. Myrecal didn't say shit to me but she was staring at me like she wanted to. "A... Annie... I'm bout to walk over here... I see something." I walked to the end of the parking lot. I seen a group of dudes form the Chi. I knew they were from there because they were the only dudes that rolled short body Cadillac's or 98's. They were all dressed up with hats that had skin on them. I didn't say a word but Wonnie's side kick Lump, was talking to some fine ass nigga with slanted eyes. He had Moca skin, a nice build and stood about five nine. He kept staring and so was I. Lumps ass was hollering at some hoes as usual. I didn't know why Wonnie wants his ass so much after her cousin was fucking him first. Like I said she always talking about bitches fucking behind her but from the looks of it she fucked behind everybody. Even family. "What's up Veronica... Ms. Veronica...with your hot ass." Lump always had to make himself known. "What's up Mr. Lump... with your flamboyant ass." I wanted the dude to say something so bad but he wouldn't. He just stared. "What you mean flamboyant... I can't help it cause I got cheese and hoes want to fuck." Everybody thought he was fine as hell. He put you in the mind of Alan Iverson but betta. "Ha... funny big head." I decided to walk past Lumps crazy ass had tried my luck. "What's up." He was shocked by my boldness. I wasn't use to chasing but I just thought it would be fun. "What's up… I seen you looking at me." "Nah…y'all was looking at me too." He was smiling form ear to ear. He had a beautiful smile. "I was… um huh… so." Oh I see he wants me to sweat his ass. He walked up on me. Myrecal was rappin to his friend that she must of known because he was feeling on her ass. "What's your name girl… stop playin with me." Damn he walked all in my face this nigga is bold, but I like it. "Shine" "Don't tell me that shit Joe… baby…your Momma didn't name you Shine." I put my hand on my hip and put my finger in his face, then shook my head. "My name ain't Joe… so don't refer to me as Joe.…Nah my Momma named me Veronica… nigga so that's what you call me." He was a little pissed I called him nigga. "Joe is what we say in go girl…Chicago. ." He pushed my hand down out of his face lightly. "Don't call me nigga neither… my name is Low" Here we go with these nicknames again. What could I say , I have one as well. He took my hand and walked me and Annie to the car. "I'm going to call you… Low" He bent down to talk to me. "You do that." He touched my face. "Beautiful… Bye." I watched his fine ass walk away until I couldn't see him in the crowd. "See… see bitch and you wasn't even going to go out… you ain't even dressed up and pulled a fine ass nigga." I started pulling off because Myrecal was flagging us down. "I guess that's true when your Momma says that it don't matter what you look like if you got it… damn it you got it… bag lady or beautiful queen… if he wants you he wants you." To every fine man becomes drama.

Chapter 18

"Glam slam –n- Riverview"

Trying to juggle two niggas at a time. That shit is hard as hell. I was officially Pimp's girl. I didn't see him that much but when asked he told people I was his woman. That was cool cause when I went on his set to make money, they bowed down to me. He was giving Me and Annie ounces for 2 hundred. That was a straight come up. Even though I was fucking his 2 minute weak four play ass. I felt I should have got my work for free or cheaper. Shit not to Pimp. He stood by his name, after 2 months of no ass and breaking me off 2 hundred here and there chump change. When I finally gave it up he was sweating like a fat pig and breathing like he just ran the Boston Marathon. I hated fucking him but I had to pay bills. "Ring" "veronica… get the phone I'm in the tub." "Wait… I'm talking to Tip in the window… you get it Annie." I was tryin to let Tip know not to come by my house no more! "So it's like that…answer the phone." I was talking to him through the screen because I know he wanted to fight. "Don't worry about my phone… just get away from my… "Swish… hawk spit… funky bitch." He threw a bottle of pine sol in my screen and spit into it. I had hot pine sol running down my new DKNY dress. "You punk ass bitch… you fucked up my clothes… haten ass pussy." He hyped up as he laughed and walked back to his car. "Fuck that dress bitch… go spend that G I gave yo ass." "That shit been goon nigga… yo weak ass bitch… wit yo dirty dick." He was pulling off because people started looking out their window. "I'll show you dirty… hoe… yo better watch your back." Annie was out the bathroom thank god in my son's room getting dressed, as I cleaned myself off. "Annie who was that on the phone?"She started whispering. "Their still on the phone. "Who… stupid?" "Low is on one line and Pimp is on the other." Oh shit I had to get my story together because I know they heard my big ass mouth. "Hello." "What took your ass so long to get on the phone girl?" "It was Pimp. He didn't pose a threat. "I was getting something out my car." "Oh… you was huh… um sounded like you was arguing with some lame to me." "What… boy please you know I live in the hood… that was the girl upstairs." "Yeah… whatever… that's why I don't come over there… shit nigga's might set me up he really pissed me off. Now he's accusing me of setting people up. "Fuck you nigga…you ain't nobody to set up… I don't fuck around like that your scary fat ass." "Oh… I'm fat now… why you talking to me like that… I never talk to you like that." He had a point but he still had me fucked up. "So what… don't you ever put my name out there like that… I ain't never set nobody up and never will shit." I had to make myself clear. "Ok damn… I was just saying… shit, you like in that fucked up neighborhood and..." "And what nigga... I'm bout to move in 30 days nigga... so don't be try in to come over then." I wasn't saying..." "Click." Annie was cracking up cause I was hot. "Ring." "Calm down Shine before you answer the phone." Sh was right it was too nice outside and my Mom had my son for the week. "Hello." "How you doing... Ms H-e-l-l-o." I straightened my tone. "My fault... I'm fine." "What happened... Annie had me on hold for a minute so I hung up." "Oh... she thought you hung up... what's up?" "You... I wanted to see if you wanted to go to the movies tomorrow night." That's cool Low...what time?" I loved his sexy ass voice. "I'll come get you about 6 so we can go eat." "Ok... I'm with that." We hung up and I told Annie all the juice. "We going out this whole weekend." "Good... then lets hit the block hard." "Yeah I got to since I fucked up with Pimp... I got to get some new furniture... I ain't taking none of this shit with me except the baby's stuff." Me and Annie decided to get Bird and walk around the hood. "It was a lot of people hanging out on Selby Ave. I seen this dude name Gen that use to bye work from me. I was really happy to see him. "Hi Shine... how you been doing?." He was sweet on me but I couldn't fuck with him because he was too soft and he fucked Ty. "I'm fine... you got some work?" I took advantage of his kindness by having him sale my shit for free because he liked me. "No... but I'll get rid of yours from you... if you need me to." See works every time. Bird and Annie walked ahead of us trying not to listen. "Ok." I pulled my cut up work out and gave it to him. "Hay... where's sweets at?" This was his cousin I fucked a couple of times. I stopped because I suspected he was gay. His dick was good but I just wasn't feeling him because he was broke. He didn't have a car and he stayed with his sister. "Why... you still like him or something?" I could see it's time for me to walk on cause he might change his mind about my work. "Hell No... I told you I don't trust him... that's your cousin... shit un...I can't fuck with nigga's that's suspect." He busted up laughing. "Give me a hug... you my girl. ...you say anything out your motha fucking mouth." I gave him a hug and we walked to the VFW. This was the hood restaurant that everybody in MN went to. It was a small bar and grill. Mrs. Ann sold the best cheeseburgers and soul food in town. Bird ordered a cheeseburger fries and a grape soda. Annie ordered fried chicken wings, fries and a strawberry soda. I ordered a smothered chicken dinner breast and wings with greens, man and cheese and corn with a cornbread muffin and a Pepsi. We were stuffed after we waxed that. Nobody said a word just straight grubbing. The old timers were hollering at Bird, she was with that. I wasn't and Annie didn't know what was going on. I had to sit and talk to the women behind the grill. While Bird was talking some old man out of his money. Annie was in the corner of the bar exchanging money for the aluminum foil pack that I seen her and Pimp with that day. "Oh hell no…I'm leaving y'all hoes." I jumped up and paid for every thing and left. Annie and Bird came running out of the bar. "Wait… wait girl." Bird was tryin to explain to the old man that she had to leave "Here I come Shine… wait…I'm tired." She was always acted wired or nodded off and I didn't understand. They finally caught up to me as I made it to the next block. "You are tripping girl… what's wrong with your ass?" "yeah you just jumped up and left." I was ignoring them at first. "You was jacking that old man out of his money… knowing you wasn't going to give him no pussy." Then I pointed at Annie. "Then you… your ass been snorting some shit… and I don't like it…you been falling asleep often and been spending money like crazy." Bird was ready to fight me but wouldn't hit me. "First of all… you don't tell me how to hustle… I don't tell your ass how to sale dope…don't tell me how to jack no nigga… I don't give a fuck who they are." I could tell she was heated but I didn't care. "He was somebody's grandpa or something… you are wrong Bird and know it girl." "I don't give a fuck… he ain't my grandpa… and if my grandpa wanted to pay a young bitch that looked as good as me he can." "Whatever… hoe." I started off running a little, I just wanted to get away from them. "Wait… and the reason why I was asleep so much is because I'm on my period… the foil packs is dope… and I ain't snorting shit… so stop accusing me of this." She was lying through her teeth. It was there life not mines. I just felt that it's certain things you do in life. "Whatever." We made it to my house and they didn't talk and neither did I. Bird came in behind me. "I need my vacuum." Just like a petty bitch, when you get mad at your friend you want to take shit back. "There it goes." I pointed at the vacuum against the wall. "Nobody ain't stopping you." She stood there for a minute snatched her vacuum and headed out the door. "I ain't fucking with yo ass no more." I jumped up to shut the door behind her. "Good... I'm moving and you won't have to see my ass no more neither."

— One Month Later —

"Annie...you ready?." We were on our way to the Glam Slam. I knew everybody was going to be out. Annie talked me into letting Myrecal and Mya come with us. I never understood why when you get into a fight with some women their dumb ass still wants to be your friend. We made a stop at the gas station. "I'll go pay for it Veronica." I walked to the gas pump and put it in my car. ""spss...spss." "Oh my god... what the fuck is going on." Gas shot straight up in the air. I stopped it before I got it all on my clothes. "Mamma... do you need some help?." A man seen me struggling and offered to help me. "I put 20 on the tank... what happened Shine?" "Girl the damn gas won't go in...it splashed all over my hand." I went in the gas station to wash my hands off. The man was nice enough to check my gas spout. I made it back and I had a surprise that I didn't like. "Baby... somebody don't like you at all..." "Why what's wrong... is it anything I can fix." The only person that would fuck with my car was Tip or Bull. Pimp thought he was too good for that and bitches around here was punks and I really didn't have any enemies. "You have Oreo's and snickers in your tank...if you have at least a half a tank you will make it till the morning but you have to get that fixed before that sugar gets to the engine." I thanked the man and gave him $20 for his time. I road two blocks down to a hood shop. He checked it out and told me in the morning he could take out my whole gas cap, clean it and I'd be straight. "Who in the fuck would do this Annie." "I don't know... but if a bitch did it... I'm whooping her ass." "Me and you both... don't say shit in front of Mya and Myrecal." "I won't shit... I still don't like that hoe Myrecal but... I'm going to chill cause Mya is cool." "Yeah she straight I guess." We road over to pick up the haters. "Hi y'all... thank you Veronica." Mya started off kissing ass. "I'm sorry y'all... I should be a better friend... I know." Myrecal said while tryin to give me a hug. "Nope... you straight... get in." They knew I wasn't feeling them but they didn't care. Annie talked to the haters the whole ride to the club. When they made a Smalltalk I would answer them and that was it. As soon as we made it to the line we saw Wonnie and Olivia, that was my break away. "Hey... y'all what's up." "Hi Veronica... you look cute... where your ass been girl." Wonnie gave me a hug and told me to walk with them. "Why you with them anyways girl." "I don't know y'all... let that hoe Annie talked me into it." We kicked it all night. I didn't see Pimp or Low up in there but I knew they was going to be outside. When I made it in the bathroom to do a check, I seen a childhood friend Yoyo. I tried to avoid her because she was a scrub. Yoyo was the kind off girl that fucked and sucked anybody for crumbs or for free. She wore you as a jealous person knowing she was. "What's up... Veronica... long time no see." She was with this stinking ass bitch Nella. Low hoes run together. I guess to them they don't have nobody to watch but themselves. "What's up." "Damn that was dry." She was pissed cause I went to the counter and paid the maid of the lady's room 5 dollars to use her DKNY cashmere perfume and spray some spirits. Damn Prince had it going on in his club. The maid of the Lady's room had everything from lipstick to panty hoes. You hook her up and she would hook you up, courtesy of the Glam Slam. "I don't feel no need to be no other way." Nella said like she was waiting to start some shit. "Shine... I ignored the hoe at first. "Ok... be like that... I got something you might want to know." I kept talking to the maid and fixing my hair. I thought, damn she was fucking with Bull...she might know something I want or need to know. "What... what would you have to tell?" She came a little closer. "Do you know Low?" "Yeah... He's a dog and I heard he tried to get with you but we went to the movies the other night." "Girl... he ain't my man I don't give a fuck about that." I pushed past her and YoYo's ass. I wasn't worried about that nigga shit. "No... wait... well do you talk to Zero at all?" What was this hoe getting at. "Don't walk away Veronica... she really got shit to tell you." Yoyo's flunky ass would jump on any free damn ride she could get just to be down. "Let's go of my arm hoe." She stepped back because she knew I'll whoop her weak ass. "For real... Zero was at my house talking about how he wants to fuck you." "And... that's my son's aunties man...what the fuck you telling me that shit for?" I know this jealous ass hoes is tryin to hate for some reason. "Because... I just think it's wrong what Bull did." "What did Bull do... that you know about? I knew she was fucking with Bull and now she wants me to know she's fucking Low too. "I saw him put sugar in your tank." I turned around ready to beat the shit out of her when Annie walked up. "What's up." "Dis hoe just told me she saw Bull put that shit in my gas tank." Annie pulled me to the side to whisper. "Dummy make that hoe think you like her so you can get some info." I stepped back in both of their face. Annie got everything out of Yoyo because she loved telling everybody's business. "What was you doing there?" Mya and Myrecal started standing around and I chilled because they were nosy as hell. "I was going with them to make a run and he put the stuff in your tank at about two in the morning." "So Zero was with y'all too... when he was saying he wanted to fuck me." I know that nigga didn't say that shit in front of Bull. Not that he won't but he's on some sneaky shit. "No... he said that when I was over T.T.M's house... he thought I could hook him up with you but when he found out I use to fuck him cause her jealous ass wants me out the way. "Um thanks for tryin to get some brownie points." I walked away from that stinking hoe before I whooped her ass. She was yelling saying something but I couldn't hear her. "Wait Shine." Annie was calling me and on my tail. Mya, Myrecal and Yoyo was right behind her. As soon as I made it outside I seen Low. "What's up nigga." I knew that would make him mad while he talked to some hoe. He was still mad because after the dinner and movies two weeks ago. He tried to do it to me and I told him it was too soon. The next morning after we woke up, I seen cum all over the front of his pants. He wanted this pussy bad and couldn't get it. Embarrassed, he asked for a towel to wash his face. When he came out the bathroom it looked like he tried wiping off his jeans. His dumb ass should of known it's hard to wipe white sticky stuff off of black jeans. "What did I tell you about calling me nigga." He grabbed me by my weave and put his arm around my neck. The girl just walked off. "Stop playing boy...this shit cost too much." Everybody laughed as they watched like we were in a circus. "I told you about wearing that shit anyways." This nigga was very demanding and he ain't even hit it yet. "When you start paying for shit that's when your ass can say what I can do about mines." The club was letting out and I seen

Nella and her crew watching me and Low play in the street. "You got a slick mouth girl... but I like it though ." I was cheesing from ear to ear as we played all the way to the parking lot. Zero and his Cali people rode by and yelled "I can do better than he can", Low broke his neck tryin to look cause Annie and them didn't respond. "Who's them nigga's yelling at." "Look at you... you say don't call you nigga but you use the word too." I had to change the subject so he would forget about them. "You right... a... .when we going to... you know." He was smiling so hard I didn't want to ruin his flow. "Soon... soon enough."

— One month later —

I moved out to Edina, MN. It was an upscale town and predominantly white. I was glad. The only thing I had to worry about was neighbors and that I did. The Mall of America had just opened and I lived 5 minutes away. Tuesday was happy about that because it was open season for her and every booster in town. I went to an alternative school called work Opportunity Center –WOC for short. When I got there they told me that I had a lot of credits and I would only have to go to school until Dec. and then I would receive my diploma. That felt good because I was ready to start college. Graduating at 19 was better than not graduating at all. I called my Mom and told her the good news. She was so proud of me that she offered to keep my son during the week so I won't loose focus on college. That was music to my ears being as though I go out Sunday through Thursday anyways. I let the haters miss me on Friday and Saturday. Annie and Ty went with me so that was cool. "Honk...Honk." Some dude in a blue blazer was honking his horn while I was walking towards the door to go to school. "A... you don't know me now that you're all grown huh." I knew that voice from anywhere. You know I thought I was cute so I turned around slow. "Yeah... you know me big head... you still think you're cute... it's bumpy... bumpy from the block." Oh I knew it. Bumpy was the homeboy who had one foot in the game and one in the corporate world. You never knew what he was doing but he always kept paper. He didn't curb serve anymore but he bought a new truck every year and always took care of every homeboy in prison. He was good peoples. "Hi Bumpy... how you been?" Now you know me huh... I knew yo ass would remember when I started talking about your ass." I walked to the truck to give him a hug. "Shut up... you still Manish as hell... what you doing up here... you're out of school ain't you?" He must was getting at some hoes or something. "Oh... I'm just waiting on my homeboy to come out." "Ok...bye... I got to get to class." "Yeah... stay your ass in school... cause I heard you been hitting the block pretty hard... you ain't no nigga so you need to chill that shit out." "Ok Bumpy... damn daddy always got shit to say." "Yeah nigga's digging out here for petty shit... I just hate to see shit happen to you ok... if you ever need me... or I can do anything for you let me know... love you girl... you a strong women." His word stuck to me like mashed potatoes. "Thank you Bumpy... love you too." I ran in to school and couldn't get those words out of my head. It seemed like time would never end. The day went by slow so I decided to get Annie and leave early. "Spss... Spss...Annie." I was trying to get her out of home ec. She hated it because she liked nothing about sewing. "Wait... grab my stuff out my locker... I'll meet you at the car." I walked real fat away from the door cause the hall monitor was coming. "Hay... hay...you got a pass Momma." I hit the corner and down the stairway. I ran to my car and ducked down cause I saw him walking behind Annie but he wouldn't say nothing to her because she was known for cussing them out. "What took you so long?" "Girl I had to tell that stupid Ms.whatever that I had a headache." "Oh... don't you got a hair appointment?" "Yeah in about 3 hours... you going with me." "Yeah." We rode around to get something to eat. Ty would have to find a ride from some nigga cause I ain't waiting on her ass. After riding over North to reminisce again. I dropped Annie off at the girl's house to get her hair done. I decided to roll around and go see some people. When I turned on Logan Ave. I seen Bull and his crew. "Yo...yoyo .... pull over." I fucked around and rolled all the way to the Riverview. It was one of the oldest and best clubs in the city. Right off the river front it sat high up on a hill. When I made it back to get Annie she still wasn't done yet, I was bored so I just sat and waited on her. "Somebody page Shine." "Yeah... dis Bull." I was about to hang up. "Wait... I know you don't want me... but let me give you some money for my son." "Meet me at the Riverview." I felt it wasn't that much he could do to me there. It wasn't club time but it but there were a lot of police in the area. I made it there and he jumped in my car and told me to drive back to the block. My first instincts told me to stay in this area but I didn't. "So how you been... I heard you got a boyfriend now... yeah you go with that nigga Pimp huh." He was fishing, reaching for something. That ain't your business... you said you got something for my son." I pulled over to let his ass outing front of Burger King on Penn and Broadway. "Turn right here and answer my question." I could see he was getting pissed off and I don't know why because we were way done with each other. "I got to go." "Bitch, click...click." "I screamed... what the fuck is wrong with you." I pulled up on the block where Tweedy got killed and didn't know it. "I didn't tell you to stop hoe." He slapped me and put the gun to my chest then my neck." You ain't got shit smart to say now huh... hoe, you bout to suck my dick...you suck everybody else's." "No...no I don't." I started grabbing the gun from my chest. "You better stop hoe." He kept punching and slapping me. "Kill me... kill me motherfuck... I screamed." I jumped out the car and started running. "leave me alone." "Boom... blocka...blocka." The nigga was shooting at me as I ran to my old school. "Bitch you better stop or I'm going to kill you." Somebody called the police from me screaming because I could hear the sirens. "The police are going to get you Bull...I'm crying... don't do this... I don't want you...please." The Po Po hit the corner and he took off running. From this day on he would never see me or touch me again.

Chapter 19

"California Crippin"

"I told you don't call me Rockma aight." That's what his ass said to me after I met a couple of his people, Chico and Ricky the real folks from Cali everybody else was fronting. Biren and Frank were right from the Northside. Oh I better get it right as they would say. Frank is T.TM and Biren is Big Boy. Bullshit I knew them nigga's real names round here and so do everybody else. "What don't call you that in front of other people or what... shit I'm use to calling you your name and so does my son. "He thought about that shit for a minute cause his son and my son are cousins. Even though we don't fuck with Bull or Cat it still remained that our kids are related why does he want me. I don't know but I'm going to get whatever I can out his ass without fucking him. "Man... whatever... I said call me Zero or 59 ok... not what is it that your fine ass wants." I looked at him like he was crazy. "No... I don't mean like that didn't you say you needed some work." "Yeah." "Well... how much can you handle?" I wasn't going to jump straight out the window be cause I had finals to do. "Just give me a half ounce...that's cool for now." "Here ...if you need something else then let me know." "I will." "A don't be telling Cat or that nigga Bull about..." "Hold up... you know I don't fuck with them at all... they ain't allowed no where around me... you got me fucked up." He just looked at me for a minute. "A... Um I'm trippin aight... I just got to know I can trust you... ok." I slammed the door of his truck t make it look like I was mad. That always works.

Chapter 20

"Hyatt Regency Hotel"

"Damn cuz... stop hold them dice nigga." "That's you nigga... drop that 5 g's nigga... and play." It was a hotel full of nigga's from Cali ready to set up shop. Nigga was looking for any dumb hoe that was able to hit the block or put a trap house in their name for them. "Come on T.TM... man put my money down nigga." Dis nigga thinks I'm playing he better quit tryin to front off nigga's. "Zero... cuz don't be acting funny ...you know I'm good... just play." "5 before 9 nigga bet." He all in my business. Number one rule don't tell my homeboys about her pussy cause everybody been waiting for her to get away from Bull's punk ass. "Don't try and throw me off nigga... pay up... cuz." I just won that whole 5 g's, nigga better focus and stop worrying about pussy he ain't going to touch. "I quit nigga." The whole room busted out laughing. "Cool cuz... I got mines and I still ain't telling you if I hit it or not." "All... cuz you being funny like that nigga... fuck you then." "Fuck you... that's why we call yo ass T.T.M that shit fits talk too much. ...you ain't fucking up shit for me." "So what nigga... I could of hit it in high school." "You fronting now nigga." I got up ready to put it on his ass and the homie's grabbed me. "Let me go cuz." "nigga ...y'all ain't bout to fight over no bitch... nah man... that shit ain't cool cuz." He's lucky the homeboy Big O was between us cause I was going to whoop his ass. "Man that's Zero takin that shit personal... over pussy he ain't hit yet... I was just playin cuz fam." I had to shake that shit off. I can't be trippin off shit that don't belong to me. "Shut up nigga... your ass just better worry about Wonnie... cause once she finds out you fucked Olivia she might not let you hit." "You crazy nigga... she's a mad freak... man she fucked her cousin's man Lump, so fucking me don't matter to her shit... she be running that shit like she feeling that Chi Town nigga but for real I'll be loving that pussy up in a minute." He was really fronting now I'm bout to have Veronica go out to Cali for me... Um see if she wanna step her game up in da weight game." "Oh... look at Daddy... ain't even hit yet and wanna help her get rich." He just mad cause I made it to her ass first. She's a down ass bitch and he knows it. He knows them hoes he fucking is just looking for a free ride. I can see it in her beautiful eyes. She won't fold for nobody. "I got her back and she got mines nigga." "Do she know you still be fucking Cat... or that you fucked her girl B.B." "Nigga...you act like you going to tell her or something." What this nigga getting at. I'm cool on him knowing anything serious about Veronica. "No... that's where you wrong at cuz I'll never do that cuz." "Yeah right." Everybody made their own dice game. They was tired of hearing us argue. "A cuz you know that bitch Nella still tryin to fuck after she fucked you cuz." "Fuck that hoe... she got good head that's about it. She can keep my work to her crib cause Veronica ain't... I'll keep laying dis to her for that reason only... Um and pay her a few crumbs." He looked at me crazy cause he knew I was bugging. "You dig her for real cuz... damn you got it bad... don't let her know she got you open like that cuz." "No y-o-u don't let her know she got me open nigga... to make it so bad... she goes with that nigga Low." "What!... nah cuz he still fucking Nella and Wonnie's brother's women... to make it so bad... Nella and the girl hang together." "You know what cuz you gossip too much... ha... you know everything, that ain't cool." "Um... I got to know what these bitches be out here on... shit ain't none of them getting me caught up." I had to get away from his ass and think . I took 5 of the homeboys over to me and Big Boy's crib out in Richfield. The Po Po don't really be out there too tuff. Now that's out of my way, I'm a see if Shine really wanna start working with keys of coke or what. I can't have her out there on the block because pretty soon nigga's going to be tryin to kidnap her once they know she fucking with me.

Chapter 21

"Target on Broadway"

"Corn... corn...I need more than 300 dollars to get the baby's clothes... why we got to go to this cheap ass store anyways?" He better give me more money with his punk ass. "My name ain't Moca... it's Hell Girl for a reason." "Moca... I'm sorry that you think cause a nigga is from Cali that... I got mad paper... but I don't "My name is Hell Girl... don't call me that no more I told your ass." He got me fucked up. This nigga is going to do way more than he's saying. He grabbed me by my arm. "Look you're about to be a mother... your name is Moca Anderson and that's what the fuck I'll call you." "Let me go... you should have been grabbing on Rockma's punk ass when he punched me and broke my jaw." "That's what you get... you was wrong telling that man's bidness...you was causing a scene like you're doing now." Damn he was right. I didn't really like all the people in the isle watching my 8 month pregnant ass act a fool. "I ain't causing no scene... y'all can stop looking at us. ...ain't shit wrong...people can't have a conversation around here." Everybody went back to doing their own thang. "Corn... Corn... quit trippin boy... you know I'm pregnant and I can't do shit." Yeah I'm going to use his dumb ass even if this ain't his baby. Stupid motherfucker going to pay for leaving me for that bitch. "I can't tell... you act like a damn man with that mouth of yours."

Chapter 22

"Tower's Apts."

"Lump why you acting like that lump?." I swear I thought this nigga was going to be mine. I know he got a woman but she was in Chicago. I don't give a fuck. That bitch need to take care of her man. The nigga is breaking me off G's. I don't care. "Yeah... cause I told you I got a women before you wanted to fuck me... when she paged you... you should of acted like you was my boy's girl or something." Why am I so weak for him. Shit T.T.M said he'll take care of me but he wants me to keep that shit in my house. Fuck that nigga is too hot and I can't jeopardize my kids like that. "I know Lump... I'm sorry but I didn't trip about... I told her none of her business. I was... I mean I been sucking you dick and you ain't even ate my pussy yet." I knew this would change the subject. "What... you trippin... shit all this dick I'm given you...and all the paper I be breaking you off with...you shouldn't care." "You right Lump... when you coming over?" I love him so much, I don't know why he won't leave her. I mean every since he stopped fucking my cousin and given her dope, he been fucking me. He said I'm the only one in MN that he fucks with. "I don't know... shit I heard about you fucking somebody else... one of them nigga's friends that Veronica be fucking shit... y'all sneaky." Oh shit I don't want him to tell Low so I better clean this one up. "You going to believe something some bitch probably told you... fuck you shit... ain't nobody fucking around you... Veronica got her own pussy... I can't tell her what to do with her pussy." "You know what she be doing though and you hang with her." "You know what... you say too much shit about Veronica... you must want to fuck her." I know his ass likes her cause he talks about her too much. "If I wanted to fuck her...I would... quit tripping girl... I was just saying that to make you mad." "Well it worked shit." "Don't be mad...I'm bout to come suck that pussy... you been waiting on that huh." "Yeah... come on!" "Click."

Chapter 23

"Arnelia's Night Club"

I'm bout to stop fucking with Nella's ass. I can't get no money with her. She been fucking Zero forever and he still ain't ate her pussy. That bitch Veronica got him sprung. "Nella... when you going to tell everybody you pregnant." I knew this would make her mad. This is my reason to get over Shine and Annie's house. "Why bitch... with your gay ass... you keep asking me my business." "So what if I like girls but she ain't going to be telling my business. "What I know you ain't tryin to front on me... you don't even know who you pregnant by bitch... Zero, T.TM, Low and Bull been hitting it everyday." Oh shit I struck a nerve, the bitch is bout to hit me. "What... bitch you don't even got no where to live YoYo... your Mom fucks young niggas and you and your sister fucks behind each other B-i-t-c-h." I know she didn't put my Mom in this shit. "You mad cause you wanted to fuck my sister and she said no bitch... you broke ugly... gap tooth bitch... big ass say your pussy stinks bitch with your fake ass." She calling somebody fake when she fucks behind everybody. Then she cries when somebody does it to her. "You know what Nella?" "Nah... what YoYo?" I walked away from her a little bit. "I'm bout to hang with Veronica and them in MPLS... they some real bitches... they know how to get real money." "Go ahead... you slithery snake bitch... I h-a-t-e you." She stormed off from me. Now I got to get my hustle on. I should say beg. When Veronica is your friend she's your friend. I know her dumb ass will feel sorry for me and let me stay at her crib. I can get some money and she will hook me up wit some Cali niggas. Let me see if she's home. "Ring... Hello." "Hi... Um Veronica... dis Yoyo." Oh shit this bitch got quiet. She might not help me. "What... what the fuck you want girl... you want to speak Annie?." I could hear Annie in the background asking who was on the phone. "No... I need your help." "What bitch... who you think you talking to... I ain't no lame bitch... help you what... where's that hoe Nella at... that's yo girl ain't it?." Damn I'm going to have to spill all my business." "Please... please Shine... I promise I won't tell none of y'all business. I need money and a place to stay... I'll babysit...whatever please… I just need somewhere to go… I got something to tell you about Zero. .. .and Low." I knew that shit would work. She was fucking with both of them. "Come on YoYo… the first time you start that shit… I'm putting you out." I knew that would work every time. "I'm on my way… Thank you!'

Chapter 24
"Mall of America"

"Tuesday… come here… let me show you what I want." I'm sick of every time we go shopping and Veronica gets her shit first. "Wait… I got to get Veronica this Looney Tunes Coat…she paid me for it." "My money spends just like hers damn Tuesday… let me find out you all up in her ass like that." Punk ass crack head bitch, she always gets Shine ugly ass everything. I want my shit now I just don't have the money right now. "Ty… do you have the money or a little dope so I can smoke my primo." "No I was…" "See that's why I fuck with Veronica first… she's my peoples and she looks out for me so I have to look out for her." "Man… Shit I can't wait till I get my settlement… I ain't fucking with nobody not even Annie's ass… and I don't care if you tell them neither." I better shut up cause I know they can whoop me. "Come on Ty… I got the coat for you…plus we got to take Veronica her car back." Damn I still find myself needing this bitch.

Chapter 25
"Graduation Day"

"Annie girl I'm so glad… it's over… I got my diploma at 19… I got 10 G's stacked and a 9 piece in the stash… I'm chillin." "What you going to do now… I mean are you really going to move to the ATL or out to Cali." "I'm unsure… I mean my Mom wants me to wait until Victor is a little older so I might as well just go to MCTC for Business." I was so focused and Annie wasn't but she was my home girl so I could change that. "Um… I don't know what I'm going to do… I mean I could do hair… I guess." That's so sad, I don't want to make her feel out of place because I know what I want to do with my life and she doesn't. "You guess… what you mean…" "Wait… Veronica… you got a son… you got section eight to help you, your Mom and two nigga's." "And… so what Yoyo… what's your point." I knew this hoe was just trying to know all my business. "My point is… me and Annie don't have no kids." "So… me having a baby makes it way harder." These hoes are real dumb, no focus, for shit. "You think so… I mean I can't for Yoyo but with help and a baby it gives you more reason to make yourself get up and do something." "Annie you know that Ms. Hardway would help your ass if you had a baby… you both could get any nigga to cough up some cash anyday. .. right Yoyo." They both started laughing at me. "Ring… Hello." "Veronica …what are you doing?." "Huh…Mom." "We are at your school and graduation starts in 30 min." I totally forgot for a minute all into this conversation. "Oooh Mom… we are on our way." "Ok… this is your life… Victor is looking forward to this?" "I know… Mom I'm on my way… Bye." We ran out of my apt like a bat out of hell. Yoyo wasn't together so she stayed at my house after Annie convinced me it would be cool. I don't know why I felt Annie talk me into doing shit all the time. I mean I am way stronger then her, plus I don't even know if she's a true friend when shit gets rough. I mean everybody hangs at my house uses my car, needs me for advice and borrows money whenever they know I have it. The shit gets on my nerves but my Mom and grandma taught me what it is to be a loyal friend. We made it to graduation on time Annie went to sit wit my Mom, Step dad and Victor. I had to sit at the table with the other graduates. Man this felt real good to finally be done. The great thing about the Alternative school was that when you graduate you get your diplomas from your last school you went to. So even though I didn't graduate with my regular class at North High . I still receive my diploma from there. "I would like to congratulate Veronica Gittens for all of her accomplishments and achievements. "Yeah…that's right baby…get that diploma." My Mom embarrassed me cause everybody laughed. "Yeah go girl." "Good Mommy… I love you." I was crying because I finally did something good for my mother. "I just want to thank my Mom for sticking by me and pushing me to finish... love you baby and you too Annie." They all stood up to clap. We had to sit through the rest of the ceremony because my Mom said it would be rude to leave. "What are you going to do after this Veronica... have you thought about what yo want to do yet?" I knew she was going to be right on it. "I told your Mom... business or fashion... probably both." "Ok... it's your choice... you need to make a career out of something for this boy." "I know... Mom will you watch him for the rest of the week ...we are going to have a little get together for me graduating." I knew she would say yes of course... call me later and I want you to sign up for the semester ok." "Ok... Love you Mom ...gemme a kiss Victor, Smooch." I left my graduation and headed back to the house. Damn Annie... somebody is blowing my pager up girl... I'm bout to pull over to a pay phone." "cool... I'll call and see what Yoyo ass is doing." We went to the gas station and it was everybody calling to tell me congratulations and that Bull's cousin Pear got killed at the gas station the other day. Hell Girl said be careful cause they said Zero and that Cali nigga Big O did it. I asked how do they know and she said cause Pear was with Boo and Trip when it happened . They didn't have a gun so they couldn't help. Pear pulled his gun and shot Big O then Big O shot him in his face. It was another shooter on the side of the gas station and that's who they say Zero was. I knew she was lying just to pick me. She didn't like Zero at all. She was so close to Bull's family because of Lump that she was going to do anything to find out if I'm fucking Zero so she could tell Cat. "I don't believe Zero did that Moca... are you coming to the graduation party? I had to change the subject. "Yeah bitch... you know I wouldn't miss that party... a Bull wants to know if he could come?" I knew this bitch was trying to tell me that Bull shit about Pear so I would feel sorry for Bull. "Hell No... He can't come within 20 feet of me No... damn... what happen to Big O... is he ok?" I truly didn't feel this conversation but I didn't want her bringing Bull out to my house. When Low or Zero might come over. "You sure are worried about them crip niggas... damn hoe you really must be fucking Zero." "No bitch I ain't." She'll never know until she catch me with him and I haven't fucked him yet. "um... I'm on my way out there with some of the homeboys from off Plymouth Ave... they say his crab ass is in a wheelchair." "Damn... that's fucked up cause he's cool as hell." "Well his cool crab ass will go back to Cali in a wheel chair." "Bye... dumb ass... his name is Big O... click. "Who was that Shine." Annie had been sitting in the car for 20 minutes waiting on me. "Why you eating... it's a gang of food in the house girl." I knew she was hungry cause we haven't ate since breakfast. "Girl... you was on that damn phone like you don't have shit to do... I was hungry while you bullshitting." I was wrong... but she didn't have to go off. Damn Annie... quit trippin... who was the other pages from." She rolled her eyes. "Zero... Low, Gen and pimp even called as long as you was talking." I laughed at her dumb ass. "You funny as hell... what they say." "Gen got your money he owns you. Zero told me what happen and No he had nothing to do with Pear getting killed. That's another lie Bull and Cat made up to get hum put in jail cause Zero don't want Cat. Low wants you to call him and so does Pimp. Damn I was talking too long if she got all that info while I was talking to Moca. "Thank you Bitch... you don't have to act like that." I pushed her in the head. "Quit hoe... you don't know what you would do without me." "live hoe live... ' We made in back to the house and Yoyo had everything laid out for the party. She had her damn feet kicked up on my new table." Annie started laughing. "You ain't brought shit up in here." She almost dropped the phone trying to get her feet down. "I'm sorry Shine... you crazy girl." I ain't crazy shit she better be lucky she's still over here. "who's that on my phone anyways?" I knew she was gossiping even though Dr. Dre's the chronic was blasting through the speakers. "Mya... She wants to know can they come over." Before Annie persuade me. "No... hell No... it ain't no party like that... I don't want my house hot." Annie kept bobbing her head to the music she laughed and shook her head." She said ok... and congratulations." I wasn't trying to hear them hoes. Everybody from the hood came over. I really didn't want nobody to know where I lived but I guess it really didn't matter because Moca is going to be Moca. Yeah she's so grown now you can't call her Hell Girl. I'll call her what I want, she is still Victor's God Mom so it ain't much her ass would do to me. She be wanting to fight me sometimes but she don't cause loves me. I ain't scared though. We all got drunk and everybody either rode home with their plates or stayed to be nosy. I had to run next door to the Mall the next morning. I'm walking into the Guess store and who do I see Low and some Bitch. Hell Girl came with me and even though my girl gets her scrap on I didn't want her in my business. "oooh Shine... look...ain't that ole boy from Chi Town." I was trying my best to act like I didn't see him. "Um huh... that's that nigga." I said it so loud he noticed my voice and turned around. "Look... his ass looking over here... say something Shine... say something." He was watching Moca's messy ass push on my arm. "What's up y'all." Oh shit I wasn't going to say shit even though I fuck with him. I wasn't being faithful so I didn't care about no bitch. "I'm chilling Low... looks like you doing the same." I seen the women turn around and look at us, roll her eyes and say something to Low. "I'm just out here doing a little shopping with a friend. "What... oh I'm your friend huh... and you living in my house and driving my car huh." Me and Moca started laughing. "ooooh Low don't let your Momma get you." Sh was really pissed off cause I called her a Momma. "Who you talking about little girl." She was trying to get to me and Moca was ready to whoop her ass. "Nah... Low don't grab her... if she hits my home girl I'm a beat her ass." I can fight my own battles but I was going to let Moca whoop that old bitch. "Shut up Hell Girl." Pie started pushing the women out the store because the lady at the counter called security. "You always start shit... Shine... call me girl." I rolled my eyes at his ass. "I ain't calling you." Moca was still hyped up and started following them out the door. "Fuck you Low... Shine don't want your ancient ass." Low kept walking with his middle finger up at Moca. "I'm leaving your ass at my house next time Moca." "Shut up shit... if I wasn't here that old bitch would a whooped your ass." I laughed at her cause she think she's so unstoppable. "No she wasn't... I can fight hoe... don't act like you don't know." "Whatever."

Chapter 26

"Hoes will be Hoes"

How this bitch knew where I lived I don't know. I could assume Moca cause she been over here in the last month and Spade helped me move in here so I figured they probably told her. "Bam "Wup ' "Wip" "Spish" I got up off the couch and jumped over zero as his snoring ass slept on the floor. When I made it to the window I seen Cat headed towards my building. "Oh.. .. shit ....Zero....boy get up ....Cat ......done busted out all your damn windows in your car." He rolled over and looked at me, by the time it registered in his head she was bangin on the door. "What....what you mean...." "Bang...Motherfucka....I knew you was fucking that young bitch." I was pissed and took the chain off the door. "NO ....don't open it....she might have a gun." "Mommy....Mommy is that Auntie Cat....let her in m-o-m-m-y." Now this shits all fucked up. This dumb bitch is trippin way out here in the fucking suburbs and my son is here. Shit where is Annie when I need her. "Baby....go back to your room ok.....that ain't your Auntie Cat ok." Thank god he was halfway sleep cause he did what I said and cried himself back to sleep. "You must be fucking ...her...I'm going to kill both y'all "Bang"..."Bang." She kicked my door as she ran back down the stairs and jumped in her car. We watched her leave the parking lot, "I got to go....she knows where all my money is...she's going to call the police on me." He started putting on his shoes and grabbed his coat. "Hold up....motherfucker.....you must of told that bitch you fucked me....huh." "No....I didn't she.....she just thinks that because I help you out." "Nah...nah nigga oh she don't just think that....who you been talking about me too." "I got to go Shine....don't worry about it ok.....I mean you came up and I ain't even hit it. Don't trip....I'm going to send my brother over and my homeboy to get that 10 g's from you aight." I pushed him as hard as I could, opened my door "Get your punk ass out my house....nigga you tryin to get me killed." He laughed as I tried to swing on him. "Quit trippin .....I'm sorry Victor had to see this....I'm going to fix it right now." He tried kissing me. "No...bitch." I tried so hard to shut him out of my life I got me and Victor dressed and went to visit Wonnie. I had to run the story down to somebody that would understand and that wouldn't judge me. I mean she fucks behind her cousins and her sister fucked behind her so I had to talk to somebody that understood. When pulled up to her house I seen that Lump was there so I thought she might not answer. "Hunk.....hunk." It was 10 o'clock Saturday morning so I know she should be fixing breakfast for her son. She waved her hand for me to come in. As I walked in her house I could feel my pager vibrating. "Mommy that little....thing keeps moving." He was scared of it when I put the pager on the table it looks like a snake to him. "Ha ....it's ok baby.....I told you somebody is trying to get in touch with Mommy that's all." "Hey Veronica...what you doing over here this early." I seen Lump walk his half sleep ass to the bathroom. Damn his body was built like a ball player. I turned my head so it wouldn't look obvious. "Big head Shine....what's up girl?" He saw me peep him and winked his eye. "What's up baller." I always called him that because he was a flashy person. "Girl....I want to go out but you always be with them nasty hoes." I knew she was jealous when I hung with other people. "Who ...Annie ain't nasty." "No.....girl you know I like Annie." I know ....but that be Annie fucking with them hoes....she be talking me into being friends with them." She turned her nose up. "You know better then that Veronica ....I mean you just fought Myrecal and Yoyo be hanging with Nella....that's stupid for you to let her in your house." "I don't care shit....you hang with your enemies ....and that hoe gave me info bout Low and Zero...shit I do what I got to do to get what I need." She knew I had a point. She thought I forgot about her being cool with China after they fucked each other and got into it. "Well.....whatever....you do. What you want....I mean I know you're my friend....I just hate to see you going through that and you don't have to." She seems so concerned but she can't be trusted neither. The only people I can trust is my cousin Queeny and my sister Fox. My pager kept going off. "Wonnie...Wonnie." I seen her go to the back and talk to Lump. "Huh." I'm bout to use the phone ok." I knew she didn't care but I had to ask because she knew it was about business. "Girl....quit playing...go head." "Where the kids at?" I was about to start yelling because it was Steen, my Mom, Cat and Zero paging me constantly. I went on the porch and shut the door. "They are in the room playing." I fanned my hang to let her know I heard her. "Somebody page Shine?" I knew it was Steen but I just wanted to piss her off. "What...you know damn well who called you girl." I just sat on the phone because I didn't want to disrespect her. "Hello" "yeah Steen....what you calling me about now." Everything that happens with her kids, she gets in the middle of it. "You know why I'm calling ....what are you doing sleeping with

Rockma and you know he goes with Cathy." See Cat done went over there lying. "I ain't sleeping with no damn Rockma." "Cat told me she caught you and Rockma in bed and my grandbaby opened the door." Now look at this shit. She lied on me that was cool but she put my damn baby in it. "First of all Steen….lets get something straight…..I'm a damn good mother, I take care of my child without y'all help….I would never sleep with no nigga with my son in the house." "So you telling me my daughter is lying." I started crying because I know if she told her Mom this lie, she told the world. "Fuck you, your daughter, your son and who the fuck ever believes that bullshit…tell that bitch Cat it's on when I see that stupid bitch and keep me and my fucking baby's name out her mouth…..click." I cried and Wonnie heard me going off. Instead of her seeing about me, she grabbed Victor and took him back to the room to play. She understood I needed privacy. I hate Lump had to hear my business because I knew somehow it would get back to Low. I hesitated to call my Mom I had to get it over. She was at work and the way she was blowing my pager up I could tell Steen or Cat called her. "Southwestern Bell….This is Ginger speaking." My feet dropped to the ground because I was embarrassed to explain this shit to my Mom. "Hi Mom …. You want to go to dinner after work." She cleared her throat and started whispering "Veronica ….Ronny"…….Uh…..oh I knew when she called me Ronny that she's disappointed in me…."huh Momma what's wrong." "Nothing baby….Steen's judgmental ass calling here to my job and said some hurtful things about you honey….are you sleeping with Cathy's boyfriend…..Ronny?" I could hear hurt in her voice. She didn't raise me with messed up morals and I knew better. I was so furious that I didn't fuck him but I was sure going to make it my business to now. "No Mom ….she never even came in the house…..nobody opened the door to talk to her…..she busted his windows out and left." "Slow down……you mean to tell me….." "No….No Mommy she never caught us in the bed and no…..Victor didn't open no door for her Mom." I was crying hysterically. I never noticed Lump leaving and Wonnie was looking at me concerned. "Ok…ok baby….calm down…..I knew those people were lying on you…..I knew I raised you better then that. You bring my grandbaby over when I get off work so we can talk." I still cried harder. "Stop crying you hear me…..stay your butt away from those people ….you hear me." "I….I have been Mom." "Ok….call me later so I'll know you're ok." "Bye Mom…love you." "I love you too Ronny….click." I didn't have to tell Wonnie the story cause as loud as I was the whole neighborhood heard. "Stop crying Veronica…..fuck them….I would take all his money now." "I know sniff….sniff…I might as well fuck him now." "Yep….you might as well." I had to get myself together before calling Cat or Zero. They were both calling me from Cat's house. "Yeah…..what's up Cat….you told my Mom that bullshit hoe." "So what…..you lied and said you wasn't fucking my man." I could hear Zero's punk ass in the background saying "I don't fuck with her…..I just be giving her work." "So y'all ain't fucked huh…what was he doing over your house so early in the morning then?." "I ain't about to go into that over the phone shit his dumb ass can tell you….all I know is you better quit lying on me and putting my son in this shit bitch….click." It made no sense for me to argue with her. I wasn't guilty of nothing. Her man wants my ass and is ready and willing to pay a grip (money) for it. My pager kept going off. She was putting 187 in my pager. Yeah she can play games if she wants to but I got a family too.

— One Month Later —

I'm tired of Zero coming to my house, da club and school looking for me. I haven't even started college yet and somebody told him that I registered for school. My mind was on Low and me making the transition to him having a key and clothes at my house. I finally let him slowly move in after he explained that the women me and Moca got into it with was a sugar Momma. Yeah she was tired of his ass and put him out her crib. He kind of stayed at his brother or sisters house but he said he didn't want to intrude. "Ring….ring Hello." "Shine w-h-y you ain't told me you got caught fucking Zero girl." Here Annie goes with her shit. "What Bitch…. I didn't get…" "Shut up girl….I was just playin damn." "How you know that shit even happen?." "Cause Zero been looking for your ass something tuff…he said he taken you to Cali whenever he fins you." Ain't that some shit. Now the nigga sweating me after playing all them damn games. "Cali huh….he must of told you what went down?." "Uh huh….he said give him a chance….he told me to go pick up your work from Big Boy." Just like I thought. Daddy knows how to get my attention. Right on time when I need some major money. "Um …how much…..he better come correct or I ain't fucking with him." Low came from out the room with a suitcase and bag in his hand. "Girl….I ain't going to be saying all that over the phone….a w-h-o-l-e gang of shit though." Who you talking to Veronica." I put my finger in the air to tell him to hold on. "Annie get some clothes together….I'll be over to get you in a minute." "click." I didn't give her a chance to answer." "Where are you going with all of that….Low." He looked me up and down. "We questioning each other now….cause if we are, that means you my girl right." I just asked nigga….you been staying over here fucking me and got a key to my crib." He stood in the doorway with a smirk. "You didn't answer me." He put the stuff down and got in my face. "Are you my girl or what?" I wasn't ready for this because it was happening too quick. "You been staying here haven't you?" "a…..if you mines then you can't be selling no dope for other niggas….I take care of mines." He was trippin. I'm independent to the heart. I take care of me and my baby alone. "Nah….baby….I got to hold my own paper." He got mad and pushed me down. "Fuck you then girl….I'm bout to go to the Chi and I don't know when I'm coming back." He tried to pick his keys up off the floor and I grabbed them and ran to the bathroom and locked the door. "Stop playing girl….give me my shit now." He was slow, I was taking my key ring off his ring. I threw it in the toilet before he tried kicking in the door. "Here…stupid." I gave him his keys to his car and pushed past him. He followed right behind me so I opened my door. "Bye….you can go now." He started picking up his stuff and left his suitcase there. "You ain't leaving me…..I'm keeping my shit here now." He walked out with his phone and a small bag. I slammed the door and yelled out the windows. "Don't come you're stupid ass back cause you ain't getting in." He got in his car and put his middle finger up as he drove away. I got my key out of the toilet and put his stuff in my closet. When I got to Annie's house she let me know that Wonnie told her that Low was going to Chicago for a week with Lump and some friends. Cool now if I want anybody in my house then I could have them. His funny acting ass wasn't breaking me off a couple hundred here and there anyways. "We got to meet Big Boy at the mall." "For what?" To get the half a key out the locker in the mall. "That shit was scary. Who am I going to give it to. Oh Gen and Slow said they could dump it for me and I'll break the rest of it down. "Ok….that's cool." We road over to the mall and did a little shopping to kill time. I sat down while Annie went into Lane Bryant to find her something to wear. Here comes Big Boy and Zero Rollin up on me. I rolled my eyes as he held his hand up to give me five. "Don't be like that girl you know you want my boy." Big boy pushed me….. "No….I don't …you mind your own business Big Boy." "E-x-c-u-s-e-s me…. Wild girl." He called me that cause I use to fight a lot in school. He walked off and left there to talk to me. I knew Annie was up to something. "How you doing….since you left me hangin." He sat down next to me. "I'm fine." "Oh so you wasn't never going to let me explain….you just going to play me like that male nigga you fuck with huh." He was really pushing it. Low don't have shit to do with this. "Why you haten….you fuck with Nella anyways and I ain't got time for your shit with Cat." He got mad and stood up and got right in my face as I sat on the bench. Low is fucking that stank hoe…I don't want that bitch….I told you that she be havin shit at her crib for me and T.T,M. Now if you wanna handle business like that then you can shit….a nigga wouldn't play you or Lil Victor like that." I see he has a little respect for me and my baby. "Nah nigga you know I wouldn't let you play me like that." "I wouldn't try…I'm feeling you but I ain't bout to keep begging your ass." He kissed me just like that. Before I knew it my panties was wet as hell, it felt so good. I had to stop him. "Quit …boy." I pushed him back. "I ain't forgot about Cat calling me….that was some bullshit nigga." He held my hands and sat on my lap. "Stop…stop beautiful….don't fight it." "I ain't….but I can't forget how you played me." He knows he got to do some real ass kissing." "I ain't playing you….I been done with Cat…..I just had to get my money from her….now I'm done…you don't have to worry about her." He started kissing me again. "Ok…ok Romeo and Juliet….we see y'all made up now let's go." He helped me up and put his arm around me. "Shut up Big Boy." Annie's sneaky ass was laughing. "You shut up… you set me up." "Nah…I didn't know he was coming….I got what we came for." I seen her slap hands with Big Boy. "Don't be mad at her baby....she knows I'm going to take care of you." We left the mall and put the work up in the stash spot. I called Gen and Slow to let them know I was happy to break them off with something. Thank god Low left town. Today because Zero was meeting me at my house to spend the night after I took care of my business. After making my rounds to Gen and Slow. I dropped Annie off to her new boyfriend's house. He was Tricky from grade school. We called him Tricky because he was always slapping people on the back of their necks or pulling girls pants down. As he got older, he was real skinny with a big nose so it was hard for him to get pussy. He didn't care, he would pay for a girl to get a black eye down below or to get sucked up it didn't matter to him. So now the name fits. I took a shower and put on some cute shorts that hugged my butt and a tight fitting tank top. Zero been breaking me off for months without getting any so I guess after him blessing me earlier with that whole half a brick. I could give him some. "Ring....Ring." I was running to the phone. "Hello." "I'm outside....open the door." I was nervous as hell. When I opened the door he kissed me and walked right on in. "You look good." He said after licking his lips. I shut the door behind him. It was late and there was no need in playing around I grabbed him by the hand and lead him to the back. My black and gold lacquer set was going to be messed up by moving. "Don't get yourself into nothing that you can't handle." He was talking directly to my giggling ass in his face. "Um...I won't......I just want to be comfortable when I talk that's all." I watched him pull off his shirt and slowly push his pants down to his boxers. His skin looked so smooth and silky like fresh melted dark chocolate. His pearly whites were nice and clean with the exception of the shining gold's that glowed at me. As he laid in the bed next to me I put my head on his soft chest. "So you going to tell me if you fucked B.B or not?....she said y'all never fucked." I had to start somewhere because I was nervous as hell. My home girl said she didn't fuck him. Now I don't know if she just said it because she was hangin with Cat and she knew that was snake shit or if she just didn't want the clique to know. I could feel him laughing inside. "Why you laughing....Zero?" "Cause....you funny as hell....is me fucking B.B going to stop you from fucking me now?" He had a major point. I was horny as hell. Shit I don't think the building burning down would stop my pussy from getting beat up right now. "Nah...it wouldn't but we could of never got this far....I don't fuck behind my friends." I could but honestly don't fuck behind my friends." I could honestly say that because everybody has fucked behind me so far. "ha....ol man ha." He was rolling hard as hell. "What's so funny Zero." "You ....I can't blame you for trying to have morals but....for real....everybody fucks behind everybody....what you don't do is....don't fuck your friend's husband....anytime you have to question if a nigga fucked your home girl....she ain't your friend cause if she was you would already know....now wouldn't you. He had a major point, when I shouldn't of asked him because I did think she was my friend. "You're right....I also heard you had a big ass dick." "Who told you that ha.... Ha .....you funny." He turned his body towards me and his dick rubbed up against my leg. "I don't know....ha....I just heard...so..." "You want to find out right now?" That's all that was said. He grabbed me and flipped me on top of him. I started kissing him slowly as I grinned on his dick. He flipped me back over and kissed me down to my hairline. "Yes...oh....Um huh...Zero....put it in." I felt and seen his rock hard dick. I was ready. I helped him take my bra and panties off. As he sat in between my legs ready to raise them up. "You ready to take all this?" He was smiling and unsure if I could handle it. "Can you handle all this manhood beautiful." I loved when he called me that. "Yeah....huh...ol shit put it in." I was getting sick of him teasing me. "Oh....o....o....my .....goodness.....yes baby." He stuck it in hard and deep. I wrapped my legs around his neck and slowly grinned my hips. "Yeah Um huh....you got s-o-m-e good....oooh....yeah....Shine....you so beautiful.....dis pussy good....Un huh....it's good girl." I flipped his ass over, tightened my walls on him, raised up to the top of his dick slowly grinding the tip, and then went down real fast. "Girl....oh....man....yes....why don't you be my girl....Veronica....girl....you got some.....OOOH....yes....dis pussy's good....g-I-r-l." I was riding him like a wild women. He didn't expect it. He picked me up and put me up against the wall, then to the floor. "Z-e-r-o...sis...please....o-o-u-c-h---slow down baby." He was killing me from the back. His big hands were locked to my hips. He was hitting it fast as hell. I started crawling to the kitchen and he was right behind me. "Um oh …um….where you going….huh…I….thought you could handle it Veronica." Sweat was pouring off of both of us. Sex was definitely in the air. This was some wild and funky fucking. "I can handle…..whatever you bring me….baby….give me the dick….d-e-e-p." With him still in me I stood half way up, he stood all the way up and hit it deep and boy was it deep. I felt the whole 11 inches and 3 in. width. "Oh….yes….girl….yeah….take that…..yeah….dis pussy is wet….yeah." I walked bent over and stood in the kitchen butt ass naked I pulled him out of me. "No…..sis…..sss…..no….you ……girl…..no….I didn't come yet." I put my finger over his lips, put my butt on top of the stove and put him in me. As he held my ass I put my hands on the stove and my feet on his shoulders. "Girl….were….did….y-o-u-…..Shine I….L-o-v-e……this…..girl…..your shit is…..bomb as hell." That was my goal. Nigga in love with the pussy on his first hit. We finished after another 30 minutes. We showered together and his ass was out snoring in five minutes. I was ready for another round and I couldn't get it so I called Wonnie and Annie to tell them the details. They were mad I woke them up but when I finished they were laughing their heads off. The next morning he let me know how good it felt being inside of me and gave me a g. I really felt like I sold pussy. "Why you give me this?....I already owe you 10 g's for the half a brick you gave us. He ignored me at first as he grabbed his things and headed for the door. "Take your time with the work….you got to build your clientele up ok…" He kissed me long and hard. The g is for you to buy all lingerie….that shit was good. He put his hand between my legs. "You can't ever get rid of me now….tell that nigga I ain't going to be sharing you too much longer." He kissed me again and left. I can't believe I just fucked Zero. The biggest dope nigga in the Sota. Damn and I put this pussy on his ass too. A g huh…..if I got that and all that and all that work out of his ass it got to get better.

Chapter 27
"Minneapolis/ St. Paul Airport"

"T.T.M....man I feel good." I can't get that shit out of my head. Good pussy but she ain't mine. "You feel good about what nigga....bout this paper we getting?" He don't even understand....she's beautiful.....I'll kill her if she ever leaves me. "Wake up...cuz ....damn what's up.....we bout to board the plane." I grabbed my sack of paper. I hope these motherfuckers don't ask to see in my shit. "Can I have your ticket sir?" "Yes mama....Thank you." That was close. We sat down and got comfortable for the long 4 hours to L.A. "Nigga.....what was you thinking about....you was slippin....you know you got too much money on you to be trippin." "I know cuz.....but that pussy was so good last night damn." "Nigga....that pussy almost got you caught up.....we don't need no feds on us....we getting too much doe." "I know dog...it just had me bad." "Whatever nigga....you act like you in love already." "I am nigga on the first hit too." "All shit ...you hit Shine's big head ass didn't you?"....you got to tell me cuz." "Nope....I'll never tell."

Chapter 28
"Balling out of Control"

Damn it's poppin out here and I'm running out of dope. The hooks (vice lords) got park and Franklin sold up. Dirty Red got heat for me in the bushes but I see him tryin to plot on me and Annie. "Shine.....you see them hooks over there....yeah cuz I'm telling you they tryin to set us up." "Fuck them.....I ain't going nowhere....I done made 1500 in about 10 minutes just off of these bolders 150 pieces)....you got to be nuts if you think I'm a let them punk me." Annie had a gang of blue on. The vice lords didn't like that. They are already mad because California niggas has taken the whole drug trade in Minnesota. "Nah....baby girl.....you see all money ain't good money.....they have out numbered us.....see homeboy right there..." Dirty Red was talking about a dude in a black and gold Iowa starter coat. "Yeah....I see him Dirty.....and what.....everybody that look suspect you going to leave this paper out here because of it?" Annie had the heater on her but she was acting nervous and pissing me off." Annie .....dog....you straight ....you look like you bout to piss on yourself." I said while turning to serve a pregnant girl that looks about 16. "Yo....you smoking .....dis shit girl?." "No.....I'm tryin to get my paper too.....just like you." Hold up, I never seen this before. How does she know me "A.....how you know my name....girl?" "Everybody knows you....if not from Bull.....the word around the hood is that you fucking that ball in nigga Rockma....and you know he got the best shit on the street." She knew a little too much about me for me not to know her. Dirty Red and Annie was right, I got to just work the pager. I've gotten too big to curb serve. "See...see what I mean baby girl....to much....too many people know you.....you too big for dis shit I told you." Dirty said while watching the whole park close in on us. I watched them as the girl walked away with her half ounce. "Um....ah I'll holler at you.....be careful with that baby in you." "Ok....Shine I'm a holler..." As soon as she was about to finish her sentence the hook with the coat on and some ugly bitch snatched the dope and the girls bra making her bra break and money went flying everywhere. "Oh.....oh God.....please don't hurt me. I'm 6 months pregnant." As the girl screamed and tried snatching her money back the dude pushed her I socked the girl. "Plow....bitch......you don't run shit.....plow...." Annie moved in and put the heater to his head." "Don't.....move nigga.....and you won't get hurt." I beat the shit out that weak ass bitch. "What...the fuck y'all tryin to pull huh." I kept slapping that hoe. "Y'all niggas.....back the fuck up....or somebody going to die." Dirty Red said with me, Annie and the pregnant girl walk towards the car backwards. "Dis .....VL's block....y'all know what's up....y'all better come deep ....or y'all going to die." One of the dudes put his thumb and index finger at me like a gun and pointed it at me. I laughed at his ass while Annie threw the crip sign up at them. That pissed them off. We knew they didn't have know guns on them because by now with all the people they had and the two guns we had want enough. As we got closer to the car the pregnant girl was crying so hard I gave her an ounce off gp(general purpose) because I understood she had things to take care of. "Baby girl ....chill form out here for a minute....ok." I gave her a hug I didn't even get her name. Dirty Red and Annie started busting the heater so they wouldn't follow us to the car. "What y'all doing?" I started running. "They don't need to know what kind of car were in." Dirty said while running backwards. "Yeah….they going to try and get us later."

Chapter 29

"White Castle On Lake Street"

"Wonnie…what you want?" I was ordering our food after a fun time at Gatsby. It was poppin. I had to shake Low because every since he got back from Chicago he's been sweating me about another house key. "Get whatever….me and Yoyo….got to pee." I laughed and ordered our food. As I sat down to start eating some ugly jay-z looking nigga came in the restaurant and started trippin. "Motor City…..D-Town in the motherfucking house." He was drunk and foaming at the mouth. I ignored him. "Girl….what's wrong with that nigga." Wonnie was all frowned up. "Yeah…..Veronica you know him or something." I shook my head no. "Oh….you hoe's going to act all boogie and shit…like you don't know this money making D-Town nigga. "He's ….kinda cute?" Yoyo is a stupid hoe. Naw he just called us out our name and she talking about this nigga is cute. "I know all y'all freaks…..and y'all know me. I tried to throw my pop at his ass. "Nigga ….you ain't going to keep disrespecting me." I got up in his face and pushed him. His boy jumped in between us. "Nah….y'all going to go to jail up in here." Wonnie and Yoyo looked scared behind me. "Bitch…I'm a kill you." He said as he fell right on his face. "Ha …look at his drunk ass….he couldn't fight if he wanted to." His boy was so embarrassed and tired to pick him up. "y'all….he's just drunk…..don't trip off my people….he really straight…..I'm telling you." Me and Wonnie grabbed our food and started walking towards the car. "Look Veronica….ha…..he spit all over himself girl." I looked down as I stepped over his legs. "Yuk….and Yoyo…you said his fake ass was cute." She helped his boy walk him yo the car as we waited we watched her get his number and run over to us. "Y'all…that's that….D-boys….y'all know them ones that got the Southside blown up……he got paper!." She was acting just like a chicken head. "You tweaking like that's the only nigga out here balling or something....shit that nigga just disrespected you.....girl." I was pissed off at Yoyo's broke ass. "Yeah...Yoyo....you act like he's really cute....you don't really know what he got." "I'm telling y'all.....I did a three some with his boys....when they paid me....I remember now....he gave me the money for them." Damn I knew it had something to do with fucking when it came to her. "Yoyo.....when you going to stop fucking for crumbs....that hood rat shit .....you're a petty fucking hoe." She put her head down as Wonnie laughed at me. "Call me what you want.....I'm going to get my fuck on cause I like it....Nah I love to .....and if I can get some money while I'm at it then cool....shit you fuck for paper shine....you fuck with Low and Zero." Oh she was feeling herself so I gots to put the check down. I stopped the car in front of Wonnie's house. "Yoyo....who you tryin to front on." I got up out my seat and put my hands in her face. "Quit....Veronica.....don't fight her." Wonnie said while grabbing me. "Nah.....I ain't going to hit her let me go." I moved Wonnie's hand. "First of all......No I ain't innocent one bit.....but bitch I get G's for my shit before I drop my draws you dig.....I'm a hoochie if anything that's what the fuck you call me......I'm real hood as if you don't know and I'm a chick with sassiness ok....I'm classy and don't you ever forget it." I pushed her head with my finger.....stop.....Veronica." She was about to cry.....I was just saying cause you always go off on me.....I wouldn't be no woman if I didn't take up for myself." Her point was made but she wasn't bout to be getting slick at the lips with me. "Call me tomorrow Veronica.....Yoyo.....you'll be aight."

Chapter 30

"California Love"

"Oh.....Veronica let Zero sit next to me on the plane." Wonnie got shit all fucked up, what does she mean let my dick sit next to her. "What girl." Zero thought the shit was funny. "Girl quit trippin.....me and Veronica will be right behind you ok." She was nervous because she never been on a plane before. "N-O-.....please I'm nervous." "How in the hell you going to be nervous.....Zero already paid for your ticket girl." T.T.M is going to pay him back." Zero turned around. "Nah….even if he don't…..I paid your way so you could kick it with beautiful. He knows that makes me feel real good when he calls me that. "So….that nigga better come up off of something when we get there and I ain't playing." She stormed off and gave the stewardess her ticket as we all boarded the plane. Wonnie had her lips poked out as she sat down next to a real skinny man with long hair. He looked like he was an actor or something. We took our seats and Zero laid his head on my lap. "When I get you out here…..we going to take this shit to another level." A whole lot of shit went through my mind. Does this mean he's going to try to marry me. Is he going to do something bad to me. I don't know! "What do you mean by that Rockma." He looked up at me. "I told you to call me Zero….don't fuck up and call me that out here around these niggas….you got that." Oh I pissed him off. He kept his head on my lap and turned the other way. I kissed him on his cheek. "I'm sorry…..I won't make that mistake again baby." He smiled "aight." I let my seat back and relaxed as I watched the movie "heat" play over the screen. "Wonnie….you ok." She was talking to the man like she knew him from school lunch or something. "I'm fine." "Yeah….she's ok….I'm taking her mind off the air right now." The man said as he and Wonnie smiled back at me. "Ok…..I'm bout to go to sleep." She was so into the man she just shook her head at me. That felt cool. God works things out for a reason. Even though T.T.M was sending for Wonnie. I'm glad I told Zero to pay for it. She was the best looking friend I had so when he said bring a banging friend that's older, I had to pick her. Plus she would have been pissed if I told Olivia to come. I wasn't going to be messy like that anyways. When I ran that by Zero he told me No. As we made it off the plane we walked through the airport like true glamour girls. Woo…..Veronica…..my first time on a plane and we in Cali. "Zero hugged me and gave me a kiss. "See your friend is happy now….she didn't want to come a hour ago. "I know look at you Wonnie….you happy you came huh." "Yes….I'm glad y'all invited me…..thank you….." She hugged me. "Thank you Zero." She skipped off to the cab stand. "Where y'all walking too?" Zero was walking towards the arrival service. It was an all gold Lamborghini parked up with all the limo's and luxury cars. "ooooh…….Veronica look." Me and Wonnie's eyes lit up. "Girl…..I know T.T.M ain't doing it like that." "Yes…he is…..look that's him walking towards us." Zero grabbed our bags as T.T.M grabbed Wonnie and kissed her. "Wonnie….girl you look good as hell in that guess suit….you handle your business with this dick and you can trade that shit in for Channel." Me and Zero was rolling as we got in the car. "Shut up Frank…..I'm still mad at you." "All girl…..dis dick will make you forget about that." Zero drove to the Beverly Hills Hotel. We all checked in our room. It seemed like a whole day before we seen Wonnie and T.T.M again. Me and Zero would have wild butt ass naked sex take a rest …. Go back and make love again. He wasn't eating pussy yet but he was close enough to it. "Who you talking to Zero?" I could tell he was talking to a girl because he was whispering. "Huh….nobody." He pushed the elevator and rapping 2 Pac. "I get around.." He thought it was funny and kept….Nah man ok cuz…..Um a call you back." That shit is game. You can't run no over lay for the underplay on me. Yeah I'm a cheater myself so I know how the fucking game goes. "Gimme that …..fucking phone." He held on tight to that motha-fucka like it was diamonds. "Stop….playin ….girl….you trippin shit." He held me in a bear hug and walked me off the elevator. "Stop…you must be talking to that bitch Nella or Cat." He was laughing as we walked into T.T.M and Wonnie. "What's wrong Big head girl." All these punk ass niggas keep calling me big head. They got me fucked up. I got a big ass if anything. "Shut…quit calling me that." I rolled my eyes and smacked my lips. "Dang what's wrong?" Her and T.T.M sang together. "Nothing." Zero came and sat down next to me while we waited for the car to come. "She'll be aight… I just gave her dis good dick for 24 hours shit… she shouldn't be trippin." He was tryin to send me off I'm not going there. I won't ruin this trip for Wonnie's sake. "Shut up…I just won't you to know…you can't out slick the slicker…know that nigga!" I grabbed Wonnie's arm and walked to the doorway entrance. I let her know why I was trippin. "Quit…Veronica…girl were going to kick it ok…he ain't your man remember… so don't trip." She was right the nigga was going to play games in front of his friends, so I'm a let him while we out here. "You right…he can't leave a bitch stranded out here and shit…ha." Right…Right." T.T.M waved to tell us to get into the all white drop top 5.0

Mustang with chrome D's and silver flakes. "come on girl...we aint got time for you to be playing." Zero was yellin over the music as we got in I asked "were we going?" I took that as to sit back and be quiet. We rode all over Cali, L.A. , Hollywood, Guadiana and San Bernardino. Over the last two days we went to the comedy store and almost got into a gang fight with some people from another crip gang. Shit I thought all crips were the same. I was nervous and Wonnie was so happy to be flossing in Cali like we were some movie stars. She never paid any attention to the Astros Van full of niggas with heat. Every time I asked Zero why they were going with us everywhere he would tell me not to worry about them. "their for your protection." We would get up in the morning, go shopping on Rodeo Drive and the Beverly Hills Shopping center. Wonnie was getting upset because T.T.M got some pussy he was being Cheap. He got her the Channel he promised her and that was it. "I'm ready to go home." I ignored her while I was looking at the designer glasses. "Zero...you like these. I held up the chore frames that were in my hand. 'Yeah ...get them baby." He walked off to use that damn phone again. He's been using that phone a lot but I know he was talking business with Chico. He peeled me off like 3 g's just to get the glasses so I brought Wonnie a pair. I wasn't ready to go home yet. "you straight now...you still ready to go?" I gave her five hundred dollars to the 200 hundred she had. 'Yeah...but I ain't gone keep fucking dis nigga... shit he ain't breaking me off shit." "What you expect...he sent for you...he's spending you home tomorrow, you ate you got a Chanel suit right out the boutique and you rolling with some ballers. We went to the gram slam out here and we kicked it with the stars...so what....I mean you ain't paid for shit." I had to le her know because I could see jealousy setting in. I mean with her own insecurities. You should never allow yourself to be jealous of or envious of the next person because you can't get what they got. "Yeah... but he just acting funny now...all talking to bitches on the phone and getting smart. "girl please... didn't you tell me not to trip... shit follow your own advice...you came with nothing and leaving with something... and he knows you fuck with Lump." You're ...right I guess." She sat quietly while we finished the day out. She asked Zero to get her own room but he talked her out of it. After he put a bug in

T.T.M's ear, she seemed to be cool on the elevator going to the room. "Y'all ready to leave tomorrow...Shine.' I didn't know what T.T.M was hinting at but it didn't sound right. "Yeah... but for real I like it out here... I could live here." Wonnie looked at me surprised. "you could...I don't know...I'm more laid back... it's a little fast for me." Zero grabbed me to go in the room. "Well we will see y'all tomorrow." He slammed the door pushed my bags out of my hands and laid me on the bed. He started ripping my clothes off and planting soft kisses down to my mid section. "I said the next level...so you know if I do...you do." I tried playing stupid like I wasn't in here earlier before we left." I could see it was money or dope because of the way he looked at me. "Worry about that...later.' He was up to something and I could feel it. "Now...I said the next level." He then took all my clothes off. Then he spread my legs and went to town. "Um huh you do it like that...Um huh... boy... yeah... yo head game is the bomb." All of a sudden he turned his whole body around and I had balls, dick and sweat in my face. I was forced to do it so I started rubbing his ass and licking his balls. He stopped eating me and lifted his body up. "Suck it... baby... suck it." I started sucking like he said and he continued to handle his bidness for real. After finishing the 69 we made love all over that Beverly Hill's suite. The next morning I thought me and Wonnie were leaving but plans had changed. "Put this on... I have to take you to the airport in 3 hours...so I got to prepare you." "prepare me ...why you handing me a driver's suit?... this is for people that work out and want to sweat or for scuba drivers." I was a little confused because he didn't want me calling over Wonnie and T.T.M'S room. Then Chico came to the door. As soon as he came in the room he headed for the suit case. "Go in the bathroom and put this suit on..." I looked at him crazy. "Go ahead...you getting paid." Chico said before Zero could speak. I grabbed the suit and went in the bathroom. I cried for a minute because this nigga didn't ask me to do no dirt for him before we left. I wiped my tears, looked in the mirror as I blew my nose and told myself "next level..bout to be paid up...get it together." I came out the bathroom and like I thought it was about 15 kilos all over the bed. I was amazed and they sat back and laughed at me. "Baby... come here let me put this on you." Zero loaded me up with bricks as Chico looked on to make sure it was correct. "But... what about Wonnie... she don't sell dope... she ain't built for dis." Chico didn't know what I was talking about so Zero told him. "She's talking about... the water that's in the room with T.T.M... she ain't acting right so she's going by herself tomorrow." My heart starting beating hard as hell. "Oh... a... um I got to do this by myself... shouldn't Wonnie be with me so It won't look suspicious?" Chico stood up to help Zero stuff the work to my body. "No... you are better alone...you'll be fine... just act normal." That wasn't no prep talk. "Baby... you bout to be able to buy you a house and a brand new car." That made my greedy ass calm down. After I put my long ass shorts , tank top and button down shirt on with glasses and sandals. I was ready to go. I looked just like a college student. "You ain't coming Chico?" I just knew he was going to take me with Zero. "Nah... I got to make sure you straight on the other end." "Yeah... he got to make sure that your flight is straight." We got into the car that looked like an old Delta. I could barely get out the car because I had two kilos in between my legs, two on my back one on each side and two in the front. Damn if I got caught I would go down forever. I promised myself if God let me make it home, I vowed to never do this shit again. "Smooch... Thank you Baby... I'll meet you at home tomorrow." I was pist off. I thought this nigga would at least be behind me a couple seats. "Ok... gimme some money... you know if I make it home... one of these is mines and I want 10 g's too ." He had a little smirk on his face but his ass couldn't do shit cause I was on my way to board the plane. "Aight... whatever you want baby.' I gave him a hug and kiss then gave the woman my ticket to board the Plane. "No... luggage today mama? Sweat started pouring down my face. Thank god its summer because I would of gave myself away. "No mama... just my purse." "ok... right down the walk way to crew." "Thank you." Zero sat and waved until we pulled off. Everybody on the plane was the police to me. Thank God I didn't have to use the bathroom and I wasn't going to drink nothing I fell off to sleep for the whole four hours. I woke up every time the plane shook. Once I seen that everything was ok I would drift back off. I finally made it off the plane. As I walked to the cab stand I seen the undercover dumping some girls luggage out on the ground. "Oh... My God." I said almost too loud cause one of the dic looked at me and quickly turned his head. I walked real fast and called everybody I could to come get me. No one I men no was available. "Fuck." People were looking at me as I walked around and cured for about 20 minutes. "mama...are you ok... are you lost?" The older man with a janitor's suit on "No... I just have to find a ride... shit."I was sweating even harder in this fucking scuba suit. I had bags in my eyes and all this fucking dope on me. "Ok....get on this cart and I'll take you to the car service....ok....don't cry!' We rode right past like 3 more people that were getting their luggage checked. "Could this go any faster ....please...I got to pick my son up." He stepped on his little petal a little faster. I have to be careful honey we don't want no accidents around here....then it would really take forever." I didn't day nothing cause this man just don't know he really saved me 25 years or whatever in prison. We made it to the car service and I was lucky. All cars were available and I hopped in the car with a young nerdy looking white boy. I gave the old man $50 because I only had hundreds left. "No....honey.....this is my job....ok." I ignored him and shut my door. "No...take your wife out to dinner." He kissed his two fingers and waved me off. I had him drop me off to the Marriott Hotel in downtown MPLS. It was 9 o'clock so it was kind of packed downtown. I had to walk around until Annie got a smoker to get me a room. I put the work up in the ceiling of the room and went to my house to take a shower and relax. Annie thought ahead and took the smoker's ID and kept her on a short leash until I got my shit the next day. "Ring...Ring." It was too damn early and it seems like I just went to sleep. "Ring...Ring...Hello." Veronica....how in the fuck you going to leave me in Cali...you are wrong....girl the motha fucking police...." "A...Chill....wit all that...were you at now." "My house...and click." I jumped up put my clothes on brushed my teeth and ran out the door. I knew Wonnie wasn't built for this that's why it's good she didn't know nothing at all. I had Annie to take a cab to the hotel to wait for me to come and take it to the safe house. Zero wasn't in town and Wonnie let me know that when her scary ass rode back by herself. "Now what happened...Wonnie?" She had her same clothes on from the last time I seen her. She let me know that the FBI asked her was she me. They dumped her shit on top of the cab and then let her go. Zero's shit wasn't tight because somebody knew too much. I got something for his ass running his fucking mouth. He probably was fronting when all them niggas was rolling around out there with us. "Here....just be glad you didn't have shit on you....don't mention this to n-o-b-o-d-y...or I'm cool on you." She was all quiet and smiles for now anyways as I handed her $1500. Hush money works all the time.

Chapter 31

"Responsibility Of A Woman"

Me and Ciara was in the house after a long night at the glam slam. Ciara woke me up talking to Bunny's staking breath ass about her boyfriend Grease. Damn that girl's breath smells like somebody shit in her mouth. I know she has to know her shit stinks. To make it so bad, niggas be getting at her. I'm going to tell her buck ass one day. She plays like she really likes me but I know she doesn't. Low told me to stay away from her. For some reason I feel he only said that shit because somebody is tryin to fuck. They want me out the way but if her game was as tight as mines she would of snatched the nigga from me. "Where is the damn boy at?....shit y'all talking too loud." They got a little quiet and kept looking out the window. I walked to the front of the apt as I brushed my teeth. "Get down....get down Shine...girl he got a red beam....he pointed it in the window." I fell to the floor, not having any idea of what the fuck was going on. I crawled back to the bathroom with slobbery tooth paste running down my mouth and hands. After I finished in the bathroom I could see Ciara and Bunny laughing while they still crawled on the floor. "Ciara...Bunny...oh hell naw....what the fuck is going on?" "Girl...get down...Grease is trippin ....he seen me last night...when I got into the truck with Grimmy Loc...he said he was going to kill me." They thought the shit was funny but I didn't. I was too deep in the game to be having heat at my crib like this. "Ciara...who in the fuck told this nigga where I live...I ain't with this shit...girl." I was pissed off because if Zero knew I had this shit going on I would get cut the fuck off. "No...please don't...don't open the door Shine....please he's going to beat my ass." I went straight to the window and bam the red beam was right on my chest. I could see his bitch ass trying to get in the building. Every button he pushed nobody answered but I could see them looking out their windows. "Yo....Grease....nigga you better get from in front of my building with that bullshit nigga." "You....you in the middle of this shit....I'm getting you too....nasty bitch." He pointed the gun up at me as he cursed at the door tryin to get in. "See...I told you Shine, I'm calling the police and telling them about him killing that man in the alley." I instantly snatched the phone from out of her hand. Bunny kept looking at Grease out the window. "Girl....you stupid motha-fucka....ain't no fucking pop o coming over my crib....see ...you foul as hell....you was fucking dis nigga now yo ass wanna call the police on his ass. Nah....bitch....my house ain't getting no hotter then it already is." I unplugged all my phones in my crib and took my cell phone out the door. "No....he is crazy....he going to kill you Shine." "Bunny....y'all hoes better find something to do because I'm bout to holla at this nigga." I put my 9 mille in my DKNY zip up and had my bitch beater in the other hand. He seen me coming and started backing up. "Nah....Shine...I'm a kill that bitch.... I seen her with the enemy." "Come on.....Grease....dog....you can't be doing this at my crib man....you know who I fuck with...man....and nigga you got the beam out here in white folks land....nigga I'm surprised the popo ain't came yet." I was making a lot of sense to the nigga. Bunny and Ciara were looking stupid in my window. "Oh....God...why she do this to me doe....I give her everything." I listen to him as he cried and kicked his car. He put his gun away. "You strapped huh..." He put his hand in my arm. "Nah...kick back...boy." I snatched away. "man....you gansta as hell....I been hearing how you got shit sold up out here." I didn't say shit I just smiled. "Um a send her out here aight....but you got to leave here with that bullshit." He was thinking about what I said. "Yo....take dis heater....so I won't do nothing stupid." "Aight...be cool Grease." I grabbed the heater and went back to my house. I told Ciara that she had to go. I gave Bunny the strap and told her to put it in her car. "I'm ...scared....Shine......he's going to beat my ass!" "I'm bout to shit, shower and bathe....by the time I'm out ....y'all better be gone...I can't have this hit at my crib." Bunny just laughed at me. "Damn Shine....you talking to us like we ain't cool or something." No this bitch ain't tryin to run game. I didn't grow up with this hoe. I met her at the Riverview on a humbug. I introduced her to everybody and now she think we family or something hell nah. "You know who I roll wit….I kick it with y'all on a humbug sometimes but that's it….I don't trust hoes like that ….for this reason right here." Ciara made her way down the steps because Grease kept honking the horn. After I got out the shower everybody was gone. Ciara left me a note "I'm sorry I brought drama to your house and I hope this don't end out friendship….sorry- Ciara." Then Bunny left a note on my door as I was leaving out to my car. "No…I ain't like everybody else to be in your ass because you got money….I won't disrespect your house cause I make money too…but anytime you want to take it to the street…holler at your girl….Bunny." I laughed at her stinking breath ass. She's just mad cause I gets my paper and niggas she throws pussy at wants to fuck me.

Chapter 32

"28th and Penn Ave"

I was rolling my bike with Victor on the back. It was a nice summer day and I had to make sure that I spent some Mommy time with him this week. I rode down Penn Ave and these Detroit niggas were yelling "hay…hay baby….I got 300 on it." Another dude was like "Yo…that's a Queen right there….that's Queen B….she be running shit." Now I had my son with me and I had to keep my mother image. No dope slanging, No rubbing or kissing, No sex with him around, No cursing, with this in mind I stopped my bike. "Mommy…who is that….Mommy….you know them." My baby was having fun in his little seat. "No…baby….Mommy don't know them….but it's ok." I had my bitch beater on me but no heater. I was a little nervous cause I got into it with that nigga Motor and pushed him down a while ago. "Yo….baby…you don't remember me…" It was Motor and two other D-boys with him. I grabbed my bat and they seen me. "No…I don't." I turned my bike wheel to pull off. "Nah….we ain't trippin like that baby….I just was drunk that night." Motor tried explaining as his boy gave Victor 10 dollars and played with him. "Mommy…look…I want some candy." Victor didn't understand what I understood. "Yo....get away from my son." I started pulling off and Motor jumped in front of me causing the bike to jerk and my son hit his head on my back. "See....motherfucker....you made my baby cry..." I swung on him and pushed his boy. "NO....Queen B....quit on that....we dry out here and niggas say to holler at you." They all backed off and the cool one grabbed my son to comfort him. "Why y'all surround me then." They started laughing. "Girl....you crazy just like they say ....Yoyo told us you got the hook up..." "Yeah she said your man Zero....be holing you down." Now I should whoop Yoyo's ass for telling my business. She never seen me do shit with Zero. She don't fucking know what I do. "Oh...yeah....hum...I see Yoyo's don't know what she'd talking about...." "Well she was on your tip .....she says you're balling out here...shit so do everybody else." Motor was really kissing ass. He needed a MN connect and that was cool but Yoyo would have to deal with this nigga and not me. "Mommy... I'm hungry." My baby was tired by this time. "Ok....were going home in a minute baby. They were real friendly to Victor. One of them went into the house to get him some chips. "Thank you Dog. ...you didn't have to do that." I gave him dap. "No problem Queen B....anything for you." Why in the fuck do they keep calling me Queen B. "Yo Motor ....I'm going to have Yoyo holler at you aight....!" "Why I'm mean I been fucking da bitch but I don't want her in my business." She's so stupid. She can't even get a nigga's heart before given up the draws. "Well....y'all had a lot to discuss with me not being invited to the conversation so....you going to have to deal with her....aight." He was a little mad but he'll get over it. "Hey...uh....let me give you my info." "Me too...Queen B." they gave me their #'s and I then found out homeboy's name was City. I gave them Annie's # and had to ask. "Yo....City....why you call me Queen B?" He was a cute chocolate nigga that was ready to pay for some ass but I have enough problems already. "Because... you got shit sold up....and you got heart like the real Queen B in Dolomites movies back in the day." I put my baby back in his seat and laughed. Now I'm about to run out of shit on a constant base I'm going to work Yoyo's ass for running her mouth.

Chapter 33

"On the Block"

"Veronica ….I want you to have my baby." I woke up to Zero whispering in my ear after two day length of love making. The feeling was getting deep but not that deep. I mean I got a baby bull and he has one Cat. Yuk that wouldn't be cool at all. Cat or Bull didn't know we really fuck around but neither one of us fucks with them I mean at least I know I don't. So there for we have no explanation. "We got time for that later…but what would your ….Mom say about that?" I'm sure his Mom thought I was some kind of hoe or something. I mean she knows I use to go with Bull. "What…my Mom don't say shit…she's the one that got me calling you beautiful because she never seen me doing that for no other girl." Oh he really got me gassed up now. His Mom approves but my heart is still with Low's no good ass. "I don't know Zero… I love Ms. Maybel …she's sweet to me but you know our kids are still young….that just don't look good. "What." He jumped and was pissed off. I been doing all this shit for you and you think I'm going to keep on letting you fuck me and that nigga….you got me fucked up." He was on one of his tantrums today. This means he wants to sneak off and be with Nella or one of his other hoes so he needs an excuse. "What ever nigga…you think I forgot about how you played in L.A… huh….fuck you." I jumped up and put my clothes on. I locked the bathroom door while he banged on it. "Open the door… Shine… beautiful…My Mom wants to holler at you. He's lying . His ass feels bad that fast about the shit he pulled. I guest me spending the last week with him he wasn't use to that. I finished in the bathroom after he kicked the door in damn near. "What…do you want…I'm done with y-o-u." I stormed out and ran up the stairs. It was a sunny day outside and you couldn't tell being in that basement. "Hello… beautiful… baby you never come and talk to me when you're over here." I was really trying to make my way out the door. "I'm sorry…how you doing?." I gave Ms.Dupri a hug as I tried walking out the door. "I'm fine…I would like to have a talk with you sometime." I knew this had to be about Zero wanting a baby. He wasn't ready for that and neither was I. Too much drama for nothing. Pussy whipped world make niggas think their in love but really their not. "Anytime…Ms.Dupri…and I appreciate your kindness when I'm over here." Zero thought the shit was real cute. He stood back and watched me and her but I had a trick for his ass. "That's no problem… beautiful… you're welcome anytime… even if you're not here to see Rockma…you can come see me." "Thank you… I sure will ." He frowned up off that last statement. His mother was real so what could you say. I made a run for it out the door and he was hot on my trail. "Come on… let me give you a ride at least…" "Nope… I'm cool on your ass." He was going to learn to stop playing games with me. "Cool on me… well fuck you then… I ain't bout to kiss your ass." I kept walking and he turned around and ran back to his Momma's crib. I understood he didn't want me walking because people would of seen me coming from that way. I made it a block away from a bust street so I could catch a cab. Here comes Zero and his crew. "Hey…. somebody said you need a ride in this neighborhood?" I ignored all of them and stuck my middle finger up. "Ha. ….ha… ooh… cuz she pissed off at you." "Yeah… she's doing the silent treatment ha… ha." T.T.M and Big Boy thought the shit was funny but I didn't. I seen a cab, flag it down and jumped in it. They rode all the way to my house and I never paid them any attention.

Chapter 34

"Valleyfair"

"Veronica… girl… come here… let's play dis over here." It was hot and I was very involved with Low. I knew it was an unhealthy relationship. He cheated and I cheated. It wasn't worth it but I guess love is blind. I have to make up lies about being with Annie. Then what about the days I have to fuck Zero and come home and fuck Low. This shit is beginning to be too much. I don't see how niggas can do it. Going with two people at the same time is nasty. "I want to get on the roller coaster… baby." After he tried getting me a stuffed animal we went to the roller coaster. Low started kissing all over me. "You're in a good mood… what brings dis all about?" He frowned up. "Now see…we can't have a good time without you starting an argument." "I'm not... I'm just saying... I ain't use to this from you." We started boarding the roller coaster. "Well get use to it....cause your ass is going to start being at home with me and Victor." Oh shit. He's been hearing about me being with Zero. Probably from that hoe Nella. "um huh...and what about you low....what you going to be doing?".....You going to be there with me?." "If I said you're going to be home wouldn't that mean you're going to be there with me...I don't just talk cause I got lips." I cracked up at his smart mouth ass. "dis ride bout to make me throw up." "Girl... don't do that shit on me." He leaned over away from me. "a u...a... u... .l...la ha... ha." "Quit playing...girl... I thought you really did it." "Gotcha... but... I do feel like that I have too." We made it off the ride and I went to the bathroom. I didn't have to so I checked myself in the mirror. My stomach was getting thick and so was my ass. I instantly got emotional. My cheeks were full and I knew from having Victor that I was pregnant. I whipped my tears away and knew if I was for sure, I wasn't keeping it. For the past month I been fucking Low and Zero in the same month. Oh hell no bitches won't get a chance to say no maybe babies came out of Veronica's pussy. They both would clown the fuck out of me anyways. No nobody would know about this at all. "Girl... what took you so long...I thought you was making the damn toilet or something." I was scared because Low watched my body more then Zero. He was around me more and he watched me. "Oh I was just having a girl's Moment." We walked hand and hand as we went to get something to eat. On our way out to the car he started again. "Baby ...I'm ready to get serious...when we made love the other night....it was real hot in there....that only happens when a girl is pregnant." I knew it! Damn this boy knows too much shit about a women. "Boy...you are trippin....I ain't pregnant...I had my period this month." I tried to play it off and skip to the car. He had this serious look on his face and he knew I was covering something up because I wouldn't look at him. "Veronica ....stop baby....you're pregnant and I know you are....were going to the doctor." No oh god please help me. I can't have this baby. "We can stop at the store on the way home and get a pregnancy test....you'll see....I'm not pregnant." He didn't say nothing and just shook his head. We made it by our house and he still wouldn't talk to me. He had the music blasting as I ran in the store. I bought two pregnancy tests. The first one I was going to wet with water. I be damn if I let his ass watch me pee on the stick. "I'm going in the bathroom with you." He said while we walked up the stairs to my apt. Nope he's not. "What...you don't trust me....that's nasty...I ain't pissing in front of you boy." I acted like I had a attitude....I knew that would work. "Ok...but baby...I just want to know....cause I know your body...look at you....you're getting thicker....a little on the chunky side." I sucked my teeth and rolled my eyes. "What the fuck you tryin to say....I'm fat or something." Tears began to wail up in my eyes. "See...now baby....I didn't call you fat....stop trippin." I went in the bathroom and slammed the door. As soon as I pissed on the damn test. It was positive. Tears just started running. "Hurry up...it don't take that long." I jumped and dropped the damn thing in the toilet causing it to say both. "Fuck...can't I flush the toilet and wash my hands." I quickly ran water over the other one and it said negative. "Here boy....I pushed the negative test out the door and shut it back. I could hear him outside the door cursing and mad because of it. I came out like I was a happy camper. "Plow...Bam....you think you're slick....bitch...I know your ass is pregnant." He slapped and kicked me so hard I flew into the tub. I was damn near knocked out. "What....is wrong with you." He grabbed his car keys off the and walked out. I got up out the tub with my head banging. When I made it to the window he was pulling off. How is it that I get these psycho niggas. I don't know.

Chapter 35

"Chicago and Lake Liquor Store"

"Cuz....ain't that them niggas from that Iowa Posse...bullshit." Damn that's them little niggas that was running their mouth about Pearl's murder." Yeah cuz....that's them hook ass niggas." I went in the liquor store to grab a couple of 40 ounces and some yak for me, Grimy Loc and Pop One. I checked my heat, got my brass knuckles check too. "What's up...Rockma....you don't fuck with the Iowa Posse no more huh." This nigga think he's funny. I'm bout to show his ass. I ignored him and paid for my shit. "Lil nigga….you need to stay in a boys place …you know dis is cuz…one tre duce… you know I ain't with that shit…hook ass niggas." I turned my back and put my set up. Oh…so they got back up huh. Two little niggas was banging with Grimmy and Pop One in the parking lot. "Zero…nigga you was down with I…I…Iowa Posse nigga…now you flipped to a crab…you too grimy. Y'all niggas is some bitches. "They laughed and thought that shit was funny." Before I set my lick down Pop One got to busting on them niggas. "Blow…blah…blah…dis rip or die niggas…one ….Tre…Duce….you hook ass niggas." Damn I knew fucking with these young ass niggas was going to get me twisted. "Come on…I hear da po po…" Pop One kept busting people in the store screamed while watching the whole thang." "nah…cuz I'm a make sure them niggas don't never front on me again….y'all hear me….Blah….Blah….dis Grimy Loc…cuz ….Blah…Blocko. Damn Grimmy let them niggas have it. They ran and scattered like roaches after he let that 9 Millie go. I pulled the car up and had to snatch both them niggas up. "Come….the fuck on…shit….the po po….is coming for us dog." We peeled off and seen some old bitch writing my license plate numbers down. "Bitch…Blah…Blah…ha…bet yo ass….won't have a hand to write shit else down." "Damn Grimmy you was gone peel that bitches wig back cuz." "I told you that's why da call me Grimmy dog." I dipped to the to the Mississippi River so we could dump the burners. I had to dump mines and I was pissed cause I just bought it. "You niggas is buying me a new heater." "Ah…Zero…big homey….you know we had to pop shit off…day was fronting on you!" Grimmy was really tryin to get them brownie points. He knows his ass is still under the scope from When I whupped his ass in front of Veronica for running off with my paper. "I can handle my own dog….y'all don't need to jump the gun for me…you know I puts in my own work." Yeah I had to tell him as I looked at the top of his eye, he still had that gash from my pistol. "Here big homey…you know I still owe you a favor dog…you know I had to pay you back." I knew I was showing off. Damn now I might go to jail for dis bullshit. "Nigga….Grimmy…$350… I ain't letting yo ass get shit for me….you might fuck around and kill me with my own shit." Pop One started laughing. "Nigga you know I got yo back…I'll never do …."

"Grimmy…nigga give me the loot." He passed me the doe with a smirk. "We even cuz." "Yeah…we are if I don't get caught on dis bullshit you just pulled."

Chapter 36
"Hit Park and Franklin"

Today was a good day to get some paper. It was the first of the month and the hooks weren't out yet. "Good…Annie…ain't nobody out here." "Woo…girl I know…Dirty been bringing new to me." I put my 100 and 50 pieces in a Doritos bag and went to sit on the bench, I seen this lady with a bankroll of money so I picked my shit up and ran over to her. "No…baby girl…let them get it….I think she's an undercover." I didn't listen to Dirty Red and I should of. "Yo…Yo….I got em….double ups boo…..come here….mines is bigger." All the niggas backed up ….. "All….Shine…..you making us loose bidness girl….yo ballin ass come out here with that big shit…" The women was so high she turned on their ass. "Yeah…I know how to treat them…ha ha…I got the fire." The women pulled her whole stack of hundreds out, got all the shit I had except an eight ball and walked away. "Yo…Shine…we got to go….look….the po po's is watching us." It was a cop car that just pulled on the park's grass. "I ain't going nowhere…I'm bout to stuff my shit." "I'm going to the car…Shine." Annie and Dirty Red jumped off the bench and went to the car. "I told you baby girl…all money ain't good money." Annie had all the money on her so I wasn't worried about it. I was sitting out their all by myself and the cop car wouldn't move. Everybody kept yelling…Shine….they watching you….so I got up and started walking. I couldn't walk to the car cause that would of made Annie hot. As soon as I made it to the stop light. Get down…get down on the ground ….with your hands up." Fuck they told my greedy ass. What the fuck. I make too much money selling weight and I'm out here curb serving. I got caught with the little 2.5 grams. Everybody in the holding cell told make to say I was smoking so I did. I had to call Ginger and that pissed her off. "Yes…Veronica….baby…I heard what happened." "Who told you Mom?" "Annie….and some boy named Low….your boyfriend." "Damn

Annie was on her JOB shit she works quick. "Mom….you going to pay my bond?" "Yes…that boy Low is going to bring the money now." Damn I haven't seen or talk to him in a week. "Ok…I'll see you when you get here." The detectives told me they watched me get something and give it to numerous people. Being as though I was on camera I couldn't fight it. Since I said I smoked, which was funny as hell. I had to go to treatment, 1 year probation and then it would be a misdemeanor. I spent the night in jail and YoYo and my Mom came to get me. I got off cool that time. This was definitely going to be my reason to not carry sit for Zero on that fucking plane or nothing else. I know his ass is going to be mad about me in the park but ole well. I need extra money for my abortion and the buster. Shit I had $30,000 stacked and waiting to buy a house at 20 years old. I wasn't going in it for nobody. "Baby….are you ok….you know you don't have to do drugs…I can get you some help." YoYo was winking her eye at me. That was the lie they told my mother so I had to stick to it. "Thank you Mom." I hugged and kissed her with that stankin ass jail scent on me. "I am going to get help and I start school next month too….ok. "Ok baby…..we will talk about it later." Damn that was easier then I thought. It's a damn shame you are grown and on your own but you still lie to your Momma about shit you shouldn't be doing.

Chapter 37
"On Top Of The World"

Waking up in the morning without knowing who you are is sad. The phone was ringing constantly and Low didn't budge and Annie had company. The lord knows I was glad for Annie, she was beginning to scare me. She stopped havin sex for about a year before she had met Tricky. He was an ok looking cat that was very skinny. He had a bald fade and two gold teeth in his mouth. Well all I could say was if she likes it I have to like it. "Shine….girl…get the phone." "Who is it." I was rolling over from under Low. Every since he bonded me out of jail, he won't leave my side. "Just get it." That meant don't ask no questions because it was trouble. I turned the fan up and left out the room so Low couldn't hear me. "Shine…why haven't I heard from you." My heart dropped to my feet. He never called my house, he always paged me or Annie. "Um...cause I said I was done fucking..." "Let me tell you something...you can't cut me off like that....do you realize...who the fuck I am." I was scared because he never talked to me like this ever. "Yeah...Zero .....I know who you are." "Well you better fucking act like it....meet me in two hours...I'm going to hit you back and let me know where....if you ain't there...I'm going to your punk ass nigga and tell him all your damn bidness"....click." Oh this nigga is tripping. He's bogus for even coming at me like this. He don't even understand what's been going on in my life. Does he think I'm trying to run off with his 50 g's for the 8 kilos he gave me or what. I put my clothes on and made Annie and Tricky get up with me. "Why you in such a hurry...Shine...you damn near dressed girl." "Cause....Zero called here trippin." "A....Shine you didn't hear about all the shit him, Pop One and Grimmy Loc got into." "No...what happened." Tricky gave me a briefing about them getting into it with the Iowa Posse at the liquor store. I seen it all over the news but they didn't have any suspects. Two people were shot up but they didn't really have any witnesses. "Damn is that why he's trippin." "Hell yeah girl.....cuz he probably needs your help...I know them niggas is on the run." I never responded to Tricky because I wasn't that cool with him. I know Zero wouldn't want me to be discussing anything with the help so I won't. I left a note for Low to let him know I had bidness to take care of. After we dropped Tricky off we met Zero at the Embassy Suites in St.Paul. I guess since the shit happened on the Southside of MPLS. They sure wouldn't be looking for him over her. "What took you so long girl?" He hugged and kissed me as soon as he seen me. "What y'all want me to do?" Annie didn't want to see us rubbing and kissing all on each other. "Yo....Annie since you down with the homies...I need you to take care of something for me." She nodded her head in agreement. She took his orders and left us in the hotel for two days. He paid for it up to a week but after two days we had to move in case the po po's came snooping. "Zero...baby...oh my god....wake up....y'all all over the news again." He rolled over real slow wiping the sleep from his eyes. My baby was so exhausted from putting it on him for two days. Now that he might be going to jail he had to get all the pussy he could. "I heard enough....turn that shit off." I did what he said and he grabbed me for another round. I wasn't really into sucking dick. That day it seemed like I sucked the skin off of it. When we finished he had a new attitude. "Baby...if I go lay down for a minute...can you take care of business for me." I was already in trouble and waiting for probation or treatment for my own case. "You know I'm already inn trouble baby...if I got caught with you now....I'll really be up shit creek." He sat quietly for a minute. I'm not going to go into what I told you about fucking with that curb shit....but you are getting major doe....you don't really have to worry about the police...you can pay some people to handle your business like you been doing." He had a point and if I'm going to handle his business then that would be cool I guess. "Yeah....I will but let me see what's going to happen to me just...ok." He grabbed me and kissed me softly." I told T.T.M.....you was a down ass female...I'm really digging you ....and it's so fucked up cause you won't leave that nigga alone." His pager was going off crazy....where is Pop One and Grimmy...who is that, that keeps on blowing your pager up." He ignored it for a while thinking that it was a girl. "Pop One ran to Miami until shit settled down.....Grimmy Loc is in the hood somewhere....you know his hard headed ass thinks if you hide out then you're guilty of something.....shit this shit is fucking with my money....I don't like dis bullshit." I felt sorry for him. He hadn't done anything but stay real to the streets. By him being the biggest nigga in Minneapolis getting paper since Pookey Duke then obstacles was going to come his way. Niggas put in work for him because he was being disrespected by the enemy. He was definitely in a fucked up situation. "You'll be ok baby...I got you." Smooch....that's all I need to hear from you." I seen him pick up his pager and frown. "What's wrong...zero." Everybody is paging me with 187 behind it...even my Mom Annie." My heart started pumping and so did his. "Ooh.....what do you think is wrong .....oh god....I hope nobody ain't dead baby." He shook his head. "That's the way the game goes....somebody will always plot to get you...you have to watch your enemies and friends...because they be the first ones to set you up." He wanted to call but he couldn't call from the room. "Baby....give me the pager...I'm going to walk two blocks down to that car and use the phone in there." He handed it to me without thinking. I had another motive to get my hands on that pager. I was calling every number back. The only people that called was all the homeboys to tell us about Grimmy Loc getting killed by Spade. Ms. Maybel wanted to see Zero because she was very worried about him. She understood the code so she sent her love after realizing he was with me. I told Annie she was to check all mirrors and suspect cars and to come get us in two hours. I took my time making it back to the room. As I looked up at the building I seen him waving to me, so I blew him a kiss. He was watching out that window with his paranoid ass. I had to laugh out loud at that one. Damn I had to tell him the bad news. Nobody likes finding out their friends got killed. I made it up to the room and by the look in my eyes he knew something was wrong. "Baby…what's up with my man." I was going to make him laugh by telling him I called every number back it wasn't his hoes because the damn hood called so much, that they bumped all other numbers out. "Your Mom is cool….but she needs to see you….she's worried." "She'll be alright…..I'll holler at her when shit blows over." "I told Annie to come get us in two hours…..she's bringing us some under clothes….I told her to stop at target and get some." I walked off and started running bath water. As we got in T decided to break it to him. "Baby….everybody said Grimmy Loc was in the car with Big Boy and Grease." He looked up at me with fear. "What….tell me…what's wrong?" I started washing his back. "They are all kicking it and pulled up to the weed house on Knox, Grimmy was driving, Big Boy on th passenger's side and Grease was in the back….Able started set tripping as Grimmy made it back to the car from getting his weed and from out of no where Spade just dumped on the car…he really let loose on Grimmy as he tried to pull off." He put his hands over his face. "Don't cry baby….you'll be ok." He moved his hands. "I'm not crying….I just hate when hard headed mother fuckas don't follow orders." He was pissed off. "Damn." He splashed the water real hard. "I can't even go to the fucking funeral." "Why not." "Girl…don't act stupid…you know the fucking feds will be all over the fucking place….there really going to be looking for me and Pop One now." I washed up and got out to give him his space. After Annie made it, I gave him his under clothes. "Are you ok baby." He looked so good standing there butt ass naked. "Yeah...I'm straight." I needed to drop Zero off so he could get himself together. We went and checked with T.T.M and Chico. Everybody was gearing up making preparations for the work that had to be put in. Retaliation was a must. They paralyzed Big O, aired out Lano, now they done aired out Grimmy Loc. Niggas mad because the only ones there aired out was Pear. They been getting shot up but only one of them has died. Me and Annie left him with his boys. I had to get away from all that shit. Annie was down for that bangin shit. I was past that bullshit.

Chapter 38
"MPLS Court House"

"Please state your name as you raise your right hand." Me and my Mom and lawyer were at court so I could plead guilty for probation. I had registered for school resources until this happened so now I must change my major to business management. I have to run shit. I can't or won't let no bitch be my fucking boss. I gave my name as she read the charges to me. "Do you understand that if you stay in school and out of trouble for a year...you will not have a felony on your record." "Yes...your honor I do." My Mom was very pleased. I had to check in with the P.O's office. She was a young women that seemed to be pretty cool. She told me after I finished out patient treatment that she wouldn't bother me unless I get into any trouble but that she will be making sure that I'm in school. "See baby it worked out fine." "I know Mom...I can't wait to start college." We went and ate lunch and I gave my Mom a kiss and left. All I thought about was my life. When I went to the abortion clinic the other day I seen Mya. She claimed she wouldn't tell nobody so I decided to treat her to the mall Friday if she goes with me to get my abortion tomorrow.

Chapter 39

"The Next Day"

I woke up feeling nervous. I hadn't heard from Zero in two days. Low was trippin with me again. "I'm just saying...you been.....saying you going to the block to beat your feet....but when I ride around out there people say they ain't seen you." He was tripping this morning about some bullshit. I was tryin to make it to my doctor's appointment. "Whatever...I was out there I told you...why you got to be looking for me anyways...I don't go looking for you ....when you disappear and shit." I rushed to put my clothes on cause I seen Mya and Zero paging me so I picked up the phone to call Mya. "You ready." "Yeah....but my nosey ass sister keeps asking where I'm going." "Don't tell that hoe shit....start walking down your block till you see me." "Ok." "I'm on the way ....click." Low watched me comb my hair in the mirror. "Nah....where your slick ass going this early." "I got to go up to the college...and I got to go pay the day care where Victor goes to." He knew I was lying but couldn't argue because I had a good lie going. "Baby....I paid for you to get out of jail....and you still haven't spent no time with me." I put my shorts on." "I will I just got to take care of shit so dis P.O. won't be back ....and don't be having no work up in my house neither." I grabbed my purse as he looked at me with a screw face. "A....I pay bills in this bitch...you don't tell me what the fuck to do." He started down the stairs and to the car with me. I jumped in and started the car up. "I got to go Low....I'm on paper now....I can't jeopardize that." I backed up and pulled off. I knew damn well I still had a hundred g's and 3 kilo's at the stash house. Low had no idea of how much money I was making. I could of supplied him but he was a very jealous hearted person and I know it especially when I dressed up to go out and I wasn't with him. I know he heard about Zero but he couldn't question me. Nobody didn't see us together much because we were together in the crib or hotel. When we went out of town that's when e enjoyed each other the most.

Chapter 40

"The Funeral"

Me, Annie and Ciara rolled up in the funeral to pay our respect. Grimmy's Mom was upset because of all the gangbangers. She checked everybody at the door to make sure her family was safe. "Shine…girl I ain't feeling this… look at all this fake hoes falling out and shit." We went to sit down by the family. "Look at that hoe Myrecal… he just split on that hoe last week now she acting like he really cared about that bitch. I should a whupped her ass when he told me too." Ciara was mad because when she was with Grimmy two days ago, he pulled up to Myrecal's house to let her know he fucks with Ciara. She was getting on my nerves because she knew all along that he went with Monique. "Chill Ciara… I already had to stop you from whupping Ty's ass…" "Yeah… and you lucky I wasn't there cuz… I would had to… Slap… your ass up side your head." Annie gave her grim look as she demonstrated. "Chill… girl we at the homeboy's funeral…" "ha ha… oh… you right cuz." Ciara didn't say nothing cause she knows Annie would beat that ass. I just had an abortion two days ago. My damn feet is hurting in these Sergio Valentines, shit this Escada Rain dress is itchin me like a mug. My French twist bun is about to come down too if they don't hurry up. After all of the homeboys stood up to speak their piece we rolled out. I felt so sorry for Big Boy?" "yeah some girl… I'll be cool… a you talk to Zero?" " Nah… not in a couple of days… he's layin low you know ." he wiped the tears from his eyes. "I think you need to holler at him… tell em… niggas tried to take my life cuz… I ain't letting this shit go easy… that nigga Spade got to die… woo… you just don't know that nigga dumped on us hard." He kind of had a smirk on his face as he remembered the event that almost took his life. " You know he ain't letting that shit ride… y'all niggas is going to do a sneak attack on them and you know it." He nodded his head and agreed. "Hey… Big Boy… I heard what happen." Ciara and Annie gave him their love. "Well I'm bout to see if I could spot some undercovers for Zero… so he can stay low key right." "Yeah baby girl… y'all stay out the line of fire… y'all know niggas be plotting on y'all cause you fuck with us." "Oh … Annie is always strapped cuz- you know me." Annie started doing her little crip signs with him. That cheered him up cause he was laughing. "Ya'll funny as hell … be careful." "Ok Big Boy… Be easy baby." I said while giving him a hug. We made it outside and I could see detective on each corner. "Damn Shine… their looking for somebody cause they ain't even in no undercover cars." "I know Ciara… stop looking at them so they don't follow my truck shit." I just bought a dark green Yukon and didn't want nobody to see me rolling I kept my little Fiesta so I could move my weight out of it." Yeah… stop looking spooked Ciara… Grease ain't going to get you… when Grimmy got killed you know they was together because they was plotting on your ass." "All… Annie stop playing… that ain't funny girl… you be trippin." "ha… ha… shut up and roll the blunt… with your scary ass." Ciara was so jumpy. She knew Grease had something to say to her about that murder shit she was saying over the phone and about her fucking his homeboy Grimmy Loc.

Chapter 41

"Edina Apt."

It was pouring down rain outside. I looked out the window and drank my tea as I thought about Zero. He had been in jail for a month now and was facing attempted murder charges. He stood strong like a real solider should and told the prosecutor to fuck himself. They wanted him and his crew really bad. They couldn't get him or T.T.M on their operation so this was their perfect chance to send Zero away for 20 yrs. " Annie… what is that paper under the door?" I assumed it was something about my school or treatment. Huh… " I don't know." She half ass answered me as she played a game with Victor on the floor. I picked it up from the door and opened it. "Attention Ms. Gitten's on behalf of the tenants and the management office. We are to inform you that your lease is up in 30 days and at this time we have no desire to renew your stay here. "Thank you." Oh my God. I hope like hell they haven't been investigating me. "Annie … girl look." I shoved the paper in her face and she read it. " Girl… don't even trip… I seen a lot of side by side bungalow over South …we can move over there." "Where at… not in the hood I know… I can't do that… it would be too close to the stash house." I could hear Low in my closet rummaging around. "Nope ... its over by Calhoun Lake going towards St. Louis Park," "ooh bitch ... you be on shit don't you... I'm going to get us a paper today so we can find something until my house is built." "Damn you getting a house built at 20 years old... you go girl... you know your ass be way ahead of yourself... that's why niggas and bitches be hatin." "I know... and they need to congratulate and get like me instead of player hatin." "Right Right." I kissed Victor and went in my room to see what Low was doing in my closet. I tried opening the door and he wouldn't let me in. "Hold up... girl." I pushed because I could tell he was doing something sneaky." Let ... Boy let me in my ... fucking r-o-o-m." I shouted to the top of my lings. Annie and Victor peaked around the corner. "Mommy... what's wrong." "I'm cool baby... keep playing the game with Auntie Annie ok" I gave Annie the wink and she pulled Victor back. I stood back and kicked the door open. " Boom ..." Right before my eyes this motherfucker had a big ass triple beam scale, crack all over the bed, plastic bags all over the floor. "Nigga... you got me fucked up ..." I screamed out. "Chill... baby... I... I... I'm bout to get it out now." "You been having this here with me and my baby here... you bitch ass nigga." I clocked him right in the eye and was swinging out of control. "No ... baby... I'm sorry quit... the neighbors are already watching us." I was going crazy like a mad woman. " You pussy... you put me and my baby in the line of fire... nigga I don't even have dope in my own house ..." I slapped the piss out his ass cause he grabbed me with all of his force and pent me down. Annie came to the door and seen dope and paraphernalia all over the room. "A... Shine you need to... "She looked down and seen shit all over. " Yeah Low ... nigga... oooh... you dirty." " Shut the fuck up and get out my house bitch." He kicked the door shut. "You don't tell my friend to get out bitch ...fuck you." I started scratching his pretty boy ass up. "Bitch... I'm going to kill you." He looked at the long scar down his cheek and started choking me. I was gasping for air until Annie knocked on the door and said. "Yo... be quiet for real ...the police are in the building." We both jumped like clock work and started cleaning that shit up. "Low... oh my God... how much dope is this." I started crying. "Quit... crying... I won't let you go to jail for me... fix your hair and go see what's going on." I put my hair in a ponytail and washed my face. " they been knocking on the door... so I made Victor go in his room and be quiet ." I got my lie together and stepped outside of the door ... "Hello." It was two younger cops patrolling the buildings. "Hi mam ...we got a call that there was some bumping and yelling going on is everything ok?" The white cop said as he focused on my neck. I'm red as hell and had marks all over it. "No sir ... nothing wrong ... I was playing a game with my son and watching the rain that's all." "Are you sure..." He tried looking behind me so I shut the door so he couldn't see in. "No... I'm fine really." "You sure are beautiful... you wouldn't be letting anybody beat you on that pretty face would you." I gave him a sexy look and stuck DD's all in his face. "No sir ... . I'm to smart of a girl for that." They both smiled and focused on my titties. "Well if you ever need us ... give us a call." They both handed me their card. "Thank you... have nice day boys. I winked my eye and shut the door. I watched them run back to their car and leave. Annie busted out laughing. "Good one... now tell that nigga don't call me another bitch." "I'm on it... right now sis." I looked in the room to check on Victor he was knocked out. When I went in the room it was spotless. "Low... don't disrespect Annie no more... she's like my sister and she didn't do nothing to you." He rolled his eyes and grabbed his bag. "Aight... I'm bout to take this." He shoved me a duffle bag with money, the scale and the plastic baggies. "I'll be back to get the work." I stared at him like he was crazy. "Man quit trippin ... I can't take all that shit at once." He had a point and I didn't want him to get caught up. " It's raining... so the best time to move it is now... before the night is over... I want this shit out my house nigga. " Aight." He pushed past and left out the house. " Annie watch and see if that nigga pulls off." I went back in the room and pulled all the work out and put it on the bed. " He pulled off... Shine." " Watch that window... as soon as you see him pull up ... anybody else... let me know please." "Aight... I got you." I gotta trick for this nigga. He going to leave dope in my house without my permission, I'll teach his ass. I took each ounce out one by one and put it on the scale. I took 5 grams off of 100 ounces. That meant I had a whole half a bird. Yeah that was a quick 12 g's I was going to make for free. He wasn't going to miss it shit, somebody put him on and he didn't want me to know about it. "Come on Annie... we got to go to the stash house." I put my clothes on and headed for the door. "Victor is in the room sleep... what you in such a hurry for now." A girl got to do what a girl got to do and lots of times it's nobody bidness. Not even your best friend. "Oh... shit girl... ha ha I forgot his ass was so quiet." I had the work on my body so Annie had no idea what I was doing. "Um I got to go check on something stay here with Victor and when Low gets back, make sure his ass leaves with that brown duffle bag." "Aight ... be careful." I made it to the safe house without any problems. I called up YoYo, Gen, Slow and even Danger. They were to meet me tomorrow to get these packages. I took a look at my hundred g's and smiled. Zero was in jail and he still helped me a whole lot. I got emotional thinking about him. "My father please give Zero a favor in trial. He knows not what he does lord. Upon his release lord make him changed man. Lord also forgive me for the wrong things that I have done in my life and help my Guardian Angels guarded around me, my Mom, Victor and family. Thank you for the Angel that kept me out of jail today and yesterday. In Jesus name I pray, Amen. Just like a hood bitch. Pray when your ass just peeled off your own nigga's dope. Can't knock the hustle, got to get it anyway you know best without getting caught.

Chapter 42

"Old Money"

I felt like a new woman. Money was flowing like running water. Zero had been in jail for almost two months. Me and Annie been making a lot of paper by working our pagers. It felt really good not to be out there on that block. I mean the way I as working nigga's . I didn't have to be anyways . I found me a little bungalow row house on the Southside of MPLS. Today was moving day and Low didn't know shit about it. I mean if a nigga don't care about me and my son's safety then what the fuck am I with him for. "Shine... I finished packing your bathroom stuff up... you want me to help you in Victors room?" " Nah... Wonnie... it's good... help Annie in the kitchen." " oh." I was finishing everything in Victors room. The more I packed up, the less I had to pay the movers. " Hay yall wanna cook tonight?" Annie and Wonnie was finishing in the kitchen and the movers were ready to take everything out." Girl... you know I can burn..." " Who is that coming up the stairs... running and shit." I haven't heard from Low in two weeks and now his ass shows up." I don't know shit... oh ." he kicked the door all the way open. The movers had it cracked as they took everything out. "Oh... um huh. You didn't think the devil would appear while you was being slick... now did you" He was frowned up and punched his fist to his hand. " What's up Veronica... looks like you're moving somewhere huh ..." I finished pushing the boxes to the front door. "Yeah... Lucky I'm moving into a nice place." I made sure I stressed that cause Low wasn't going nowhere with my ass. Lucky started talking to Wonnie because they always had some sneaky shit going on. " Come here... let me talk to you baby" Low said while grabbing my arm. I followed him into the empty room. I could tell by the look on his face he was pissed. I was smiling inside. Yeah all them late nights coming in when he wants and leaving town without calling me and letting me know um huh... gotcha." " So... its really over huh...and you was just going to dip and not tell me ?" I stood up against the wall because I knew this was going to end in some swinging. " Yeah... I was going to tell you..." "When...when you was fucking gone" he said thru clinched teeth. I got worried and tried to open the door so one of the movers would hear. If they couldn't help they could at least call the police. I heard the phone ringing crazy but nobody would answer it. "I was going to tell you Low....but I think its best we..." "Hold up....you ain't breaking up with me like dis." He started putting his hands in my face like he was going to choke me. "I pushed him back and stuck my head out the door. "Annie...Wonnie....are they done yet ...why ain't nobody getting the phone?." Low was getting impatient because he knew my nonchalant attitude. "Yo...Shine stop ignoring me." Wonnie walked to the door and handed me the phone. "Here...they say it's important,....you have to come on cause we're almost done out here and the people got to follow us to the house." "Oh here I come." Low sucked his teeth. I mean he was stuck. I had all his shit packed up at the door and it was perfect that he had his brother to help him move. "Damn...that...you ain't leaving me." "Yes the fuck I am." I said while pushing him back and not realizing somebody was on the phone. "Girl......I....I'll kill yo ass." He pushed me into the wall. Wait...quit ....Low....HELLO....HELLO." I never realized that somebody was still on the phone. "Yeah Veronica...I thought you told me that nigga was going to be out your life." My fucking heart almost fell out my chest. I had Low in my face and Zero on the phone from jail. "I am." I wasn't about to play him while he was awaiting trial. Shit this was my bread and water, and to top it off, he got good head and dicks a bitch down. "I am what...you fucking with that broke ass mother fucka....I told you how shit was going to go when you started fucking with me." "Who in the fuck are you talkin to." Low tackled me and tried to get the phone. I had it so glued to my ear he couldn't pry it off. "Quit stupid...fuck it's my dad." He backed off. I'm so glad that worked. He walked out the room and gave me my privacy for a minute anyways. "Hello..." "Yeah. I've been gone two months damn near and you still got games. I put food in you, your family and even friends mouths!"...."But baby..." "Nooooo......here me the fuck out." "Ok?" I was sweating of the thought of Zero cutting me off. I had to let him know that I was down for him. I was confused. I loved two nigga's at once. The enjoyment of us creeping made it even more exciting. He was falling for me but I kept my guard up knowing it wasn't right. "Veronica....I'm facing 20 years girl.... These Tom ass moth-fucka's playing with me....if you ain't no good for me while I'm going through trial then....what are you good for?" I swallowed real hard and was nervous as hell. "I'm good for you...and I know you don't think so right now but I got your back." Low entered back in the room, "A....I'm bout to go...I call you later." I fanned him off and he slammed the door. I'm so glad there was only one phone in the house because of the moving or else he would of picked the phone up. "Baby....I'm going to take that to heart right now....if you are a women of your word...you'll be here to see me Wednesday....click." Damn I got the dial tone right in my ear. He was pissed and I and I knew it. Well I at least got 3 days to make it sound good. When I left out the room. I could see Low and his brother taking his shit to their car. I helped the movers get the last of the stuff out the house. Annie and Wonnie was in my truck waiting for me to come. I gave the movers all the info and the address that I was going to. I let them know that my Ex was stalking me and I needed a little more of their time to stall them. They agreed to leave ahead of me after I gave them an extra 300 hundred dollars and offered to cook them a meal. As they pulled off, Low, Lucky and their brother 20 pulled up along side of me. When Low got out I thought it was going to be another episode. "Let me talk to you Veronica…please." He grabbed the door and opened it for me. I got out and walked over a little so nobody could hear us. I didn't want him clowning in front of his family. "What's up?" "Um…did you take any of my work last week when we got into it?" "Oooooh I had to keep my face straight cause he will kill my ass. He's not like Zero. He's the fucking help. "What…you mean take your work?" I frowned up and put my hands on my hips, "Well….I'm just saying….Um…when I came back to get my duffle bag that night….I could tell some of my packages been messed with." "So what you saying….I took your shit or tampered with something?" I had his ass good. Here goes the over lat for da under play. "No…baby…when I took the shit to the spot and weighed the work over again…they all was five grams less on everyone." "Hold up…when you was weighing them was the work still wet from being cooked?" I knew this would get his ass. "Yeah…baby but….it shouldn't shrink 5 grams dough." "I don't know why your shit was short nigga but you know I holds my own down….I don't have to steal shit from yo yes man ass." I had to keep up my attitude. "all….baby why I got to be a yes man…I help my big brother out that's all…you ain't tryin to help me." "Nigga I helped your ass enough….shit your ass jeopardized me getting locked away out here…" "But I gave yo Mom's 5 g's to get you out …I didn't trip and that was my last….I had to do what I had to do to get back on my feet." "Yeah…and I had to do what I had to do and move around on your ass." I stormed off and put some pep in my step to my truck. I was pulling off and he kept yelling something. I heard Lucky tell him "fuck her dog…you got more hoes." I don't care as long as I came up on his ass. I got all his bond money back when I went to court. So I just gave it to my Moms. I mean she did deserve it. Shit Victor might as well be her son as much as he's over there. Plus she is the one who told me to move from way out there. I guess that's a mothers institute so I had to take heed to that. I had to listen to Wonnie and Annie try and sing Erika Badu's. "Get Out The Game." They had my shit blasting. I didn't realize how loud factory speakers could be. We made it to the house and helped the movers un-pack. My little sister Fox was there with Victor. After putting everything in each room I was suppose to go, I had to make a run. I was so relieved that Low didn't follow us to my house. He probably had something up his sleeve because he was fatal attraction like that. I had Wonnie to ride with me. She wasn't cut out for dope slangin but she was game to ride just to pick up money. "Where we going Veronica?" She was the only one of my friends from a snot nose who wouldn't call me Shine. I guess she was to much like family for that. "You know I'm not about to take your money your scary ass on no dope run girl....anyways have you talked to T.T.M since all this shit went down." "Nah....girl she creepin with Phat boy lately...I mean I'm so glad Lump ain't catch us." "Girl catch you what....I'm late." She always had drama In her life with somebody. "Oh.....I must have been telling Olivia." "Yeah cause I ain't heard shit." "Well I was getting ready to go out with China and Phat boy was over my crib with Mistro and they was getting drunk. Girl the next thang I know the nigga kept saying...I bet you can't fuck, I bet I can turn that shit out better then Lump." "Oooh...what you say ...girl don't tell me you let that nigga mack on yo ass like that." "Yeah...girl...I was ridding that nigga o top of my table." "Oooh...where was Mistro?" "Oh...he had some hoe in my son's room so he wasn't coming out, shit dude was in there fucking so hard, pictures was falling off the wall and shit." "Yall nasty oooh and what else happen." "Well he started fucking me from da back and Lump was unlocking my front door." "What!...what did yall do?" "Shit that nigga knew he wasn't fucking up my money....shit we stopped and he ran to the bathroom and out his clothes on." "Now I know that nigga knew something was up....shit all that hard fucking I know it smelled like dick and pussy in the air." We both busted out laughing." "Nah girl....my shit don't stink." "Ha...ha...you know damn well if it's fucking going on it just smell like that in the air." "Yeah well...if it did he didn't say shit." "Ooh girl you nasty." We laughed our asses off. I'm no nastier than you girl." "I know that's right." We laughed and talked until I met my workers. I had been paging YoYo but I wasn't getting no answer. I swung by her crib and she wasn't there neither. Crazy shit was running through my mind. I hope this hoe didn't get with these Detroit nigga's and think that she was going to run off. I could just be trippin cause I ain't heard from her or Motor. I left a message with her sister to let them know I wasn't happy about not getting in touch with them. Her sister didn't like me so I knew she was going to repeat that message real quick. When Wonnie seen her she turned her nose up. She was always game to whoop her fat ass but I was too busy getting paper so it didn't matter if them hoes hated or not. Her or no other bitch was going to stop me from getting it. I was out to use who ever the enemy was. When we made it back to the house, Annie let me know the movers were gone and that she gave them an extra hundred to get them something to eat. Annie had caught a cab to the grocery store while Fox decorated the house. My little sister was only 15 but she has a gift for design. I let the chicken breast marinate in the sink while I prepared the jiffy mix. We didn't have time to make no real hot water corn bread like we wanted so we went the quick route. Annie had the greens and yams already going when we walked in the door. That's just like a friend. They know how to get shit done sometimes before you think of it. "Damn this house is the shit Veronica...and Annie ass got it smelling good!." "I know....Fox....I like how you got the pictures up and how you put my plants around." "Thank you...now give me some money" "Look at you....that's all you know." I wrestled her to the ground. "I want to go shopping with Victor tomorrow." "Ok...I got yall....you know that." I showed Wonnie the whole house with 3 bedrooms, a basement and a small outside sauna. "Girl...your room got a mirror over you're bad on the closet doors, oooh....look at those long picture windows." Wonnie was in amazement about this place. "Come look in my bathroom girl" she loved it. "Girl no you don't have a gold and cream marble tub with matching sinks and marble floors." "Yeah me and Annie found it in the paper....I'm going to stay here for about two years. By then I'll have enough money to get my house built." She looked at me hard with her mouth open. "You doing it like that Veronica....girl bitches is going to be hating you for that...how much you got to have to build your own house?" "Now what in the hell makes you think I'm going to tell her ass my damn bidness. "It all depends." "On what." "If you can show and prove how you bought it....and if you can put down a big down payment." "Oh...well I guess I can't buy me a house until I'm in my thirty's....or at least find some nigga to buy one." So stupid, I won't ever wait for nobody to buy shit for me...never. A girl got to do what a girls got to do to get her own shit. "Nah...just save up Wonnie that's all." "You right." I had to end the conversation because it was going nowhere. I finished the chicken and everybody sat on the floor to eat. "Hey....everybody get on this table right here.....and yall going to have to drink at the counter because I don't want no stains on my carpet...."I don't blame you Veronica.....this house is super tight" "Thank you Wonnie...I plan to keep it that way." After everybody ate we finished putting the house together. I took a shower, checked my pager, climbed in the bed and called it a night.

Chapter 43

"Visiting Wednesday"

I was exhausted standing in this fucking line, all these hoes down here coming to see their baby daddy's. Zero better be glad I have a point to prove otherwise I wouldn't be going through this shit. I check my watch and it's like 5:30. Now I been standing here for 30 minutes. Visiting hour is over at 7:00. Oh I know I didn't just see some damn girl cut the line. "Yo...a....uh excuse me but um...were waiting to see somebody just like you are." The slick bitch had her back to me so I couldn't make out who she was. "So....I'm getting in right here....where this girl let me in at." For some reason she wouldn't turn around so I walked up to her. I told the girl who I was standing in front of to hold my spot. All the women there was smiling and ready for shit to kick off so of course she was going to hold my spot. "Hey...you." I started taping on her shoulder but she wouldn't turn around. "Hey...since you ain't going to answer." "STOP....you stupid BITCH." "She said while diving on me. "Oh...no...no....No you didn't Nella." I grabbed that hoe by her damn weave and pushed her head into the glass. She hit it so hard the police lady behind the glass looked up. "Hay...you come here!" All the women jumped back in the line as Nella tried to pull herself together. "Who me...I didn't do nothing!" I tried to put my sad face on while Nella was running her mouth. "No...you with the big mouth." She pointed at Nelle. I was snickering with the other women. "What" she said while giving Lacy all attitude. "You come in here at least once a week and jump in the line." "No...I don't....it ain't me." "Oh yes it's you...you are here to see Rockma Dupri aren't you?" Nella put her head down "yes" "Well since you keep jumping the line and can't follow orders...you get to the back." I cracked up. That's what that hoe gets. She been running her punk ass up here to try and get brownie points and now her ass going to have to wait. "Bitch...stupid ass Lacy cop." "What...what did you say...if you still got lip service...you won't see him at all." She told Nella as she stormed off to a seat. "Nah...I didn't say shit." It was my turn to get buzzed in. Damn Nella wanted to kill me. I stuck my tongue out at her and she gave me the finger. I laughed as I stepped on the elevator. The things some do to fuck with niggas. When you're waiting to see a nigga in jail or prison the visiting room is packed. That's not the case when you go see a women. That shit is wide open. By the time I made it up to see Zero, I had another area to wait in. Thank god it was shorter. The court house makes sure that you don't try to break out or get out. When I sat down I could see Nella through the glass. They had 4 floors of different grades of niggas, so all those women waiting must have been on the other levels. Damn I screwed my face up. I smiled my ass off when the lady told me I could go back. I made it to the window and picked up the phone. I heard somebody yell out Shine, but I couldn't make out the voice. Zero came to sit down and had his mad dog on me. "Hi...what's wrong with you?" I tried to keep a happy mood. He was facing attempt murder charges and I didn't want to fuck up his mood. "You ...what took your ass so long to get here?" "Boy...I had a long ass line to waitin ...shit!....you need to holler at these people." He better chill shit I already wish I could jump through the glass for having this bitch Nella up here. "No...I told you to be here early!" "Um huh...I know so I wouldn't run into Nell's ass huh." He gave me a weird look. "Don't look at me crazy boy...you know that hoe been coming up here to see yo ass." "Yeah...I do but I told her you was coming ...and not to come today." Now that's a first but I still ain't letting my guard down. "DO you want me to believe that….shit…what do I …look like?" He shifted in his seat as the Guard told him he got 10 minutes left. "You look like beautiful…the one who ain't my women…the one who keeps playing with my heart…the one who got this no good ass nigga living in her crib, the one…" "Hold up….chill…ok…boy…" "Boy…I'm a grown ass man." "Rockma." He looked at me like I was crazy and so did everybody else. "Girl don't be saying my name all like that." "Shit you're in jail and about to go to trial…they know your fucking name…shit, I didn't come here for this." He laughed at me real hard and punched the glass. "Now…you should understand how I feel in this mother fucker….shit ….you suppose to be taken care of business." "I am…why are you trippin like this Rock?" I made him smile again. "I don't know shit! It is you but…girl you make my hard just looking at you." I was smiling from ear to ear. I still was in there. After him calling with Low in the background I just knew it was over. "Well your name is Rock ain't it?" He licked them thick sexy lips. "Yeah…um huh and my dick is for your thick ass too." We had to rap things up. I let Zero know that I had everything under control and that I was going to have him straight when he got out. He told me not to come to trial because he didn't want them to investigate me for nothing. Bullshit! He really doesn't want me to come because Cat is going to be there. People hear about us getting money around but they don't know if we fucked around. Cat is suppose to testify against Kanie, Able and Kobe. I guess she knows shit about them because they are all Bull's homeboys. Well whatever, I'm not in that shit I can't get his ass out of here I guess! Whatever! "call me when you think I'm home." I told him my new number to the house until he memorized it. I stood up to leave and blew him a kiss. "A Shine." I grabbed the phone back. "Yeah what's up baby…don't go out here trippin when you leave…aight." I knew he was concerned because I was on probation and he knew I'll slap a bitch. "I ain't baby….smooch." I blew him a kiss and he threw up the peace sign. I walked out the visiting door and Nella was standing in my way. "Move girl…shit you don't won't none." I pushed her to the side as I stepped to the window to get my I.D. "You think you are slick hoe" I grabbed my I.D. as the guard watched us. "Slick…I don't have to be slick." "You know I was out here waiting to see him and you took up all the time so I couldn't." I laughed and had the women to buzz me through the door to get to the elevators. Her stupid ass was right behind me. Damn she knows I'll whoop her ass if we wasn't in this jail house. "YO dumb ass need to take that shit up with Zero…I mean you do fuck with him don't you." I knew her stupid suckin dick in the back of the movie theatre, ass was going to try and say some slick shit. "Yeah I sho am now…but ya think you the shit, ass keeps getting in my damn way." "Doin…what? Now that's your problem." We stepped on the elevator and all eyes and ears were on me. At first I didn't want to get real nasty because peoples parents and kids was out there. They wasn't Ginger or Victor so I really didn't give a fuck. Where is Annie when I need her. I hope she sitting down here waiting on me so I can really shut this hoe right in front of her. "My problem is you….you ain't as cute as you think you are…my pussy is the shit cause Zero and Low be all up in it." Oh no she didn't have to put Low's ass in it. These hoes know how I feel about my dick. "Well let me tell you something Nella, for one nigga's never admit to fucking your sloppy pussy ass #2 you fuck for crumbs, #3 you'll suck a dick anywhere and with anyone." I pulled my 3 g's out on that bitch that danger just gave me. #4 and both them niggas keep me paid." I then slapped her in the face with the money. Everybody laughed as she ducked and weaved. "Oh how much money is that an old lady said as we stepped off the elevator. "I'm glad you told her ass, she been talking shit since she been coming every Wednesday ." Nella walked off as I walked over to Annie. "Girl I had to just check Nella." "Where she at?" Annie was looking over the group of people walking out. "No Annie over there." I pointed at her as she stood there frowned up. We walked by her as we left out. "Fuck her Shine….she ain't got shit on you." She rolled her eye's and sucked her teeth. "Yeah I know Annie and she don't got shit to say now…yeah keep them cock suckers shut…shit that's all you're good for anyways…your pussy don't get wet as mine, as both them niggas told me." I told Annie to go get the car because I knew I was getting to her. "W-h-a-t…who told you that?" She was pissed. She wasn't quiet no more. "Both of them did..um huh that's how I know I ain't neither one of them leaving me." Annie pulled up and I jumped in the passengers seat. "Whatever...you're lying...I'm going to ask them." She so stupid why would she argue with me. That's a no no. You never argue with the bitch that's getting more because her goal is to get more info. "Ask them what you want and why you're at it, go gargle and get my pussy juice off your breath from sucken them nigga's dick." Me and Annie pulled off crackin up. I could see her stumping up and down with he finger in the air. That'll fix her ass the next time she try's to see my dick when he told her ass not to come.

Chapter 44

"Not Guilty"

I'm enjoying the college life now. These business classes are harder then I thought. Usually when you think of taking classes you always think, that you are going to take the class that you're majoring in. Nope you have to take shit that doesn't have anything to do with business management. Like biology of women, what I do I need to know about the body to get a degree in business management. I hope it will all fall into place sometime down the road. "Hey Veronica ...how you doing?" I had seen a lot of familiar faces in school but I didn't know where the voice was coming from. I looked around in the cafeteria but I couldn't see anyone. "Over here...it's bunny." Damn I didn't know I was going to be in school with this hoe. "What's up girl?" I hadn't talk to her since her smart mouth ass left my house that day. "What classes are you taking ...I'm taking computer programming." "Um...for real!" I didn't want her knowing shit about me. That's why I don't say to much stuff around Ciara. I know her big mouth ass be telling her everything. "I haven't figured out yet....but I'm going for something." Her nosey ass looked down at my bag and stepped a little bit too close. "Oh...I see you're taking Economics and Biology of women." Damn I had to step back a step. Her fucking breath was on fire. "Yeah...um I am." "What's wrong...you stepped back like I was offending you or something." Yeah her fucking breath did. "Here...it's still morning." I laughed and handed her some gum. "Ha ha....girl you still stupid...thank you." I might be stupid toher but my fucking body and breath sure is straight. "Well let me get going...I got shit to do." I said while walking off. "Hey...Veronica...Ms. Shine....um I know you ain't mad about that shit a couple of months ago." "Nah..I'm straight." I kept walking to get my food so I could eat in peace. As I stood in line I seen her at a table waving her hands and talking shit with some hoes I didn't fool with. I grabbed a fruit salad, cheesecake, chicken sandwich and a lemonade. I see all the girls in school are some weight loss program so I guess I'll get to kick it with them. When they say you should stay around people so positive change will come. That's a definite statement and true fact. I sat down and watched all of the rich kids eat and enjoy themselves. Well I guess my Mom can no longer say I'm not pursuing my goals. I'm so tired of going to them treatment classes. You have to lie and say you're a user. I mean I tried crack mixed with weed before. I didn't like it. Bird's cousin offered to smoke a blunt with us once. By us being so young and silly. We didn't realize his ass was a straight ass fiend. We was bouncing off of walls. When everybody noticed how we're zipping around the party and acting crazy. They let us know that he sell primo's and not weed. I wanted to have somebody whoop his ass. Bird talk me out if it because that was her cousin. He's lucky cause it sure would have been a done deal. I could only take & courses at school because of the treatment classes. On my way out to my truck I seen Bunny's ass again. She didn't have her little flunkies with her so she acted like she wanted to chill. I acted like I didn't see her and opened my door. "Shine...um...I need to ask you something." "What's up?" I said while starting it up and having the door cracked. "I wanted to know if you have anything?." Like what." She needed a favor and she was haten cause I'm ballin and she can't take it. "Um...whatever...you can loan me." I knew it. I ain't the fucking front girl. "Loan you...what you don't even have any loot?" "Well yeah...I got like 3 g's." "SO what do you need a favor for?" I knew why but her ass is going to tell me why. "I just need a 9 piece so I could get on my feet...I've been having a little hard time paying my bills and school ain't making it no easier." I know how shit could be but this hoe don't feel me for real. "Well...I'm going to keep it real...you don't even cut with me...shit you're Ciara's home girl...I could help you I ain't tryin to get into no funk with nobody about my paper." "I know....I...know and I would never fuck the hand that feeds me." "Ok well....I'll have you get up with me later." "Ok...thank you!" I slammed my door and backed up. As I drove away she honked the horn. Damn her ass was happy as hell. I don't know how I feel about fronting her anything. I'll have to look into that.

Chapter 45

"Trial week"

I decided to go down to the court house. I just wanted to see how Cat was going to perform. I only had 1 hour to spare my business law class started at eleven. I went in the ramp and seen Bulls car parked right next to a spot I was going to pull in. That fucked me up cause Zero don't fuck with Bull. Hell he's on trial because of homeboys. I found a spot right next to the parking attendant in the ground level. I had my all peach Donna Karen suit on with my Kenneth Cole heels. I'm sure nobody was expecting to see me looking so good. As soon as I opened the door, the whole room turned around to look at me. I gave them a twisted look and rolled my eyes. Cat was on the stand and Zero had his eye's on her. The prosecutor was asking her how well she knew Kane and Able. She let them know that they were known drug dealers and that anybody could have shot them out of retaliation of that type of life style. Everybody was itchin in their seats. I could see Bull and them shaking there head. I heard Spade tell Kobe to "get up there and lie on that nigga... you got to get them 20 years he's getting to much money." Kobe nodded his head. As he stood up to walk to the stand he pointed at me and said "you are a cold piece." Everybody looked at me. Dana, Bull Steen and Cat. Cat took a seat right in front of me and put her mug on me. I could feel the tension in the air. I was just waiting for Zero to turn around so he could know I was there. "What you looking at?" I said to Bull and rolled my eyes. He turned around. As Steen cleared her throat Zero turned around and saw me. I mouthed "good luck" to him. He smiled real hard and winked his eyes. That's all I wanted to do. I showed my fly ass face, ain't nobody going to tell me where I can and can't go. As I said "excuse me" to move out the row I was sitting in.

Everybody watched me walk out. Bull was right behind me but I wasn't worried. It wasn't no way he was going to trip up in this court house. I put a pep in my step to the elevator. "Veronica let me talk to you... I just want to see my son!" He was lying, his ass was happy to see me and just wanted to talk. "You know you could have your Mom come get him from my Mom." I didn't want him walking by me cause I didn't trust him. I stood until more working people came, it was lunch time. "I've tried that but that's to much of a hassle." "And who's fault is that?" He stepped closer to me. I put my guards up because I was unaware of what he was trying to do. "Ha ha...girl you're trippin... I ain't going to hit you. "I know you ain't because yo ass will go to jail down here in these peoples court house, trippin plus my restraining order stills stands player." All the white folks were looking crazy as I rushed to step in between them and got on the elevator. His stupid ass jumped right on it with me. "Come on! Please Veronica, I just want to see my baby. I mean I'm not even trippin about you messing with Zero." I Knew It. His ass was tryin to get conformation about Zero. Nope not from me. "What... all nigga, whatever... you just better worry about if Popone or one of them nigga's don't get at yo ass." A white older woman looked at me and cleared her throat when she heard my foul language but I didn't care. "You're so stupid... they caught Popone ... ha ha in Ohio tryin to be pussy ...nana." He's still childish kid. He just knows them nigga's is going to be head hunting his ass. "Oh well... I guess that's only one you don't have to worry about." I stepped off the elevator and he grabbed my arm. "Help... A h...please leave me alone." I did the fool and had everybody looking. "Oh girl stop playing." "No... no don't touch me.' I screamed and the police came running. He tried to push the elevator to leave but he had nowhere to run. "Mam... what's the problem?" A crowd of people had formed and people were walking by being nosy. "Him right there... I have restraining order against him and he just grabbed my arm!" "She's lying sir... please sir." I laughed and jumped on the next elevator behind me while that asshole tried to explain his self. I jetted to my truck and made it out before he could see what I was rolling. When I made it back to school I seen Bunny again. This time when she approached me she was smackin like a hungry cow. "Shine... girl that was some cool stuff Yoyo gave me... thank you... um a ...I'll have your paper in two days." "Aight." I kept it moving cause I was 10 minutes late for class. "A... and I'm going to be ready to get my own." Can't her dumb ass see I'm on school time not hustle time. "I'll holla at you bout that after school." She smiled and nodded her headed. I slid into my chair and my teacher was right on me. " Excuse me Ms. Gittens is there any reason why you couldn't be here on time like the rest of the class?" Everybody looked to me as if I had shit on my face or like they're never late. "No sir... I apologize... I won't let it happen again." "O.K... you need to know that you're an adult and responsible for your grades and if you're not going to be here you need to at least let me know." "O.K." The girl next to me let me write down the lecture that he had before I came. "Thank you." I said in whisper. "You're welcome... my name is Ellen... what's yours?" "Veronica." "Anytime and I love the way you dress..." "Thanks... anytime you want to go shopping let me know o.k." She smiled and shook her head. The professor was looking directly towards the back. I put my head down and prayed he didn't buss me out again. After class Ellen gave me her number and introduced me to her friends Chan and Paris. They all looked like struggling baby mother that couldn't wait to get out of school. I didn't realize how popular I was until they gave me a little history lesson on myself. They knew that I hustled. That I had a baby by Bull and I went with Low. I laughed it off as if they didn't know what they were talking about, but they did. All of the them sold weed on the side or wrote checks. Shit to me that's slow money. But I can't knock them because at least they wasn't setting around making any excuses. I told them I'll get up with them for dinner sometime and went to my truck. I was so glad school was over. My Mom had something to do so I had to ride all the way to St. Paul to pick up my son from daycare. When I got there I could see all of the parents picking up their kids and how happy they seemed to be. "Hello...I'm here to pick up my son Victor." The woman looked at me crazy." Who are you mam?" "I'm his mother." I said with my hand on my hip. "Oh... well since your face isn't familiar then I'll have to call the administrators office to check and see if your name is on the list." I was fuming as all the kids and their parents walked past looking happy. As she got up to walk away I had to calm myself down. "Hi... lady... you're pretty. Who's Mom are you?"A little boy said as he walk pass with his mother. "Hi... you're a cutie yourself.... I'm Victors Mom." "Oh... ... his grandma comes to get him usually." His Mom tried pushing him through the door. "Well not today baby... I'm here to take him with me." "Can I go?" he said while tussling with his Mom. "A... maybe next time baby.' "O.K... bye... pretty Victors Mom." "Bye... cutie." That did it. I've been neglecting my son because I'm huggin the block. Tears came to my eyes as I thought about how this little boy just checked me. I was in a daze thinking about all the times Victor would fallout if I didn't take him with me." Mam... excuse me ...mam.' "Oh... I'm sorry... yes." "You can go up and get him now." "Thank you." I ran up the steps in my heels and was so happy to be doing something parental. I thought Victor would of ran over to see me but he didn't... He was standing at the door with his backpack and coat on. The teacher was preparing to leave "Hi Victor... ain't you ready to go with me baby?" "Where's my grandma?" He said pouting. This made me feel even smaller as I fought not to cry. "She had something to do... so you're coming home with me." "No... no I want my grandma." This boy did the fool in front of this white teacher. I wanted to beat his ass for doing this but I couldn't. He was right. He doesn't see me enough. "Please... come on Victor I'm going to take you out for pizza." I grabbed him by his arm and picked him up. I almost fell trying to get down the stairs . "Veronica do you need me to help you to the car." "No... I'm fine." I said to the teacher with an attitude. They all watched me like a hawk. I guess they thought I was going to beat my child. "And what yall looking at?" "Don't be angry Veronica... our best interest is in Victor." I set him down so I could wipe his nose. "Well I'm not going to hurt my own son." I was crying by then and this must of hurt Victor because he wiped my tears and said "don't cry Mom... I love you." I gave him a hug and put him in the truck. After convincing him that I would buy him candy and pizza he calmed his self down. I enjoyed myself with my son. At three years old he knew a lot. I'm going to make it my business to always spend time with my son no matter what.

Chapter 46
"Zero's Verdict"

For the past two day s I've picked up Victor and brought him home. I guess my Mom missed him because she told me I didn't have to get him tomorrow. Good I'll kick it for the weekend. I was dozing off after school while watching video's with "Tigger in the Basement." I opened my eyes all the way when I seen Nas on there. Damn that nigga is fine as hell. He kinda looks like Butchie a little. I want to tell his ass that though. Damn if that nigga and Spanky was around to see that shit that I saw I n the courtroom the other day. Bull, Kane, Able and Kobe's asses would be gone. Oh well they got 2 years in J.C. for getting caught with un-registered guns. So I won't see them for a minute. As I got up to go to the bathroom somebody was ringing the phone off the hook. "Hello" "you have a collect call from… Rockma" oh shit, my heart stared racing. "To accept this call press 5, to not accept… 5555." I kept pressing 5 so I wouldn't have to wait. "Hello… Hello…baby you there?" It was so much noise in the back ground, I couldn't hear him. "Yeah… beautiful… what's up?" "Nothing I'm chillin with Victor." "Where's Annie… did she handle that for me?" "Of course… did you see me the other day?" "Yeah I was glad to see you… you're as is bold as hell. I seen that nigga bull follow you too. I wanted to jump out my seat and follow his ass." "I know but my only purpose was to make you happy." "Good cause I'll be there in a minute to make you happy too." I was smiling from ear to ear. "How do you know that… baby?" "Cause… Pop one's lawyer told them that he shot them in self defense. He said he did shoot them and they shot first. Cat testified, you seen her right?" "uh huh." "Well her testimony helped me a little baby…don't be mad, I can hear it in your voice." I was pissed because now since that hoe got us there and put a show on for his ass he was going to come with that over lay under play." I'm not mad… I just don't want it to change shit between us… I'm not accepting you fucking her because she helped you get out of trouble." "Nah… baby… I want you for real… but I got to at least act like I like her." "Whatever." "Well when they say that I'm released I'll come get you so we can talk about this… aight?" I just sat there for a minute. "Hello… beautiful"

I got so weak when he called me that. "I'm still here… a they found you not guilty?" "Yeah… but the judge said he needs to talk to my attorney." " For what?" "Cause they have questions about the prints on one of the guns they found." "What's that got to do with you?" "Shit" the recorder came on for him to get off in 3 minutes. "O.K… well I'll be there I promise." "I hope so." "For-real them prints don't got shit to do with me, I promise you." "O.K… Baby." "My Mom will page you when I'm on my way home so that means to meet me over there." "O.K… Bye." He blew a kiss into the phone before hangin up. I know he don't think I'm about to share him with Nella, Cat and all the rest of them hoes he's fucking. I put my clothes on and got Victor dressed. We had to go tell Annie the news and go to the stash house. I had to drop my baby off first because I couldn't have any accidents. When I got to Annie's she was outside talking to Myrecal and Mya. Me and Victor got out the car. "What's up Annie and Mya?" I wasn't feeling Myrecal and she knew it. "

Hi…girl what you doing?" They said together. Myrecal started picking up Victor and playing with him. "Shit…I need him to drop Victor off and go to meet Zero." "Oooh…id he out?" "Yeah…I heard nigga's testified." I ignored Mya and answered Annie. "Nah…not yet, but we got some shit to take care of. I gave Annie the look to stop answering questions. As Annie went back in the house to get some clothes to come over for the weekend at my house, I snatched Victor out of Myrecal's hands. "Dam…Shine…you seen me playin with him…why are you being like that?" I kept walking with him. "I ain't being like nothing…you know yo ass is shady and sometimey." "No….you are…shit…you need to let that old shit go girl." "Nah…I'm grown…..shit I let shit go when I feel like it." She rolled her eyes and smacked her teeth. I sat in the truck and listen to "Flavor in you ear" by Craig Mac. "Hunk…hunk…Annie hurry up." She was talking to them I guess about getting a ride. I knew it, now these hoes need to be dropped off. Then it dawned on me. Mya hadn't sweated me about taking her shopping for keeping quiet about that abortion. "I'm sorry…but I was going to go with them to the mall…but when you said you needed me….I changed my plans with them." "So what's up now." I could tell she wanted to ask for me to give them a ride home. They stopped outside the truck looking stupid. "Well I can't just leave them here…you know my Mom will trip plus you know Ty don't get along with Myrecal." "Aight…get yall ass in." I pulled my money out to make sure I could give Mya $300 dollars. Damn, here I am acting funny and she kept her word and didn't even ask me about it. They both climbed in. "Thank you Shine." Myrecal said. Mya looked at me and mouthed. "I didn't say nothing." I shook my head and smiled. We rode over to their house and I was about to turn on their block. "Shine…can you stop at the store so I could pick my Mom some cigarettes up." "Um huh." I blasted the music as I pulled up to the kings Liquor store. The block was still hot on Plymouth and no, I can't go back to that curb servin shit but it show was funny watching the daily events go down. Mya jumped out and I was right behind her. "Here…here take this." She grabbed it really quick and put it away. "Why did you give me that?" "Give you what?" Myrecal had walked up on us. "Nothing…shit, where yo ass come?" "I came in to get Victor some chips and…me a pepsi…please." She said while smiling and walking away. "Yeah…I got you." I made sure she was all the way back in the truck. "Damn my sister is nosy huh?" "Yes…I wish she'd be more like you she'd be more like you." She laughing. "I know…thanks for the money, but you didn't have to give me this just for being quiet…I would do it anyways." "Thank you…girl…I'll remember that." We got all of the stuff for Ms. Danyell. After making it to the house I dropped them off. Myrecal begged Annie to give her a hundred dollars to match the hundred she already had. She did of course. She ask me could she come over to my house and kick it sometime. I just nodded my head yes. I rolled down Knox Ave. Just to get a good look of where my stomping grounds use to be. "Why you turn this way…its going to take us longer to get to the freeway." "I know I just thought about Tweedy that's all!." "Girl you know we can't be down here with Victor in the car." She was right. As soon as she said that, Bull and his whole crew tried following my truck but I dipped to the freeway so they couldn't get on the side of my truck. "Go…go down to Olson Hwy and dip through the projects." "I am girl…you see the popo following them so I can't speed girl." Annie was nervous cause we didn't have no heater on us and we had Victor in the car. Victor started crying from all of the screaming we was doing. "It's alright

Victor, Quit crying…Mommy can't drive good if you cry." Annie passed him his chips and a juice. "He's ok….I'll give him a sucker." I kept my eye's on the road but went right through lights. The po po put on their lights but they didn't want me. I pulled up and over but he pulled right next to the three cars that were following my truck. The officer fanned me off and told me to go on. I went right on the freeway and was glad. "Woo…girl I didn't want them to know for sure that this was my truck." "I told you them nigga's still be holding down Knox….shit Tweedy been gone a minute they don't really give a fuck about that when it comes to getting that paper. "You're right Annie…I guess since I use to or should I say we use to run these parts. I just was remembering the old days." "Girl…please fuck them hook ass niggas….let me find out you still got Bull on yo mind." We both busted up laughing. "Hell nah….you know I wouldn't even let that nigga pay me to smell…this pussy." "Ha ha…I know I remember when that nigga use to pay you to fuck him. Then you would dog his ass right after that. You really trip me out when you use to tell him that in order for your headache to go away, he had to take you and the cutie pie posse to Red Lobster." "Yeah um huh…that shit worked…see I was never selfish…my hoes had to eat too….dog." We cracked up laughing at Bull and his slow ass. It's funny how when you don't go with somebody no more you realize it was never a reason for you to trip off of them to begin with. We made it to Mom's to drop Victor off of them to begin with. We made it to my Mom's to drop off Victor and Ms. Dupri paged me. While in my Moms, I had to get Victor to wound down because he didn't want me to leave. "Go in the room and get your toys baby." My Mom looked at me crazy. "Now yall hurry up because you know his butt is going to act up." Me and Annie ran back to the truck. "Bye Mom…I'll call you." I said while pulling off. As I pulled away Victor was pouting and waved bye. "Girl…at least you know your son loves you." I know….I just have to make sure I'm around to see him grow up." "You will be. I turned up the music and called Ms. Dupri back on my phone. "Hi…Ms. Dupri….did Zero come home yet?" "Yeah…he did but he left." "Where did he go?" I don't know baby…but I tell you what….he's glad to be out and you know how men are." "SO what are you trying to tell me Ms. Mabel….I mean did he tell you something….or …oh did you see something?" I knew this was his Mom and she's only going to tell me something to a certain extent no matter how much a nigga's Mom like s you. She will always cover up for her son especially when they are Momma's boys. "Oh baby…um I'm going to tell you like this beautiful…when a man is taken care of you and you get any and everything you ask for…then it's no need to question them about what their doing. You know where his heart is so don't worry about it!" She was right but I didn't want to hear that. "Ok…Ms Mabel…tell him I just hate that I didn't get the dick first." She was shocked. "Ok..ha ha baby."

Chapter 47

"On da Grind"

"Beautiful….honey come here", Zero's Mom called out to me. I don't have time for nobody in that nigga's family. I'm bout to dip out this aisle… Damn I know his Momma didn't do me wrong, but I'm cool on that nigga so I'm cutting all ties. I needed some popsicles for Victor and some crab legs for Low. Oh shit here her ass comes right up on me. I'm bout to keep walking like I don't see her ass. "Excuse me …is this checkout lane open?" The young girl looked like she was just getting to work. "Yes, you can come right here." I started throwing my stuff on the line counter. "Are you in a hurry Mam?" Didn't she understand I wasn't trying to conversate with her ass. "Yes I am, so could you please be quick." Ms. Maybel just stood behind my two carts and watched me. "No problem Mam." The young girl was zipping my stuff right through the line. The bag boy was just as fast as her. Damn, I was going so fast I dropped all of the cereal on the floor and one of the boxes fell on Ms. Mabel's foot. "I'm sorry, I started to say…" "You don't have to say sorry…. but you are being very sorry by the way you just treated me when I called you by your name." I ignored her because she was right. She helped me pick my stuff up off the floor. "Thank you Ms. Mabel." "I told you Veronica, I really like you and just because you courting with my son doesn't make me like you more." "What are you talking about." "You know just what I'm saying." She raised her voice a little louder then usual. "Ms. Mabel, I'm not going to be disrespectful towards you....I just didn't answer you because I'm done with Zero." She frowned up at me and it made me really nervous. "You what?...let me tell you something Veronica, you have a lot to learn about these young men out here that you call niggas." By now, the whole store watched as she dog checked me. The young boy and girl that were checking my groceries out were completely done, so they stood there and took the lesson just as well as I did. "Ms. Mabel I..." "No, you had every opportunity to speak your peace and you didn't, now sit back and learn from an older woman." "Yes mam." By this time, I was damn near in tears. She was right and I was being fake. It wasn't her fault that Zero was acting an ass. "I told you that if a nigga is takin care of you and your son then you shouldn't never trip, and if you choose to stay with a boy then that's your business. My son is a man and I can't control what he does nor will I try when it comes to the women he's involved with. I do know this- he's in love with you, but he won't allow himself to be because you have a man and a baby..." "Oh...ok Ms. Mabel...I get your point." I wasn't about to let her tell all my business in that damn Super Value. Shit, we in the hood and all kinds of people were walking pass just to get an ear full. She smiled at me. "Oh I see you don't want me to bust you out." The check out girl busted out laughing. I shot her a look like, you better shut the fuck up. I then looked at the bag boy and he put his head down and smiled. "No...I don't..." I turned from her to make sure I wouldn't look her in the face." "How much, I asked the check out girl?" "Oh...$337.00 mam." I handed the girl three hundred dollar bills, two twenties and a ten. "Why did you give me so much?" She asked me. Ms. Mabel and the bag boy left the lane. "Take that as a little something to keep your lips shut." I winked at her as I left. She smiled and winked back. That might stop her from spreading rumors. When I made it to the truck, the bag boy put my groceries in real nice and neat. So I had to break him off a dub ($20) so he could continue to do his job better. "Thank you....beautiful", he said as he chuckled and walked away. Ms. Mabel just shook her head. That boy had heard her the whole time. "I'm sorry Veronica...I didn't realize how loud I really was." "I needed that and you're right, it ain't your fault what Zero does in the streets." Ms. Mabel and I continued our conversation until she received a page from Zero. "Well, that's my cue...I'll be in touch Ms. Mabel." I jumped in my truck and rolled my windows down. "I'll be seeing you at the house sooner then you think beautiful." I just waved my hand and pulled off. I was about to get on the highway when Zero started blowing my pager up. I had to laugh at myself because I knew his Mom was going to tell him it was me. When I made it to my house, I was on overload. My phone started ringing. "Wait....I'm coming." I was talking to myself as I ran up the stairs. "Ha ha...who in the hell are you talking to Shine." Annie said as she saw me dash for the phone. "Hello.." The person just sat there breathing. "H-e-l-l-oooo....stupid...bitch." I flopped down on the couch. "Girl, that phone been ringing and they just sitting there." "Hum...how long has that been happening?" Annie shrugged her shoulders. "I guess since yesterday. I know when you went to school the other morning a green Taurus was parked down the block for about two hours and I've been seeing him around lately." My mind started racing. Damn, I just moved here. Nobody has been over here so why would my house be on the jump out list. "Ok hold up, I've been beaten my feet real hard so maybe when I go to the D-boys spot, I might of picked up their beat." "Yo...have you hollered at YoYo?" "Yeah, her and Bunny said their all out and they wanna holler at cha." "Word...well why didn't you break em off." Annie put her hand on her hip. "Now you know I had to holler at you first." That's my dawg, Annie had to check with me first. Hum... and hoes try to say she don't got my back. "Right....right I'm glad you thought about that first, since we almost out. Did Zero call?" "Yeah...he been ringing the phone off the hook too." As I started pulling my shoes off, Fox and her home girl QT came from the basement. "Hi big sis...where you been?" QT started laughing and sat down next to me. "Yeah...we missed you". "Bullshit, y'all think y'all slick." They both kept laughing. Annie started smiling and asked what they was up to?" "You know when they start kissing ass they want something, shit they wanna be put on." Annie was smiling from ear to ear with both of them. I know I didn't hear what I thought I heard. "Fox...what the fuck gave you the idea that I would put you on?" I screamed at the top of my lungs. All their smiles turned to frowns. "Shine, me and QT see you getting paper...shit we wanna beat our feet too." It's funny how young people are so easily influenced. They didn't understand the whole headache of hustling. "You ain't beating your feet with my mother fucking work. "QT, what the fuck have you put in my little sisters head, huh?" They knew I was hot as fish grease. My sister would never get in this grimy ass game. QT put her head down. "Um... we was on the block." "With who...huh....what mother fucking block huh?" Fox backed away from me after realizing I had the phone raised in the air like I was going to hit her with it. "Oh...on Knox and Plymouth with Polo."

Damn, that name took just half a second to register. "Polp the young pimp?" Everybody busted up laughing as if I had jokes. "He ain't no pimp...he's digging on me." Shit he been spending money on me." She didn't even see his game. "Stupid... that's what the fuck niggas do dummy." She put her head down. "Damn Shine, you don't have to keep calling the damn girl names and shit!" "Shut the fuck up Annie...shit you letting these young bucks think that it's cool to hustle." Annie was mad at the way I raised my voice. "You ain't got to be screaming at me and shit...I was just saying." "You know what..." I pulled out a bunch of money. "End of discussion, Fox, you won't be getting no dope I said as I got into the shower. As I cleaned myself up, I thought about how I just went off on the whole house. I just couldn't let my sister get into nothing on my account. I put my Gucci sandals and dress on. It was a little chilly out, so I had to put my boots on instead. It's a shame how people get a little taste of sun and think that they could wear anything they wanted. "Yo QT, come here." She made her way into the room with her head down. "Yeah...Shine." I could see that she wanted to get smart with me but she didn't have the guts. "Call that nigga Polo right now." She frowned up at me. "Fox...what...he ain't my man, shit." "I know who the fuck he's fucking with but I know Fox ain't going to call the nigga." She sat on my bed in hesitation. I picked up the phone for her. "Here, what you waiting for." I said while shoving it in her hand. "What am I going to say Shine?" "Shit...I'm just going to give him a piece of my mind." She still didn't wanna do it. "That would be snitching or setting my best friend up for the bo bo. "Girl, call that nigga now!" My blood was boiling but she did what I said. "Here Shine, he's on the phone." "Polo the pimp huh." "Who in the fuck is this?" I could tell by his cocky ass voice his lame as thought that he was somebody. He was one of them punk niggas that plotted on young girls. He would buy them shoes or an outfit, take them to dinner and make them turn tricks with the ballers or set them up to get robbed. "This is Shine nigga." "Um...what's up?" "Don't you ever ask my motha fucking sister to sale shit for you!" "If I do, what's going to happen?" Oh this nigga think I'm a joke. I know Zero's little brother told his ass about me. "I'm going to handle yo ass!" "Oh, so you threatening me?" "Nah nigga, I'm promising that ass!" "You can't help cause yo sister is a freak that wants to be down to get some paper." "Guess what?" "What?" "I sho can't, but yo bitch ass won't be having her part of your stable and if you keep tryin to make her...Zero will be to see ya....click." I didn't have to hear the nigga respond. Shit, the mention of Zero's name made my heart skip a beat so I know his ass knew not to fuck with Fox or me. QT sat there looking at me like I was crazy. "What, you got something to say?" She was shook up thinking I was going to tell Fox about her calling Polo. She stood up to leave my room behind me. "Shine you are crazy", she said as she shook her head. "Just don't tell Fox ok." "I won't, but I ain't playing, y'all better stay the fuck away from Polo!" Hustlers are born not made. "The next thing I know, y'all ass will be strung out...dis shit ain't no game to be fucking with." She was right behind me as I entered the living room. "What ain't....what y'all talking about Shine?" Fox said as she handed me my pager. "Nothing here." I handed Fox $500 dollars. "Y'all split that, maybe that will get your minds off hitting the block.

Chapter 48

"Out Patient Treatment"

Damn, everybody was in there melting except me. I hate that because they always pull me up on my tardiness. I walked straight into drama. Tara was crying hysterically about child protection services taking her kids because she dropped dirty and everyone was comforting her and I wasn't tryin to hear it. I had two weeks left and I was ready for it to be over. "Hello everybody...I have donuts and coffee for everyone if you would like some." I damn near got knocked down as I sat the box on the table. "That was nice of you Veronica, you've been doing this for about a month now." "Yeah Ms. Wise, I know she must be messing with a baller or she's still out there slangin them thangs." Flow was about to get her head busted right up in this meeting. "Hey Flow, that ain't the way you treat a young girl who feeding us this morning." "Yeah, you of all people needs to shut yo ass us being as though you don't know where your next meal is gone come from" Tara said. "Shut up Tara, your ass needs to worry about them damn kids being molested and turned out in that damn foster home." It was on now. Them dope fiends got to bombing in the meeting...."you fucking bitch"... "I'll kill you for putting my kids name in your mouth"...bam...bam...crack. Tara drilled Flow all up side her head then busted her on the head with a flower pot. "Ha ha ha...you crack heads are a trip" I said while standing back to watch. Ms. Wise was in her late fifties so she really couldn't handle the breakup. "Help me....please Veronica...please" she begged. They had Ms. Wise all tangled up like a twister board game. All the dope fiends dogged the donuts out and watched on. I never realized that this was probably the only time they were sober or received a meal. "Yo...y'all get over here and break this shit up...damn it." They all damn near choked and rushed to help me. "Tara, let her go...." She had Flow in the headlock and was upper cutting her. "NO....she disrespected my kids and you." "Let her go cause you're hurting Ms. Wise." "Yeah, let me go, Ms. Wise is about to lose her mind." I put both of them in chairs across the room from each other. They acted liked they were juveniles so that's how I treated them. Ms. Wise sat down and stared at them with tears in her eyes. "I'm still going to whoop your ass Flow." She ignored her and tried to fix those matted up tracks she had in her head. One side was real nappy and the other side was hanging on by a strand with a bobby pin. Flow was a pretty crack head. She stood about 5'10, B cup with a little booty. You could tell about 10 years ago she had it going on. After catching her husband in bed with her twin sister, she lost her mind. She was a stay at home mother so she didn't know how to survive on the streets. She met Tara through a man that they both were messing with. He turned them both out on crack and Flow started selling her ass on Hennepin Ave. for dope. She was on tape sucking the Chief of Police's dick and landed her ass in a whole pornography conspiracy. That's how she landed her ass in treatment. Tara was caught stealing from TCF Bank. She was the President of the bank, jacking them for 7.2 million. Being as though her family was rich and owned part of the bank, they made her confused ass go to treatment and took her kids. White people always make it so easy for their children. That's why when shit hits the fan, they have no understanding of how to survive. Thank God that I'm black and was raised to struggle because I would be stuck just like her. "Have y'all cooled out now?" I said as I sat in the middle of the floor. Today was my day to get in the middle of the floor. In treatment terms, that means that you had to get grilled and answer every question that your cohort asked. Ms. Wise had to step out the room to get herself together, so I took advantage of the opportunity. "Yo...Flow....the nasty ass H-e-n-nepin hoe...you better check yourself before you try busting me out" I said while staying in my chair. Everybody chuckled as I kicked my lame rap. "What you mean...I mean you do have a lot of money for somebody that stopped selling dope and has a habit." "See Flow, you always let your mouth overload your ass." "Shut up Tara...you ass kissing half-breed, you don't have a say in shit." And why is that Flow? Because you say so...?" "Nah...Shi...I mean Veronica she's an oreo cookie... she can relate...she don't know her ass from a hole in the wall." Every snagga tooth dope fiend in the room bust up laughing. Tara's beautiful light skin turned beet red and she was ready to leap out of her chair. "No...No...No...Tara." I pushed her back down lightly and made her sit back in her chair. "Don't sweat her, she has a jealousy problem and you don't." Flow turned in her seat. "I know Veronica, she's just mad because my family cares about me and has money...now." Tara stuck her tongue out at Flow like a third grader. I think when people do drugs and go through recovery, they become chemically unbalanced and think they're children again, reaching out for attention and yearning for love. If you as a person, take the time to love yourself then you'll find that you don't need drugs to fill that need. "Money ain't everything Tara, maybe you need to pay attention because that's what got you in here." She looked at me like I was crazy. "I guess you not amongst us then Veronica, I mean, everybody in here knows that you only fuck with ballers and one of them happens to be Rockma Dupri." Flow was really about to get her ass kicked for telling my business. "Flow, what makes you think you know my business so well" I asked? Flow looked at me and said, "you act like this is New York or something." "Shit, this is Minneapolis, MN damn it....the place where Prince made Purple Rain a fucking classic!" "Girl, that's what we're known for...the pimps, hustlers and players in this town are peons compared to the ballers in the big cities, so therefore everybody knows your business...shit ain't no damn secret. "Um damn she really tried to check me but I got her ass," "All I know is you better keep my fucking name and Rock's name out your mouth." I paid as I put my finger all up in her face. "You don't want it known you a fucking strawberry...sucking a dick for a hit bitch." "Veronica...what are you doing?" Right when I was about to smack the shit out that hoe. Penny Daniels and Ms. Wise walked in on me. "She wasn't doing nothing Ms. Wise....she ....she was just protecting me form Flow that's all. All eyes were on Tara as she tried to explain my behavior. My heart and eyes were quickly focusing on Ms. Daniels. What the hell was she doing in here. "Everyone sit down",. Ms. Wise tried to get the meeting together after an hour passed. I had to be at school in 1 hr so she's lucky that it just got started. "Everyone I would like you all to meet Ms. Daniels." I watched her walk to everyone in the room and shake their hands. When she made it to me she broke down crying. "Penny what's wrong honey...you said you needed to do this." My eye welled up with tears. She was embarrassed and so was I. "Ms. Wise...Thank you so much for my recovery...but Veronica is my daughter's friends...I thought I could do it with no problem but I can't....I can't...I failed as a mother and a role model." All of us in the room couldn't stop crying. Penny was functioning crack head. She never had money for Mya and Myrecal but the house was always clean and they never went without food or a place to stay. I guess that why they always wanted to stay out all night. Their mother let Scotty get her hooked and she couldn't shake it off. "It's ok Ms. Daniels....I would never ever let Mya or Myrecal know that you were in treatment with me." "I know baby....I know....I still need for you to stop doing what you doing....you sale to your own people....it's destroying our nation daily....if you stop...it will soon cause everyone else to stop." "Hold up now. This ain't about to be get on Veronica day. Just because I fucking sale dope and they decided to smoke the shit ain't my damn fault. "I understand that everybody wants to dog me out because I sold people like y'all but I will not let y'all get on me for your own mistakes and choices. I'm the youngest person here so that alone lets me know that nobody put a fucking gun to your head and said smoke that glass dick." Everybody looked at ,e with hate and evil. "That's a very mean way to say something Veronica." Ms. Wise said. I cried even harder. "I'm sorry Ms. Wise for cursing, but it's just the way everybody is getting on me like it's my fault they using drugs. Everybody hugged each other and continued to conversate. I stood up to blow my nose and looked out the window. As I wiped my eyes I saw Zero standing in the window looking for me. Before he could ring the buzzer I ran out to stop him. That's all I would need is for these damn people to see him and keep up more shit. "Where you been?...Baby I've been calling and coming by the house what's up?" "Stop...Rockma....you can't be here...go Rockma....to my truck and wait." "Why...do they know me or something...I don't know them junkies." I didn't have time to exp[lain." "Boy...just do what the fuck I said." He seen my face and understood me well. As I watched him get in my truck I made it back in the meeting. Everyone was in deep discussion. "Veronica...where are you going?" I tried to grab my coat without them noticing. "To school...I'll see y'all next week." Ms. Wise and Penny just shook their heads.

Chapter 49

"It's on and Poppin!"

Morning traffic on 94 west was a trip. It's so damn early I'm not even functioning. Zero has been on my ass after popping up at treatment center the other day. I haven't been able to get rid of his ass. When you give a nigga the silent treatment, they usually get some act right about themselves. He confessed to me that since I was playing games, he had to get some pussy form Nella and Cat. That's bullshit though he was just making up an excuse to why he did it. Well at least I got me three bricks (kilo's) out of it. Yeah playing games with me is very costly. I'm a twenty piece shit he didn't show as I pulled up to yoyo's spot I seen her ass standing outside butt ass naked. I parked in front of the building and jumped out. "A YoYo, girl what the fuck are you doing out here, it's cold?" I startled her and she jumped. Before I could reach out to put my coat around her Motor's crazy ass came running out the house. "Don't give that funky ass hoe shit." He snatched my coat and grabbed my hand and pulled me in his direction. "Let me go...stupid....I'm her friend not yours." I grabbed YoYo and started crying with her. I tried covering her up with my body. Her face was all beat up and her head was bleeding. "YoYo are you ok." All the neighbors were walking up from the commotion. I thought going to their house before school would be a good idea. I wished I would of never come to this mess that I was involved in now. Money was on my mind though. So I had to come get my 25 g's. "Come on get in here...I ain't going to hit her no more." He was becoming embarrassed because all the kids were coming out the apartment and pointing at her. She wouldn't talk and I couldn't understand why. "YoYo...what is going on girl...are you high?" She would snort cocaine from time to time- a habit she picked up from an old pimp that had her stripping up in St. Cloud, MN. Every since Al Capone days. That was a place where work girls could go and make some cheese for selling pussy. "I'm ok." She said with a low tone and walking towards the door. It looked like it was a normal thing for her because she wasn't embarrassed about being butt ass naked and looking like a wild women. After getting the apartment YoYo went in the bathroom and I took a seat down on the couch. My money was in two crown royal bags on the coffee table as I reached over to count it. "What....you think I jacked you or something?" Motor said in between breaths of his weed smoke. This nigga was a trip like he just didn't beat the shit out of my friend for breakfast. I knew it was a reason why I didn't like his abusive ass. He's lucky that he brings in a hundred g's a week. Other wise I would have got Zero and his boys to whoop his ass. "Nah nigga...this is business...I count my man's fucking money." He shook his head and continued to blow weed smoke my way. "A...nigga....open a window or something shit...I got to go to school in an hour." He jumped and pushed the window open. "Anything for you...your majesty." This nigga had jokes this early in the morning and I wasn't for his little humor. "Anything huh...that means a lot Motor....I'm so honored." I said sarcastically. "I'm for real....I respect you Shine....see you ain't like your home girl...she's not about shit...nasty ass bitch." He got up and started banging on the bathroom door. YoYo was in there so long I almost forgot my purpose for being there. She started yelling something from the locked door but I couldn't understand her. I guess calgon took her away and she probably fell asleep in the tub. "See...this is why I treat that hoe the way I do." He pushed a tray with white residue on it along with two straws. Just like I thought. YoYo was back to snorting. I assumed that she was running with some of her old stripping buddies because that's the only time she done it. "Why don't you get her some help Motor....shit you keep fucking her and y'all live together now." I was sweating from counting my money. I stood up to wash my hands in the kitchen sink. My hands had green ink on them. There's no telling where this money came from. Blood money as the old heads would say. "A....I care about her Shine but she's a freak and that shit got to change or I'm out." He knew damn well hiss ass was lying. He wasn't going nowhere. YoYo yelled as she threw an empty crown royal bottle at Motor's head. He ducked just in time because it busted against the wall. "Aright girl....you don't want me to do to you what I did to you last night." "Y'all both need to break up...shit y'all fight too much. I stood to walk towards the door. "I am....I'm going with you Shine." "YoYo broke out running like she was Flow Joe. "ha ha...ha see I told you that bitch was shady." Motor thought shit was funny. I knew there was a reason for her running. "Nah....she's just tired of you whooping on her that's all?" he went back to the window and watched YoYo hoped in my truck and lock the door. After Motor told me about catching YoYo's head between some dope fiends legs. I decided to leave before his ass starts tripping again. "A...Shine when are you going to hit me back with some more work...I'm out and City is finished his last big eighth (4 ½ ounces) right now." See how niggas are! He was just talking about his girl sucking a dope fiend's pussy. Now he got his mind on money. I'm going to hit you when I'm ready you got to come across town to get it....I think that when I've been meeting up at your spot...Um the jump out boys been watching me ....have y'all been raided or something? Because I haven't had no heat on my end. He looked a little worried like I might cut him off. "ah...nah....I mean we've been having the same shit that happens on the block." "Oh yeah like what?" I knew it was something that his ass wasn't telling me. "A...ah...I know you have to get to school so...I'll just meet you where ever you say you need me to be." At that Moment YoYo started honking like crazy. "Aright I'll hit you up." When I made it to the truck YoYo was on my cell phone. "A...that shit cost more money in the daytime girl." I said while snatching my phone and hanging it up. "Damn..Shine...I'm sick of everybody treating me like a nobody...shit." "Nah...people treat you the way you want to be treated." "And what why is that...I'm human...I want to be respected like you are." "You can't or won't be YoYo...you're not me." She looked real confused. "I know I'm not but just because I like to fuck girls and like giving head...that doesn't mean your better than me." "Nah YoYo it doesn't but you disrespected yourself for pennies and think about the shit after you do it, you were on the hood porn tapes letting a dog lick your pussy while sucking his owner's dick, you was just caught last night giving head to a strawberry neighborhood hoe while she snorted your man's dope up her nose, you..." ok...ok...stop...I've heard enough....Veronica....sniff sniff....you're the shit and everybody knows it." YoYo was saying in between cries. I was so busy trying to make it to school on time that I was running my mouth and missed my damn exit. "Ah...fuck" I screamed out. "What, am I getting on your nerves" YoYo asked. She wanted my full attention and I couldn't give it to her right now. I weaved in and out of traffic and made it downtown Minneapolis 10 minutes early. Now YoYo was still crying and looking out the window while I was breaking my neck to get to school. "YoYo...quit tripping...girl...you're good at what you do shit...I just call it like I see it....but don't be mad cause I don't get down like you." She still ignored me as I pulled up to my school. At that Moment I just remember that I was in my truck and she didn't have nowhere to go.

Chapter 50
"Car wash on Broadway"

"Man...I'm hungry as hell....I'm going to have to hit up Amos and Amos to get me a Polish Sausage." Kane said to himself out loud as he looked around to see what happened to Kobe. "Yo...Kobe...man quit fucking with them hoes nigga...I'm done vacuuming so we can dip." Kane saw Kobe hollering at some hoes next to the spot where he was cleaning his Caprice Classic. At this present time, his car would come in hand because of it's speed. No wonder why the police used it back in the day. Kane got in his car to back up so he could see where Kobe disappeared to. "Kobe...Kobe...man what's up." It was a little dark outside so Kane cocked his 9 mille and thoughts of Zero entered his mine. His heart instantly started racing. His hands were sweating and he could barely turn the steering wheel. "Kobe...nigga quit playing." He jumped out with gun in hand and walked pass every self help garage opening. The first four were empty, when he made it to the fifth one he seen a puddle of blood. He almost pissed on himself. "Oh...my god...somebody help me." He screamed with his gun raised. He shook Kobe and his neck almost rolled off. Kane jumped back. "Kobe....no dog...who did this...oh my God...don't die on me dog...no." Kane cried for about an hour while he held his boy Kobe in his arms. HE felt like shit because he didn't even see it coming and there was no witnesses around. Kane had the music up so loud that when Kobe walked off to talk to them girls that's when it had to happen. Zero's face kept flashing before him but he was unsure. I mean Zero would shoot you in a heart but only a true professional would take the time to give somebody a Columbian neck tie (slice your throat). His thoughts were broken by the police shining a flash light in his face. How was Kane going to explain this one. A 9 Millie in his hand with his boy's neck halfway off. "Put your hands up...you have the right...." "No...No sir this is my boy. I didn't do it please...don't." Kane didn't realize that the gun was pointed right at the officer when he tried explaining and raising his hands. "B l o c k o w blah blah."

Chapter 51

"Downtown Skyway Theatre"

I'm so tired of going to the movies in the hood. Same shit is about to pop off and I can feel it. "Veronica....what are you doing?" I had dozed off and was thinking about what would happen if a gang war broke out. This menace to society" was thick with bangers (gang members). "Nothing...I'm in line to get the popcorn and candy." "How in the fuck are you in line...way over here by the damn exit door?" Zero was showing his ass because I didn't give him no pussy last night. He had me sitting at his Momma's for two hours and when his ass finally came he was buck eyed like a crack head with beads of sweat pouring off his face. When I returned to the movie and started walking down the aisle looking for Zero I got nervous. "What up folks....GD's up in this piece." Some dude in a blue rag said while throwing up pitch forks. "Shine...girl what you doing here." I didn't know where the voice was coming from because it was so dark. I almost pissed my pants thinking that Low and his boys was in here. Zero had that big ass 44 on him so if any nigga got out of line they was sure going to die. "Sunshine..." "Oh shit...Zero you scared me." "What are you jumping for...that nigga ain't in here." He grabbed my hand and made me sit down. "One-tray- duce....shot gun cri I p....Cali love niggas." T.T.M was on some banging bullshit. It was so loud that we couldn't hear the movie start. Everyone started whistling and clapping when the movie started. Y'all niggas need to shut the fuck up...I paid my loot so I want to watch this shit." Hell Girl's baby daddy Corn said while telling all the homeboys to be quiet. This was the part I hated because we couldn't never do shit by ourselves. "You ok....baby...why you mugging niggas." Zero knew I wasn't feeling all of this. The police was in the lobby locking for suspects of a murder that took place a couple of days ago. When Phat Boy and his crew whispered it to Zero, his whole attitude changed. "I'm not bugging baby....but it's off the chain in here." He looked around and we watched Phat boy set trip with the Champagne Queens. I haven't seen Princess in a couple of years but she was still the same. Messy then a mother fucker. "Blood love....what's up Phat Boy....you a crab or a donut now nigga....you don't hang with family no more." He didn't take her fronting him off lightly Zero sensed it as they argued. "Yo....T.T.M...lets dip out Cuz." Zero didn't wait for my response, he just snatched me like a rag doll. I stumbled over people as he pushed and shoved me. "Ah, Zero....boy I'm spilling pop all over my Nike suit shit." "Through that shit away..." Zero started skipping to exit when he heard gun shots ring out. "Zero...oh my god...I can't see nothing." I could feel the heat from bullets fly past my head. I was stumbling over people as they screamed. "Stop talking so damn girl...come on." Zero looked like some Mafioso right out the godfather movie. His gun was silver plated and pointed at anyone who made a false move. The police patrolling the room didn't even matter to him. He was trying to get to that damn truck. When we made it to the parking ramp, Zero took off running. "Wait boy...damn...somebody might shoot me." He ignored me and kept running I could hear the police sirens and ambulance picking somebody in front of the movies. When I made it to the truck I could see him bent over like he was putting something away. "What are you doing on the damn floor...boy." I screamed so loud he bumped his head on the ash tray. ""Girl...stop fucking screaming, shit...you want the Po Po's to start harassing our ass." He was real irritated for some reason. We pulled up to the ramp window. Zero handed the attendant the parking ticket. The young boy was all up in the truck. "Hey...you sure do have a balling ass ride man... what kind of TV is that...oh dog...damn is that a Nintendo...ooh...is that a radio with out a face on it." "Hey mother fucker, quit clocking my shit." Zero pushed the animated boy back and muffed him in the face. Zero...chill..he's just admiring you." The boy put his head back in the booth and frowned up. "Nah, that's what I'm saying...you don't be up on shit like this...niggas will rob your ass girl." He pushed my arm back. The boy held his hand out to try and tell us the price. "Mother fucker, you think I'm playing with your ass" Zero said while swinging on the boy. Thank God he stuck his head back in on time because Zero's hand hit the door instead. As loud as it sounded, it would of given the boy a black eye for sho. "Zero stop" I screamed and pushed him in the head. "You'll fuck around and go to jail down here." He looked at me and shook his head. "You ain't built for this shit Veronica... I thought you was smarter than that." "What the fuck do you mean nigga?" Oh, I see...yeah... overlay for the underplay- start an argument so you can go fuck one of your hoes." The young boy chuckled until Zero looked at him. "How much is it nigga? ain't shit funny" he said. "$21.05 sir." He pulled out a fifty and handed it to him. "I ain't your fucking sir... sir is a white folks term nigga... you better recognize." The boy tried handing Zero his change." Let the gate up mother fucker, you slow or something?" "I was tryin to give you your change sir, I mean dog" the boy said. "I see you catch on fast, that's what I'm talking about...keep that shit and go buy yourself something to eat. Shit, I know your ass is hungry" Zero said while laughing. Zero swerved off and I ignored his ass while he bumped Mary J. Blige's "What's the 411" . I loved me some Mary. She had that "ghetto love" on lock. Zero knew just what to do to get me in the mood. As we road around downtown, Zero kept the music bumping. I guess he didn't want to holler at anybody. Everybody and their daddy was trying to get his attention. When I reached over to tell him that T.T.M and all the homeboys that were at the movies with us, were trying to get his attention, he blew me off. This was his funny style mode. He acted this way when something was wrong. I watched out the window as he drove up 7th Street to Plymouth Ave. This was shocking because I still knew we were a secret. I mean, the only person that I didn't want to see us was Low. As funny acting as he was, I shouldn't have cared, but I did. We were going out to Golden Valley, an upscale area where a lot of rich people lived. Some blacks live out there too, but not many. He stopped at a park that was very dark. I got a little nervous because this could mean death. I mean, I haven't done anything to him but I knew he was nothing to fuck with. He parked and turned the music down. "So Ms. Sunshine... tell me, where do we stand?" he asked. His eyes looked like worry was beating him in the head. "We stand where ever you want to baby" I said. "Don't give me that baby shit girl" he snapped. He held my chin in his hand and dug his nails into my cheeks. "OOOUCH...stop Zero" I screamed. He grabbed my legs and jerked me towards him. "Nah... I think yo ass like getting beat or something" . "No... no I don't... stop... please" I begged. I should've known sooner or later he was going to flip out. No man on this earth is going to keep your pockets fat and except you being with the next nigga. He hasn't tripped in a while so I took him for granted. "Yeah... you like when I trip" he said. Before I knew it, he slapped the spit from my lips at least three times before I started fighting his ass back. I felt a little sorry for him at first, but then I had a flashback of all the times Bull whooped on me and made me piss on myself. "You mother fucker" I screamed as I snatched the remote for the stereo and beat him in the head with it. "Why are you doing this Zero... you don't love me?" I cried. I kept fighting him until he punched me in my chest and almost knocked the breath out of me. "Stop... girl..." "No... you stop." I love you... Sunshine ...and you keep playing me... I give you everything... and you play me." He was screaming like a mad man. I was so scared that I tried jumping out of his Suburban. "Touch that mother fucking door and I'm going to blow your face off" he threatened. The chrome 44. was right in my face. He had it hidden in his secret compartment and I forgot all about it. I was breathing heavy but I wasn't stupid enough to touch the door." "What?" I said as I sat back in the seat. "I'm listening now." "Oh now, you'll listen when I draw the heater." I was sniffing and swallowing snot. "you pointed it at me... you're No different then Bull." The mention of Bull's name in the same sentence as his pissed him off. "No the fuck I didn't he screamed." I told you I would blow your head off if you leave me. I just continued to cry and shook my head. I was so mad at myself for fucking with him. What made me think this dope boy would be any different. Pussy whippin a nigga is always unsafe, shit, at this point it could have been deadly. "I'm tired of this shit Zero" I said. "I am to girl, you not going nowhere" he said while looking at me. "I already told you what I'll do to you if you leave, so you need to prove to me how down you are." This meant that he wanted me to put in some work and I told him before that I wasn't with that. "So how am I supposed to do that" I asked with an attitude. He looked at me for a minute, then said "you got to put fear in one's heart."

Chapter 52
"Thangs Done Changed"

It was Sunday morning and for some reason I felt like church. It had been so long since I went to church but at this time I really needed it. "Yo Annie... let's go to church." By it being so early in the morning she wasn't feeling me. I guess Tricky had been on her nerves so much that she was cool on him. She hadn't been talking about him lately and he hasn't been around. His name stood for itself because a trick he was. He hung out with Butchy and his crew. They always jump on him about buying tainted pussy. So one day I asked them what did they mean by that. They all busted up laughing and said, anybody that has the bottom knocked out of it. If you can't feel no walls. Well I'm glad I still have mines. His name also meant that he was trifling and shady. He always befriended people and then about a month later you ask him where is the person that you was just running with, he'll get to mumbling or just straight up ignoring you. Then the rumors spread that he has jacked about 6 people at gun point. I tried telling Annie that he was bad news. Her being her, she flipped it on me and told me that I had no room to talk. She had a point. I didn't have no room to say shit, so shut up. "Annie...get up." When I went into Victor's room she was knocked out next to Victor. I shook the both of them. "Um...Mommy...I'm sleepy...I don't want to get up...Um...Mommy." "Stop crying boy....get in there and go pee. My little son was sure going to be something in life. His little butt can fin for himself already at four years old. I guess that comes from being an only child. "Annie...come on....get up...girl, I want to go to church while I got this feeling...where is QT and Fox?" She finally woke up. "Damn girl....it's too early for you to be in a good mood...QT should be in the front room or the basement." "Where is Fox...hot ass at...I'm going to bust her head if she keeps fucking with that Polo." Annie got up and took her shower. While she got dressed, I laid out Victor's Docker slacks and striped shirt to match. I had so many hootchie clothes that I was going to have to piece some things together. Even though I dressed appropriately for college, I still felt there was nothing that I could set off for church. So I settled with a long skirt, lace up high heel, open toe shoes and a tight fitting Chanel tank top. I had a money green leather Escada jacket to go over my outfit because it was real chilly. "QT…where is Fox?"…get your ass off of my couch like that girl." I had to pick my Oriental pillow off of the floor. I really hated for people to sleep on my custom made furniture. This hoe don't know shit about no money so I see why her ass was sleeping on my shit all sloppy. "Dang Shine…your ass up and straighten up my shit…you obviously like me shit…you keep bringing your ass over here." She got up with an attitude. I went to get myself together. After getting Victor ready and watching Annie tackle with her weave ponytail. It dawned on me that I didn't have any money on me. After me and Bacon went around collecting my money, I dropped it off at the safe house. When I made it to my room, my gut feeling told me that something was wrong. I checked my panty drawer to see if I had 5 g's in there for the sackers. Being in the game, you have to always keep at least a thousand dollars laying around so if somebody robs you, they might think twice about killing you. "Where in the fuck is my money" I screamed at the top of my lungs. "QT….Annie….Victor." I was wrong for that. I know damn well a four year old didn't take 5 thousand damn dollars. "Chill….girl….it's Sunday remember." Annie had jokes and I wasn't trying to hear it. "My money is gone out my room and I want to know who been in here stealing." QT had a scary look on her face but she didn't look guilty. Annie had a look of, I know you better not even think that I did no hoe shit like that. "What." "What do you mean what Annie…girl 5 g's is gone like it got legs and just walked off." I don't go in your room for nothing and why in the fuck would I take from you." "Nah…hold up dog…I know you didn't take shit…that's not what I'm asking you….I said who been in my room?" Annie or QT didn't want to sat Fox so they got quiet. "So you don't know neither QT?" "I mean I never go in there without your permission but you know Fox always gets clothes for us out of there." I didn't want to think my little sister clipped me. Every rumor the hood had been saying was true. That nigga Polo done turned my sister out. Either she was letting him pimp her or she stole to put herself on. "So you seen Fox in here yesterday?" I asked. Before she could answer, Victor said "Mommy…my…my auntie bought me a G.I. Joe and us some new Jordans."

My eyes was blood shot red. I knew it was her. How in the fuck did she 15 years old to buy my baby anything- some fucking Jordans at that. I gave her ass everything. She had no reason to steal from me. "Come on….Victor let's go start the car." They were shocked at my instant change in attitude. I wanted to kill Fox. I, not going to tell my Mom because she'll wander where in the hell did I get 5 g's anyways. I should call up Percy and let him know. My dad and I weren't that close but at this time I need to know where in the hell was Fox. If he asked why I'm looking for her then I'll tell him. If he doesn't then I won't. "QT if Fox calls find out where she is and tell her she better not let me catch her ass because I know she got my shit." Annie walked past me and went to the car. "Ok!" Um Veronica I would never do that to you…and I don't think Fox did it neither." "Look QT don't try saving Fox's ass you know and I know that nigga Polo her up to it…. I ain't stupid. That….I keep telling y'all to save your virginity until you get married. Once you give that up and get turned out, it's over. The nigga will have your ass robbing banks. "As I jumped in the car and pulled off. Annie and I noticed that same Taurus sitting down the street from the house. We didn't even have to speak a word, I just drove right up on the car. Sure enough when I came closer to the car it was a man and a women sitting there watching us roll by. We just shook our heads and made a mental note of what they look like. After ridding around for an hour to try and figure out what church to go to. I decided to go over North on Plymouth and Owens. I can't remember the name, I think it's called Salem Baptist. Victor was getting irritated by the crowd, so we walked across the street to another church. It was ok for what we were there for, but on a more organized day we would have stuck with Reverend McAfee. I was more familiar with that Reverend because he use to mentor us at The City Inc., an Alternative High School. The City was good for me, but thinking about it reminded me of that nigga Bull and right now wasn't the time to have his ass on my mind. God was my main focus this morning. We went in and took a seat right in the middle. All eyes were on us. I could tell they had dollar signs on their minds because smiles spread across their faces as they looked us up and down. "Hi baby….what brings you to the Lord's house today." A lady with a all blue skirt outfit said to me. "Oh mamma...Uh I was just feeling him that's all." Annie turned her lips up. "Why do you ask...do you want us to leave or something." She looked at Annie with a little hate for being questioned. "No...oh no baby.....I was just asking because I never seen you here before." Annie shook her head. "I use to come here when I was a little girl...but I see nothing has changed." I nudged Annie and gave her the eye. The Reverend was preaching about lying, stealing and cheating. I guess it hit me in my heart because I cried uncontrollably. I felt heat all through my body I was never one of those people that acted a fool in church. I don't like when people perform. You never know when it's real. My Mom always said when someone has the Holy Ghost you don't ever question it. You know it and God let's you know you have it. So will everybody else. He told me it was in me because I couldn't shake the feeling of his presence all around that church. It was time for us to put our offering. I seen Annie go in her purse and put 20 dollars in there. Whispering I said "Why did you put 20 in there....you got to put 10 % of your earning or close to it." She rolled her eyes and put 60 more in there. "If you put 10% you would never know what 10% is....plus this is blood money and god knows where it comes." My heart dropped to my feet. It didn't down on me that god knows everything you do before you do it. He's definitely present when you're doing good or bad. "It's ok baby...put whatever your heart desires...because he's going to bless you anyways....you god's child and he knows you're hurting baby....he hears you." I cried even harder. The sister of the church put a lot on me. I'm glad Victor was knocked out because I would have to explain why I was crying. After I pried my purse from under Victor's little body. I put $200 in the offering plate. I should of just put $2000 but I didn't have it on me. The sister made me and Annie stand up and say our names and tell a little about ourselves. I seen some known crack heads in there so I didn't want to talk too long. Guilt was coming at me in every form. I'm strong though and I knew the battle wasn't mines. Church was over and Victor was irritated and crying. I picked him up and we headed to the car. "Yo...hay....Shine." That voice sounded too familiar. As I turned around I almost lost my tongue. "Hi Dirty Red...oh my goodness." He walked over and gave me and Victor a hug. "You look so good Red...man...have you been to treatment?" Annie said what's up and took Victor out my hands and walked to the car. Me and Dirty Red talked for about 20 minutes. Victor started honking the horn and Annie thought that was so funny. "I'm glad to see that you got yourself together and I wish yo the best." "It's a struggle baby girl...a don't call me Dirty any more....I love you like a little sis and I want that name to stay in the past...ok." I gave him another hug. "I understood...God bless you...Red." We walked away from each other with big smiles like a never ending story.

Chapter 53

"Valentine's Day"

Damn its taken me forever to find a parking spot. "I know Veronica...well oh well I'm going to get the same custom made beget earrings and the bracelet and Chain to match...what you think Annie?" "She going to like whatever you buy her Zero...nigga you going all out...ha ha you must be up to something....a there goes a spot right there." Annie said while pointing. This nigga is really whipped shit Veronica better take advantage of this situation because I'm kind of loving us rolling around with his hot ass. "Come on let's check out Goodman's Jewel or the wholesale Diamond Exchange you know they always have a deal." Um hum see his ass still going to be cheap but I'm going to get my home girl the matching tennis bracelet for the ankle as well. We went all over downtown MPLS to find this damn girl a nice present. I'm going to tell her ass she owes me big time for this. "Zero lets just get her some clothes or something....I'm tired of walking." He copped an attitude. "Damn this is your girl...I thought you would be glad I'm hooking her up....shit what kind of friend are you." He kept talking mad shit all through the mall. People kept looking at us like we were a couple or something. Thank God he wasn't my man. I didn't see how Shine could hang with his ass because he snaps out over shit and it ain't even that serious. "Annie...come look at this...Damn why your ass got to sit down at every store we go to huh...you're lazy...shit. I'm going to have to watch that." Oh shit I don't want him to cut my paper off, he might think I'm not loyal. "I'm sorry Dog....I was just in deep thought...oooh let me see." As I reached out to pick the earrings, chain and bracelet up, I seen another one I liked. "Look at this one Zero." The old man looked a little nervous because Zero had a Du rag on his heads and was sagging with a Crip rag in his back pocket. "Excuse me, mam, can you sit down before I show you that piece please." I knew it. This white mother fucker thought because a nigga had a certain look that we were here to jack his shit. "What you trying to say old man..." Zero pulled a fat ass knot out. "Nigga...I got 15 g's on me to buy my beautiful Queen a banging ass set." His gold teeth didn't make it any better. The old man's eyes almost popped out of his head when he called him a nigga. "No...No sir I'm just saying..." "Saying what nigga....I came to spend money and this is how you treat me...me...Rockma Dupri." He got to waving his hands and causing a whole fuss. Every white person in the place had disappeared. "Calm down...Ze...Rockma...chill boy." I grabbed him. "You know you will go back to jail." That must of hit home because he through his hands down. "Fuck this shit." He through all the money down and walked off. The old man helped me pick it up. I watched him like a hawk. "Mam...I'm sorry....I'm not a racist...please believe me." You could tell all he had was money on his mind because when he handed me the money, I had to damn near snatch it out of his hand. "I'm not the one should be trying to convince...sir...just let me see that set...with all them big ass diamonds." He pulled out every one of a kind diamond set he had. He even pulled out sets that weren't on display. I ended up spending 7 g's on earrings, bracelets and anklets. It wasn't my money hell. Zero threw it down like it was trash. The man gave me free jewelry cleaner and a life time cleaning guarantee and on anything broken. He walked me over to where Zero was sitting. "Sir I'm sorry for making you feel uncomfortable." "Oh yeah does that mean yo gave me a damn discount then?" Zero said while standing over the White man. "Yeah...yeah and I also gave her a lifetime guarantee on anything that breaks." "Um hum I said a discount nigga!" The man still didn't understand why Zero kept calling him a nigga so he kept frowning and backing up. "I did...sir, I gave her a one of a kind set...I'm sure you'll like it....if not then you can bring it back." Zero smiled "Aright....I like how you said sir...I see when I called you a nigga that made you feel uncomfortable...that's how I felt...shit." Zero snatched the box out of my hand and walked off. Leaving the old man there looking stupid. I swear that nigga has calmed down and if this would have happened 6 months ago, he probably would've hit that old man. On our way back to the car, we ran into that nigga Low. I tried my hardest to not let that nigga see me. "Boy...a...a....Annie come here girl." Zero look real hard and he recognized him. With that big ass grin on his face I knew he had something up his sleeve. "Go see what that nigga want." Zero told me while nudging me in Low's direction. I walked over to him with Zero in ear shot of us. "Where's my baby girl at....see what I got her." He had a box of candy, a big human size card that said "no matter what, you are my soul mate." A dozen of roses and a small box. "Oooh that's nice, she'll like that." Zero stepped a little closer "What you got in the box dog?" Damn Zero was pushing it. "Oh....this yo man or something Annie?" Low looked a little suspicious about Zero asking him questions. I couldn't budge to say a word. "Nah dog she's a friend helping me pick my girl something out." Shit, this made me feel real uncomfortable. "Um oh....well...I got my girl this." He pulled out a baby looking tennis bracelet with a matching ring. The diamonds were so small they looked like sand rocks. I turned my head because I knew Zero was about to blast his ass. "Oh...nigga....who ever yo broad is.....she going to be mad cuz....let me show you how to do it. Zero opened up the box with the matching set that would blind a nigga a block away. "Um...yeah...that's raw, but I don't got it like that Joe." "Nigga, my name ain't joe.....you got that cuz!" I knew Zero wanted to whoop Low's ass right on the spot and Low had no understanding." I'm not tripping with you man." Low said while walking off. "Later Annie...tell my baby to be at the crib in bout an hour." "O.k., bye Low." I grabbed Zero so he couldn't say another word. They both walked backwards staring each other down. Shine just didn't know that these two will have it out one day.

Chapter 54
"Low's Thoughts"

I know damn well that was that nigga Rock. I swear, if I ever see that shit on her neck, hands or wrist, I'm going to cut it off her. I'm going to have them Crip nigga's robbed. What, he thought cause he got this shit sold up in Minnesota that I'm supposed to back down... I'm a mother fucking Gangsta! Damn, I should have bought her a bigger bracelet though. That nigga been fucking my bitch. Rachel told me she always see Veronica sneaky ass with him all the time. I should set her up like she asked me to. She wants to be in her house one day so she could kill her. The only reason why I wouldn't is because I love her. I didn't want to risk Victor being there either. That bitch Annie is down with it. She's the one that hooked them up with her want to be crip ass. I got her though...

Chapter 55
"Zero's Thoughts"

Before long beautiful will be mines. What the fuck did that nigga think? I'm every inch of my dick down. Plus when she gets her mind right a hundred g's and a new crib will make her ass choose up. If that nigga keeps playing, I'm going to have one of the homies from the city smoke his ass...

Chapter 56
"Annie's Thoughts"

I'm real tired of Veronica and her orders. Maybe everybody is right. When she say "jump" I do. I'm tired of doing her damn foot work shit. I mean she does look out for me. I live room and board free. It really ain't her fault that I spend my money on boy (heroin) dro(weed). Shit, if I would of spent that 70 g's I had saved at my Mom's I could of started my own nursing pool like I've always dreamed of. I don't know maybe Bunny,

YoYo, Ty and Wonnie are just jealous of our friendship. Ty especially is a hater. She'd always fucking people's man and shit. Her and Wonnie needs to be sisters cause I swear they're in a race to see who could fuck the most nigga's and stay broke. Well I'm just going to stay on board until this ride is over.

Chapter 57

"Valentine's Night"

"Veronica…come here…I got something for you baby." Damn I told Annie to act like I wasn't home. How in the fuck am I going to explain why I got this fucking teddy on under this full length black sable coat. Whispering I called out to Annie "Annie a…..tell him I left." "No….bitch he's going to whoop your ass…please Shine…put some clothes on." "No…go stall him…I'm going to the Fantasy Suites with the Jungle room theme, no …..no I'm bout to get dick down good." "Oh….no….he's coming up the stairs Shine…get in the closet." I jumped in the closet and put all my new clothes over me. I wasn't bout to let Low fuck me out my beget diamonds Annie told me about. "Where she at?" He busted up in the room "She gone Zero…oh I mean Low she gone---" I head him punch Annie. So I jumped out the closet. "Get off of her…you bitch ass nigga." I clawed him in his eye and my titties popped out all over the place. "Oh so bitch you thought I wasn't coming through hoe…I knew you was tryin to get with that nigga." Low beat the brakes off of my ass. My nails tore down to the meat around my cuticles. My hair weave was shifted every which way and my lip looked like I had a pound of seafood. We fought so hard Annie had to call the police. Thank god Low ran up out the house before they got there. I gave them a fake name because I didn't wanna see his stupid ass go to jail. I got back in the shower and fell right to sleep. Any other time I would of ran to the man of my dreams but my pussy needs a rest and I knew Zero wouldn't give it to me. What a way to spend Valentine's Day. All alone by choice not force. Um hum hoes with they could have it my way. Damn thangs really done changed.

Chapter 58

"Making Choices"

The last day of treatment oh I'm so glad. I have my twelve step program down. I'm hoping like hell we leave on a good note. I feel sorry for Tara, Flow, and Penny. I really got attached to them. For what it was worth!. "Ms. Gittens are you ready to do your presentation?" I knew Ms. Wise would pick to do mines first. "Yes....I sure am." I started off with Serenity prayer. "GOD grant me the serenity to accept the things I can, and the wisdom to know the difference." I gave all my twelve reasons of why I should involve myself into drugs. At that Moment I felt like a hypocrite. Here I was faced with my own reality of being a dope mans girl. These people problems were beginning to wear me down. I broke down into tears. "What's wrong Ms. High and Mighty...the guilt shame devil dancing on your head...ha ha, is it getting to heavy for you?" "Shut up Tara...she's a solider, she's young, she's going to figure it out." "Yeah..yeah Tara you always take up for her...yall must be lovers or something." "Hold up...Strawberry...the neighborhood hoe...you gave me fuck ...on um I mean I messed up." Looking at Ms. Wise I couldn't disrespect her so I changed my tune. "I understand you don't like me Flow but you will respect me ok!" She rolled her eyes and put her head down. "I understand that you're mad because I chose to sale dope instead of using dope. This ain't no joke to me. Shit I have a money addiction! I can't function if I don't fuck two or more men and in so many words I'm a prostitute in a classy way." And how is that Ms. Gittens?" I don't fuck...oh I mean mess with no nigga that ain't movin weight (kilo's) and if I hear he's a trick, I'm on him like free cheese." "So you know that's not cute Veronica?" I had to gather myself again because my voice was cracking." "Nah...Ms. Wise, I'm full aware of what I'm doing and I'm proud of it to a certain extent... I mean I always felt numb to men and it's all a game. They play by my rules and my rules only." "So what if you get some psycho...or an abusive man like Bull" Penny was pushing me because she knew me. I know Mya told her a lot of my business. She was more respectful and closer to her then Myrecal was. "I've been there many times Ms. Danyels...I'm sure you heard!" "I have but the rest of your cohorts haven't." I gave them the story about Bull, Zero and Low. The abuse that I've been through with all of them. The fact that they've all abused me in different ways. All these older women taught me a lot. I must of taught them as well because there wasn't a dry eye in the house and everyone asked me for advice on overcoming my addiction. "Thank you Veronica. I'll be giving you your certificate today so I advise you to take it right to your P.O." "Thank you Ms. Wise and all you beautiful women that I've come to meet." Everyone stood up to hug me even Flow. She finally seen that I wasn't the stuck up bitch she thought I was. I finished listening to everyone else's story and left. When I made my way to the P.O's office I was in a good mood. She let me know that I had one year left as long as I didn't get into any trouble. I showed her my certificate and let her know I'll be finishing my degree in Fashion Management. I had a felony at the time but if I successfully complete my probation then I'll get dropped to a misdemeanor. That was cool as hell. I won't have to explain to none of them white folks about my past. Even though the Fashion Industry has a gang of corrupt people working in it and I probably wouldn't have to be squeaky clean. I will still feel good to not have a felony record.

Chapter 59

"At Queeny House"

"Shine...girl...I got us a ticket to go down to the freaknik...you game." I was stretched out on my auntie's couch watching the Real World. I wasn't even into it all like that because of the freaky shit that go on down there. "How much are the tickets?" "Damn cousin...you got the paper! Why are you trippin...plus I got the room too!" She was up to something and I was about to find out. "Why...Queeny...why yo ass want me to go...come clean little cuz." She watched me walk to the refrigerator to get me a glass of Kool-Aid. "Um...I just want to make sure somebody there got my back." "Um hum...and yo home girls don't got you're back..you shouldn't be fucking with them." All....man...you always be trippin Shine...you always coming with that street ethic stuff....why can't you just have a little fun."

She never understood me when It came to friends and family. Zero always thought I wasn't paying attention but I was full aware of what was going on in my surroundings. "Yeah…I'll go but who's going with us." She started smiling and I knew I wasn't going to like it. "Well me and you are flying together but Tiff, Shar and Chyna will be there when we get there." Memories started running through my mind. Chyna was one person I didn't want to be associated with. She was a swinger, stripper and home wrecker. I also heard she was into setting nigga's up and killing them. If I'm going to be in the same presence as her I'm going to make sure it's known that I'm rollin with Qweeny and Qweeny only. "I don't know Qweeny…I mean you know I don't fuck with hoes like that plus I don't think Zero would want me around Chyna." She frowned up. "You sho be worried about Zero would for him not to be your man…shit what's up with Low?" "He's around." "He ain't your man now let me know cause it sounds like my big cuz is losing her pimpin skills shit." I busted up laughing. "You're funny girl…I'll never ever loose my skills girl." "Ok….that's what I'm talking about." "When we leaving stupid?" I said while putting her in a playfully head lock. "Tomorrow…so go pack up." "Damn thanks for the notice….Hailey ha ha." She threw a pillow at me as I was heading for the door. "Don't call me that…you know I hate that V-E-R-O-N-I-C-A <u>Taper."</u> I kept laughing on my way to the car. "Taper don't bother me…my pimp uncle gave me that name….R.I.P to him baby." "Whatever just be here tomorrow at 8:00 our flight leaves at 10:30 and you know we got to be there by 9:30." "Aight Hailey." She slammed the door and stuck her tongue out as I pulled off.

— Later that Night —

I made it home to a nasty house. I was pissed off to see Fox's bag of dirty clothes on my floor. I wasn't washing her shit and she stole from me. My dad caught her at his house one day when he was at work. She spent 2 g's of my money and he found the rest of it. Returning it to me he had a thousand questions about how I had so much money. I gave him a story of how my male friends gave it to me for school. He knew that it was a lie but so what. Shit what was he going to do to me, whoop me? No shit I'm grown. "QT...you talk to Fox?" I said while walking into my room watching T.V. with Victor "no." She screamed with an attitude so I walked back to the front. "What's up..you pissed off about something cause I don't appreciate the slick way you said no." She looked up at me and set the remote down. "I wasn't being smart with you at all....but I don't think Fox stole it because Polo said she didn't." My blood shot straight to my head. I wasn't about to let Victor see me snap so I chilled. "You know what, you QT....you are so naive you know and since you act like I'm a damn joke and y'all take me for granted....get the fuck out." Annie came from out the basement. "What's up Shine." The smoke hit me right in my face. Ty, Barbie and Mya came running from the stairs "What's up Shine." "Yeah you be M.I.A. all the time." Ty and Mya had conversation I wasn't trying to hear. Maybe a vacation would be the perfect plan. "What's up y'all....Barbie when did you get up here. She was Ty's home girl from Texas. The home-boys named her Barbie because she looked like Barbie and was very stuck up. She could relate to me because her motive to get paid was similar to mines. "Girl I had to get out of that country town shit...Dallas's is slower than her plus I need to make some paper so I'll be here for a while." I totally forgot about me cursing QT and telling her to get out. She had little bag in her hand and bent over to give Victor a kiss. As she wiped cookie crumbs off his mouth he started crying with her. "What's wrong?" Annie asked them while looking at them back and forth. Barbie, Ty and Mya was so high I had to snatch that blunt up. "Ooh...girl, what you doing...you're on probation." Damn just like that I forgot. "Ooh Mya...girl why you pass it to me...shit." I was a little un-focused but I felt good. "Shit fuck it now...you done hit it now." Everybody kept laughing except QT and Victor. I felt a little bad because Victor had fun with Fox and QT but I had to teach her a lesson. "Quit cryin yall....Victor you're going to granny's for a couple of days and QT...I'll take you home and when I get back I'll come back and get you ok?" She nodded her head. "Annie you wanna go to the ATM with me?" Everybody looked at me wondering why I didn't ask them. "Why you going there?" Mya ask. "Yeah dog what's down there?" Barbie said while passing me the blunt. "I'm straight Barbie." I didn't want to make it worse. "I'm going to the Freaknik." The whole house got loud. "All bitch we wanna go." Everybody knew if I went they wouldn't have to pay for shit. "Nah...dog...I got to be there to make sure the paper is straight....I'll watch Victor if you want." I was going to be gone for four days. My son would need to be with my Mom. She would come pick him up anyways, so I'll save her the trip. "I'm cool...he's going to his granny's house...a did Zero or Low call?" Everybody was still looking for their investigation. "What's up Shine?...we wanna go!" "Yeah...who's all going?" I wasn't going to mention Chyna's slimy ass until I got there. "I'm going with Queeny but some of her friends are going to be there." Annie turned her nose up. "Oh...I'm cool dog..I don't do bitches that I don't know to much...Queeny is cool but the other I can't roll like that." "aight cool....you ain't got to rub it in girl....I just need a vacation." "Good...do that...I got you on this end...Zero called and said call him ASAP....Low came by but he left looking for you." "Yeah he seen a house full of hoes and left." "Yeah what was that all about?" Barbie said while raising her eyebrows. "He don't like me hanging with a bunch of people and he sho don't like a bunch of company." "He must be dicking you good girl." Oh no I'll never disclose my man's bedroom business. "Whatever he's doing, yall ass won't know, believe that." They all busted up in laughter. I finished getting myself together. I paged Zero like three times and he didn't call back. So to save myself sometime I took Victor to my Mom's. Everybody wanted to ride with me, so I made them think I had something to handle so they stayed at my house. I let Annie know that I didn't want any company before I left. I don't know what it is but everybody thinks my house is the Do Drop Inn Hotel. I'm going to have to let them know when I get my new house it ain't going down. I appreciate the love but damn nigga's act like they don't want to go home. I made it to my Moms at around 10:00PM. Still no damn Zero. "Hay Mom...I need a vacation so I'm going down to Georgia for the Freaknik...will you take Victor for about a week?" She was ending her phone call. "Let me call you back girl...Veronica is talking crazy ....ok....ok girl has...bye." Mom must have been sick of that conversation because she never get's off the phone that soon. "Girl...what does that say right there Veronica huh? Anything that has to do with freakin is dangerous girl....I tell you....you come up with some crazy things." Damn If I thought I was going to get lectured I would of just skipped the freaknik part and just told her ATL. SO much for being honest. "Mom it's cool...I need a beak ok." "Ok...Girl as long as my grandbaby is here, take as much time as you want baby." I took Victor off the couch and put in his room. Even though he had his own room at Mom's, some how in the middle of the night he'll end up in the bed with my Mom and Terry. I really respected my Step Dad. He never says much of anything. I guess that's because he says it all to my Mom and she get's on me about everything. Right when I pulled from my Mom's Zero calls my phone. I didn't want him to know where I was so I stop at the Amoco on Lexington and University in St.Paul. "What's up." "Damn girl....where you at and why it take you so long to call me back." "Nigga don't play ..you haven't answered my calls at all so don't be trippin about where the fuck I been shit...I'm bout to dip to the Freaknik anyways." I could tell he was doing something or somewhere he shouldn't of been because he was talking shit to somebody in the background. "Girl...I know that damn.....I was tryin to give your smart ass mouth ass some money damn." I sat quiet for a minute because I need to recognize that voice in the background. "Hello....Hello...yo stop touching me." "Who In the fuck are you talkin to Z E R O." I screamed at the top of my lungs. "Ah...oh um damn ah...fuck it, I'm at Nella's house." Now I don't know why his ass calls me from his bitches house. He knows I know exactly where they live. "Zero ...you got me fuck U-P...boy, I'm done fucking with you." "No...No Shine baby I love you....Ple...click." As I drove down the 94 highway the memories of my last recovery meeting. The thoughts of me admitting the fact that I was addicted to sex and money, I couldn't understand why. I pulled up to my crib and Zero beat me there. HE had a lot of nerves to show up at my house and Low's car is parked right in front. I hopped out and headed straight for the door. I hope like hell that Low ain't looking out the window. "Wait...please...I'm sorry beautiful...just listen." I don't know what it is but when he calls me beautiful I get weak. "What...Rockma Dupri!." He looked at me real crazy. "Aight girl....I understand you're mad but don't get beside yourself." We both busted up laughing. "Shut up...I'm mad at you." I started trying yo go in the house. He grabbed me. "Oh un un….you ain't leaving without kissing me and no I ain't been kissing her." He knew me to damn well. "Give me some money nigga." I didn't need none but he was going to pay for playing games. "Here…" He broke me off a knot. "Smooch…I love you baby." He didn't want to let me go and neither did I. I was bold as hell to be kissing on Zero in front of my house but at the time I didn't give a fuck. Annie got rid of all that baggage. She knew I meant business about my house. I appreciated her for that. Low was knocked out on my bad so that's where I left him. I didn't want him knowing none of my business, he'll see me in the morning.

Chapter 60
"ATL Stomping"

"Shine…Shine girl get up." I rubbed my eyes and wiped the slob from my mouth. "What…damn why are you hollering at me girl." I had to stretch in my seat. I was tired from the morning sex Low made me give him. He was going to mess my hair up and hide my bags if I didn't give him some. It wasn't the same. He still could put it down but I didn't feel the same way about him. He gave his dick to too many hoes. "I'm not…but we are about to land." Damn we been on this plane for four hours…it seems like I been sleep for about two days." "I know ha ha…yo ass was snoring and you farted too." "Ha ha you stupid…quit lying girl." "Ha no…no for real you did a couple of times." I seen a group of niggas I thought I knew and looked back at them. "Don't worry…they didn't hear or smell you." "A h h…oh my goodness…ha ha you're stupid as hell…good looking out lil cuz." We made it off the plane. He told me that he had my paper and he heard I'll be staying with his girl Tiffany. See that's why I would never tell my plans to anyone because people know your business before you do. "Yo..Yo…yo lil Momma where you going?" Me and Queeny kept walking because the voice didn't sound familiar. "At Cuz…she acting fucked up cause she out of town…her ass wouldn't be doing that shit if da homeboy was here." I knew it was smart mouth ass Crip nigga's. "Come on Shine….we got to get on this train and it takes us to the point where the cabs and family picks you up." "Oh…ok…" I turned around to see who kept hollering at us.

"Wait Queeny let me holler at Big Boy and them." I stopped to talk to he homeboys. They were staying at some Radisson Hotel downtown on one of those Peachtree's. It seem like every street there was called Peachtree. We finally made it to our hotel. All I could do was talk how beautiful the people were down south. All the men said Hello mamma, Ms. Lady, Beautiful, Sexy, Sista Queen. WWhooo well I've never experienced that in my life, I'll fuck around and move down here just for the fact of the courtesy along will make me move. I grabbed me a bite to eat at the Wendy's that was downstairs from our room. Queeny walked off to leave my ass because she knew I was in for a surprise. When I walked in the room it was a gang of niggas and bitches with shopping bags all over the floor. The Dro hit me dead in my face as I closed the door behind me. "What the fuck is dis shit? I yelled at the top of my lungs. "What you thought this is girl…,it's the motha fucking freaknik….you know we bout to party." Joe said while he tried pumping his dick on my butt. "Boy." I pushed him back. "Don't fucking touch me…do you know who the fuck I fuck with?" The music went down and the whole room focused on us. "Fuck you bitch…I don't give a fuck about that shit…you came to get fucked hoe." "Fuck you bitch…I don't give a fuck about that shit…you came to get fucked foe." Before I knew it I spit dead on his shirt. All hell broke loose. "Oh…no nigga, let my cousin go." Me and Queeny fought his ass all across the room. "Stop…Stop Shine…let go of his hair." Fuck you hoes Tiff…yall hoes should be helping me." Shoe and Chyna was so high and worried about getting with some Miami niggas they thought we were playing. "Get out bitch…" Queeny threw his shit out the room because she paid for it. "Everybody that don't got no bidness here yall can go too…shit!" "Ah…come on Queeny…quit trippin…he was bought to pay for everything." "Chyna…me and my cousin got our own stacks we straight." "Yeah Chyna you go out there with them cause you're the one that brought them up here anyways." "You know what fuck yall stuck up bitches…I'm going to get my freaknik on…dis is the damn freaknik." Chyna yelled while slamming the door. After me, Shone and Tiff has a talk. I crashed out for a few hours while Queeny drove them all to the undergone to find something to wear. The next two days Chyna was M.I.A. We partied so hard at the platinum house, and hung out in Magic City's parking lot. I wasn't into watching no bitches strip but I got to give it to them, every kind of man was going up in the club. Parking lot pimpin was what we were doing. We saw so many nasty girls shakin titties, showing pussy and one girl was sucking her man's dick while a girl was eating her out in the middle of traffic jam. I seen enough sex for that vacation. Even though the Freaknik was the most talked about event from year to year, I might have to pass next time. Queeny enjoyed herself. So I did a good deed for her. Next time I'll make a better choice.

Chapter 61
"The Up and Up"

My mind was playing ticks on me this Friday morning. I know my message box didn't tell me that 3 of my workers got robbed. The other 2 told me they had money for me and one was from my boy Bacon that was ready to put me on to some new money. My whole body was hurting from hanging out in the ATL. It's been a whole week and nobody even knows I'm back in town. Every call Zero from Low and the rest of "how can I be down crew", had no clue I was in the house spending sometime with myself. My grandma always told me if you don't love or spend time with yourself nobody else will. Economics was kicking my ass and I had to study for a test. Annie had to put a code in to let me know every place she was calling from because I was really on some incognito shit. "Ring Ring....Hello...somebody call Shine?" I knew who it was but I was playing everybody. I was tired if being the damn charity friend. "A...yo man what's up?" The nervous caller said. "What's up Gen...the only time you and sweets call me mean's there's some funk popping off!" "Um oh...yeah....I got tied up and robbed while you was gone." "By who nigga...damn let me find out you're slippin on the hustle." Gen had a major crush on me. I could get him to slang anything I wanted but I never took advantage of that. I was full aware that the news was just as hard for him to tell it. Then it was for me to hear shit. "Nah...baby I'm not slippin. Niggas that I fuck with set me up." "Who was it and what kind of niggas do you fuck with that would do this to you?" He cleared his throat and coughed a little. I heard him getting a little down and my heart soften a little. "I was on my way to meet Annie to give her 5 g's of the 20 g's that owed you." Oh god I'm so glad they didn't get everything. "You there Shine?" "Yeah…go ahead." "On my way out the door my boy asked me to drop him off on Selby Ave. When we got there the block was hot so he didn't want to get out. He talked to me into taking him to the UFW to get something to eat. When we got there I seen that nigga Scrappy with his crew. I knew then they was on some bullshit because my boy started acting shady and stuttering. He jumped out and I had my head down dialing sweets number. When I put my head up one of Scrappy's boys had the 9 to my dome. "Damn where was your heater at and where is that dirty nigga you was droppin off?" I said really agitated. "He convinced me I didn't need one cause he had one. "That was stupid Gen…damn how you going to get the rest of my cheese…shit." "Chill out mean…damn don't act like I ain't never helped you out before. Girl a gang of nigga's be plotting to rob you. Them nigga's tied my ass up and beat me in the head with pistols and there fucking feet. Shit I love the shit out you. I don't ever want shit to happen to you. They tried getting you and Sweets address out of me." "Did you give it to them?" "Hell no." He yelled into the phone. I knew he wanted me more then anyone. I couldn't do it though. I had fucked Sweets a year before I met him. Plus I just felt him more like a brother. He tried convincing me that since I hook Sweets with Myrecal and she had a baby on the way by him. He thought it would work. I told him no because aside from Sweets, he fucked Ty and Mya. I wasn't taken their sloppy seconds never. They'll never get to say Shine fucked behind them. I'm the shit, nobody will get the chance to put my name in the dirt. "I told you mean I got your back…I'm serious." In this game you're going to have to take losses. So I guess I have to get use to this." "Aight…baby..as long as they didn't hurt you…I'm cool." A sigh of relief went through the phone. "Thanks Shine…I don't like when you're upset…how was the ATL?" "It was cool…I tell you about it over dinner, aight." "you cooking?" "Nah boy…your ass is taking me to Apple Bee's or Friday's." (laughing) "Girl you know your ass is don't never quit." "I know and I ain't starting no time soon." I ended my call with Gen and was very hesitant to call everybody else. Ciara gave me a story about Bunny's cousin going in her purse while she was sleep. Dangers money supposedly got taken by the police. I was glad that his paper had nothing to do with me because he own Zero and had been dodging him for about a month. I felt a little better when I got Bacon and Motors message. Motor was waiting on me to come pick up my dope and Bacon was ready to make 25 girls (25 g's). As I made myself get up and get dressed. I seen a letter on the table from Fox. She must of come by while I was gone. When I got back in town. My dad had her staying up at his house. She was caught with my money. It was in the same bills I had stacked. I promised my dad I wouldn't whoop her ass but I really wanted to beat the brakes off of her ass. Zero told me that, that's what I get. I was flossin in front of her too much without putting her on. Please...that's why he got the silent treatment this week. I threw her apology letter away. I was pissed off about everybody getting robbed while I was gone. On my way out the door I decided to call Low before I went looking for Zero. "Ring Ring." Damn the phone went dead after two rings. I told his ass to get a new cell phone. After trying him two more times I finally got him. "What's up boy?....you been calling me like crazy?" I could tell he was at some bitches house because she was hollering in the background. "Yeah...I been calling your ass all week..where have you been?" "It's over bitch!" A voice that sounded like Rachel. "It's over...who in the fuck is that Low?" "Man nobody...quit trippin." "Nah nigga you obviously told that hoe it's over....who is that Rachel?" He didn't answer right away. "Hello...nigga." "Damn that's what I'm talking about you don't ever respect a nigga." "Nigga please your ass don't even respect yourself...shit your dick is slung from MPLS to Chi Town nigga anybody out here can fuck you." "Oh so you feel like that huh." "Hell yeah...I don't know why I keep fucking your ass...Thank god you ain't gave me that package." "Oh so you going out like that huh...well good I'm bout to let Rachel pay me then" "Yeah young girl...you don't know what to do with a real man." "Tell that old bitch she got to pay nigga's with her fat hater ass. You stay the fuck away from me with you dirty dick." "Fuck you bitch...you ain't shit...you can't even give head right...you tell that nigga Zero he can have your old not knowing how to make a nigga have a nut ass…bitch…click." Oh this nigga didn't hang up with that bitch cheering his ass on! That was the OVERLAY FOR THE UNDERPLAY. Something is up and I'm bout to get to the bottom of it.

Chapter 62
"Wonnie's House Party"

"Wonnie girl where is your girl Shine at?"Nella's cousin asked. Wonnie had invited a bunch of hoe's I don't fool with so I didn't go. "Girl Shine got it going on….I'm not on her list of kicking it…I guess." Wonnie said sarcastically. "Oh…um I heard that her man Low got a baby on the way and that she be bringing all that work here from Cali for that nigga Zero." "Oh…for real well that's her…shit a real nigga wouldn't let his girl do no shit like that." "I know and I heard her girl Myrecal is trying to push up on Low. The only reason why he hasn't left her ass is because he's plotting to rob her." "…for how much…shit I didn't know she was balling like that. Um huh…what kind of friend is she." I heard she's getting a house built right now…that's what T.T.M and them nigga's be saying." "Yeah she is getting a house built..but Zero is buying it for her and she only fuck's with Low because he got some good head. Damn I'm going to have to tell her about that baby though." Now Wonnie was wrong for telling all my business to this bitch. She was so slow she couldn't get what she was fishing for info.

Chapter 63
"Meeting at the Hyatt Regency Hotel"

"T.T.M…cuz you been running your damn mouth to much. "What you talking bout now cuz….I told you I don't be saying shit on the phone nigga." He knows damn well he be on the horn talking to much. I'm sick of his ass. "Yeah….aight but if you ever get our ass indicted I'm a have something for your ass nigga." I felt the police presence. I know I'm getting to much money out here and I know their coming for my ass soon. "Quit all that politican and shit…yall niggas just count this money up so we can get them 50 kilo's on the road. Chico said in a irritating voice. "Yeah yall argue like yall ain't family or something. That ain't good to work like sat." Ricky said as he put a stack of money in the money counting machine. Zero gave T.T.M. a look that let him know to shut up. This was a major deal and he couldn't mess this up. This deal would set me Veronica and my family straight. I could sit down and let these youngsters handle this. "We work just fine cuz." "Yeah…we family right Zero?" "Of course." I'm getting tired of TTM but I can't let these nigga's know cause it could fuck up my paper.

Chapter 64

"Calling Zero"

"Hi baby…did you miss me?" I had to charm his ass since I've been dodging him for a week. "Yeah..uh come get me…I got to go find that nigga Danger…he ain't hollered at me in a minute." "Ok….where are you at?" "I'm at the homies crib right off of Broadway and 4th St.." "I'm on my way…click." Damn Zero sounded like something was really bothering him. I hope my baby isn't about to go to prison. Tears of fear streamed down my eyes because I knew my fun was about to come to an end. I got off of 94 highway on the Olson highway exit so I could see something. I rode up Glenwood Ave to Penn. That was a hot spot that always jumped. To my surprise the hooks (vice lords)had the spot blown up. I seen all of Zero's enemies out there. When they saw my truck coming I could see people holding there waists and throwing up there signs. I just bumped Prodigy's "Shook Ones" and kept it moving. I had a feeling that it was her beef or the popo that had my baby on the edge. Once I pulled up the homies crib Zero jumped off the step and jogged to the truck. "What took you so long?"He was looking around as I adjusted my seat belt. "Pull off girl…damn." "Ok boy…quit trippin…where are we going?" my heart felt a little fluttering because I could see worry all in his eyes. I got on the highway and had all the way to the Holiday Inn in Hopkins, MN every time I tried to say something. He would turn the music back up and stair at me. I knew he was packing his 9 milli so I felt a little nervous. When I pulled dup to the hotel he jumped out before I stopped the truck and signaled for me to come in.. After I grabbed my bags and walked towards the room. I seen a car full of crips pulling up T.T.M. was driving so Chat let me know they had been following us all along. "Zero did you know T.T.M. and the homies were following up." "Yeah...I always make sure somebody follows me...you just know catching on to that." He said while shaking his head and coming out of his clothes watching him pull his shirt over his head made me tingle instantly. I seen him chuckle as I watched him. Don't worry...you bout to get it." He grabbed his dick and dropped his jeans to the ground. "Him what makes you think that's why I was looking at you." He walked right over to me and stayed crying. "Oh..my goodness what's wrong Rock....I held him in my arms and subbed his head." Tell me please what's wrong baby." He continued to cry and burry his face in my stomach. "I tried baby...I'm confused and worried." About what....where is all of this coming from?" He pulled all of my clothes off of me and said laid me on the super king size bed. "Wait...what's wrong please don't shut me out like this Rock...tell me what's up." He laid on top of me with his Rock hard dick stuck to my leg. I was so horny but I had to know before we got into anything. "If I tell you....you have to promise me that you won't tell nobody." "I won't...I swear...I got your back I told you." "You know that nigga Pimp you use to fuck with?" "Yeah" "Well he got caught up...its like 12 niggas 4 girls on his case." "What's that got to do with you baby?" "Nothing but a gang of people he was fucking with I fuck with now and since they got indicted I know there going to go to talking." "How do you know baby?." Because this bitch Big Boy use to fuck with told him that Pimp is still jealous because she left him for Big Boy and he's snitchin on Big Boy and anybody else he use to serve." "Damn Big Boy was getting paper with Pimp?" "Yeah..yeah back in the day." "So Pimp told the bitch that Big Boy is indicted or something?" "Yeah Jo's baby daddy got indicted on that case and he told everybody who the informants were and said there watching us right now." "I felt my heart drop to my feet I guess he felt my heart beating faster because he tried assuming me that I wouldn't get indicted. "Don't worry..I would never involve you into anything." I started crying, thinking that my life was over. "Beautiful...you said you got my back....stop....stop....crying right now...Here I is this nigga is crying in front of my ass and now he's talking about stop crying." "I can't...I don't want to go to prison...I have a son and them damn mandatory minimums are given niggas buck Rodgers time for real." "ha...you crazy...Buck Rodgers I ain't heard that one in a minute." "I'm serious....Rock baby...you know niggas ain't no solider like you....you know niggas will tell everything they can on you baby." He put his head on my chest and softly sucked my titties. As he made it to my belly button, he made licked around it in circles. Turning me over he licked my hips from side to side while sucked all my juices out of me from the back. I grabbed the sheets and screamed out "Zero...I love you baby....please don't leave me." This made him aggressive because he lifted me up and down motion. My legs well shaking uncontrollably. After I came all over his face. He softly kissed me up my spine and entered me from the back. He held my waist and whispered in my ear. "Beautiful...I only trust you baby.... I got to tell you....I'm scared baby....I'm a killer.....I'm a dirty nigga...and you the only person I trust baby...If you ever cross me...." He opened up in this stroke. "Oh...Zero...you're hitting me." That made him hit it even harder. "I'm pony...girl...take it....take this dick." "Zero...please...it h-u-r-t-s...p-l-e-a-s-e." The gun fell off the bad and went off. "What was that." He jumped straight up off of me and ran to the window. His dick was brick hard and sticking straight out with a slight curve to it. After he noticed it was his gun that went off he tried getting back on me. "No....no baby....I can't take no more!" I rolled over and tried to close my legs. "ha ha all...baby you going to leave me hangin." "Nah just let me take a break." We laid there and shifted off to sleep. The next morning I couldn't get the things that he said to me out of my head.

— One Month Later —

"What's up Wonnie?." I was real furious because her fake ass went and told some Pimp nigga that I said he has aids. "Oh..ah nothing....what's up?" "Have you talk to Mya's baby daddy lately?" "Yeah why." She was getting an attitude so I know she was guilty. "Well I seen him at the club last night and he told me that you told him I said he had aids." "Um yeah...I did say that." "You know what ....Zero always told me you was a hater." "SO...you listen to Zero now huh...he ain't even you man." "So the fuck what.....he got my fucking back that's what I know ...you foul as hell. What if that nigga would of slapped the piss out of my ass...he could of easily rolled my ass up and you didn't even give a fuck." She sat guilty and let me went. "I didn't mean to tell him but you know I fucked him so I wanted to know." "One you slow or what Wonnie...you're fucking his boy now! So you really think that nigga would tell you if he had HIV girl!" this let me know right then and there that she meant me no good. I couldn't tell her ass anything. "Quit trippin Veronica...his not going to do shit to you. I already told him that his baby Momma was at school yelling it out because she found out about him fucking with Jessica." "Your ass is just tryin to clean your name girl...thank god his ass didn't flip out and that its not true." "Yo....are yo coming to the Barbeque with me...my Mom is cooking that pasta salad you love." She was always tryin to cover up her wrong. "You know what Wonnie?" "What" "I'm going to go but you need to start realizing that you're no better then nobody else, you always talk a good game but you never do what you speak about." "were all you going with this Veronica? I mean you been in college and you think you got it all together don't you." "I do got it together out I...." "a...girl just come put me and will talk on are way to the park..." "Click." Damn just like that. She didn't get shit I was trying to tell her but I wasn't even going to worry about it. I'm just going to pull away from her slowly. As I put all my homework in my backpack, I realized that I didn't have any money on me. When I paged Zero his brother called me back to tell me he was busy. Normally I would of copped an attitude but he told me that he had logs for me to go shopping so I shut my mouth. When I left, I seen that same undercover car from two months ago. Maybe my mind was playing tricks on me but I'm sure I seen that car. I don't know but I will put prayer and the bible in my life a lot more. When I pulled up too Wonnie's house she was sitting on the steps waiting for me. She was walking towards me with the barbeque grill. "What's that for girl." I said while opening my trunk. "The grill fool...I told you we was going to grill today." "Damn Wonnie why do I got to be all of that?" "Quit trippin damn...you know how I talk shit...." "I see you're still mad about that shit ain't you." She makes me so sick, I don't understand why I keep fucking with hoes that don't give a fuck about me. "You know that Wonnie I'm not mad....Nah ah...not at all but I do know one thing I'm a loyal mother fucker believe that." "Oh so I'm not?" "whatever...what store do you want me to take you?." "Nah..wait you said I'm not loyal...what do you mean by that?" "Fuck it Wonnie! Do you want to go to the same store or what?" She huffed and sat back into her seat. She wasn't use to people standing up to her way of no way. "Super value...on Nicollet and Lake." We drove in silence all the way there. I could tell that really though he didn't do anything wrong. As I was making a left into the grocery store parking lot. We were getting pulled over by the police. "Oh...my god Veronica...what did we do." "Nothing just chill...I got license." She started sweating and rubbing her head. "Do...do...do you got anything on you?....was this car in a robbery or drive by....or did something happen?" "you're so damn scary Wonnie...girl I wouldn't put you in jeopardy of shit." The officer heard me as he was walking to my side of the truck. "License and registration please." "Sir did I do something wrong." He was a young white cop that resembled Brad Pitt. "No mam you didn't...now if you give me your info we can get this over and you can go on your way." I handed him my info and from the other side I seen a Indian woman coming on Wonnie's side "mam could you step out the car and come with me please." She said while opening her door and pointing to the police car. Wonnie looked back at me with fear. Damn did she think I could save her I heard her asking the women what was going on but I couldn't hear what she was saying. I seen the male cop coming towards my door, so I tried my best to do what Zero taught me. Play it cool especially when I'm not dirty. "Mam could you step out and go get in the car with your friend." "oh man what did I do sir?" "nothing mam just do what I said....ok." I could tell he was a rookie because any other asshole would have been very aggressive with me. After the women opened the door for me, I got in and Wonnie went to questioning. "What's up Veronica?....what the fuck is going on?" "I don't know." I screamed. "Shit I'm just as nervous as you are." She knew I was pissed off so she just folded her arms sat back and watched. They checked my whole truck and set the grill, my school books and bag of condiments all over the ground. I felt relieved when I seen them neatly place everything back into my truck. They returned to the car and let us out. The women told Wonnie to get her license taken care of because she had revoked on her record. The man let me know that my truck was suppose to be in some kind of robbery. I knew he was lying but what could I do. I just listened especially since he gave me my fake ID back. I got lucky this time because I know this was the feds investigating me.

— The Next Day —

"Zero...do you understand that the feds is on me baby..what am I going to do?...I mean you act like you don't care!." He walked back and forth in front of me butt ass naked while he fixed me breakfast. "Damn girl....you told me that already!....shit I told your ass that if I have anything to do with it....I'll never let you go to prison behind my shit." I know baby....but I'm scared...I don't want you to leave me....." I love you....I can't make it with out you!! He turned around with his beautiful black ass. His bow legs and thick brick hard dick will make any bitch crave on her knees for his attention. "Hey...what's wrong with you?." He walked straight to me and bet my plate with eggs, turkey bacon and two slices of toast on the table. "I heard somebody sounding like they was weak...is that what I'm hearing?....huh?" I just studied his dick that was sticking right in my face. I felt hypnotized. "Nah..ah...I'm not weak baby...." He started laughing at me while he grabbed my chin. "I love you too. Beautiful...I told you you're special." He said as he guided my head back to his dick. I handled my business for about 3 minutes. He always made me stop sucking his dick. He said it felt so good that he didn't want to come to fast. Once again we didn't finish our conversation because if the lust of love. I don't know which even it was I knew in a matter of time the fun was going to end.

Chapter 65
"Dick's Detail Shop In Crystal"

"Yo...cry...ain't that...that nigga Danger right there?." Zero said while passing the blunt to Big Boy. "Yeah..that's him cuz. But don't trip out here...than...you know these white folks will call the police quick...plus your d's are almost on your truck." "Nigga fuck that...I know you ain't getting soft...and turning pussy on me?." Zero said while gripping his hip and walking towards Danger. As soon as he appreciated him he thought he saw a ghost. "ah..oh Zero just slapped the shit out of him. "That's what I thing of niggas that try to dodge me over Chump change....you fucking pussy." He yelled as he continued to punch and kick Danger all over his head. "Wait...here...her man." Danger screamed while handling him a wad of money. He snatched the money nigga...you tell the rest of these pussy ass nigga's that even think about asking me that they'll die next time." He took Dangers keys off the ground and started to walk away.
"Yo...Rock...man people don't take my car man that's all I got dog." Zero ignored him and walked back to Big Boy's car. All the people at the shop didn't say a word. They must of seen the look on Zero's face that he meant business. "On the real cuz....ha ha ha...you handled dude." "On the up and up nigga...you was suppose to be helping me nigga ....so you know I'm going to clown yo ass in front of the homies." "Nah...come on cuz....you didn't need my help cuz." Zero just shook his head and continued to smoke his weed. "Niggas just ain't built like me I guess."

Chapter 66
"It's Going Down"

Five months have passed and it was just about over between me and Low. His two nieces moved in with me and Annie. The adjustment was cool because they kept my business my business. Most kids at twelve fourteen would run their mouths off to their uncles about his women, but they didn't. I felt good about influencing them to be better young ladies than I was. I told them to tell people that their mother was having problems. I could afford to let them to stay with me while there mother and brother stayed with a friend. Zero didn't like it at first because he thought they would keep up shit between me and Low but they didn't. "NeNe, do you want to make a run with me before I let yall drop us off at the Quest?." "Oh my goodness...you going to let us drive...oh thank you Veronica....we love living here" NaNa said while jumping in my lap. "You know damn well that Low is going to snap on your ass when he see us pull up." "Annie you always try to philosophy shit don't you." "Aight...watch his ass going to snap when he see our ass rollin up." I grabbed my purse and headed towards the door. "NeNe go start the car up! NaNa clean up and straighten out my closet for me." "Ok...I got you Auntie that made me smile because they had the most respect. "Here...this three hundred is for yall to go get you some summer clothes and buy your Mom something." "Thank you...oh god we can buy a bunch of stuff....I'll see if my friend can come...he got a truck." "Hold up...what you doing with a friend at twelve years old give....I'm going to have to watch you!." "Yeah...you too damn young to be talking about going out with some nigga." Me and Annie just smiled at each other because it all sounded so similar we were young and hot at there age. At least they were still virgins. "That's NeNe out there honking...hurry up Shine it's already six and you know how long it takes for you to get dressed." "Aight I'll be back, tell Mya and Myrecal they're going to have to get a ride over here if they wanna ride with us." "Aight...just hurry up." As soon as I got in the truck I started schooling NeNe. I let her know that her waiting to have sex was important and once her virginity is gone, you don't get another chance. I was honest with her in everyway. How it felt the first time and how she will get her heart broke the first time. She laughed at meat me and told me I was trippin. Even though it was just a six year age difference and a eight year difference between her sister. I still felt I could save them from sex money and drug addiction. Since I couldn't save my little sister Fox who was very naive, then I was going to try and school them. People always tell me I could be a counselor but I didn't find that to be my calling. I had to meet with the contractor. My Mom let me know that it was going to cost another twenty go to put a fireplace, tall ceilings and a jacuzzi tub in my bedroom. I had already spent well over a hundred g's in bits and pieces, thanks to Zero. Low never questioned me about where I got the money from. NeNe and the streets were talking loud and proud of how scandalous and nasty I was. Cat and Bull never caught me and Zero together so it kind of feel on dead ears to them. When I did take Victor to see his grandma Steen. She didn't have the guts to speak on it because she didn't want me to take victor out of her life again. I know all of them were being fake, so I just played the fake game with them. "auntie...did I make the right turn?" NeNe was doing a great job driving while I handled my business over the phone. Bacon, Gen, Sweets, Bunny, Danger, Ciara and Slow didn't beat there feet with dope. They sold weight so I was at ease with that I didn't have to worry about my shit getting taken in no crack house. "Right here baby...." We pulled up in to the contractors building in St. Louis park off of Lake Street. Every time I went to meet the short nice build white man. He often stared down my throat so I tried to get my business done fast. "How are you doing today...I know I'm a little late but I got the twenty thousand in cash." I said while he locked the office door behind me. "Hay why you lock that door?" I clinched my purse and backed up. He smiled and walked past me sat down behind the counter and go to typing into his computer. "You have twenty grand in your hand honey....if any hoodlums were following you they could easily come rob and kill us dead with any one knowing." "but I got....." "Oh and your friend that's I your truck would have been dead just...listen to how loud you have the music playing...it calls all kind of attention to yourself honey...if you want to last in any game, you must handle business be a little more professional." Damn he pulled my hoe card like a mother fucker, "well nobody is going to be jacking me cause I'm very careful." He shook his head and smiled. As he stood up to hand me my receipt and to unlock the door. He said "your house should be ready in about a year...I hope you listen to the wisdom I tried to put on you. Be careful not to slip cause you may not have no one to catch you by next year." I grabbed my receipt. "Thank you sir....I'll have Terry my dad to meet you next time....I don't cause any attention to your business ok." I said with an attitude. "Ms.

Gittens..honey I didn't mean harm ok…you're so beautiful…I just hate to see something happen to you…it's an ugly word out here. I fanned him off and hopped into my truck.

Chapter 67

"That Night At The Quest"

"Damn Myrecal…don't you got any pull with all that pussy yo give out." I said with my hands in the air. "Fuck you Veronica…I don't have time for your shit tonight." "Whatever hoe….just work something shit…you always talking bout how you be pimpin nigga's shit…I know you was fucking security not to long ago so…work it." I snapped my fingers and twisted my hips. People in line started laughing at her. "Chill…Shine…you know we came to kick it dog…chill out." Mind your business Annie…I don't say shit to you when you do shit… so don't sweat me aight." Annie rolled her eyes and turned around. Mya was so into sweating one of Zero's friends from Cali, she never even paid us any attention. After about ten minutes went by I seen the homeboy Bumpy. "a…Bumpy…you got me and my girls dog." I said while waving my hands. "Oooh…my baby girl Veronica come on…you know you a diamond….why are you in line you know VIP players always roll with the ballers." I grabbed Annie's hand and grabbed Myrecal. "See this is pimp shit right here…when you know niggas that got it like that." She stuck her lips out and rolled her eyes. The club was super packed because Total and 112 were in town. I didn't see them in the club but I'm not a groupie like that so I wouldn't have called either way it went. I made it through the club to show my appearance to let hoes know I'm still the shit. I seen nobody up in there that I would holler at so I was ready to go. "Annie I ain't feeling this shit….I'm bout to go back down stairs…VIP is boring tonight…looks like da niggas are all downstairs." "I know let Mya and Myrecal say up here….I ain't really feeling them either." "What…not you." "Shut up Shine…lets just kick it." I couldn't say shit because I enjoyed the fact that she didn't want to hang with them. As we where going down the steps I seen Myrecal arguing with somebody and Mya on the side. Annie pointed and I nodded my head in the other direction. She was probably arguing with some hoe about there man. Being as though I only fool with her because of Annie. I wasn't never getting in her shit. I fought her so you know animosity was still there. Plus when its time to smash on hoes she don't have my back. "You...yo...Shine...yo girl and them are you over there scrapping." I had just bought my anger with line back. I was ready to get my fuck on and fighting was no where in my plan. "T.T.M....yo ass knows I don't fuck with her like that and where's Zero anyways." I said while yelling over the music. "He's out side" "a...Annie cuz...go help that girl over there..." He started pointing. "She's getting whooped." "I'll be back Shine...don't leave me." While Annie went to play captain save a hoe, I walked outside to look for Zero after slamming another drink. As soon as I stepped outside who did I see went over in his BMW Ms. Drama Queen Nella. Yeah she got that name after Zero told me she cried and begged him not to fuck with me. He said after she had five birds shipped to her crib, she threatened him for some attention so he took her to the movies. Afterwards he tried dropping her off but she wouldn't get out the car, she started giving him head and that still didn't convince him to go in and hit it. So she through a tantrum and begged him to fuck anybody but me. Dumb bitch, don't she understand niggas don't want know weak bitches. You never show his ass how much you dig him. Not even your husband. Soon as they see you don't love yourself half as you love them. They'll be cheating on you in an instant. I moved through the crowd made my way to the car. Yeah all the thirsty ass look a likes knew I was about to snap. "Shine...ah...ha...your man is pushing up on the next hoe." "Yeah he ain't sweating you tonight...he's on da hoe hunt tonight ha ha." Some bitches were yelling as I walked up. I just threw my middle finger up at them and switched my hips a little harder. "Watch this pimp shit doe" I said and walked right up to the passenger door and jumped in the car. Nella stood in the driver's doorway and continued to try and convince Zero to take her home with him. His music was so loud he didn't know I was sitting next to him. "T.T.M....aye cuz hand me my phone out the glove compartment" he said with out turning around. I played the game with him and handed him the phone. I slightly rubbed his arm as he turned. "What ....what the fuck....ah...man when you get in here girl?" he asked with a little smirk. "Yeah...I'm smoother then you think...nigga I could of killed yo ass" I said while playfully putting my hands around his neck. He kissed me and rubbed my pussy. "A...I'm bout to hit that tonight....I got some where to take you aright." I sat back in my seat. "You better get rid your problem then." Nella stood back with her hands on her hips. "What's up Zero....you said I was going with you tonight." He stood up outside the car and shut the door so I couldn't hear. I winked my eye at the two hating ass hoes that were throwing daggers at me when I rolled up to the car. They walked off mad as usual. Whatever he was saying to Nella had her pissed off because I saw her push him. He grabbed her and walked off with her. It didn't matter to me because I knew what he was about to do with me. Plus I had to make sure I put it on his ass so the next time my mom met with the contractors I make him pay that next 20 g's. About 10 minutes later I seen her walking with T.T.M. as Zero got into the car, Annie Mya and Myrecal came rolling up at the same time. I rolled the window down. "Annie I'm going with Zero tonight...you get the keys to the truck." "Yeah and don't tear my baby's shit up neither" he said while kissing me. I smelled Hennessey all over his breath. Mya and Myrecal stood there with a crossed and lips poked out. "I got the hey...dog.....O be there...call me in da morning." "Aight you bout to drop them off." Myrecal rolled her eyes. "You didn't have to leave us like that Shine....that shit was fake." Fuck you bitch...you ain't my friend hoe...you Annie's friend shit." Zero pulling off. Annie was laughing .....don't have them hoes in my crib." I yelled as we skirted up 7th street. Zero started checking me about not having Mya and Myrecal's back. I let him know that I only fuck with them because of Annie. They don't have no love for me period. There just in it for the fame. Everybody knows that niggas respect me for what I do. Bitches know that if they run with me all the ballers will be on them. Plus Myrecal done fucked behind me too many times. I told the hoe, her pussy will never be mine. Annie and Ty say the bitch acts like she wants to fuck me. Nah....I know that ain't it cause I don't do bitches under no circumstances. We were so into our conversation that we never seen the yellow 98 pull up next to us. "Ah...damn beautiful...baby look to you're right." I stopped in mid sentence and whoa I got a shock. We were at the light on Olson highway and James Ave. "Damn baby...you could of warned me before I turned around." I felt a little nervous but I smiled and would. "Girl...ha ha you're silly." Bull was so pissed off. You could tell he wasn't comfortable sitting next to the hoe he had in the car with him. Tomp laughed threw up the piece sign and skidded off. "Oh....did you see how that nigga looked at us...ah...ha...da know we fuck around for sure now." Zero was cheesing from ear to ear. I know Bulls punk ass called Steen and Cat right away. It didn't faze Zero at all because nobody was going to whoop j=his ass. I wasn't worried about that to much neither even though I'm sure Cat and Trina could whoop me. They knew I wasn't no punk bitch though so they never tried.

— Two Months Later —

Business was going good. Chico and Ricky fell out because Ricky jacked Chico's connect for 20 birds. Damn that was well over 2 million dollars, so it was hard to find another reliable source. Zero never stressed about it because he said it had nothing to do with him. Chico always made sure Zero and T.T.M. was straight with some product so that they wouldn't loose there clientele. "Shine...baby...I feel some shit is bout to go down baby...here...take this money and pay your house off even though I probably won't be around to see it built I want you and Victor to be straight." I walked around two bedroom apartment he shared with Big Boy butt ass naked. I heard him while I was making him some chicken gizzards. I walked over to him with his plate in hand. "Here...eat....you're talking crazy baby." I said while kissing him on his thick juicy lips. "You want some ketchup." He watched me with his lustful eyes as I went back in the kitchen. I knew he was hungry for me a plate so as I sat the ketchup down, I made my double D's shake, he watched and ate his gizzards while sucking on his fingers. "Girl come here....you just make a nigga hard every time I look at your fine ass." "Nope...until you stop talking crazy...cause yo ain't leaving me I told you." I didn't eat gizzards so I grabbed my sucker off the table and twirled it around in my mouth. "I like how you eating that candy, you want to try that on me." I couldn't respond before he grabbed me and bent me over the couch. I worked my pussy muscles and he hit it.

He couldn't take it that way so he wouldn't come to fast he let me ride him. Yeah it felt so good to be in control. "He cupped my titties and let me work him. "Oh….Shine I'm bout to come baby." I heard someone turning the key to the door so I stopped. "Why you stop…come on." He said while grabbing my waist. "Somebody is unlocking the door." Just as I finished my sentence Zero picked me up with me still inside of him. Big Boy and two girls was with him. "Ah…my fault dog…you want me to come back" he yelled as they stood at the door. Zero slammed the bedroom door and through me on the bed. "Yeah…nigga and next time call first." He yelled and finished his business with me. That day I would of savored the Moment if I would of known that it was really about to come to an end.

Chapter 68

"Monday Morning"

"Veronica…auntie ….get up…you're late for school….somebody is ringing the phone off da hook." NeNe said while shocking me. "Who is it…..I'm tired." I rolled over and wiped my eyes. Before grabbing the phone I felt my heart drop to my feet. The noon news was on and I seen three dudes with blue rags in there pockets being put in the police car. "Hey hey NeNe turn that up girl." I had to cover my mouth and talk. "ha ha….why you cover your mouth auntie." I grabbed the phone at the same time. "Cause…I got that little thing in my mouth…hello." "Yeah…a cuz nem just got popped off by one time." My thoughts and worse nightmare has come true. "What…who is dis…what are you talking about?" "Dis SA home boy….I ain't finna be on dis phone like that but ah…I was to let you know to clean house and yo boy. Rock T.T.M, Big Boy and the old man got picked up…..oh…and they still looking for people." "Why…you call me with this shit….how you get my number?" "A…I was told to let you know….I got to go…." "click." I looked at the news for a whole hour and nothing came back on. "NeNe…did you see anything on the news about Zero and them getting popped by one-time?" "No…but I kept hearing them say that they had a big drug bust. Something about a drug….." "It's true Shine….they got them at T.T.M's peoples house….cuz was a snitch and he had them meet at his crib and they …..." "Hold up…Annie how you know all of dis….damn why didn't nobody wake me up?." "I tried to when Zero called but he said let you sleep." "What the fuck….oh my god….I might not ever see him again." I screamed and cried my heart out. "You should of woke me up….my baby is gone….dis is what he was talking about….oh my goodness." Everybody was awake now. Nobody said a word they just let me cry my heart out. After giving myself a pity party for about ah hour. I finally got up the strength to get myself together. I checked my pager and phone and both of them were over loaded with messages. It was about 90 degrees outside so I know everybody was out running there mouths about the latest indictment. "Annie…do you feel like making some runs with me…you know niggas is out running there mouths about shit." Everybody in the house was ready to go. School didn't start for another week so Victor was at his peoples house. They probably was jumping for joy. Shit Bull and his boys was praying for Zero's down fall anyways. "Yeah, we all were waiting for you to come out the room…everybody been calling too." "I figured that…did Zero call yet?" "No but his Mom called and said they all go to court tomorrow so she wants us to go…the more people the better it looks for them to get a bail." We all got in the truck and drove nowhere. I schooled NeNe and NaNa not to repeat anything that's going on within my house hold. Even though they knew better I just needed to remind them because I knew people were going to pump them for information Annie informed me that everybody was out of dope, so all I need to do was go pick my money up. I could see it now. Back to the block I go. Maybe I'll just stack and get me a job. Nah that thought went right out the window. I think being a better mother and stop thinking about sexual positions before I go to bed would be a good idea. Thank god I hit everybody up before they wrote me off. When nigga's here about there connect getting caught up, they get to breakin bad on yo ass and spending up your loot. "D-Town…you still got them houses over in St. Paul?" I had everybody sit in the truck while I talked to all of my workers. Annie knew somethings but from what's going on. I don't need her ass knowing everything. "Yeah I still got em…why?" "Cause I'm going to be sitting in them….shit I might be working for your ass in a minute." D-Town never worked for me. He was just one of them cool ass nigga's from Detroit that respected me for what I do. I grew to be friends after Coco introduced us a couple of years ago. "You doing bad Shine...why didn't you tell me?" "I'm not doing bad but I will be....don't play boy....you know you heard what happened." He frowned at me...."Girl I ain't heard shit...what's up....Spill it out." I let D-Town know everything that I knew from the streets talking. "Damn that's fucked up....but it ain't over for you doe." That was cool to hear I didn't want to use D-Tows spots to work out of until I really needed it.

Chapter 69
"The Court Date"

As soon as me, Annie and Wonnie stepped off the elevator. It was like a celebrity was going to court. The whole hood was like a celebrity was going to court. The whole hood was there maybe for support out most was there to be nosy Nella and her crew was there along with all the hoes that they all were fucking. I saw Zero looking a little confused but worried at the same time. I made my way to he front of the crowd. Some one reached out to touch me. "Veronica ....hay ....come sit up here with me." I took the frown off my face immediately. "Oh....hay Mrs. Dupri...ok." We follow Zero's mom to where she was sitting right behind Zero. As we scooted threw the aisle to sit, Zero put a big kool-aide smile on his face. "I'm glad to see you baby." He said while puckering his lips out at me. "I'm glad to see you baby...yo gone be straight." We all broke our neck to turn around to see who said that. "Shut up hoe....he wasn't even talking to yo ass." "Fuck you bitch... he was with me before he got caught! Now!! Mrs. Dupri grabbed my arm and Wonnie grabbed the other. "Baby don't pay that no mind...we're here for my son. "All rise for the honorable judge." I rolled my eyes and stood up. I had plans to whoop her ass as soon as I left court. Zero kept looking at me to see if I was mad as he winked his eye and trued to pay attention to what they were saying to all of them. I smiled and listened on. The judge read all of the charges off and their bail was denied. T.T.M. went off. "Suck my dick you old shriveled up mother fucker." "What....bang bang...order in the court...you will have respect in my court now." "Yo cuz chill...you fuck it up for all of us Frank." "Fuck that my name is T.T.M. nigga fuck these pussy ass one times." "Get this man out of my court room now." The judge yelled so loud I thought his frail little body would give out at anytime. Everybody laughed to the top of there lungs at T.T.M. half the people in the room didn't know his real name but they do now. My baby was up shit creek. With out a paddle. There changes were Drug conspiracy, CCE, cancer criminal enterprise conspiracy to commit murder and possession of fire arms. The least they would get is ten years but since nobody would snitch at this time anyways. They all will get Buck Rodgers time or at least Chico T.T.M. and Zero will. As of now Chico was a fugitive. So the best bet for him is to go to Mexico to hide out. "Mrs. Dupri...what is going to happen now?" I was so confused and I need to know where all that dope was that they found. "Well baby...its like this, if they don't get there money together for a good attorney then they don't have any luck!!!." "Does Zero have any money....I have some for him." "Yeah he told me how to handle this situation...They go to court next month so he'll be alright...If you want you can go see him tonight....I was going to go but he'd rather see you instead." She was always so thoughtful of me. I couldn't hold my tears back and I didn't, I didn't care who seen me. It hurt real bad to see somebody you truly care about go through some deep shit. "Thank you Mrs. Dupri....I really appreciate that." "Stop crying baby...save those tears for a day you need them." I felt her pain. She held it together for her child who was I being weak and she wasn't. "I'm sorry...I just know this is very serious and he looked real nervous in there." "Just make sure you see him ok....I'll let him know when he calls." "Thank you again." I gave her a hug and we walked her to her car. Downtown was full of one time. I guess that thought we were going to break them out or something. "Yo...lets go see if Nella is over there... I want to whoop that bitches ass." "Quit this Shine....yo need to be worrying about Zero...shit that nigga don't need that stress right now." Annie said frowned up and we walked to the parking ramp. "I know Veronica...he's really going to need you now....just focus on going to see what's up with him....you'll see that hoe out somewhere." I walked even faster and was headed to know where when you pissed off you always think you're invincible. "Yall sound real stupid to me….that bitch disrespected me for the last fucking time….I'm whooping her ass and I mean that shit." "Aight…you go head…shit all des police out here…in da middle of downtown." Wonnie said while pointing them out. "Yeah….that's a one way ticket to a cell right next to Zero." I started laughing. "Shut up Annie….you're silly." "Uh huh…I thought you would rethink about it." "Yeah…and where is Nella at anyways Veronica." I just kept laughing as we made it to my truck. "I know you'll think I'm loosing my mind…don't yall?" They both looked out each other and laughed. I started my truck up and backed out. "Think you crazy….huh we know yo ass crazy…don't we Wonnie." "Yeah…I must say …you got a slight case of sprungtitus ha ha ha." "ha..ha whatever I just want him to know I'm there for him." "Oh…he'll know that even if you whoop Nella or not…ha ha he'll know." That's a shame that out of all the times Nella has pissed me off I never wanted to whoop her. I needed to take my frustration out on somebody and I decided it will be Nella.

Chapter 70

"Reality Check"

The summer was here true in deed and the events that have taken place I sure wasn't prepared for the ones that were to come. Yo Yo and Motor had caught a dope case with some niggas from his town. Annie and Thicky were getting close and so were me and Butchie. It was hard for me to tell Low that I've moved on but I had to play him for having a baby boy on me. I don't understand why niggas step outside of commitment and fuck the next chick raw and then expect us to still fell the same way about them. Naw nigga, I can't picture you sucking and fucking that bitch like you do me let alone have a baby on me. "Auntie….its my uncle on da phone." NaNa said as me and NeNe got dressed for Rondo Days. "Ok I'll call him back later." I didn't feel like arguing. He heard about me going out of town with other niggas and I don't have to explain shit to him. I pay my own and make sure me and my son are straight so no nigga can't even leave us stranded. "Na Na get little V ready go…and could you please hurry up cause we are going to miss da parade." Thank god for Low's nieces. They were very sweet and respectable girls. I was so glad when there Mom let them live with me to help babysit little V while I hustled in the street. I hated when Wonnie and Fox had so much shit to talk about NeNe and NaNa being up under me. They made me think they were jealous because I didn't kick it with them as much. I felt good about that too because people seem to think when you need them they can do whatever they want with you. Me, my son and the girls went to Rondo Days. It always rained when they had this event but for some reason anytime a black function went down some shit always kicked off. "Hey yall…go over there and get them ribs and chicken from Big Daddy…that shit is good as hell." Olivia said as we walked and talked to people "Ok girl…have you seen my mom out here…. I'm trying to get rid of Victors little ass." "No…but I seen Queen with her crew and Wonnie Is over there with Lump." "Oh shit…he bought her ass out…huh is that ol girl from the chi (Chicago). Must not be in town huh." I don't know but….they are together." "Ok…well let me find my Momma." I let "O" walk her way as we looked for my Mom. We made it over to Big Daddy's stand and ordered out food. "Mom, I don't want no cheese on my cheeseburger." "Shut up boy you'll get what I get you." "But Mommy I don't like cheese." Little V cried as I tried to make him eat cheese I guess that was the irresponsibleness of a teenage mother. "When yo lil ass stop liking cheese nigga." "I never eat it." My son was right when I think about it he always took the cheese off his pizza and then ate the crust. "Ok Mommy is sorry…come on boy lets go find your grandma." We laughed and talked while watching the parade. Next thing I know a fight broke out and my son slipped out my hands. "NeNe…where's Victor…my baby." Everyone was running and screaming and bullets raced over our heads. "I don't know Auntie NaNa grabbed him and ran." NeNe said while starting to cry. As we hid behind a tree we could see the end of NaNa's shirt sticking out behind a table. "Oh look NeNe there they go." I said to her while pointing. We could hear the police sirens so the gun fire had stopped. The parade was over and as we made it over to Victor and NaNa my Mom was sitting right next to them. "Oh Mom I'm so glad to see you…please take lil V so we can go up to Central High and watch the dancers compete." "Now Roni I don't have no problem getting my grandbaby even though I'm know I'm not supposed to get him until tomorrow for the week but are you being responsible by taking NeNe and NaNa and people been shooting out here." Wow this woman sure knew how to ruin somebody's day. Shit this wasn't shit to us people shoot all the time. "Ok Mom, if anything gets to poppin off...will leave with no problem. We went to the dance contest and like always another fight broke out. This time some little girl got shot along with her pregnant mother and the dude that was driving. It started over the 60 Crips and the Bogus Boys. Every news channel and barber shop was talking about it for months. The police questioned so many people and still couldn't get to the bottom of it. It's a true fact in the hood. Don't believe none of what you hear and half of what you see. If you do, the hood will know and you'll be watching yo back for the rest of your life.

Chapter 71
"Talkin But Ain't Sayin Nothing"

"So NeNe you talking to Gotti huh" I said to her so I could catch her reaction. "Um...yeah auntie I have." "How did you do that without me knowing?" "I met him at that party Annie had with that girl from the Southside." I could tell she was uncomfortable but I had to keep her in point. "Well NaNa he is one of Bunchies friends and he hangs with the Shot Gun Crips so you know that brings a lot of hoes and drama ok.... He's older so I just want you to stick to a nigga yo age ok." "Thanks auntie but I'm not tripping off him no way cause my baby lil Dirty will be out in a few months." "Girl you and your lil sister is always doing time with a nigga....Yall are to damn young for that." "No auntie I ain't meaning sexually just mentally ha ha." "I don't care....please me I can't wait for no nigga in jail at all....Shit they don't wait on yo ass." "I know Auntie its ok... I'm good." She didn't want to hear shit else I said. I wanted to let her know he already slept with Mya back in the day and he has a women with a kid don't know nigga want to be faithful out here so she better do what she got to do to get what she can out of his ass. "Ring Ring Ring." I walked to my room to answer the phone. "Hello...Bitch. Damn who's playing on my phone now. Ring ....Ring...." "Hello ...Bitch." "Hold up girl...damn its Butchie "Oh nigga I thought some bitch had me fucked up and was playing mind games with me." "Nah....I need you to do something aight." "What boy." "Damn you always talk crazy to me but I never talk crazy to you. "Ok...my bad you can holler at me when you get over here ok." "Laugh...click." I loved my 3 bedroom house even though at my age I was set on her thing like a new Mercedes Benz and a big beautiful house on lake Calhoun with a closet full of clothes and a pool in the back yard. I probably wouldn't get it with 80 grand. "Auntie what are you doing?" Nana yelled "Nothing trying to get some sleep so we can get on the road tomorrow." "Ok...I ain't gong...I'm going to stay home with Annie ok." "That's cool Pinky wants to drive down there and see this young nigga she's diggin on so she'll probably drive most of da way ok." "I'll watch little Victor too." "Ok." I changed my clothes and got into the bed. As I laid there all I could think about is what Butchie wanted to talk to me about. The next morning I got dressed while NeNe did the same. As I started up the steps to put my bags in the car with Pinky I seen a funny colored Cadillac pass my house. I put my stuff in and waited for NeNe to come on. I seen her on the phone so I walked back to the door. "Come on NeNe cause I don't want to be on the road at night." "Wait Roni its somebody like a...." "Like a what?" I said while kissing Victor and hugging NaNa, "Auntie when will you be back from Chicago...will you tell my grandma I'll see her this summer." "Yeah I'll let her know that were coming for the fourth of July." Her eyes lit up. "Yeah" "What you mean you're going to see and take everything." NeNe yelled and started crying I snatched the phone. By this time Pinky was out the car and at the door. "What's wrong NeNe" Pinky asked. "Hello...who in the fuck is dis in my line." The phone hung up. "NeNe who was that?" We all said at the same time. "It was some white man that said he was representing Phat Girl and Clue in a law suit against you and Mrs. Ginger... he said all these different codes and legal terms I didn't understand but he said since I answered and let him know you lived here. He will be sending you the papers in the mail." "Damn....oh....fuck my Mom is going to be pissed off." All kind of shit was running through my mind. "Come on Roni…. Fuck it lets just kick it so you can get this off your mind." "laugh." We walked back to the car. As Pinky and NeNe talked and tried to cheer me up. I couldn't focus so I laid in the back seat listen to Faith Evans "Soon As I Get Home." The mellow music just made the tears roll down even harder. "Are you ok girl?" "Yeah I'm good." I didn't feel like talking to nobody. Is this what life's about people just sue you for some shit that they did to themselves. Damn I've always thought when you grow up with people and they're your friends its certain shit that you just don't do. Sleep has become my best friend. The ride was so cool till we made it to the gas station to fill up and get some snacks. "Veronica wake up." I whipped the slob off my mouth. "What." I knew it was some bull shit because they both used my real name. As I leaned up to look them both in the eye. Whoo it looked real serious. "What's wrong yall" "So call the house… your pager been blowing up." "Oh no Pinky is it Dom or my Mom…what." I grabbed my purse and ran to the booth where NeNe was standing. As I put the quarters in NeNe started crying harder. I was shaking by now. Pinky had gone in the gas station. "Hello….NaNa what's wrong baby?" A male voice came on. "Hello…Roni where your home girl?" "Who's this?" "It's me girl… they killed your boy." The butterflies and tears started rolling. "Who." "Please don't let him say Butchie or my other baby dad even though I couldn't stand him. "Its Gotti they…they killed Spanky." "Oh god…. He was just at the house yesterday why…. What happened?" "I don't know they said that somebody that looks like him had robbed the weed man and then he did. "Damn Gotti I didn't need this right now." "I'm sorry baby I had to tell you first cause I know that's your boy." "Wow we're at like homie number 10 or some shit huh." "I know cuz I swear I'm sick of my people dying for dis shit." I wiped my tears and said a player. "Where's Butchie at…does he know?" "Yeah he was with some of da homies a the tattoo shop when he heard and he already got him tatted on him." 'Aight Gotti I'll see you in two days ok." "Aight." Damn the jack game is a dead mans hustle. Everybody looses and nobody ever wants or thinks I'll be them.

Chapter 72
"Death Means Everything"

The trip to Chi town was very relieving. I was so relaxed that I didn't want to come home. The three days away seemed like eternity especially what I had to face when I walked in my door. "Where you going Annie." As I walked in the door and watched Annie and Tricky take them there bags of clothes to the car. "Oh a while you was gone we found us a crib." Annie said. "Yeah so now you ain't got to talk shit bout al the homies coming up over here without calling or asking." I was put off about Tricky's statement. I felt Annie was acting funny as hell for a while now. But jumping into her own crib with a nigga that would put yo ass out the moment he feels you're off your square is the weakest shit she could of ever done. "Fuck you Tricky... yo ass needs to pay me my paper nigga." He stopped in his tracks and thought about it for a minute and started laughing. "Ha ha... you mad ain't you...yep you girls coming to be with me now.... But ha you can come stay whenever you want home girl." I smacked my lips and rolled me eyes. "Yeah....ok nigga." Annie walked to there trap car to put her stuff down. "Yeah nigga I know you just was nice cause you worried bout me telling her you been paying these ole flip flops to suck you up huh." "What... I don't give a fuck what you tell her... she ain't going no where." He was right if that nigga left her ass she would loose her mind, she already looks like she's a blink away from a break down anyways. "You ain't worth it Tricky.... I'm good....just pay me my money." "When I'm ready to." Before he could finish his sentence I just slammed the door in his face. It had been weeks and I haven't had my period yet. I was a little nervous because I watched Wonnie go through the confession of who she got pregnant by and the shit was depressing. You should never sleep with two different dudes in the same month I knew that it was Butchie's baby if I was pregnant but Low was a possibility for sure. I done it two weeks apart so that's still a close call. "NaNa what's been going on since I've been gone?" My son ran and jumped right in my lap. "Hey lil V how much did you miss Mommy I hadn't seen my son and I know his other family didn't come see about him while I was gone. "A lot...Mommy I love you." He sure knew how to get me on his good side. "My uncle called and said you haven't returned his page....but I didn't tell him where all was." "Oh good but I'm sure he knew cause we seen Sandra and Laura in the Chi on 63rd and Halstead shopping in the sneaker store." "Oh well maybe that's why he was trying to question me but I wasn't answering him. "Damn I sure appreciate that because I didn't want him try to come fuck on me. I just wasn't interested anymore. The next day QT was asked to do Spanky's braids for the funeral. Man I couldn't really take it. I didn't realize what was going on until the day of. "What happened when you and Annie went to do Spanky's hair?" "Girl I was nervous as hell." "Knock knock." I jumped up and looked out the window and seen Annie and a few homies standing behind her. Instantly I thought about what Tricky said so I didn't catch an attitude like I would of. "What up yall?" I said while standing to the side letting them into the living room. I had a split level house with 2 bathrooms and 3 bedrooms. The great thing about having company was that none of them had to use my bathroom. "What up Sunshine." "Yeah what up before you get to snapping and she." Cassidy and Gotti said. Tricky didn't speak "so you know I had to get em." What up nigga.... You don't live here and I didn't sleep wit yo ass last night." Annie rolled her eyes. "Don't start Roni... this ain't the time aight." "Yeah and yo ass might want to stay on my good side girl.... For real." Tricky gave me a look that made me worry a little. What you mean nigga." I said while running downstairs to brush my teeth. When I returned Butchie was standing at the door. "When you'd get here." I had my scarf on and I did want to comb my hair. "Oh I just came through.... What you on." "Shit...chilling." "Um didn't you find out if you're pregnant or not." Damn this fool was worried and I don't even like him like that. "Nah but when I do I'll let you know ok." Everybody that back and listen to QT and Annie talk about how Spanky looked dead. OT told Fox and Annie that the nigga had a nice size dick. Who looks at a dead mans dick when shit like that doesn't matter no more. If that nigga knew that when he was alive he would of asked OT to put it in her mouth. That's just how that fool was. He said anything to anybody and dared you to step out of line. Annie was mad at him one time cause he told the whole house her pussy stunk when he walked in the bathroom behind her.

Chapter 73

"Funeral Day"

Me, NeNe, NaNa QT and Fox sat in the second now. Annie and Tricky sat behind us. We watched the preacher speak and talk about all the murders that took place in the past year. At that time it was well over 10 homicides in both the Southside and Northside of Minneapolis in the big city's it didn't matter but here 100 was well over the amount we were use to. Spanky's uncle was uncomfortable with the Crips wearing there rags and pouring out liquor at the grave site. He made an announcement that his sister which was Spanky's Mom didn't want her son buried like no gang banger. His grandma just cried and the family wasn't having it.

— Two Months Later —

Butchie knew I was pregnant and had dipped to California. I didn't understand why but I just took it as he needed to get away because his best friend had died and the stress really got to him. I confirmed to him that yes I'm pregnant and I knew it was his. He called every other day but that wasn't enough. I needed some affection and he wasn't there to give it to me so I had to give Low a chance one last time. "Roni when going to let me come suck that pussy good." I was shocked at Low. I guess that's how niggas get when you hold out on there ass. I was a little irritated and needed some because Scrappy kept calling me and when I finally answered he told me my homeboy Coolaide was about to get sentenced to some big time and wanted to talk to me. I didn't know what to say to him. Damn he was facing two counts of attempted murder. The people that got up on that stand and lied on him so his cards were stacked against the wall. I told Scrappy I would get up with his ass tomorrow. "Yeah Low you can come on over if you're real hungry." I said while planning the phone down and running to jump in the shower. After I got out I fixed NeNe, NaNa and lil V some tacos. It seemed like all I could make was fried chicken, hamburger helper, chili and sloppy joes and steak. Shit they was sick of the same thing and so was I. "Knock knock." "Auntie you want me to get it." "Go head NaNa its your uncle." After she let him in he went straight downstairs to my room. I laughed to myself seeing that he meant business. I had on my short lace teddy that Whiz bought me for Valentine's day. Huh he'd be mad if he seen what was about to go down. "So Ms. Veronica you done fucking with me huh." "Nah you here ain't you." I said while rubbing on his chest and kissing him. "Well wait I want to be faithful and move with yall to Atlanta." Huh that nigga is on bullshit, not now I'm pregnant what do I say. "Ah yo came to let me drip my juices down your face so lets just stick to that." He instantly got an attitude so I licked all the way down to his stomach. "You like that baby." "Yeah but I love you and I don't want yo loose you Veronica." I continued to ignore him and lick around his belly button while rubbing on his dick. He got hard instantly as I watched him get aroused I thought about having Butchie's baby in me and giving myself to Low. "What's wrong baby why don't you suck it." "I don't know where you been boy." He laughed and set me on my chest. "Put your legs on my shoulders." I did as he said and enjoyed watching him lick me from the roota to the toota. "Oh boy damn I miss dis dick." His face was filled with my pearls laced all over his face. "Turn on the bed and set your butt in the air." I was uncomfortable but I just did it. He was going in and out of me like a race horse. "Slow down Low." "Nah dis is my pussy and I'm going to make sho you know dis." "Ah…..no I didn't like it." I screamed. I wasn't feeling it no more. I'm sure it felt extra good because I was pregnant. "Ok be still I'm…cumin girl …oh damn." I broke loose from his grip and ran straight to the shower. "What's wrong baby you don't love me no more." I ignored his ass and stood in the shower until my fingers turned to prunes. When I got out he was sleep think god. I went walking around the house to look for the phone and my pager. I seen Butchie had called. "He… what you doing." "Nothing Butchie when will yo ass he back shit." He had the goofiest laugh. "Why is that funny nigga?" "Ah… man I told you bout that nigga shit didn't I …. I'll be back Sunday and just have that pussy ready." Wow he was ready to break me off. "Huh nigga I know you been fucking down there haven't you."

"Nah... not at all.... But I'll be back dis week end for that good shit." I really wanted Low to leave now. The next morning I jumped up for school when I got dressed I made Low leave out with me. He kept trying to talk me into letting him move in. I wasn't having it. My boy Chico was on the run and needed me to get rid of some bricks for him so that made me feel a lot better when I was getting in my car I seen that Cadillac pull up. The window rolled down and Chico's face appeared. "Damn nigga you move quick don't you." "Yeah baby girl I do... I rolled up a few weeks ago and I seen some niggas coming out the house so I just kept going. "Damn Chico needed a shave and a hair cut. Life on the run wasn't to good for his ass. "Ok what you need me to do." I said while fanning Low off as he road down the street and I walked over to the passenger side of the Cadillac. "I know Chico don't trip my home girl and her nigga moved out so you safe." "What's up Feet... you have to stay nigga." His old ass had a lot of girls names tattooed on him and look real mean but was cool as hell. "Yeah till were done with dis load." "How many yall got." Chico spoke. "Bout 10 but I got five and um give you five." "Ok I got you call me when yall get situated and I'll come to yall." I watched them pull off and was nervous as hell. I hadn't been in the game in a couple of months so to be pregnant and get back in it with a nigga on the run was playing deadly.

Chapter 74

"Jack Move"

"Scrappy what why do you keep calling my house and playing on my damn phone nigga." I was ignoring his ass because he wasn't nothing but trouble plus I know that him and his boys is the one who tied up Gen and Pistol whooped him. Thank God Gen was strong enough to not tell where I lived. I used the nigga for what his trick ass was worth. "Cause Bitch I spent my bread on your car getting fixed I treated you and Ty's nasty ass to California and Bitch I heard yo flip flop ass was pregnant." "Damn how does everybody know this? "So what punk ass nigga we also road out there for yo ass to get on nigga and you put us in a cross with them nigga James and Floyd shit that nigga was knocking at my door... fuck you." I slammed my phone down and the nigga was right out side my door. "Bitch come out here… um beat yo ass." He was scaring everybody so I went outside to calm down. "What Slappy what." I said while jumping at him. I seen he had that 9 millimeter on his hip so I played cool. "Yeah you better had a faced me with all that shit walking." "What nigga." "Here ya boy Coolaid wants to talk to you." He knew that was the only way to get me to calm down. "Hey Coolaide how you doing in there." "I'm good… girl you better watch them cats out there… they trying to get at you." I read between the lines and understood what he meant. I listened to him explain what happened and let him know how much I prayed for his release. "You have 2 men left on his call." The recorder came on. "Oh you got to go." "Yeah….you be careful sis." "I will… I love you homeboy… make sure you read up in there ok." "Oh yeah I am so you cant tease me about not knowing how too." "Ah ha ha you remember that boy." "Yeah how could I forget you yelling it out in the class room?" Thirty seconds remaining. "Oh I got to go baby girl." "Ok I ." "Click." Damn I was pissed the phone hung up. "What did he say?" "Shit Scrappy… leave me alone nigga." "Yo ass is bad luck… I got a new man so bye." I walked back in my house stood by the door and locked it.

Chapter 75

"Sunday Night"

Butchie was back and like I needed he gave me what I needed. I didn't realize that QT had been calling cause I sent her and Feet went out of town to get the rest of the work for Chico. "Hello QT are yall alright." "Yeah we almost back"…. "Oh ok …. Yall good." "Yeah." Feet grabbed the phone. "Enough with the questions aight." He hung up on me. I could hear Victor upstairs I had one more finale to finish before summer started and I was done. "Butchie are you good I'm bout TO GO TO SCHOOL." I said while giving him a kiss. "Yeah." He turned over and was butt naked. I smiled and knew I did my job before I left I seen Sandra and her two kids in Victor's bed. "Sam… what's up girl… where is NeNe and NaNa?" "Oh they'll be back they went with Mya to the store." Damn I didn't even know that

Mya or Myrecal had been in my house. "Ok I'm going to school." I made it to school feel good all of a sudden I kept getting pages from Low back to back. I tried finishing my final then more was coming from Butchie. I asked to take a break and my teacher told me to leave my papers and let me take 10 minutes. I felt in my gut that something happened so I called Sandra because she was watching Victor. "Hello... Sandra what's up...? Butchie still there." "Oh god I didn't know he left." "No what happened." I was so scared to ask. "Girl lil V opened up the door for Low and I was in here sleep." "No what the fuck girl....why wasn't you watching him." "I was." He heard Lows voice and he opened the door Low went straight t your room." "Where were you at?" "The top of the steps and then I seen Low walk out shaken his head and cursed at me." "What did Butchie do?" "Girl he walked out behind him." "Damn Sandra... Where's Victor...tell him I'm going to beat his little ass?" "Ok... he's scared already though." I couldn't function. I finished my final and went back to the student room and called Low first. "Hello." "Hello Veronica what you doing...were you at?" I was so nervous. I could hear tears welling up in his voice. "Oh I'm at school where you at." I tried to sound like nothing was wrong. "School huh.... Who's that nigga in yo crib." "Oh that's my friend your friend yo high price prostitute bitch I been giving your ass all that money bitch you got my heart into you bitch and you talking bout you got a friend." I was laughing at Low because he was off his square. I finally got his dog ass for all the dirty shit he's done to me. "Yeah I do so what." "Oh... ok bitch you doing it like that well I ain't given you yo 2 racks and I'm killing yo ass when I see you click." I was so scared I thought he was outside Minneapolis Technical Community College looking for me. When I played what he said back that must of meant he took my two ounces I had behind the dresser. I didn't care cause he made me 8 racks already and didn't ask for nothing off of it so he deserved them two he took. "What's up Butchie?" "Man what's... girl somebody almost died today.... You being foul." "Oh wow I had to get my self out of this one. "How am I foul nigga you still be fucking yo baby Mom nigga as if I don't know that shit." He paused. "Nah but I'm with you.... Are you sure that's my damn baby." "What nigga you got me fucked up... hell yeah I know." "I mean Roni what you want me to think shit a nigga walk in your house while I'm in your bed sleep....as soon as I seen that nigga I reached for my pistol." Oh shit I don't know what I would of did if that nigga would of smoked Low. "Well that wont happen again." I hope not... and why is that nigga Scrappy going around talking bout he fucked up." "Nah... haha that nigga's mad cause I won't fuck with him straight up I ain't fucked him in 6 months on my momma." When I said that he was convinced and it was da truth. "Aight." "Aight what nigga I know one thang you better give that girl her keys back and do what you got to do." "So you going to let me move in with you then." "Nah Butchie you go to earn that baby." "Aight I'll see you later right." He paused for a minute. "Yeah Veronica girl." I smiled huh got another one.

Chapter 76

"End of June"

"Auntie do you no that nigga lil Dirty been out for a week and he just called me." I told our ass bout waiting on a nigga." I didn't really trust that little boy even though I was cool with his Mom and big brother. I got real cool with his Momma when his brother was killed by a hell of bullets on Golden Valley and Newton Avenue. It was sad because the word was that when they were having a shoot out his friend shot him in the head twice while trying to shoot at the fools that unloaded on there nigga. I felt that by his little ass going through the lost of his brother he didn't give a fuck bout nobody else. I just got a call from Chico telling me the police was in front of my house and QT had three bricks in her orange truck. I got nervous because nobody could stand to go to jail but me. "We was waiting on our order at Amos & Amos. We ordered chicken wings two burgers and fries. "Come on yall." Me and the kids got into the car. I pulled on my block and watched the police tow the car. I seen Chico QT and Feet sit in that Cadillac was quiet and we all watched the police had dogs out all around my house and the car. They didn't find anything and when they pulled off we all ran in the house. I waited for an hour and called to see why they loved it. Come yo find out the car was reported stolen by the owner.

When QT bought it from this dude off the street she didn't no that he changed the VIN numbers and the license plates and sold it to her. This was a new hustle that somebody came up with and it wasn't cool. My Heavy Chevy was damn the same way. They only difference was that my plates came from an older Chevy that I had. "Damn baby girl... it was work in that car baby." "I know but we can get somebody to go into the impound lot can't we." "Shit fuck that shit... if you can't get it back through the impound lot fuck it then! It's a loss!!!! Shit not to me I was determined to find somebody to get up in the Minneapolis impound lot. I thought all night about that shit who do I tell. I talked it over with QT to see who we should ask without them cutting us off. "Girl you can't tell Annie or Mya and Myrecal." "I know Roni.... You don't have to tell me that and I won't tell. Fox neither ok." QT yelled with an attitude. I wasn't sure if I wanted to cut her ass in neither shit she talked to much and she wasn't used to 500 dollars let alone the snacks (thousand) that I was going to give after dumping the work. "I think the only person that wouldn't jack you is Butchie." "Why you say that QT." "Cause you got his baby in you." "Ok I'll tell him and see what he says what he says. I called Butchie to tell him to come through he told me it would be a minute because he was moving into his auntie's house. I smiled and waited on him "Auntie... Mya is at the door." I didn't really want to be bothered with her right now Myrecal was fucking with some new D boy that she had to her care of her and her daughter so she was missing in action. Plus she didn't get along with Barbie. Ty's best friend from Texas and I didn't want no drama at my house. If I didn't let her in she'd swear I was picking sides. "Lat her in." I closed Victor's door so Barbie could sleep peacefully and not hear Mya's voice. "Hey girl where you been Mya." I said while looking her up and down. "Getting payed and seeing if you wanted to get dis money with me." "What money girl." "With Ken me and him been traveling and making money." "How Mya." This girl done flipped out. "Hoeing, escorting, tricking or prostituting should I say ha ha." I wasn't that shocked cause my girl was always desperate to get her own money. "Now why is Ken with you...? He's pimping on you Mya.... Are you crazy?" "Girl he protects me and if a trick tries to pull anything he'll pop there ass... you should come…." "HELL NO MYA… girl I sell dope to fiends and pussy to the dope man for his sack and that's it Mya." "No… I'm telling you Roni you can get more then you do selling that shit… girl with yo shape and them big double D's you got girl them white men will pay yo ass." "Shut the fuck up Mya that nigga Ken got yo ass brain washed girl… you're stupid you can pay me to be yo pimp." "He's my daddy… call him daddy." I rolled my eyes at her ass. "Yeah and you wish I wouldn't never pay no nigga for seeing my own pussy… bitch yo ass is crazy." She grabbed her shit that she left at my house and headed towards the door. "Well Veronica seen you don't want to get paid with me and Daddy I'll see you later ok."

Chapter 77

"Minneapolis Impound"

"You see the truck cuz." Butchie was saying to the little homie. "Yeah cuz but I'm soaked and my feet keep sinking in this mud." It was a swamp around the bob wire fence where the truck was parked. Butchie told the little homie that it was a gang of pistols in there so he would be more eager to get to the truck. He put the ladder up against the electrical fence threw the blanket over the bob wire and pushed the little homie over when he jumped over and got into the truck, Butchie seen a patrol car come. "Get down cuz and don't move." He whispered and laid in the mud. The dick passed by them and didn't see them. "I got it big homie I got …. ah." He seen that it was dope so Butchie stood up almost setting off the motion light. "Lil nigga throw the shit over the fence now." He yelled. HE threw all four bricks over the fence and smiled. He put them in the duffle bag and pushed the ladder back over so da homie could get out of there. "Come on cuz go slow." Butchie prayed that he would set off the motion detector. Right when he flipped over the lights and sirens went off. "Run lil homie run." Butchie ran as fast as he could. "Huh…huh…. O god don't let me get caught up behind dis bullshit." "I'm right on you big homie." Me and QT sat in the window with binoculars to see if they were on there way back. We heard the sirens as well. I lived right next to downtown and the impound lot. When they made it back to the car they both laid down and waited until they all knew the police had passed. "Where rich big homie." "Shut up shit... you don't know who's listening." Butchie was nervous as he kept trying to start my car this noise would come on and it was loud. "Damn why now is dis mother fucker doing dis." "Big homie you want me to run with it." "Nah nigga shit you ain't running off with my shit." "Nah I wouldn't never do that." Butchie kept trying to get it right. "Oh yes... thank god it started." He yelled. I seen them rolling up. "QT...wake up girl there here." I hung open the door and almost woke up Victor, NeNe and NaNa. "Girl that was some hard shit Roni... ya ass better be having my baby." Butchie said while throwing the bricks down and kissing me. "I am nigga." I said with a half attitude half smile.

Chapter 78

"Down As I Am"

Chico and Feet had went back to California. Thank God we didn't have to face them they didn't care as long as nobody went to raid they could get that shit a dime a dozen. QT did just what I said she spent all her money up on Bull shit and was mad at me when it was gone. "Fuck you QT... I helped you and you acting funny." "No... I ain't Roni damn you just jump to conclusions all the time." "Yeah cause you been hanging with Annie." "So I met her threw you shit cause you stop talking to her ass I'm suppose to?" "Nah that would be real fake... shit do what you do." I knew she was telling that fat bitch my business. "And no I ain't told her ass shit about what happened hell I ain't trying to die." "Ha ha you're crazy... die come on QT die from what girl." "Shit them niggas wanting there work back." "I ain't worried about that shit they took the L (lose) and they wasn't trippin." She was so scary man I should of left her ass right with my little sister were I found her ass.

Chapter 79
"Talk of taking a Trip"

"Hell girl yo want to go out of town next weekend." I wanted her crazy ass to go cuz she would make us laugh like hell. Even though Fox stole from me I invited her to come as well. Me and Butchie was just spending money and didn't need too knowing we had a baby on the way. I'm five months now and showing. NeNe wanted us to come get her so I told Boo, Gotti, Wild man, Fox, QT and NaNa. Hell girls Mom had rented us a car and we took the park avenue that me and Butchie went half on. Butchie 5.0 was in the shop getting painted silver with chrome rims on it. He loved that car I bought for him. So I would shut up he bought me an old school drop top 79 Cutlass Supreme. He got it painted black with gold flakes the seats were a peanut butter color with gold rims. Yeah we was dong it to be 21 and 23. So we thought when all passed up and jumped in the car to go Tricky called as we were leaving out the door. "Butchie Tricky is on the phone for you." I said while everybody sat and talked and waited for Butchie to get off the phone. "Yeah cuz…. Aight cuz Yeah ain't nobody on funny with you cuz that's my baby Momma and she wants her paper shit nigga if it was yo girl and I owe her nigga you going to be mad at me." I was so pissed that he was explaining to dis clown ass nigga. "Lets go Butchie." I yelled and slammed the phone down. "Stop being so disrespectful girl… what did I tell you about that." He said while pushing past me and walking to the car. We smoked and drove smoked and drove. In our car we had me, Butchie, Boo and QT. In the park avenue was Hell Girl, Fox, Gotti, Wildman and NaNa. Nobody wanted to hit the blunt after Boo cause his mouth had a odor that smelled like death. It came from the gut and he needed some cleansing. "No… I don't want no more." I said while looking at QT with a smirk. "Girl here…. Give it to your nigga shit." I grabbed it and passed it to Butchie. He drove with his knee and ripped a piece off the part of the blunt that was wet. "Ah… ha ha… good one." "Yeah I know." "What yall up there talking bout." Boo asked while looking out the window. I looked at QT out the rearview and she was rolling. "Yeah… nothing boo." We made it to Chicago and couldn't find a room no where.

We went down town and it was an event so everything was full. "Damn Roni I'm tired of driven girl you should of checked on dis shit before we got here." He had an attitude because I made him drive the whole 6 hours. "I'll drive baby... but we got to go get NeNe... she been blowing me up." "I don't care just get me a bed." I drove on seventy first and Jeffery to pick up NeNe. "Hey Auntie I'm so glad you came to see me." "Yeah I'm glad I came to see you to get you too girl." Gotti was happy to see NeNe. "Uh baby what's up you came like you said you would." We made it out to the hundreds to get a hotel. Once everybody got into there rooms they were happy. Wildman was so drunk he was knocking on other peoples door. Thank goodness that nobody got mad enough to kick off no shit. We were in a rinky dinky motel that looked like one big long shock. It was under motel 6 and when I grew up that was the most slummiest hotel I knew. The next morning the muffler fell off on Park avenue. Hell girl got to snapping on the drive over to River Oaks Shopping center. "Shut the fuck up Hell girl yo ass got a free trip so why you trippin." "Cause nigga my Mom rented the car nigga that's why." "So what you black ass bitch I paid for this whole trip and yo ass is running it now." She was so pissed off at Butchie she threw the keys. "Ah oh no give." Everybody said in one accord. "How are we going to get home girl." Fox yelled and ran into the bushes to find them. "I don't care... catch a bus." Hell girl said while crossing her arms. "Speak for yo self with yo shit starting ass." Wildman was mad and Hell girl was afraid of him. We had heard from our friend Ree Ree that he was a murderer. Shit I didn't want no problem with him either. He was bald headed with green eyes, light skinned and short. He didn't look like he could do much but when he got mad he would play with guns. Me and Butchie left and went in the mall. Everyone followed except hell girl and Boo. By the time we came out the mall they found the keys. "Lets go mash I hate Chicago shit." Boo was irritated. "Nigga shut up I got some chronic for your ass." Butchie threw a sack at Boo and his whole attitude changed. "Good let me roll dis so I can chill." Boo said while smiling at Hell girl! "What nigga." Butchie had a way of staring at people and she felt like shit. "You aight now since yo got everybody's undies in a bunch." Everybody busted up laughing. "Yeah nigga gimme some money to eat." "Look at yo ass you kick off shit and still need my nigga." I said while putting my bags in the trunk of the rental. I pulled out a fifty and gave it to her. "Thanks." She said while snatching it. I never understood Hell girl and all that damn Drama, I don't think she can breathe without kicking up something daily. Everything was all packed up and sold out. So we dove back to NeNe's people house her auntie was the sweetest and so was Low's mother. Even though I felt a little uncomfortable about bringing Butchie over to Low's people house we still went so NeNe could get her bags and we could pick up NaNa.

— One Week Later —

After the Chicago trip everything was going good. NeNe had been kicking it with lil Dirty real tuff but I warned her that she had to meet him two blocks away and she did. Gotti was older so you know with that she found out, older niggas play games. I was glad she didn't hold shit to him. He wasn't shit just like my other dude. "Oooh... NeNe what you wanna eat." I was looking through the cabinet. Butchie was through the cabinet. Butchie was over and laying on the floor while listening to KMOJ radio. They were playing smooth R&B. I guess he was in a mellow mood. "Chicken and macaroni and cheese with string beans." "Oh I make some good kool-aide cause its too sweet." "Ok auntie don't make it to sweet." As I started my dinner I seen that Butchie was in the bathroom whispering. I put my ear up to the door and I could hear him arguing. "Nah cuz you cant do no shit like that to my baby Momma nigga." Was all I heard him say. "What the fuck you doing listening at the damn door... wasn't you cooking." Butchie yelled when he caught me listening. "Let me in or cut me out with the bull shit Butchie.... Who was that on the phone talking about hunting me nigga." Tears started rolling down my eyes cause I had a feeling it was somebody I know and care for. "Nah don't worry about it... I'll handle it ain't nobody going to do shit to you cuz." I know so let me know who it was on your phone so I can handle my own business." NeNe was watching and listening. "Nah you're pregnant I got it." I could tell Butchie was upset and so was I. "Tell me now Butchie... I need to know for when you're not around so I'll know." He wouldn't tell me cause he felt like he was snitching so I laid into him. "Oh so if that was me and I didn't tell you bout some nigga tryin to jack you or kill you I would be wrong huh nigga well guess what if your loyalty lies in the hands of some punk ass gang or some weak bitch then yo bitch ass can get." He jumped up and grabbed me. "What did I tell you bout yo mouth." I was crying like a first grader that missed her bus on a field trip day. "I don't care boy... I got your baby in me and you got me convincing you to tell me who's out to hurt me." I must of touched his heart. "Aight girl." He sat back down on the couch while I stood up over him. "Ricky called to see if I was over here and asked me to leave so him and somebody could come in and jack you." The tears were none stop. "What.... Oh what the." NeNe shook her head and ran in the room and woke Victor up. "What did you say." Butchie stood up to hold me. I felt good when I seen the chrome 44 magnet on his hip. "I told him what I look like letting somebody jack me people." "Who was coming in with him." I needed all the details cause I was going to get my little cuzin that was a blood to blast on all them pussy's." "The dusty thieves from Cali and big boys little brother." "Who and where in the fuck did they come from." I was shocked because one of the nigga's I went to school with and Tricky huh I got something for his ass." I don't know Shine but auntie we got to get Victor out of here." NeNe was so nervous that she was lost for words. She didn't have any understanding about Tricky tryin to jack us. This is what Annie has become over some punk ass dick. That punk bitch can die. That's how I felt. You will allow yo nigga to hurt me and mines over some punk ass money. I did as NeNe said and so we all jumped in Butchies blazer and road out to Brooklyn Park to drop Victor off. Ms. Steen didn't ask any questions at one in the morning she just grabbed my baby and shut the door. When I returned to the car NeNe was knocked out. "Roni let it go baby.... Them niggas will get there you know Tricky is jealous." "How in the fuck is his ass jealous I'm his bitches best friend and that weak bitch ooh I hate that hoe." I had so much hated in my heart for Annie and Tricky that I had to go to church on Sunday. For the next three days I slept I felt like my world was ending. When Sunday came I got up and went to New Salem Baptist church. It sat right on Plymouth and Queens kitty corner from Momo sweet shop. My pastor

Jerry McAfee knew just what to say to me whenever I needed it. When I walked in the big white church I seen how packed it was and scared to walk past all the people. Tiffany looked at me and would I left a little wetter. Damn I had to sit down right next to Rachel's ass. "Hey Veronica... the road called you back huh." I didn't answer her I just shook my head yes and smiled reverend McAfee was talking about how people gossip and disrespect there selves by not feeling loyal. I left him so much that I stood up and clapped. The tears rolled through and my body felt like a sauna. After church was over I felt real good. It seemed like I could take on a army. "Hey Veronica how are you and where have you been baby." I knew he was going to catch me at some point and I couldn't lie. "In the streets rev in the streets." I said with my head down. He pushed my chin up in the air. "Hold your head up high girl... you're going to be just fine make sure you keep him up stairs first and everything will work out." "Ok I will Rev." I whipped my face and walked to my car sad and lonely but one thing I wasn't was a back stabbing ass liar.

Chapter 80

"26th and Aldrich"

"Auntie come on he lives out here." Me, QT, NaNa, NeNe, Fox and Hell girl walked with the half a brick of cocaine in a duffle bag. I didn't feel nervous because lil dirty had the lick from dis nigga name Big. I knew the nigga had just got shot six times and didn't really want no trouble because he was wearing a shit bag. That shit didn't stop his ass from hustling. I left my 380 glock in the car like a fool. Tricky bought it for me after going in motors pockets. I couldn't get that off my mind. Robi had whooped the shit out of motor and so did Tricky. Man they couldn't I get them days back damn Roni I don't know bout dis.... Shit dis is a dope spot(crack houses)." I was so thirsty for the thirteen grand that I didn't pay any attention to the niggas poster at the door. "Who's Big." I looked around to a group of young niggas smoking weed at the door. "I am...what's up." Damn dis nigga was fine. I watched him walk to the kitchen, "Come on yall." I had NeNe and Hell girl walk to the back with me. "Big where is lil

Dirty at?" I wondered why that nigga wasn't here and dis was his luck. "He's in his way now where's the work." He said while rubbing his hands together. I thought this was a nigga with some paper. Huh dis nigga was full of shit. "Nigga where's that paper at." "When I see the dope you'll get yo paper its right here." He said while pointing at his hip. "Will just wait till Dirty comes." NeNe said as she kept paging lil dirty. It had been about an hour and dis fool still hadn't shoved his face when I walked to the front QT NaNa and Fox was making friends with the man of the house name Pac. HE smoked them out and him and his boys had a lot of jokes. "We are out of here Big." The nigga thought fast. "Wait and you one of them crip girls." "Who." Hell girl said because her baby daddy Corn was from Gardena California and was one of the first shot guns to come to Minnesota from California. "Nah I'm talking to her." He said and pointed at me. "Why you ask me that... nigga are you da police or some shit." I seen he got real pissed off and started laughing. "You funny joe." "I ain't no joe nigga." I understood this was a term that Chicago niggas used when they talked to people. "I know baby calm down... come back in the kitchen and count dis cheddar(money) wit me and relax." I held the bag tight and stood at are end of the kitchen while he stood at the other. I couldn't see what he was doing because he had his back to me. As soon as he turned around out came that black 9 millimeter glock. "Drop it bitch with your shit talking ass." "Oh shit." NeNe ducked and yelled. "Fuck I dropped the dope and I'm at 6 months pregnant. "What's wrong yall." NaNa yelled while running behind me Hell girl and NeNe. QT and Fox was so fucking high that they stayed on the porch until that bitch ass nigga pointed that gun at them. "Wait Roni wait for me." I could hear her dumb ass yelling as if I could protect her when we made it to the car I felt fucked up and NeNe had to answer a lot of questions.

— One Month Later —

All the stress of me falling out with my so called friends, Butchie acting real wish washy with me and finds getting Low was enough for me to have a nervous breakdown. "What's up Roni." "Hey Wonnie what have you been doing girl." "I been so into Butchie that I haven't kicked it with her lately. "Nothing I'm bout to come over and talk to you about your baby shower." My heart felt up with joy. At least somebody cared about me. I got up to walk around and see who's in my house. NeNe, NaNa, Barbie and little Victor was all in the bad sleep. Butchie Gotti and chill was at the table smoking a blunt. "Good morning beautiful." "Yeah what's up Roni." Gotti and chill said before I could respond to Butchie. "Good morning everybody." I started to pull out eggs, sausage and milk. "Nah bay we going to breakfast." "Ok I'll go get dressed I woke up everybody in the room. "Roni we want to go to Bennihana's we don't wasn't breakfast." Barbie said while holding her blankets. "Yeah Mommy I don't like eggs." "Boy yo ass don't like nothing do you." I watched his cute self shrug his shoulders. "Yeah auntie can Barbie take the station wagon." "Yeah NaNa go get the keys out my room." I watch all of them get in the car so I hoped in the shower. When I put my clothes on Wonnie was at the door. "hey girl it took you long enough." "I know I had to drop the kids off." "Oh who got them and how's my baby's doing." "There good." "Hey what's up with you Wonnie." Gotti said to her while looking her up and down. I could tell it was about to be some bull shit. "Shit chillin what yall been doing." She said after walking to the table. "We bout to go get something to eat." Butchie told her and walked downstairs to get his hat. I went downstairs with him to let him know that Gotti been asking about Wonnie and I didn't wanna be in the middle of no bull shit. He understood and gave me some money so me and Wonnie could go to a restaurant by ourselves. When I made it back upstairs I seen that nobody was in the house. "Come on Butchie everybody's at the car." Chill was in his suburban and Gotti was standing outside the truck talking to Wonnie. I kissed Butchie "Call me baby so we can go to the movies later... k." He told me while rubbing my stomach. I seen him frown at Wonnie. "Why you look at her like that baby?" "She's sneaky... I don't know why yo ass calls her your best friend." "Cause I've known her since u was eight years old... I love her like a sister." "Hum... yeah well... she ain't straight." "oh baby I'll see you later." I said while pushing him. "Don't be talking bout her neither nigga." He walked to the side of Chills truck and got in the passenger seat. He told Gotti to get in and when I seen Wonnie walk to Butchie's blazer I could hear him ask

Wonnie for her number. She said it too him and I just shook my head. When she got in the car I let her know what time it was. "Wonnie you know Gotti fucks with NeNe and gots a girl and a baby." She looked shook. "Nah I didn't but um I asked him did he fuck with NeNe he said not like that but she's a little girl." "Huh... come on girl you know I told you he be fucking with her." She frowned up at me. "I mean he said he don't and I don't give a fuck shit I like them guys but they are your little friends not mines." "Yes you're right girl what's up with the baby shower... I want you to make it before or after November because the first weekend of that month were going to Vegas to see Mike Tyson and Evander Holyfield fight." She sat there and was shook off how I changed the subject. "Oh uh well we can talk about it when we get to Milda's." "Why... what's wrong?" "nothing I was going to surprise you but I had to tell yo ass cause you be into so much shit that I wont be able to find you." "Nah Wonnie I wouldn't do that to you."

Chapter 81

"Element of Surprise"

I went to my God dad to get your tickets to the fight of the century. Barker my dads best friend was a pimp and he had one of his hoes that worked Vegas go get our tickets from the box office. Yeah I was cold like that. Butchie didn't realize what he had at all. By his birthday being in October I gave him a party and bought him a watch and gold chain that said Butchie. Everybody use to trip off me doing for him but I had the bigger picture in mine. I ain't never going for no dude that don't do more for me first. You got to give a little to get a lot. Damn I been dis boy since he left this morning. "Butchie I been calling you all morning nigga... where the fuck you at." He didn't know I had tickets for him Wildman, Chill and Bumpy to go to Vegas. They've been good on keeping quiet so I was dealing with a lot of Butchies shit so I wouldn't ruin anything. I couldn't take the fact that he didn't come home though my pregnant emotions was getting the best of me. "I'm at Chill's hotel." "What nigga and you ain't called or answered my page." My gut was hungry instantly. "I just woke up shit... I ain't doing shit... damn you ain't my Momma." "Fuck you punk ass broke bitch... I made yo ass nigga you didn't know shit till I showed you bitch." "See that's why I didn't come in cause your mouth is foul and I'm going to punch you in it one day... click." I kept calling back and he wouldn't answer. I got up and went down to the basement right to his weight set. I picked the 10 pound weight up walked upstairs to my balcony and stood on the top step and through the weight right threw the back window on his 5.0 mustang. "Spush... boom." Everybody in the house jumped up. Wildman jumped up off the couch holding his pistol. "Girl you ok... what the fuck was that." I didn't say a word. I ran back down to the weight room. "No Veronica gurrl cuz is going to beat yo ass." I had snot running out my nose and was crying so hard I could see. When I made it to the top of the steps I was stopped. "Roni quit girl... please." "let me go Fox... now." We tussled back and fourth so hard that I didn't hear Butchie pull up. "Bitch let me in hoe... Wildman... cuz .... Oh fuck." "Oh shit that's him." Fox said and ran to the window. I shot past her and ran back to the balcony. "Nigga stay out my business Wildman." He knew I was pissed. "Cool baby girl but my nigga wants me to let him in so what should I do." "Mind yo.... A a a a h." The same way I use came straight through my front window. "Yeah bitch I can fuck yo shit up to." I picked up the weight and ran back to the balcony to drop it in the front window and he was pulling out the yard so the weight hit the ground. "Are you done Roni... shit... I hope so... you got me and my baby in this motha fucker freezing shit." "Fuck that the nigga didn't come home." "So what & you're slippin in yo pimpin cause I ain't never seen you give a fuck bout no nigga." My baby sis was right... I'm loosing myself and as soon as any man see's that that yo got it's a fact they will dog your ass. I went to my room and just cried. Fox was so responsible she got em the yellow pages and found a 24 hour glass replacement. "Knock knock.." "What Fox I'm good." "Girl Butchie been calling like crazy and I need the 400 to give this white man." "Hey why you got to say white man... just say a man." Me and Fox was rollin. Oh I needed that. "Here tell him sorry." "Its ok I can see you're not doing to good." I laughed again. "Damn Fox these walls are paper thin huh... he can hear good as hell." "I know... get you some rest ok... that baby is going to be mean as hell... you really been through a lot." "I know thanks."

Chapter 82

"Las Vegas Trip"

"Thanks baby for everything... but did you pay for everybody." "Nah now what you think I ain't... boy them niggas paid for there own shit I paid for ours... why." He sure was tryin o count my pockets. "Cause I was tryin to see where your money been going." "Why." "Cause girl we bout to have three kids shit and dis shit ain't cheap." Huh he was right his daughter and my son and now the new baby. "Who did your hair anyways.... I told you I hate the weave in your hair you look good without all that shit." He did always say he loved that plain rap. "Shit and it be a lot of people in there all the time." "Yeah a bunch of hoe's talking about nigga's huh that's why you need to go to them classy hoes." "Shut up Butchie you don't know nothing." I was so glad when the plain ride was over he was getting on my nerves already. We checked into the room and went shopping for something to wear. The fight was the next day and I couldn't wait. Me and Butchie found matching coogi sweater he had a coogi coat that he found in this specialty shop and I was cool with the sweater I had. We both had on Gucci shoe's and he topped my outfit off with the purse. The next day we got dressed and meet everybody in the lobby of our hotel the Flamingo. On our way to the flight we seen Don King, Andre 3000 from Outkast but when we seen Butchie's favorite he got to acting like a groupie. "Hey...what's up Nas look bay there goes Nas." All of us busted out laughing. "Damn nigga that nigga don't know you... shit you acted like a girl." Bumpy said. "So what.. fuck you nigga you got here cause of my girl nigga and you wouldn't of seen him neither." " Oh don't get mad baby." Bumpy said while rubbing Butchies head. Butchie laughed it off. "Shut up nigga." We kicked it and had a good time. We sat in the 1000 dollar seat s so we were surrounded by celebrity's. I watched Holyfield whoop the shit out of Tyson wow history right before my eyes 13 rounds and he finally knocked him out . Hustling show has taken me to my highest heights.

Chapter 83

"Baby shower"

"Hello… NaNa where is Veronica everybody's over here waiting on her." "Oh she's in the shower." "Tell her she needs to hurry up… how she going to be late for her own baby shower… shit… click." I could hear NaNa walking to the bathroom door. "Auntie Wonnie called and was snapping… she's mad man she said you're way late." "Ok." Shit I didn't have to rush they way. Al u needed was a crib I bought all the other stuff on my own. I made it to the baby shower. "Hey miss late." Olivia said. "Hey girl I ain't seen yo ass." I gave her a big hug. "Oh Wonnie stop with the attitude." I reached out to hug her. "No you're always late." I chased her ass. "Give me a hug for I start crying." She ran from me and I caught her but. "Thank you." I picked her up. She still was a little mad. "Don't be late no more." I wont." I enjoyed myself and ignored Butchies pages. He was acting stupid again. He didn't pull that sleepy out shit because I only had two weeks before I dropped my load. I ate real good and talked all my problems out but I still didn't feel good. Thanks Giving was three days away and I was starting to feel contractions but I didn't tell anybody.

Chapter 84

"Doctor Appt"

Me, Wonnie and Butchie went to my last appointment. "Hi Veronica how have you been feeling this last week." Right when I was about to lie. "oh damn she been having pain." "Shut up boy." "Wait why are you not wanting to tell me Veronica that's important." The Doc said while I looked in the air. I know." "Well lay back." I did what she said and looked at the wall. Wonnie sat guilty. The Doctor noticed that my baby was breach so she called another Doctor in. They informed me that I was going to be uncomfortable because they were going to turn my baby around. "OOUCH No..please." "Honey this is the only way you're going to hear a natural bitch." The doctors tried to calm me down, I got to go... I cant watch you hurt her." Butchie jumped up and left out." I'll stay Roni relax so it will stop hurting. Wonnie said. I feel bad for Butchie but it let me know he does love me. After the visit he explained to me why he left when we pulled up to Wonnie's house she grabbed her stuff. "Veronica call me cause I got to tell you something." "Ok." I said and laid back in my seat. The next day I had to get everything together for the hospital. I called my Mom to come get Victor and to let her know to be on deck because labor was coming soon. "NeNe... you wanna go eat." I started to put my shoes on and put Victor's stuff at the door so my Mom wouldn't have to wait. "Yeah where we going." "The fish house." "Ok." "Auntie Wonnie's on the phone" huh I was wondering why she hadn't called yesterday. "What's up girl." "Oh shit will you come get me." "From where girl." "the hotel... um I'm down here with Gotti." I instantly got pissed off and I wasn't going to be fake and tell NeNe she couldn't go. "Yeah I'll come." I put on my coat and walked to the car. "Why you so quiet Roni." NeNe said as she jumped in the car. "You'll see." She didn't question me because she seen I had an attitude. When we made it to the hotel Wonnie and Gotti was standing right outside. "I see what you meant Auntie but I'm cool." "I just didn't want you to think I had anything to do with them getting hooked up." "I know you didn't auntie." The ride to the fish house was kind of quiet. Wonnie stayed in the car while he ordered out food and asked to be dropped off when we got back in the car.

Chapter 85

"Thanksgiving"

"Oh Butchie my water broke." A pain shot straight up my side. "Call the doctor." I stood there and watched water run right out of me. "NaNa bring me a towel." I didn't feel anymore pain. We had planned to go to the casino and I was pissed. "Here and the Doctor said to the hospital and for you not to eat." "Ok." When I got in the truck I had a piece of Turkey in my hand. "No... greedy... You don't listen." He stuffed the meat down. "She told you not to eat for a reason." "ok." I looked like a ashamed child. While he were in the delivery room my Mom and aunt was in the room and Butchie watched me have a cesarean through the window. When they put my uterus on my chest he fainted. "Roni your boyfriend is crazy he's on the floor." I chuckled and was mad that I couldn't see nothing. I made it to my own room with my son and Butchie was kissing all over me. "Oh Ms. Ginger I fainted and you was laughing at me." "Yeah boy I didn't know what was going on." "I seen all that blood on my girl.... Wow that scared me." "Oh you'll be ok."

Chapter 86

"Leaving the Hospital"

"Damn Butchie, I just had yo baby... why in the fuck am I carrying all these bags out."

"Damn you ain't handicap."

"Oooh, you bitch ass nigga." "NeNe you and my baby can get in this bitch ain't ridding." I was so pissed I walked with all my bags right past him. "Fuck you." I sat downstairs in the lobby and called everybody but no one would come. I watched him pull up in the front of Abbott Hospital and just sat there. I was so mad that I didn't move. Finally NeNe came in the door and grabbed the bags I had. "Come on auntie... you need to get some rest." She was right but I didn't enjoy how I was getting treated at this present time. I sat in the truck and cried. "What the fuck are you cryin for girl... you crazy." "Just get your shit give me my son and get out." "I will." When we pulled up Butchie grabbed the baby seat and two bags. He was being an asshole so I didn't bother. I forgot that I left Wildman in my house while I was gone and I had work in the car that Butchie didn't know about. "NeNe go check the trunk and make sure my brick is still there." "Ok." As she walked through the snow to get back off the house I went in and watched Butchie. Tears kept coming out. I guess this was a part of post partum distress. "So you really leaving." "Yeah I'm tired of your mouth...

you don't love me look at how you talk." He had a point I was very disrespectful and he wasn't use to it. "Ok...don't come back." I didn't mean to and I was glad he didn't respond. I put my son in my bed and called everybody to come over. Everybody came and seen the baby and that made me tired. I still couldn't get Butchie off my mind. "Hello." "Hey Roni... ah my cousin wants to holla at you." Wildman handed Elane the phone. "Hey can I come see you with my cousin." "He's going to bring you." "Yeah." "Ok.. click." My stomach was turning. "Ring Ring." Who is this now. "Hello" "What's up Shine didn't you get that from my boy yet." This was Ricky wondering if I got the brick he sent to pay on Chico's lawyer. He got caught somewhere down south and they had to ship him back. "Yeah Ricky I got you.... I'll send you the seven stacks(thousands) When I heal from the baby." "Oh you had it." "Yeah and I just got home two hours ago." "Ok baby... take your time and get some rest." "Thank you." My gut told me not to let Wildman and Elane come over but greed will make you do anything. NaNa had to leave so she could get to school while I was resting. "See you this weekend auntie." "Ok call me." She left while Wildman and Elane came in. "What's up yall... what did you want girl." I said while getting my self together. "Ah... I need to go pee but I'm I need a half ounce." "Ok the bathrooms right there." I said and pointed. While she was in the bathroom I went to the backyard to get the work and took it to the basement. At first I didn't pull it all out because I didn't know her like that. "Ok baby what you got... what color is it." She said while moving back and forth. "Sit down Elane you acting like a hype(crack head)." "Shut up bay... I'm older you don't tell me how to do business." I busted up laughing. "Come on yall... I got to get some rest." I feel the medicine take an affect on me and I was getting sleepy. "Oh ok baby you got a scale." Oh that bitch was pissing me off. She kept asking for shit. "Here girl give me five hundred." I said and pulled the whole brick out. Her dope fiend eyes got real bug. "Damn you doing that... shit I could get rid of that." "No she don't need your help... lets go." Wildman told her he see the money down on the table. She was so happy that she just shot straight up out the house. "Come lock the door Roni... you still got that 380?" "Yeah boy... I'm good." I went to sleep with my baby. And for some reason it was peaceful. I was waken up by my phone. "Hello… hello." I could only hear the person on the other end because of the static. "Hello." "Roni… its me Sandra… girl where's that baby." "Oh hi… I just woke up and he ain't up yet." As I talked to Sandra I went to the bathroom and walked around the house. When I looked out the window I seen a white truck parked in Zion Baptist churches parking lot. "Who does he look like." "Oh girl he looks like me ." I sat down on the floor next to my son and kissed him on his cheek. "I know you cant wait till we go out." "I know I'm ready… a a h… oh my god… AH." "What's wrong Roni." "No what the." "Damn damn Minneapolis police… damn." The cop was yelling and had his gun pointed right at my face. "Ok please." I yelled as I got on the ground. "Please its just me and my baby." "Stay down man is it anybody else here." "No sir just me and my new baby." The feet of the officers running all threw my house. My life was over. "Ma'am do you have any weapons or drugs on you." "No sir."

Order Form

Nelymesh Corp.
P.O. Box 65804
St. Paul, MN 55165
ihustle_365@yahoo.com

Qty	Description	Unit Price	Line Total
	Da Hood Makes Fresh Water	$15.00	
	The Overplay For The Underplay	$15.00	
		Total	

Nelymesh Corp., P.O. Box 65804, St. Paul, MN 55165, ihustle_365@yahoo.com